AT LONG LAST LOVE

It's July 1942, and nightclub singer Kate Watson has made a home for herself in bomb-blitzed London. A motley crew of friends has replaced the family she's not spoken to in years. Until one evening Kate's sister, Sarah, walks back into her life. Sarah has a favour to ask: she needs Kate to return home to Dorset for one month to look after her daughter, Lizzie. Reluctantly Kate agrees, even though it means facing the troubled past she hoped she'd escaped. As the war continues, Kate must fight her own battles and find not only the courage to forge a future but perhaps, at long last, love.

AT LONG LAST LOVE

by

Milly Adams

Magna Large Print Books
Long Preston, North Yorkshire,
BD23 4ND, England.

British Library Cataloguing in Publication Data.

A catalogue record of this book is
available from the British Library

ISBN   978-0-7505-4628-7

First published in Great Britain by Arrow Books in 2017

Cover illustration © Ildiko Neer/Arcangel by arrangement with
Arcangel Images Ltd.

Milly Adams has asserted her right to be identified as the author of
this work in accordance with the Copyright, Designs and Patents Act,
1988

Published in Large Print 2018 by arrangement with
Random House Group Ltd.

Magna Large Print is an imprint of Library Magna Books Ltd.

Printed and bound in Great Britain by
T.J. (International) Ltd., Cornwall, PL28 8RW

Jan, playmate since we were nine

Rowena, an artist who spoils me

Georgina, editor and chum

And in memory of 'Lucy', an SOE agent who was captured in France, suffered greatly, but survived. She gave Jan and me (as youngsters) lunch and inspiration in the tranquillity of her Somerset home, and the memory of that watershed day has stayed with me ever since.

Acknowledgements

I have no-one to thank for the nightclub scenes except me. I put my heart and soul into being my sultry singer, Kate, it's the closest I'll get. As for the subsequent story of Kate's past – well, sadly I have known people in that situation.

My interest in the SOE started when I met Lucy, and then there was a neighbour we had when growing up who was the quietest man, but had operated in France, and then there was the film *Carve Her Name with Pride*. I realise the older I get, and boy, do I get older, that I have met the most extraordinary people, to whom I owe a great deal.

I have always pondered how both men and women manage to undertake appallingly dangerous work when the chances are that they may well leave their children orphans. Again and again I have come back to this conundrum throughout my life and I'm not sure I have an answer, and what a cheek to think I have a right to one. We all do what we feel we must.

As for the details of training and actual activities: over the years I have read many memoirs of those in the SOE, far too many to list, and had a discussion with one person in particular. I remember thinking as we spoke of the awful loneliness of not being able to trust anyone, and the stress of being in continuous danger.

This has been brought home to me through my involvement with Words for the Wounded, a charity that raises funds for wounded service personnel. I have met those who have operated behind the lines and am aware of the difficulty of dropping the necessary alertness, or should it be paranoia, with peace. Can it ever be done? I'm not sure.

War is a dirty business, and our debt to those who wage it on our behalf is beyond price. We should remember that, and, in our turn, do all that we can to protect them when their job is done.

Thanks

Thanks to Dr Kathleen Thompson, author of the brilliant *From Both Ends of the Stethoscope,* who is also a ballroom dancer. She tangoed me through the dance, so that I could pretend I was an expert.

To Josie, who performed magnificently in the LEAP production of *Anything Goes* and described in detail her tap dances; and to Megan, her sister, who did my ironing and housework for pocket money, to free up much-needed time to write. Last but not least, to Mabel, who is always so thrilled when she sees my books in shops. Ah, there's nothing like grandchildren.

Thanks also for the hundreds of books I've read over a great many years covering the rise of National Socialism and the Second World War, and to all those who operated behind the lines, like Lucy, and in so doing suffered great loneliness, peril and too often death, in order to keep our democracy in place and us safe.

My gratitude knows no bounds. I just hope that we are worthy.

Chapter One

Early July 1942 – Soho

Kate leaned against the baby-grand piano, smiling as applause rippled around the nightclub. She sipped a weak gin. 'Medicinal purposes,' she grinned, toasting Roberto, the pianist. He winked.

'I'll Be with You in Apple Blossom Time' always went down well, especially with the few newly arrived American GIs, who seemed to have time to spend in London. 'A Nightingale Sang in Berkeley Square' was probably the second favourite. Kate had opened with it this evening and, to signal the end of the first half of her act, she would perform 'Begin the Beguine', a song that, without fail, brought the Blue Cockatoo's audience to its feet.

Roberto warned her with 'his' look, and began the introduction to 'A Foggy Day in London Town'. She replaced her glass on the piano top and straightened, picking up the microphone. The GIs wouldn't know what fog was, but they'd find out pretty soon, when autumn arrived. There was also no blossom in London, nor any nightingales – only a great many gap-toothed buildings, along equally bomb-damaged streets.

Roberto, head bent down over the keys, was into his twiddly bits, and she knew better than even to clear her throat until he'd finished. She glanced to the left of the stage, where Stan on saxophone and Elliot on bass were, as she expected, grinning as Roberto milked his moment of glory.

Stan lifted his glass of Scotch to her. Kate half laughed. How on earth had he wheedled that out of Graham? She glanced towards the bar, where patrons sat on high stools. Ah, no wonder; it was dear old Frankie serving the cocktails and he was a sucker for the entertainers, bless him. He'd lost his Gertie in the bombing and took refuge working here whenever his Air Raid Precautions duties allowed. 'It helps,' he always said, 'to be amongst other people who are trying to forget whatever it is they don't want to remember.'

Offstage to her right, Brucie, the owner, was imitating winding a crank handle and stabbing his finger at her. She ignored him and let Roberto play on, stepping away from the piano in her tight strapless, scarlet evening dress slit to the knee, her blonde hair tumbling over her shoulders. She slipped the microphone into its stand. Around the dance floor the patrons were sitting at what seemed like elegant little tables, but in this dim light everything looked better than it was, even the entertainers.

She tapped the microphone. 'Listen closely, you lovely people, the fog of winter has gone, the bombers have not returned – and perhaps won't. But, as always, the party doesn't stop, even if they do. We will continue to play for you, while you dance till dawn.'

The audience laughed, but one or two hunched their shoulders, looking nervously at the ceiling.

Maybe she shouldn't have used the word 'perhaps', but you never knew. The London Blitz was over, but the poor old provinces were getting a bashing even as she spoke. She hurried on, over the rising chatter, hearing Roberto still tinkering behind her. 'I was just thinking that although the winter is over, and spring too, Soho has no apple blossom.'

Kate waited for just a few seconds until they fell silent. She nodded towards the bar, where Teresa was stubbing out a cigarette beneath one of her high heels, ready to circulate with her tray of single roses.

'But, gentlemen, though there may not be blossom out there, inside the Blue Cockatoo we have a rose for your lovely partner. It's summer, after all, and Teresa is most ready to oblige.'

She waited for the expected laughter. It came, along with whistles and hoots. A deep voice called, 'Come to me, darling. I have money in my pocket, and a heart and soul that need obliging.'

Brucie nodded, pleased with Kate, as Teresa sashayed her way to the soldier, her suspenders just about hidden by her short black skirt, and her breasts by the strapless top. She winked at Kate as she passed. For every rose she sold, Brucie gave her a commission. Not a lot, but enough.

Roberto was now playing her in, Stan put his glass down and Elliot eased his shoulders. Kate held the stand of the microphone, closed her eyes and began to sing, feeling the timbre of the words, because she too had been a stranger in the city. Just as the song said, and hadn't known what to do. She reached that line, paused, looked up

13

and waved the audience to join in.

For a moment the patrons of the Blue Cockatoo joined together in the face of their uncertainty, and perhaps it was a comfort, much like the cocktails, for which they paid over the odds. But nothing really touched the coiling fear inside them all, and the unanswered questions: what the hell was going to happen, and when would the tide really turn?

Kate sang on, reaching the chorus. Again she waved the audience in, and together they sang. Teresa was still circulating, and the roses were going as though there was no need for money tomorrow. As Kate sang she swayed with the music, seeing movement from her left. She stood away from the microphone as Stan took her place, playing his saxophone solo. She moved to her position at the piano again, lifting her glass, swirling the drink around. It was mostly water, with no lemon of course. There was a war on. She smiled wryly.

But war was good for some. She was thinking of the spivs who did their business in the club, night after night, day after day. It must have cost Brucie a fortune. He also made one, of course, but how many lives were lost bringing the goods to their shores? It was best not to think about it. She gulped her drink. She was as bad; if she had any morality, she would only have water.

Stan was drawing to a close and tapped his foot. It was code for 'Any minute now, come and join me.' She did, draping her arm around his shoulders. They had known one another for more than four years; she was twenty-three, he fifty-three, and they were close friends, after working

14

night after night in the club, whatever raids were in progress.

The ARP wardens called all the workers at the club an 'essential war service', manned by people as brave as lions. Mark you, they were biased, because of the nip of gin Brucie would give them when they stuck their heads round the doors, complaining that they were 'showing a light'. But they were quite right, for even a sliver was too much.

She sang slowly, loving the last line, because it lifted all hearts to think that the sun was shining everywhere.

The applause was warm, and roses were thrown towards her, most of which she caught. The scent was nothing like that of the roses that grew in the gardens of her dim and distant village, but it did bring the softness of the long-ago summers into the club. She bowed in thanks and placed the roses alongside her glass. After her shift, they'd be collected and resold. She always kept one, though, and frequently wondered why she did that to herself, for Little Worthy, her village, equalled self-flagellation.

Was it still the same? Was her father still the same? She stopped: that was enough; think of the next song, the next cigarette, and perhaps another gin. Brucie wouldn't like it, but what the hell.

She always ended her shift with 'We'll Meet Again', but it wasn't nearly time for that. Yes, she had sung two sessions, but it had to be three, if you were top of the bill. Roberto left the stage and she sang, to Stan's saxophone, the opening line to 'The Way You Look Tonight': 'Some day, when

15

I'm awfully low...'

The patrons were clinging together on the dance floor waltzing, eyes closed, the men resting their heads on the women's heads. Her voice wavered; would anyone ever close their eyes and think of her with real love?

She wondered if the cheeks of the women were as soft as those she sang about, and did their partners feel there was nothing for them to do but love them? She did hope so. As she breathed the words out into the ether, she too closed her eyes. Did they hope their love would never change, and that they'd keep their soft, nightclub-induced charm? She held the last note, stepping back, making room for Stan again. She smiled around the room, wondering if Brucie had remembered that she must leave at dead-on one forty-five. Mark you, best not to say 'dead', in this day and age.

She saw that Tony, the doorman, had left his post outside the street door and was instead standing in the darkness at the back, by the curtain that hung between the corridor and the club. He waved to attract her attention. She strained to see him in the shadowy gloom. He was pointing to someone standing at his side, someone who stepped forward into the low light. It was a woman, wearing a felt cloche hat and day-clothes: a short jacket, a flowered dress and flat shoes. The light was insufficient to make out the colours.

Kate shrugged, turning and looking at Elliot, who was the only one standing behind her. Did Tony mean him? She gestured towards the woman. Elliot shook his head. She moved back to Stan, draping her arm over his shoulder again,

16

singing the last refrain. Now the dancers turned and swayed on the spot as they joined in.

The applause was almost sleepy, as though a great calmness had fallen over the dance floor. Stan kissed her cheek. 'Well sung, darling Miss Watson. But who is that woman over there, looking as though she's found herself amongst sinners in a den of iniquity and has a stare that could pierce an armoured car?'

Kate had forgotten about Tony, and now she looked again as the woman turned to him, waving her hand towards Kate, pushing her head forward to make herself heard against the noise. Kate slipped from Stan, feeling shock in every sinew, though all she said was, 'Ready for "Begin the Beguine"?' Roberto had made his way back to the piano. They began, and all the time Kate watched Sarah edge further into the light. Her older sister had changed in eight years. Well, hadn't they all? For that's what time did to people.

As Kate sang, she acknowledged Sarah. That was all. If Sarah wanted to talk to Kate, she'd have to wait amongst the company her younger sister kept, which was a far cry from the rectitude of Melbury Cottage, High Street, Little Worthy. But was she even still living there?

As she sang, Kate blessed, as she always did, the deadness, not of desire, but of memory. It had taken a while, but in the end had faded into something manageable. She sang of love, of the heaven they were in, and therefore at last able to begin the beguine.

She couldn't hold the final note, she had to breathe, and then again, but it must never be a

17

sob. Never. Stan covered for her, his notes soaring and swooping, but his eyes were fixed on her, checking that all was well. She nodded and swayed to the music, shimmying across the stage, spinning slowly and looking over her shoulder, smiling at a familiar lieutenant sitting close to the stage with three of his friends, all from the same frontline regiment, all on embarkation leave. A bottle of champagne rested in an ice bucket. He had been coming for the past week, and he was nice.

She shimmied to Stan's side, bringing the song to a close.

She hung her head, and bowed as applause burst from the patrons, accompanied by hoots and whistles. What a bloody idiot she was to think she'd really deadened the memories. She lifted her head, knowing that her eyes were full. She must not blink. She bowed again, and let the tears drop to the stage, unseen, then stood straight, smiling around at the audience, who were on their feet, cheering and laughing. 'Encore!'

She stepped away, gesturing to Stan, who took a bow, taking her hand, squeezing it. 'All right, lovely girl?' He looked puzzled.

She nodded. 'Just a face from the past – family.'

He nodded and twirled her beneath his arm. They both bowed. He murmured, 'Time for a drink, methinks. Get one for the tank-piercer, it might blunt her thrust.'

Kate stared at her sister, who was not applauding, just standing quite still. Their eyes met.

I'm a star, in spite of you and Father, Kate wanted to say. I can sing, and audiences like me. I can dance. I have friends who do the things I

18

love, all the things I wanted to do, and which you all thought so wrong. Yes, here I am. I have begun the beguine, O sister of mine. Do you even know what a 'beguine' is? It's a dance, a sort of rumba – a dance of joy, I like to think. But you don't dance. You're proper, whereas I am not. I am a polluter, Father said, not suitable... She stopped.

Sarah was looking around the club, her distaste visible. Kate kept her head up, her smile in place, saying into the microphone, 'Well, time for a break, everyone, maybe for more drinks, perhaps some food. Manuel will be here to provide a few wonderful tunes, if you are still in the mood for dancing. You see, we cover your every need. The girls will be moving amongst you, and we'll start again in twenty minutes.'

A man waited to steady her down the three steps. He kissed her hand. 'Dance with me?'

'Of course, but later,' she smiled.

Kate weaved her way through those who crowded around her. Onstage the interval musicians played. At the back, by the curtain, Tony nodded to her and disappeared to his post, leaving her sister standing on her own; a square peg in a round hole, just for once. Kate allowed herself a sense of grim satisfaction.

A young woman came up to her. 'You were wonderful, Miss Watson, but then you always are.'

'You're very kind. Thank you.'

Her partner, pristine in his dinner jacket, said, 'We listened to you in the bandstand show, on the wireless. You sound much better in real life.'

'Thank you, that's so kind. I do hope you're having fun. I see you have one of Teresa's roses.

You can always press it, you know, and have something to remind you of the evening. But forgive me. I must see someone who's waiting for me. Enjoy your evening.'

The bandstand show had been a lucky break: the booked singer was sick, and Brucie moved heaven and earth to make sure Kate was available. At last Kate was getting noticed, and soon a scout had promised he'd call in. He needed people for America.

She reached the lieutenant's table. 'Enjoying yourselves?' she asked these four friends, all so smart in their uniforms, all so terribly young. Lieutenant Bill Secker rose. 'One last dance, Kate, because I'm off tomorrow. Can you manage a tango?' He was twenty-two, and looked twelve. He could die soon. She knew that, he knew that. So many already had, so how could she possibly say no, but she wished his request had been for a waltz, as it had been last night.

'I'd be disappointed if we didn't, as it's your favourite,' she grinned. 'But after that I must leave you, to see someone who has just called in to have a chat.'

'One dance is enough,' he said, leading her onto the floor.

She signed a T to Manuel. 'Let's do this. It's time to put the waltz into storage and move on. In life it's so very important to move on, isn't it.' It wasn't a question. For a moment Bill Secker looked confused. She said, 'Oh, don't mind me, I'm thinking aloud. Come on, time to tango – it's a dance I love too, and it's been so long.'

The floor was almost clear of dancers, many of

whom were clustered around the bar or visiting other tables. She knew they would fall silent and watch the moment the dance began, because this young man was born to dance.

Manuel, who was really Ron from Poplar, slid his trio into 'Jealousy', one of her favourites. Bill smiled and swept her onto the floor and for a moment they felt the music. His breathing was deep and slow, his eyes brown and content, and Kate made hers the same, even though she feared the pain the next few minutes would bring. Safe in his arms, she moved in a closed promenade. She smiled then, really smiled, because this was heaven: this passion, this moving as one, as Bill led her into the music, their steps gliding, striding; and now it was just the two of them, in some other world.

He swished her into a fall-away whisk, which was so sudden, and so strong. There was no time to draw breath, because now he was holding her tight again and walking her backwards, and they were into the music's rhythm and her head was somewhere other than her body. The music swept them on and on, until quite suddenly the climax was reached, only to fall away as the music sliced to a stop and they ceased to move. They stayed, body to body, heaving breath to heaving breath. For a moment there was silence, then the room erupted into extraordinary applause.

Lieutenant Bill Secker smiled at her. 'I will remember this moment for ever. If I return, will you tango at dawn with me?'

She rested her hand against his cheek. 'I said, young Bill, that I would do so with my own true

21

love, whoever that might be. If you haven't met yours yet, one day you will.'

He covered her hand with his own, disappointment and sadness in the gesture.

She said softly, 'You will survive, because I insist that you do; and you will come and find me when this mess is over, and tell me all about her. You will always find me through the Blue Cockatoo. Now I must go. God speed, Bill Secker. God speed to you all, and keep you safe.'

He kissed her palm. 'I will think of you so often and, most of all, of this last dance.'

'This last dance, for now,' she said. Bill turned from her and sat with his friends. She had said that to so many since the war, and so many had not returned, and would not.

Stan slipped to her side, thrusting a gin into her hand. 'Gin from Frankie. He says you'll need it, after that fantastic tango. I'm surprised you didn't set your back off again. It's only a bit more than a year since it was hurt in the raid, isn't it?'

She smiled. 'You can stop nagging. These young men only have this moment in time. Now, I'm off to see a sister, about whatever it is that's bothering her.'

As she approached Sarah, she knew she'd rather be flung into a million wrenching fall-away whisks, than take those few steps towards a world she thought would never come to find her.

Chapter Two

Kate passed between the tables, smiling at those who called to her and stopping to sign one young woman's autograph book. Sarah had retreated into the shadowy gloom, standing in front of the rear wall as upright as a guardsman. The curtain hanging in the doorway billowed as the front door opened. Kate heard Tony say, 'Sorry, chum, we're full.' It must have been someone without a tie. The door clicked shut.

Kate reached Sarah, who said nothing, her face expressionless. As she grew accustomed to the shadows, Kate saw that her sister was thin and drawn. Well, weren't they all? It was wartime. But in Little Worthy they were out of the bombing zone, and grew their own vegetables and fruit. The farmers no doubt helped circumvent the ration cards, as happened in many villages, so Sarah shouldn't have lost this much weight. Kate shrugged. What did she know, and why should she even care?

Kate looked back at the dance floor. This was her world now, and she need never think of what once was. She smiled as the chatter and laughter rose, almost, but not quite, drowning Manuel's trio; Teresa was still selling roses, Frankie served drinks, Stan, Elliot and Roberto sat on bar stools, smoking. She nodded at it all. She was safe. She turned back to Sarah and broke their pool of silence. 'Hello, Sarah, this is a surprise.'

Sarah almost shook her head, as though she'd been brought back into the present. She said, 'Oh yes. Yes.' She stared at her feet, appearing to brace herself. She raised her head. 'I needed to see you, Kate.' Or that's what Kate thought she said, because Manuel had raised the music to another level.

She sipped her gin and shouted, 'Sarah, you'll have to speak up, or come to the dressing room where we can talk.'

At that moment she felt an arm slip around her waist and Brucie pulled her to him. 'Aren't you going to introduce me, sweetie?'

Kate smiled. 'This is my sister Sarah, Brucie. While you're here, have you remembered I'm off-shift at one forty-five tonight?'

'How could I forget, darlin'? It's in the diary, as my old ma would say, or she wouldn't actually, cos we didn't 'ave one.' He slapped her backside. 'You're on again in fifteen minutes, don't forget.' He nodded at Sarah. 'Nice to see you, love. Always a job for you at the Blue Cockatoo, if you've half the talent of this lovely young lady. Drink up, darlin', and I'll take your glass.'

He slapped Kate's backside again, and though he grinned, he would be ticking off the seconds until she was back onstage. She finished her drink, he took her glass and sidled away, his cigarette smoke adding to the layer of fug hanging over the club.

Sarah waved her hand in front of her face, raising her voice against the background noise. 'How can you work here – it's so unhealthy and

24

louche – and who is that person?'

'That's Bruce Turnbull, or Brucie. He's the owner, my manager and my lover.' Kate had also raised her voice, and watched her sister assimilate the news. Kate knew she was being deliberately vulgar to shock her sister, but she didn't care. Brucie was rough around the edges, and if Kate was honest with herself, she knew he wasn't the love of her life. But how dare Sarah come to the Blue Cockatoo unannounced and start turning her world upside-down.

'Must you be so coarse, Kate. And where is your self-respect? What would Father...?' She trailed to a halt.

Kate stepped forward and, toe-to-toe, almost shouted, 'He would say what he always said, which is much the same as you, so no surprise there. Shall we move on?'

In Sarah's eyes there was no emotion. Nothing. It was as though she was half dead, and now Kate realised that her sister's voice had held no real disgust. It was as though she was merely going through the motions.

Once again, as though more than eight years had not passed, Kate felt foolish and cheap. She gripped her sister's arm. 'I'm sorry, I shouldn't have said that.'

Sarah shook herself free. 'No, you shouldn't. But this seedy world, Kate... It's not enough.' She waved her arm around the room. 'Don't you long for fresh air, green fields, real roses?'

'Why have you come, Sarah?' Kate stepped back. She had stopped thinking about what she longed for, because she had become good at just putting one foot in front of the other and looking to neither left nor right. What's more, the minutes were ticking away, the draught was cool, and she still didn't know why this woman was here. 'Did Father send you, Sarah, and if so, why? And how are they, Father and the esteemed Dr Bates? Still golfing, are they? Still taking it in turns to be the height of respectability as captain and deputy of the golf club?'

'He's dead.'

Kate heard the words, and examined them as though they were specimens dangling between herself and Sarah.

'Father or Dr Bates?' Her voice was as emotionless as Sarah's had been.

'Father.'

'So that's why you're here? There's a funeral, presumably?'

Just at this moment Lieutenant Bill Secker appeared by Kate's side. He bowed his head, kissed Kate's hand and said, 'Think of me kindly, dearest Kate.' He straightened, handed her a rose and then, before she knew it, his friends were pulling him away, laughing. Their young faces were indistinct in the gloom. They were gone, and the curtain flapped in their wake.

Sarah stared after them, lifting her chin, as though steeling herself. 'Father died some years ago.'

Kate felt the air leave her body. Years ago? She made herself draw in breath, then exhale, then inhale again. Finally she said, 'But you didn't think to tell me?'

'No-one knew where you were and, if we had,

26

would you have come?'

Brucie approached again. Irritation swept through Kate and she snapped, 'I know precisely how much longer I have: seven and a half minutes. This won't take long.'

'Keep your 'air on, baby. I was just checkin' is all.'

He pivoted round, hurrying after a waiter who was gliding between tables in the act of pocketing a pound note.

'Sarah, Father's orders were never to return, so I would not have come, even to dance on his coffin. That leaves Dr Bates's position as captain unassailable presumably?'

Sarah shook her head, snapping in her turn, 'Do stop going on about Father and the doctor – you've said more than enough in the past. Besides, Dr Bates has left the village and is practising elsewhere. Just listen to me–'

Kate wasn't about to be controlled quite so easily by her older sister, so she interrupted, 'If you couldn't locate me then, how could you find me now? And what's so damned important?'

'I came via the Burlesque Club. That's where you were stripping, wasn't it, when Clive Burrows was treated to the unedifying sight of you cavorting with nothing on, while wafting a fan? Father had been dead some months by then, which was a blessing.'

Kate closed her eyes. 'You can see that things have changed. Back then, I had to earn a living somehow, and the little rat promised he'd keep quiet about it.'

'People lie, Kate.'

27

The air between them was instantly heavy with a tension so dense it seemed almost to drown Kate. She shook her head. 'Not everyone; I don't and never have.'

Sarah put up both hands, as though to ward her off. 'Don't start on that again. I'm here, Kate, because I need you. I really and truly do. My nanny left yesterday, without notice, just as I'm to start training for the FANYs, the First Aid Nursing Yeomanry. I've tried to find another nanny, but without success. That only leaves you. I can't leave the child on her own, for goodness' sake – Lizzy is only eight, after all. Or have you completely forgotten all about *my* daughter while you've been so wrapped in *your* life?'

Kate heard her, but couldn't make sense of it for a moment. When she did, she recoiled, outraged. 'Absolutely not, Sarah; have you lost your mind? Look around you. This might seem louche, or whatever your narrow-minded morality tells you it is, but it's my world; I have a scout coming, someone who is looking for entertainers for America, and I am an ARP warden. Anyway, you have a child and you have no right to leave her.' Her voice broke. She paused, gripping the rose that Bill Secker had given her, and fought for control. Finally she said, emphatically, 'What the hell does Derek think of it all?'

'Derek was lost at Dunkirk.' There it was at last, a welter of feeling in those eyes, in that voice, in the shoulders that slumped and the body that leaned back on the wall.

Kate's grip on the rose loosened. It fell to the floor. She said, 'I really am sorry. I liked Derek, he was kind.'

Sarah almost launched herself at Kate. 'Don't say "liked", you stupid girl, say "like". He's lost, not dead. He's probably a prisoner – surely you can see that?'

Kate let herself be shaken. Her sister was in pain, which she could recognise. She said nothing until Sarah suddenly dropped her arms. Only then did she say, 'I'm sure you're right. Yes, they'll notify you when they have some definite news.'

Sarah's face was suddenly alive with relief. 'Yes, yes, that's what I think. I'm sure some of the French help our men. He was defending the allied retreat of Dunkirk, or so one of his company told me. But they lost contact. Derek knows the family whose children I was nanny to, south of Limoges. He could have gone there.'

Teresa strolled past with her tray of roses, her eyes questioning. Kate nodded that all was well. Teresa walked on.

Sarah was still talking. 'Oh God, Kate, you must see I have to do something to help us fight this bloody war.' She hesitated. 'Anyway, I've told Lizzy you will come. Please, I'm begging you.'

Manuel had stopped playing. Soon Roberto, Stan and Elliot would resume their places, and she must too. But all that seemed a million miles away. Lizzy? So Sarah had told Lizzy that she would come? Kate found her voice, though she could hardly hear her own words over her rising fury. 'You told Lizzy? Well, you can just un-tell her.'

Sarah took hold of her hands. 'Kate, remember how much you owe me. And don't look like that.

29

Apart from everything else, who do you think persuaded Father to send you money to rent a flat until you found a job? Do you think he would have done so of his own volition?'

The noise of the club receded as the trap began to close on Kate. She'd often wondered at his unaccustomed generosity.

Sarah said, 'You needed a roof over your head, and he agreed that it might give you some security while you trained as a secretary, or something sensible. Well, clearly not.'

Roberto was warming up her act, playing 'Cheek to Cheek'. Kate thought of Little Worthy, of the villagers who would have had much to say about her upsetting her father and supposedly running away, having disgraced herself with the gypsies encamped in the woods. And she could just imagine the excited horror, at Clive's tale of the Burlesque Club.

Sarah closed her eyes and took a deep breath, just as their father had always done. 'Kate, it's time we started a new page. I say again: this is war, an emergency, and it is I who need something from you, for about the first time ever.' Her voice was cold and angry.

The trouble was that in many ways Sarah was right, and Kate's mind couldn't find its way past all the remembered emotions that were tearing back, when she had worked so hard to block them all these years.

After a moment Sarah dragged aside the curtain, her voice softening. 'Listen, Kate. Lizzy needs family around her, because who knows what will happen in the FANYs? Bombers are

30

striking other cities and towns, and I will be out and about. You are part of her family, as surely I don't have to remind you?'

It was this that found a resonance with Kate, and finally she was able to murmur, 'But, Sarah, this isn't fair. Last time we were together you never wanted to see me again. I was only fifteen when you made me leave.'

Sarah stopped in the archway. 'Stop blaming everyone else for all that you were, and all that you did. Yes, you were fifteen, whereas now you are an adult and can hopefully understand at last the nature of responsibility. Did I say that you would only have to come for a month? That's how long the FANY training is. I will telephone the Blue Cockatoo tomorrow evening for your decision. Please, Kate, make it the right one.'

Kate latched onto 'you would only have to come for a month'. She looked around the club. Well, it might only be a month, but the scout was coming, she was an ARP warden, and how could she bear to return to that village, let alone care for the child? If, on the other hand, she did what her sister wanted, then all debts would be paid. She said, 'You'll still try to get a nanny, though, so I can return if she is able to start early?'

'Of course I will. So there was no need for such a fuss, was there?'

Sarah left, and it was like a prima donna departing the stage, having had the final word.

Brucie was beside Kate. 'Get on the bloody stage. Leave the family out of it until you go off-shift. The show must go on, ducky. You know that.' She could hear the anger, but it didn't touch

31

her. Instead she stooped to pick up the crushed rose, almost cradling it as she wove her way amongst the tables. Once onstage, she placed the rose on the piano. Poor thing, she would try to revive it when she finished her shift. She called to Roberto, 'Let's do "If I Didn't Care..."'

He nodded and as she walked to the microphone, the boys began to play.

Chapter Three

Sarah walked past prostitutes puffing on their cigarettes behind cupped hands. Would a warden shout at them, as Percy in the village shouted at the lads who did just that, when they had managed to get some from somewhere? As she grew accustomed to the dark she heard music from darkened clubs, and saw doormen moving their weight from foot to foot, making a show of looking up and down the dark street, not to mention doing the same to her. The moon was full and cast a cold light, which, when she turned a corner, didn't stop her knocking over a dustbin. A cat yowled as the bin lid circled on its rim.

She hauled up the bin and the lid, but left the detritus on the ground. Someone yelled, 'What the hell is happening down there?' Sarah hurried on, but the rubbish on the pavement bothered her and she returned, kicking it into the gutter. Let the rats enjoy it. She continued on her way. It wouldn't take too long to reach Waterloo Station from Soho, which is where she'd have to wait for the early train.

As she crossed Shaftesbury Avenue she heard the faint rumble of aeroplanes off to the west, and distant ack-ack as searchlights explored the sky. There were no air-raid sirens, so they weren't heading here, but somewhere would be hit tonight.

She hoped the walk through the night would air the stale smoke from her clothes and hair, in much the same way as if she hung herself up on a washing line. She laughed, thinking of Melbury Cottage, which belonged to her now. When her father died, Derek had strung a new washing line across the long, narrow back garden, so perhaps she could dangle from that when she arrived home. For some reason they still used the pegs bought from the gypsy encampment that used to be set up every year in the woods.

She cut down a narrow street, heading south, knowing that once she reached the river she could follow the Embankment until she reached Waterloo Bridge. She should have thought to tell Kate it was only for a month right at the beginning. All right, it was a lie, but this was war and everyone should do their bit. Inside, Kate was a good girl and loved helpless things, or so Sarah told herself as she used her torch with its slit of light to illuminate her way, as clouds covered the moon. She skirted around a letter box.

Kate had been fourteen, turning fifteen, when the gypsies came that last time. Even though she'd been sent to her room each evening by their father, she had clambered out of the window at night and sneaked off to the woods, or so they had pieced together afterwards. It was behaviour that had done untold damage and brought great changes.

Sarah reached the Embankment and hurried along, hearing the wind over the river. Then over the bridge, until finally she reached the station, waiting for hours until she boarded the early train. Her brain was numb with tiredness, and her thoughts seemed orchestrated by the train's motion as it rumbled over the points. Where are you, Derek? Wait for me, I'm coming.

There were no lights in the carriage, but she could hear the snoring and snuffling of the five soldiers and two sailors who had stumbled into the carriage as the whistle blew at Waterloo. Perhaps the sailors were bound for Plymouth, and the soldiers for who-knew-where. Not Little Worthy – not yet, though it was said some GIs were due in the area soon.

They passed through dark stations lit by the moon.

Yes, the GIs were coming. Some were already here; there were a few in that club. The war would turn, and she would help it do so. 'I will help,' she whispered, repeating it in time with the wheels. 'I will help, and I will find you, Derek.'

Thank heavens she had noticed the advertisement requesting photographs of France, especially any coastal areas. She had sent some, explaining that they had been taken when she was living as a nanny in the early Thirties for two years south of Limoges. She had added that she was fluent in French.

34

She had been invited for a talk with someone in Baker Street, London, and had gone, leaving Lizzy with Ellie Summers, the nanny. She had returned, her life altered by hope. Hope that she would pass her SOE – Special Operations Executive – training, which meant that she would be parachuted into France and might at last find Derek. She stared out into the night. Saying that she was a FANY hadn't been a lie, because she actually had to become one to be able to carry arms, under international law. She had been asked if she had dependants. Warily she had said, 'A sister.'

She had not mentioned Lizzy at the interview, in case a child would prevent her being accepted. However, as the days passed and Ellie told Sarah of her decision to leave and join the WAAF, what appeared to be a disaster proved to be anything but. No doubt Lizzy's existence would be discovered, but by then Sarah would have proved her mettle. If, in addition, a relative was *in loco parentis*, surely the problem was solved.

The train was slowing. They had reached Dorset; soon she would be in Yeovil, then she had only a few miles to go. She would telephone Kate tomorrow for her answer. Mrs Summers, her mother's old friend and Ellie's mother, had said she'd keep Kate on the straight and narrow, and Sarah had to believe that. Oh, but that club; that dress, which left nothing to the imagination; and then there was all that flirting with the soldier.

Across from her one of the sailors started upright, as though alarmed.

She said, 'We're in Dorset and will soon be in Sherborne, and then Yeovil.'

'That's all right then, missus. Way to go yet.' He slumped asleep again.

The train was soon coming into Yeovil. She stood as it drew to a screaming halt. She stepped over the troops' outstretched legs, opened the door and eased down onto the platform into the darkness.

It went without saying that Kate would be needed for much longer than a month, if her training went well, but it was the least the girl could do. Anyway, there was time to sort out that particular problem.

In London, Kate sat huddled in the hut with Frankie the barman, who led her ARP shift. She kept her uniform and tin hat in her dressing room, and the other girls laughed about it. As she left the club she had told Brucie of Sarah's request. 'I haven't decided yet,' she had said when he had refused her leave, telling her she did more good entertaining the troops and their ladies than looking after a child for someone who had enlisted in the FANYs. She had replied, 'If I have to go, even for the whole month, you must agree, or I leave altogether.'

She sat on a crate alongside Frankie, cupping the enamel mug, which was warm from the weak tea he'd brewed over his Primus stove. Would she really leave the Blue Cockatoo? She had her flat, and supposed she could find work in any of the clubs, but Brucie was her boyfriend, and who else would have her, with a back like hers?

'Dawn's not far away, lass,' Frankie said, slurping his tea. 'You look as though you might need a gin, after that visit you 'ad this evening?'

She laughed quietly. 'Best not; we've another few hours on the clock, and I'll end up snoring on our beat.'

'Righto. Who was it – if I'm not stickin' me oar in?'

Kate drained her tea, shook it out onto the earth floor. The hut had been set up at the start of the Blitz so that the wardens could take five minutes' break when the bombs were quiet, or to huddle in out of the rain from time to time. 'It's a long story, but she's my sister. She's joined the FANYs and is going off to train for a month, and she needs me to fill in until the new nanny arrives.'

'Might be a good idea, Kate. You've worked non-stop for as long as I can remember. Gertie used to say you'd come to a sticky end, if you didn't take a break. 'Ow long did you say it would be?'

'Just a month at most – in a couple of days.'

'After that it's the nanny, is it, while she's 'ere, there and everywhere with the ruddy FANYs?'

She nodded.

'Ain't given you much notice.' Frankie sniffed. It was the only thing about him that irritated Kate.

'It must be an epidemic. The nanny didn't give her much, either, I gather.'

He wiped out his cup, stowing it in his canvas bag. He took hers, doing the same. She was on her feet, her gas mask over her shoulder. She pulled her tin hat down, careful to tuck the strap under her chin. Together they went out into the street and continued to patrol.

One of the terraced houses was showing a chink of light. She banged on the door, calling through the letterbox, 'Cover that window – you're showing a light. It's not dawn quite yet.'

'Okey-dokey. Sorry, luv.'

They moved on, greeting the prostitutes, who were making a better living, now the Blitz was over. 'Puts the punters off,' one of them, Gladys, had said to Kate during the Blitz. 'Talk about the earth moving – it's a bloody nightmare for business.'

Gladys was on the street this evening. She smiled at Kate. "Ow's yer back these days, luv? Them bloody bombers should look where they're chucking their eggs. Must be more than a year ago now, isn't it? Lucky you're not one of us and having to spend most of your time on it.' They all laughed.

'It's all right thank you, Glad,' said Kate. 'Best be getting on, though.'

Kate and Frankie walked further along.

'D'you ever hear from Stevie, that little toerag you saved when the bombs fell that night?' Frankie asked. He rattled the door of a bomb-damaged house, which was condemned as unfit for human habitation. It held.

Kate grinned. 'Every month, since I got hurt, he's waiting outside the club with something he's filched or found on the back of a lorry.'

'Oh, well, as long as 'e's still grateful. Your back took a right pummelling, and I don't know how you managed that damned tango tonight. Even I can tell it still pains you, no matter what you say.'

'Oh, stop fussing, it's not too bad and I can't let it take over.' They turned down the very street that had caught the stick of bombs that particular night in May 1941. It was strange the things she remembered when they reached this part of their beat: it wasn't the fear, but the smell of the sulphur, and the judder of the ground as the bombers dropped their loads, seeming to chase them as they ran faster and faster, beckoning and yelling at residents who dithered, 'Get to a shelter.'

It was then that they had seen several ARP wardens outside old Perkins's furniture shop, heaving furniture into the back of a lorry.

Frankie had called out, 'Where you from, lads?'

The men had turned, seen them and not replied, but had called to their mates who were coming out with another load to hurry up, while one of them had jumped into the driving seat and revved the engine. Frankie had turned to Kate, shouting against the noise, 'It's one of them masquerading gangs, stealing Perky's stuff. Bloody buggers – where'd they get them 'elmets from? I'll bloody show 'em.'

He'd taken out the truncheon that he had 'found' heaven knew where. She remembered holding Frankie back. 'You'll get hurt, you daft beggar. Blow your whistle; that'll scare them off, if they can hear it over the noise. We'll tell the police later.'

The bombs had been dropping closer and closer. The sky looked as though it had caught light, and buildings were burning; everywhere there were crashes and screams. The ground had shaken.

'Bloody fools,' she'd yelled at the men as Frankie dragged out his whistle. 'Get to a shelter. Leave the damned chairs.'

Instead the lorry had roared off past them, straight towards the bombs, whilst the men ran the other way, with Frankie giving chase. Another load of bombs had fallen. She remembered how the blast had flung her against a lamp post, knocking her helmet to one side. She had seen one of the gang running after the lorry, shouting, 'Dad. Dad.'

The lorry had copped it, a direct hit. She had taken off after the lad as another bomb screamed down. She'd just managed to grab him in time, but he'd kicked her away, screaming, 'It's me dad in the truck.'

Here, in the calm of a post-Blitz night, with weeds growing through the pavement cracks, she stood quite still and looked at the spot where she'd brought him down. Yes, there, where number twelve had been. The bomb had landed in the street behind, and its blast had demolished numbers ten to fourteen. She had thrown herself on top of Stevie as another bomb blasted a further three houses to smithereens. Her helmet had fallen to the ground, but she hadn't heard the clatter because of the bombs and falling masonry. Shrapnel, bricks and heaven-knew-what blasted through the air, slicing her arm, while her helmet rocked on the pavement. There was another crack, not a crash, and a burning lintel dropped to the road beside them. She had watched as it teetered, like a pillar. How extraordinary, she remembered thinking. How could it balance like that in all this chaos? It didn't, not for long, for it toppled, impossibly slowly, across her back.

There was such dreadful pain, and a smell of burning flesh, and then she remembered nothing else until she was in hospital that evening. There the nurse had cleaned and stitched the cut on her

40

arm, and applied a dressing to her back. She discharged herself in the morning, pushing away the doctor who wanted her to see the burns specialist. His white coat was streaked with soot and blood, his face drawn with exhaustion, after a night of tending the wounded. Her hand had snagged the stethoscope hanging around his neck.

'I'll look after it myself – take your hands off me, for God's sake, or I'll strangle you with this,' she'd yelled, yanking on the stethoscope. She remembered how sore her throat had been from the smoke.

She'd dragged herself to the double doors, but before she could leave, a nurse came over and gave her a large packet of burn dressings, with instructions to collect more when she returned in ten days' time, to have the stitches removed from her arm. She'd bandaged her back herself, and duly returned to the hospital when the stitches were pulling. The nurse removed them, then checked her back, gasped and called the doctor.

Kate had pushed her way past the doctor once again. He called after her, 'I'll try not to hurt, but it really should be checked for shrapnel.'

She'd just laughed, but it was a sudden, harsh sound.

She had not returned. And now, in the quiet of the pre-dawn, she said, 'It was one way to spend an evening, wasn't it, Frankie?' They both laughed.

He said, 'That's one way to put it, lass, but it's all part of the job, let's face it.' She eased her back now. Frankie said, 'You all right, lass?'

'You know I am. I always am, just like you.' She

41

tucked her arm in his. 'We're Derby and Joan, we are, Frankie, though neither of us is old enough. Did you know you're only three years older than Stan, so you could be doing the tango every night and showing us all how.'

'Not without my Gertie. Bloody bombs, they take out the good 'uns, lass.'

'Indeed they do.' She squeezed his arm. 'Do you think they have ARP wardens in villages?'

'You going then? Cos I won't 'alf miss you, if you are.'

They were heading along the main road and would take the next right and come back onto their circular route as dawn began to break. 'I've told Brucie I might, but I still don't really know. There's a scout coming, Frankie. It would be my big break, if he likes me. I could really make it then, because America would be part of the deal.'

They waved at the milkman. It was a miracle there were any milk bottles left.

'Tricky one, isn't it? Not sure what Gertie would say.' Frankie increased his stride, because a man had left his house, leaving the door open. Frankie called, 'Hey, mate, you've left your door open. Enough robbers round here, without giving 'em a bleedin' invitation.'

Just then a woman popped her head out of the door. There were rollers in her hair and she wore a dressing gown. 'Oh, stop your naggin', Frankie Dawson.'

He called, 'Ah, didn't know it was you, Lily. Sorry. And to you, mate.' The man hurried along the pavement, his briefcase knocking against his thigh, his suit smart and pressed.

Frankie came back to Kate, shaking his head. 'I don't know what's the world coming to. That Lily ain't no better than she ought to be. Her 'usband's overseas, and who the 'ell that is, I don't know.'

Kate laughed as they hurried past Lily's house. 'People said that about me in the village – and probably still do. Perhaps, like me, the truth is that Lily's an angel and he's a lodger.'

Frankie looked up at the sky. 'Just look at them flying pigs whizzing past. By that, I don't mean you ain't no better than you should be. You're a doll, in my book. So, will you go?'

'Not a word for years, and here is my sister.'

'You ain't said no, though.'

'Not yet.' They walked on, checking their watches. It was so quiet these days, so different. Would the bombers ever come back to London? There hadn't been a raid on Exeter for a couple of months, either, but did that mean there wouldn't be? Would Yeovil escape? Would Little Worthy? So many questions, so many answers not yet known, so many decisions not yet made.

Chapter Four

On Saturday, Kate waited until the train screeched to a halt at Yeovil, before swinging her case down from the luggage rack. She stepped onto the platform. Others left the train too, but she didn't recognise anyone. She slammed the door shut. The guard waved his flag, blew his whistle and for a moment she was tempted to leap back on. Instead she made her way to the exit as the train chugged on to what was left of poor blitzed Exeter.

Her feet ached in her high heels, but she was damned if she was going to disappoint the Little Worthy inhabitants, who were expecting someone who was to be disapproved of, so that's what they'd get. She even wore silk stockings, courtesy of Tim Oliver, the GI who had been sad that she would be absent for a whole month. 'Ya what?' he had said last night, handing her a rose he held between his teeth as they danced to Manuel's rendering of 'Cheek to Cheek'. 'What'll we GIs do?'

'You'll be entertained by Cheryl, who is top of the bill when I'm not here. What's more, we have a new girl starting who will take the other shift, so whatever night you come, you can dance and drink and forget the rest of the world for a while.'

His uniform was smooth, not prickly like the British uniforms. Everything about the Yanks was smooth, but they'd always take second place in her heart, because the Tommies had stuck it out when no-one else had 'held'. For her, they were the heroes.

Her case was too full, and therefore too heavy. She eased her back as she stood in the queue at the exit. The ticket collector checked each ticket as though it could be a coded message and they were spies. In the end she dumped her case down and shoved it along with her foot. She felt a resurgence of the panic that had almost overwhelmed her, as Brucie tore into her about her decision. Even when they climbed the stairs to her flat yesterday evening, he was still raging. 'We've got this scout coming. Well, he'll just have to make do with Cheryl, who bloody deserves it, because she's not walking out on me – you silly bitch.'

She had now reached the ticket collector. He was a grizzled elderly man who frowned, as though his feet were hurting as much as hers. He examined her ticket, his clippers at the ready, but instead tucked it into a tin box with others, saying, 'Not a return then?'

She shook her head. 'No. I'm looking after my niece while her mother does some war work. She's with the FANYs. I'm not quite sure when I'll be heading home, but in a month at most.'

Behind her a man sighed and murmured, 'Can't we just stop the tea-party chat and get on?'

Kate turned. 'Don't you like me talking to the ticket collector? He's doing his job, just as you are; just as our soldiers at the front are.'

The youngish businessman jerked in surprise and flushed. 'I didn't say anything. I don't know what you mean.'

She stared at him. 'Oh, I think you do.' She turned back to the ticket collector. 'Thank you.'

He tipped his cap and winked. 'Where are you heading, miss? There's a bus due in a few minutes going on past Tintinhull to the west, and another heading north, towards Street.'

She grinned, wondering how long to spin this out, but decided that mercy was perhaps in order. 'I'll hurry for the Tintinhull one. I'm making for Little Worthy.'

'You have a good time while you're here, miss.'
'I'll try.'

She lugged her case out of the station and

45

looked for the bus stop. Surely it couldn't be in the same place? It was. The bus hadn't arrived yet, and there was a queue. Another queue had formed for Street. She felt ill suddenly, and for a moment the ground seemed to lift and fall. She fixed on a point ahead, grounding herself. It was what she had done a lifetime ago, when she and Sarah had travelled on the bus, which had seemed to drive monstrously slowly as it made its way from Little Worthy to this station.

They had taken a train, and then another heading for Eastbourne, where her father had knowledge of a discreet boarding house into which he had booked them for six months. She could see him now, dusting off his hands and turning back into the house as they left to walk through the village, probably saying to himself, 'There we go, job done – problem sorted. Off for a round of golf in the morning, with Dr Bates; everything as per usual, just as it should be.'

She had never seen him again.

She drew in a deep breath. Pigeons were cooing. Somewhere a dog barked. She reached for her case, but then a voice said, 'Let me, it looks heavy.' It was the businessman. He grinned at her, lifting his hat. 'Sorry, you were right. I was rude. Let me say "mea culpa" and at least carry this to the bus stop, since I doubt you'll accept a lift.'

She thought for a moment. 'Where are you going?'

He said, 'Towards Sherborne, eking out the firm's petrol ration.'

She grinned. 'To the bus stop would be fine.'

He lifted the case. 'Crikey, what have you got in

46

this – the kitchen sink?'

He led the way to the back of a queue consisting of women tugging their cardigans around them against the breeze.

Kate said, 'I packed too much. I forgot I could wash as I went. I don't know, you get out of the way of travelling.'

He tipped his hat again. 'Nice meeting you.' He paused. 'I think.' They both laughed.

He went on his way and Kate was relieved. She didn't want to have to talk, not yet. She needed to sit on the bus and brace herself, which is what she did when finally they set off along the well-remembered roads. The sky seemed increasingly large, much as it had when they left London; the countryside seemed similarly huge, and so damned unchanging. Even the bus might well be the same one.

Here were the fields as they had always been: the copses, the crops, the sheep in the meadows, the cows in the corn. The only thing missing was Little Boy Blue blowing his horn. Just then the bus driver honked and braked as a dog dashed out between trees, or was it a fox? She grinned; how Stan would have laughed at the nursery rhyme come to life.

She missed them all, with the sharpness of a blow.

On they went, and as the nursery rhyme continued to rattle around her head, Kate wondered how nature could be so heedless of the life it witnessed every hour of every day. But perhaps, in that relentless rhythmic sameness, there was some sort of healing. She found herself nodding

47

as she became used to the lack of destruction, and to that endless sky.

She looked back at Yeovil, over which hung barrage balloons, and heard the passengers chatting about the bombing raids, as the Luftwaffe aimed for the Westland Aircraft factory and its airfield. Ah, so everything was not quite as it appeared then, like so many things. 'But none for a year, Ethel,' one young woman said, her headscarf tied in a knot under her chin.

'They won't stop flying over us, though, heading for Bristol or wherever, you mark my words,' Ethel grumbled. 'The noise they make is as bad as me bugger's snoring. 'Spect he's keeping his mates awake, wherever he is. I reckon he's somewhere 'ot, since sand fell out of his scribbled note. It did, I tell you. Making ruddy sandcastles on a beach, I reckon.' The two of them cackled at the thought.

Kate grinned across at them. They saw her and smiled back.

'Where'd you get your lippy then, lass? D'you know someone we don't?' It wasn't said unkindly, just with that certain weariness that the war was instilling.

Kate replied, 'I helped out a lad in London when there was a raid on, so now he turns up from time to time with a present; but from where, I don't ask.' She groped in her handbag. 'Here, why don't you toss a coin for it, or maybe share: I've another.'

She threw it across as the bus swerved to avoid a pothole, but it jolted in and then out. Ethel dropped the lipstick. It rolled under the seats, and off she went in hot pursuit, catching it as the bus drew up at a stop outside Tintinhull.

'We'll share, eh, Mabel? We goes out together, you see, lass, if we can get away from the 'vacees, bless 'em. There's usually a bit of a do at the pub for our bowling night. In the league, we are.'

Mabel nudged her companion; her basket almost slipped off her lap, but she captured it and resettled her potatoes. 'Tell her we're near the top and might get the cup. We'll put the lippy on then, eh, to celebrate?'

'Tell 'er yourself, Mabel – or you just have, you silly old moo. She's not deaf, you know.'

Ethel drew out her cigarettes and offered the pack across the aisle to Kate, who shook her head. There was an etiquette in wartime: never accept someone else's rationed goods. The two women lit up, blowing the smoke upwards, and began to talk between themselves about the indoor bowling league.

Kate had forgotten about the bowling alleys that most Somerset pubs had at the rear, not that she and Sarah had been allowed to join in. Her mum had liked to bowl, but it put Kate's father in a bad mood, because he felt it to be lower-class. Kate often felt that her mum had died soon after her thirteenth birthday as a way out. Either that or she was just plain tired of Kate's father. But Kate wished she was still here. Every day since her mum had died she had wished it.

The two women rose at the next stop and gathered their belongings. They'd been on the train to visit their mum. Ah, sisters, Kate thought. Sisters. Everything tilted again, and she focused on the hedges and distant hills.

49

They were very close to Little Worthy now, and in the distance Kate could see the woods where the gypsies had camped every year. She heard the accordion and fiddle-playing, saw the twilight falling, the fire flickering, Andrei and herself dancing, and his mother patting her own chest and saying, 'Feel it feel the music, my little bird. Dance with your heart and you will be brave and free.'

The bus was approaching the top road into Little Worthy. This was her stop. She rescued her case from the luggage area, thanked the driver and staggered down the steps, clutching the handle in both hands. He called, 'Next time bring some lippy for the missus, then I'll be the man of the moment and might get an extra spud.' He laughed, and so did Kate; that was something she had forgotten: country people had ears like bats, and nothing seemed to remain private or a secret.

She watched the bus leave, its exhaust smoking, then walked into Little Worthy, hoping that she was wrong, because some things must never be told, or known. Oh, how she had learned that before she left.

She caught her high heel on a clod of earth, and her ankle went over. She straightened; there was no way she was going to be seen hobbling. The pain eased as she came into the High Street. There was little in the window of Martin's, the butcher's, and it had shut for today. The haberdashery was open, though. She loved that shop, which was where her mother had bought her wool. She remembered the ache as she sat for ages with the hank around hands held wide apart, as her mother wound the wool into balls. The wool was so rough that the carefully knitted cardigans made her itch.

She thought of Tim Oliver's uniform; so smooth. He had said his father was in show business and that he'd tell him of Kate. 'He'll want to hear your pretty little voice.'

'Oh, that's so kind,' she'd said, 'I'd like that.' Knowing that no such father existed, but what did it matter, if it gave the lad a feeling of importance in this little island far from home?

She peered in the haberdashery window. Inside, the tailor's dummy was where it had always stood. There was Mrs Woolton behind the counter. She looked up from the drawer she was tidying, and then back down. There had been no recognition. Well, it had been a while.

Heading along, Kate passed the baker's, where she recognised Mrs Williams queuing, looking older, but somehow the same. Off to the right three children rushed out from the lane, throwing a ball to one another. 'Oi, my turn, Angie. Come on, gal, give it over.' A woman with the children, her hair tucked under a headscarf knotted at the front of her head, called, Angie, you throw it to 'er, or I'll tan yer arse.'

Kate laughed. If that wasn't a Poplar accent, she'd give away another lippy. So, there were evacuees here. It was as well her father was dead, or he'd die of apoplexy. Next she passed the vet's surgery. She supposed most of the dogs had been put down in the war panic, but there would be enough work on the dairy farms for Mr Sheldon, if he still practised. Across the road was the Little Worthy doctor's surgery. She didn't look but hurried on, even though Dr Bates had gone.

She reached the old stone church of St Thomas's, with its square tower. The clock still showed nine o'clock, so it really was time Reverend Hastings had someone in to mend it, though it wasn't a priority in wartime, she supposed.

She approached the lychgate. Someone out of sight was mowing at the rear of the church, but no-one had mown the front churchyard. Her father would have called the new verger a slacker.

She left her suitcase just inside the lychgate, taking off her shoes, sighing with relief as she felt the soft coolness of the unkempt verge at the side of the gravel path. She strolled left, through the long grass and wild flowers, amongst which bees buzzed. She kept on towards the huge yew growing on a line with the chancel, passing rows of tilting headstones with lettering too ancient and smooth to decipher. The yew cast such a shadow that nothing grew beneath it. She skirted it and headed for the eleventh row of headstones. Once she reached it, she turned right, examining each headstone, unsure suddenly which was her mother's. She stopped. 'Here you are, darling Mummy.'

In loving memory of Lydia, beloved wife of Reginald Watson, mother of Sarah and Katherine. Sorely missed.

'You are, Mummy, every single day.' There was a jam jar with faded wild flowers perched on the plinth, and a new inscription beneath her mother's:

And Reginald Watson, beloved father of Sarah, grandfather of Elizabeth.

She absorbed the words and wondered why the pain was so extraordinarily sharp that, yet again today, the ground lurched.

She bunched her hands into fists and focused on the flowers in the jam jar: scabious, agrimony, wild basil and cornflower, clearly picked from the churchyard. The water was tinged green; it would be the heat. She lifted her head and made herself look again at the inscription in memory of her father.

'Bastard,' she said. 'You bloody bastard. How could you not believe me, when I never lie? Andrei would never have done what you said, but you wouldn't listen when I told you who would.'

She searched around and found what she was looking for. She carried the large stones back to the grave and then hurled them at his inscription. One chipped the 'e' of his name. It wasn't much, but it showed she had been here. 'Poor Mum, stuck with you for an eternity.'

She heard someone call, 'I might have known it was you, Katherine Watson. Your sister said you were coming back, with your tail between your legs, no doubt. And here you are, behaving like a hooligan, as always.'

It was the vicar's housekeeper, Mrs Bartholomew, scurrying along with flowers in her arms. It was Sunday tomorrow, so it must be her turn on the rota to do the church flowers. Suddenly all the anger drained from Kate. She laughed. 'My tail is perky and still wagging, Mrs B, don't you worry about that.'

She stalked away, knowing she'd behaved badly, but she'd do the same thing again. The middle-aged woman called, '"Mrs Bartholomew" to you, young lady.'

As she skirted the yew, heading for the lychgate, Kate realised the lawnmower was much closer. A young man was mowing around the headstones on the other side of the gravel path. She finally reached her shoes by the gate. He looked up, completed his run towards the church and then turned, heading down again and calling across, 'Ah, the suitcase is yours, is it?'

She put her weight on the balls of her feet and tottered towards him across the path. The gravel would tear her leather heels and she wasn't having that, and they'd stick into the grass, and that wasn't a good idea, either. 'Yes, I'm back for a month. You're making a good job of it. My father, once he retired from his accountancy practice, was the verger before you and liked it to resemble a lawn, or perhaps a putting green. It's good that you've left the grass uncut, though, and given the wild flowers a chance to grow. The bees prefer it.'

He laughed. 'Purely accidental. I just haven't got round to it, but now you say that, I take your point. I might well leave that side alone. It's a really good excuse, apart from anything else.'

'You'd better be careful or that dried-up old stick, the Reverend Hastings, will have something to say, though he must be so doddery now he probably doesn't notice. Anyway, I must get going. I'm late as it is – the train and the bus took

54

much longer than expected to get me to Little Worthy, and I've been dawdling.'

He had been staring ahead as they had been talking, but now he put back his shoulders and turned towards her, and she felt the shock. He wore a black eye-patch and the left side of his face was terribly burnt, the corners of his mouth pulled out of shape. She found words. 'Oh my, where's your parrot?'

For a moment there was total silence, and she could have burrowed into the ground in regret, but then he burst out laughing. 'I thought I'd keep him in his cage until I have a peg-leg too, or at least find a dozen pieces of eight.'

She grinned. 'You'll do very well,' she said.

'Why, thank you. Where exactly are you off to?'

'Ah, so you didn't know my father, the up-right–' She stopped, and started again. 'You didn't know the verger, Mr Reginald Watson, from Melbury Cottage. Sarah, my sister, is leaving for a month's training with the FANYs. She's lost her nanny, so I'm filling in until another can be found.'

'Training for the FANYs, for a month? I hadn't heard.' He looked at the grass and then the mower. 'It's no good – the grass won't cut itself, so I'd best get on. Nice to meet you, daughter of Reginald Watson and sister of Sarah; we'll meet again tomorrow at the Sunday service.'

She looked at the church. 'Probably not. God and I aren't on good terms, on the whole. Anyway, it was very nice to meet you. My orders were to arrive on time and, as I said, I'm very late, so I must get on. Good mowing.'

She tiptoed to the gate, picked up her case and headed off, and only then did she realise she hadn't asked his name.

The Reverend Thomas Rees watched her go and felt a lightness for the first time in many months – a parrot indeed. He left his lawnmower and walked amongst the headstones, looking for Reginald Watson. One day he'd know where all these people were bedded down, but he'd only been here six months and hadn't really had a moment to settle in. Off to the right of the yew tree he found what he was looking for. He read Lydia Watson's inscription. 'Ah, Katherine Watson, I see now who you are.'

He read on down, and then reread it, astonished and disturbed. There was no Katherine mentioned beneath her father's inscription. Was it a mistake or...? He pictured her energy and beauty, her blonde hair, the laugh in her blue eyes, but the wariness too. Oh, Miss Katherine Watson, he wondered, what has happened in your life, and where have you been up to now?

He stared at the inscription again and noticed a fresh chip on the letter 'e', and the stones lying scattered around. Mrs B called from the vestry doorway, 'She's a bad lot, that Kate Watson. Left the village, she did, after running about with the gypsies in the woods, night after night, and has never been back; she wouldn't dare. She left with Sarah, to look after a relative, so they say, but that's what they always say when ... you know.'

Tom wouldn't listen to this sort of tittle-tattle, which seemed to swirl from this woman whom he

56

had inherited. Had she been the same with the succession of temporary 'dog collars', following Reverend Hastings's sudden demise? If so, why? Had she hoped that Bertie Hastings would make a wife of her? He replied, 'Are the flowers finished, Mrs B? I'll come and admire them when I've finished the grass, though I'm leaving this side. Miss Watson reminded me that the bees prefer it.'

He made his way back to the lawnmower, not bothering to check whether his housekeeper was as outraged as she so loved to be. Poor Kate Watson; not only had she lost her God, and her place on the headstone, but also – from the sound of it – her place in the village. Well, his God had gone missing too, since Dunkirk, so at least they had that in common. As he started to push the mower through the grass, he drew comfort from the fact that he was searching for his God, but suspected that Kate was doing anything but.

Chapter Five

Kate hurried towards the village pond. If any ducklings had cracked open their shells and emerged into the world this spring, they'd be long gone by now. Opposite the pond, the pub had tubs of marigolds around the entrance to the public bar. The door was firmly shut. In Soho, Brucie's clientele knew they could knock and gain admittance almost day and night. Discretion was the byword in that neck of the woods.

She sped past a queue at the baker's, wondering if the wartime regulation insisting that the wholemeal National Loaf must not be sold until it was a day old worked here? She'd always supposed that rule had been brought in because the loaf would then slice more easily, and fewer crumbs lost, but no-one seemed to know and who cared anyway? This lot looked as though they were queuing for the cheap end-of-day stale loaves, as they always had. There was Mrs Williams and her daughter from Down End. Mrs Williams caught sight of Kate and, after looking shocked to see her, turned away, whispering in her neighbour's ear. Soon the whole queue would be gossiping.

She put her shoulders back, determined to pretend she didn't care, and strode on. The baker and his wife, Mr and Mrs Harper, were nice. Would they welcome her, or was she a scarlet woman to them too? Time would tell. She stared ahead, making herself focus on whether people still cooked their Christmas goose, turkey or slab of pork in the baker's ovens. She laughed to herself. 'Come on, it's probably a tiny chicken now; or maybe they're naughty and it's something off-ration.'

Though she spoke aloud, she did so quietly. No need for anyone to think she was mad as well as bad, but she needed to hear her own voice, to remember who she was. Crikey, in a moment she'd burst into song.

Her suitcase seemed twice the weight by now and her heels were rubbed raw, but it was as nothing against the tightening of the muscles in her jaw, the gritting of her teeth as Melbury Cottage hove into view.

There it was, the only one in the street without a thatch. Her father had replaced it with tiles because he wanted gutters, and an end to the dripping rain. She had asked her mother what her ancestors would think of that, as the straw lay in heaps all over her precious herbaceous beds and lawn. Her mother had not replied, but had wept. At that moment her father had swept past them, and put his golf clubs into the boot of the Morris. He had suggested that her mother pull herself together by the time of his return, because it wasn't good for her children to witness weakness. He had chugged down the main street, picking up the sainted Dr Bates along the way. Together they had headed for the golf course where, as captain and deputy they would continue their work of supervising the improvements to the clubhouse.

She grimaced. It was strange how golf clubs were a necessary part of supervision.

In front of Melbury Cottage a taxi waited, its engine running. Kate snatched a look at her watch. She was later than she had thought possible, but she couldn't run on her sore feet. She lengthened her stride and before long turned in through the gate and along the crazy-paving path, now devoid of the chamomile that she and her mother had planted. On either side the smooth lawns still contained no flowerbeds, though there was a rusty old fountain and a red rose in the centre of the left-hand lawn, which had escaped her father's cull.

Clearly Derek and Sarah had felt the same, once they inherited. She saw, though, that the honey-suckle still rambled over the porch, as though in defiance of tidiness. To the right of the front door was a suitcase, with a pair of Sarah's gloves on top.

The door opened and Sarah stood there in her subaltern FANY uniform, stabbing at her watch. 'I've had to order a taxi because I've missed the bus to the station.'

'Hello, Sarah. I'm here – blame the train, blame the bus, blame the verger, or me.'

Sarah stepped onto the, porch, pulled on her gloves and, adjusting her hat, called over her shoulder in a frenzy of impatience, 'Lizzy, your aunt is here, at last. I've asked you once to hurry and will not ask again. I have to go, you know that, or I will miss the train.' She picked up her case, as though to leave anyway, and then replaced it, turning back to the front door and calling up the stairs, her voice softening, 'Lizzy. I want to say goodbye, please. Just come, don't sulk. I'll be back in a month.'

She re-emerged onto the porch. The taxi hooted. Sarah checked her watch, and Kate braced herself as she heard a bedroom door slam, not knowing how to cope.

Sarah said, 'I've left lists in the kitchen explain-ing Lizzy's routine, the rules and where every-thing is.'

Kate let her suitcase drop. She wore no gloves. Bad girl. Her fingers were white from the heavi-ness of the case. 'You're continuing with the nanny-hunt, and I can go if she arrives, as you promised? I have a scout coming, you see, and there's the small matter of earning a living.'

Sarah stared at her, the taxi hooted again and she dug in her handbag. She came out with change and two pound notes. 'Here, take this.'

Behind her a child appeared. Her long, dark hair hung loose, her brown eyes were wide as she looked at the money and then at Kate, whose words caught in her throat at first, because the child was so beautiful, and those eyes so... She swallowed and then managed to say, 'Hello, Lizzy. It's lovely to see you. And no, Sarah, I don't want your money. It was just a remark, probably a stupid one.'

'Yes,' said Sarah.

'Say goodbye to your child and catch your train.' Kate's voice was high-pitched as Sarah tutted and thrust the money back into her pocket. She drew Lizzy into the porch, hugging her, kissing her hair and bending low. 'I will be back in a month, remember that. And I love you. Aunt Kate will look after you.'

Sarah grabbed her case and pushed past Kate, tears in her eyes. It made her human, and twisted Kate's heart. She called after her older sister, 'I'll take care of her; you know I will. Good luck.'

Lizzy stood on the porch, staring after her mother. Sarah didn't turn, just jumped into the taxi while the driver stuffed her suitcase in the boot. They drove away with a toot. Kate watched, then picked up her suitcase and entered the house unhindered, because Lizzy pounded up the stairs ahead of her. A bedroom door slammed shut.

Kate closed the front door. The hallway was as

dark as it had always been, but there was a different smell. When she was a child they'd had a mongrel, which had followed her everywhere. Her mother had named her Topsy, after she brought her home from the farm for Kate's tenth birthday. It was love at first sight. When Kate was thirteen and a quarter, just after her mother died, Topsy had been hit by a tractor as they walked towards the fields. Kate had run with the dog in her arms to Mr Sheldon, the vet, but she was limp and her eyes were glazed. Mr Sheldon was kind and said, 'She died in her lovely owner's arms, and there are many that don't, so try not to be sad.'

Kate had carried Topsy back to Melbury Cottage, which hadn't felt like home since her mother had died, and would now feel even less so. Her father said she should have left the bloody dog at the vet to be burned, with the rest of the rubbish, and wouldn't help to bury her.

Kate left her case in the hall now and passed through the house into the garden, down the gravel path to the apple tree, where she stood beneath the branches. The sun was high in the sky, the leaves rustled and she felt the warmth of her lovely dog in her arms, and on her bed, where Topsy was not allowed, but always slept. Then the house had smelled of dog. Kate had made a wooden cross when she buried her, and it was this she searched for, but there was no sign of it.

'What are you doing, Aunt Kate?'

Kate turned and in that moment, as the shadows of the leaves danced across the child's face, she glimpsed a likeness of … him, the child's father. Then it was gone. She swallowed and said,

'I had a dog. My school friend, Melanie, helped me and Mrs Summers bury her here. You see, your mum hadn't come back from France yet, so she couldn't help. She came home two months later, to marry your dad. She is quite a bit older than me. I was thirteen, she was eighteen and looked very pretty. Poor little Topsy was only three, so she should have had more years to live.' Kate bit off the words, then said, 'Not exactly the right topic of conversation the moment I arrive, is it?'

Kate half laughed. Lizzy smiled. For a moment Kate felt a great stillness. This child was beautiful, but her eyes were so sad. She moved towards her, her hand outstretched.

'Come and help me unpack. I have a present for you, but I wasn't sure of your size, so we might need to alter it, or ask Mrs Woolton if she would do so. She's good with a needle and thread, but you'll know that.'

Lizzy ignored her hand and strode ahead into the kitchen, her cotton frock swinging, her white socks pristine. Kate waited just a moment, realising, if she hadn't already, just how hard the next month was going to be. Lizzy called over her shoulder, 'I'll show you the nanny's room. Mum changed the sheets and there's a fresh towel.'

They climbed the stairs, Kate lugging her case. Everywhere seemed so small, the landing so narrow and so dark. Even the same pictures were on the walls. Hadn't Sarah and Derek wanted to impose themselves on their home? Or were they really just like Father, who had replaced her mother's needlepoint with these scenes of golfers.

Did Derek golf? She couldn't remember. Was he even alive? Who knew, and how on earth was leaving their child to join the FANYs going to help anyone?

Lizzy tramped along the landing, head down and shoulders rounded. She was eight, but moved as though she had the weight of the world on her back.

'Your mum will be home soon,' Kate called.

'My dad said he'd be home soon, too.' Lizzy stopped outside the bedroom that had once been Kate's. The child flung open the door and walked in. Kate stood in the doorway, unable to enter. The wallpaper was still the same, so too the lampshade, curtains, even the rug on the floor. She stared at the ceiling. There was still the age-old water stain. She said into the silence, 'My dog, Topsy, used to sleep on the bed with me.'

Lizzy looked at her, smiling, breaking the spell. 'I bet Grandpa didn't know.'

Kate grinned. 'Certainly not. Can you imagine the fuss?'

Lizzy slumped onto the bed, laughing now. 'I don't want to. He had the hugest temper, hadn't he?'

'Big, massive.'

'Towering, fat.'

They were laughing now, and the child's face was alight with energy. 'He would fuss when I danced. I hear music in my head, you see, music that had been on the wireless, and it made me dance and sing. He said singing was for church, or it led you into bad ways.'

'I hear music too.' Kate still didn't enter.

Lizzy perked up, then slumped again, kicking her legs backwards and forwards. 'I wish Mum didn't have to go to war, like Dad. You haven't gone to war, so why has she? In fact you could go instead. Should we go to the station and tell her that?' She jumped off the bed and slid past Kate, who grabbed her, pulling her back. Lizzy resisted for a moment, then twisted away, wrenching Kate, who felt the flash of pain in her back. She dropped her hand.

'Your mother has a right to her decisions, Lizzy. And what's more, I do my bit in London, and did it all through the Blitz.'

Suddenly she was angry with these country people making judgements, when she bet they didn't have a back that looked like hers, and sometimes hurt almost more than childbirth. She stopped abruptly. She must continue to be careful – very careful, every minute of every day – just as she had taught herself.

'Anyway, she'll be back in a month. Let's see if this dress is any good for you?' She entered the room at last, but wouldn't look at the ceiling. She lifted the case onto the bed, opened it and a pair of shoes fell out, tumbling to the floorboards. Lizzy joined her, staring at the clothes in the case. 'It's so full. And you've brought a bottle of something.' She picked it out of the case. 'Gin,' she said, tracing the letters with her finger. 'What is it?'

'Medicine in case I get a cold. It helps a cough.'

'Oh, we have cough medicine, so you don't need this. Why don't you put it in the raffle at the musical show that our teacher, Miss Easton, is thinking of putting on near Christmas? It's to make money so the school can buy things called War Bonds, or a Spitfire, or something like that. I expect people would buy tickets for such a big bottle of cough mixture.'

'Well, I'll ask Miss Easton if she'd like it, when I pick you up from school.' What else could she say, or it would be all round the village that she was not only a stripper, and a breaker of a father's heart, but was slurping gin every minute of every day? She found the dress she had bought and held it against Lizzy. 'It seems to fit. Do you like it?'

She turned Lizzy round and stood her in front of the wardrobe mirror. The dark pink suited the child's colouring. Lizzy smiled and stroked the dress. 'It's lovely, but it's very bright. Mum said I shouldn't make myself noticed. It's showing off.'

Kate held onto her smile. 'Well, tell you what: you can't wear it for school, but at the end of the day you could pop it on. If your mum doesn't like it when she comes back, then so be it. Is that an idea? We can then find another pretty little girl who could use it.'

Lizzy frowned, swinging from side to side, watching the skirt of the dress move with her. Then she nodded. 'If you say so, then yes. Cos you're a grown-up, so it's not my fault.'

Kate squeezed her shoulders. 'Of course it's not your fault. You're only eight, Lizzy.'

'Nearly nine.'

Kate laughed. 'All right, nearly nine. Now, let's get these clothes put away.'

After half an hour everything was in drawers or in the wardrobe. Then Kate sat on the bed and said, 'You know, I think I'm going to sleep in the

66

attic. There's a lovely view up there, and it means we can keep this clean and tidy for the nanny. I'll leave my clothes here and use it as a dressing room. I have one, you know, at the theatre where I dance and sing.'

It was better to say 'theatre' and bring the singing and dancing out into the open. Lizzy nodded. 'Mum said you danced and sang, with *that* look on her face. I don't think she likes it, but you're a grown-up, so it doesn't matter who likes what, does it?'

Kate rose, leaving the room, knowing that she was already loving this child – and that must not happen. She called back, 'You're a wise little soul, Lizzy Baxter. Now, let's investigate the attic.'

It was enough to bed her clothes down in her old room, without sleeping there too. She pulled down the ladder to the hatch and clambered into the attic. It wasn't even dusty. Lizzy clambered up after her. 'Mum and Dad used this when Dad's auntie came to stay. She's dead now. Mum keeps it clean, just in case. She never says in case of what, but perhaps we'll have visitors again. She's been sad and quiet, you know, now Dad's got lost somewhere in France.'

The single bed was made up, with the headboard end under the sloping eaves, and it would be aired because it was summer. There was a camp bed folded up. Kate opened the large window. Lizzy dragged over a stool and stood on it, looking out. 'I've never done this before. Mum said I might fall, but look: the roof is sloping, so you'd slide down the slope and onto the flat shed. It's not a high jump into the back garden from there.'

Kate smiled to herself. That's exactly what she had done, and then she had run through the garden, wishing Topsy had been alongside her. She'd ducked through the broken fence at the end of the garden, over the bridge, into the woods. She'd go there because the woods were friendly, and interesting. She loved the birds, and the deer, and would head for the centre, where she and her best friend Melanie had made a camp the year before. Kate had liked to sit there beneath the stars and think of her mum looking down, with Topsy beside her. It was the only time it was peaceful enough to think of them and even smell them, because Mum wore rose perfume, and Topsy smelled of dog.

When the gypsies came as usual, just a few months after her mum died, she had found them in the clearing and hesitated, because children weren't supposed to go into the woods when they were here. They had invited her to the camp fire, where she had listened to their music as they made the pegs they would sell, and she watched as some danced. They had invited her to join them and had taught her, and they didn't tell her it was suitable. The following year they had done the same, but that was the last time they had come.

She turned away from the window. 'Yes, I will sleep here, and leave the bedroom for the nanny. But listen, Lizzy; now it's my bedroom, you mustn't come in unless invited, and never in my absence. In return, I will knock on your door and only enter if you allow me. How does that sound?'

Did she sound too bossy? Well, not only would some time alone be necessary to help her cope, but it would keep Lizzy away from the window, without being told not to go near it. She'd also tie it so it couldn't be opened, which would make it doubly safe. 'I must go down and read the lists, and make sure I know what I should be doing, and when. Together you and I, Lizzy, will muddle through. Oh yes, we will.'

Lizzy looked at her uncertainly. 'Mum said if there was a problem with you, I'm to go to Mrs Summers.'

'*We* – if there's a problem – we will both go to her. How's that for an idea?'

They headed for the hatch. Kate climbed down first, to catch Lizzy if she fell. She remembered now that Sarah had done that when she was little. Well, now Kate, in her turn, was old enough to catch Lizzy.

Together she and Lizzy returned downstairs and entered the kitchen, which was exactly the same, except for the lists. There were six, written out in small, neat writing. The first thing she saw was that Lizzy sang in the church choir, and therefore attendance at church was obligatory. She sighed, missing the club with a vengeance. But perhaps that young verger would be there. And besides, no-one in this village could tell her that anything was obligatory, so she would drop Lizzy and pick her up.

She thought again of her old bedroom, and of the water stain. How could it still be there, as indelible as the memories it evoked?

Chapter Six

According to Sarah's Sunday list, Lizzy needed to be at St Thomas's Church by ten thirty at the latest, with her hair brushed, wearing her Sunday dress. This was not only in capitals, but underlined, twice. Kate insisted that Lizzy cleared the kitchen table while she hurried to the compost with the boiled eggshells, scattering the remains of the toast on the bird table on her way back. She ticked it off the list.

She worked her way through points 1 to 5, which brought her to ten fifteen. She was now to dust throughout the downstairs. She began in the sitting room, flicking a duster along the dust-free mantelpiece, then the small table by the easy chair nearest the fire. She reached the sideboard on which her father's decanter stood, empty. She removed the stopper and sniffed. It still smelled of Scotch. Her stomach turned. He and Dr Bates would sit here, drinking and talking of their plans for the golf club. Who was captain now, with Father dead and Dr Bates elsewhere?

Lizzy said from the doorway, 'Will I do?' She stood neat as a pin, in a dark-brown dress and even more pristine white socks. 'You'll need to plait my hair. Mum doesn't like it being loose, because she thinks it looks wild. She didn't get cross yesterday, though, when I took my plaits out to say goodbye, because I was so upset with her. I don't think she noticed, because she didn't even really look at me.' She held out a hairbrush and dark-brown ribbons.

Kate smiled, 'We'll do it in the kitchen.'

'Mum says that's unhygienic, because hairs could get in the food.'

'Ah, well, perhaps she's right; but it's gloomy in here, and I'll wipe the table afterwards, to within an inch of its life. Come on, and never think your mum didn't notice you. She was trying not to show how much it hurt to leave. Let me tell you, my girl, her eyes were full of "missing-you tears".'

Kate herded the child into the light of the kitchen. She had left the back door open, to air the whole house, hoping that perhaps it would clear it of memories.

Lizzy said, 'Mum keeps the door shut, in case next door's cat comes in.'

'Well, the cat hasn't yet. And does it really matter if he, or she, visits us?'

'Mum says it might jump up on the table and...'

Kate took over, 'It's unhygienic.'

'Yes, that's what she says.' Lizzy looked amazed. 'How did you know?'

'Just a wild guess,' Kate muttered, 'Sit down and pass me the brush, please. Ah, you have kirby grips too. Excellent.' She held those in her mouth.

Lizzy said, 'Mum never puts them in her mouth. She says it's...'

'Unhygienic,' Kate muttered, biting on the kirby grips and brushing the child's hair – so dark, so like... She stopped. She created a parting and plaited first one side, tying it off with ribbon, and then the other. Finally she looked, from the front.

'There, even-stevens. You look perfect.' But in the brushing back of Lizzy's hair there was a hint of him, the father. She fetched the dishcloth from the draining board and wiped the table.

'Don't you like me?' Lizzy asked, still sitting.

Kate stopped, looked and saw, not a grown man, but a child of eight. She closed her eyes. God, life was so complicated, so damned difficult. And she wanted to be back in her world, one in which she had control. She showed Lizzy the cloth. 'Why on earth would you ask that? See, no hairs.'

She turned away and washed the cloth beneath the running water. It splashed her; well, it splashed Sarah's apron. Lizzy said nothing, and Kate relaxed.

The child appeared at her side. 'Mum looks at me like that sometimes, as though she wonders who I am. Sort of worried, sort of angry, sort of frightened.'

Kate wrung out the dishcloth, draped it over the taps and answered carefully, 'I think that a child is a sort of miracle, and that parents must be worried about how to keep this miracle safe and sound. I feel it, even though I've just been here a few hours. There's so much to think about, isn't there? If we're not clearing up after breakfast, we're getting into a sort of uniform for church; and then, according to the list, there's lunch, and I haven't even scrubbed the potatoes and cut up the lettuce, ready for you when church is finished. Speaking of which, we need to go. Fetch your cardigan, it's always cool in church.'

Lizzy had been nodding, her expression serious, as though she was examining every word

Kate said.

'Go on then,' Kate insisted. 'Cardigan, you little miracle.'

Lizzy laughed, a great pealing laugh, which Kate joined in. As the child ran out of the kitchen and up the stairs, she locked the back door, shoved Lizzy's chair back tidily, checked the list again, then met her charge in the hall.

'You'll need gloves,' said Lizzy.

'A hat will be enough. It's too hot, and we're late.' Kate's tone brooked no argument. She applied lipstick, put on her straw hat, locked the front door behind them and they half ran to the church, because it was already ten thirty-five.

They rushed in through the church door and there, waiting just inside, was the verger from yesterday, only he wasn't a verger: he was wearing a dog collar.

'Morning, Vicar Tom,' said Lizzy as she skipped towards the choir stalls where other scrubbed and brushed children waited. Kate couldn't see who played the organ. Whoever it was, they were finding some of the right notes, but not many.

She waved at Lizzy, and then smiled at the vicar. 'You could, perhaps, have told me who you are. No parrot yet, I see.'

He grinned. 'No peg-leg, either, between yesterday and today.'

'A wound of war?' she asked, waving aside his offering of prayer and hymn books.

For a moment his, smile faltered. 'It was not exactly a picnic on the beach.'

'Ah, Dunkirk?'

He nodded.

73

She said, 'It must have hurt, and probably still does. I've heard about blast damage – sort of sucks the breath out of you, quite apart from the burning flesh. I feel for you.'

Behind her she heard a whispered, 'Well, a parrot, indeed; and drawing attention to that awful face. Has she no sense of what's right?'

Mrs Bartholomew came from behind and overtook Kate, grabbing the prayer and hymn books from the vicar. 'You go and do what you should be doing, and ask again for someone to take the verger's position. The grass needs cutting properly, whatever you said about the bees. It's a dreadful mess.'

It was not a suggestion, but an order. Kate raised an eyebrow, and the vicar sighed and winked at her. He said to Mrs Bartholomew, 'No, Mrs B. I'm sure if you think about the honey situation, you'll realise that Miss Watson's suggestion is a good one. We'll leave it for a while longer.' He sauntered off down the aisle towards the altar.

The women behind Kate gasped, and one said in a loud voice, 'Coming back to the village and straight away she's taking advantage of that poor, damaged young man. What would her father think? But he wouldn't be surprised, would he? Stripping indeed. Whatever next?'

Kate moved from the queue, and waved at Lizzy again, but she was chatting to the other children. For a moment Kate watched; then, without looking to left or right, she left as she had always intended to. Mrs Fellows, from the big house, said as she passed, 'How dare she wear all that lipstick in church.'

'Her sort always dare.' It was Mrs Williams, whom Kate had spotted the day before outside the bakery, with her daughter.

Outside the church a woman blocked her path. Kate side-stepped, but the woman went with her. Kate focused, knowing she had to toughen up all over again. It was Mrs Summers, Kate's mother's old friend, and the mother of Sarah's runaway nanny – Ellie Summers. She'd recognise that white hair anywhere.

'Not so fast, young Katie Watson. I'm cutting off your retreat.'

Her laugh was booming, and she dragged Kate to the side of the path, out of the way of several women who were scurrying past, gossiping like a gathering of starlings plotting their migration.

'Don't you dare do a runner. And I insist that you do not let those tears fall, young lady. You need to face those women out; and I'll be with you, cheering you on while you do it. They'll get tired of their delicious shock at your return, and at their distinctly mouth-watering "disgust" that you were a stripper. Kate, they haven't the wit to see that sometimes needs must. And, sadly, they are encouraged by that appalling snob, Barbara Fellows, who has little to do but count her money and create divisions. Your mother would have made sure that whatever happened back then, it didn't – even if it meant going to the woods with you and learning to tango. However, I suspect she already could. Now, come along, this is not the time to be precious. Lizzy needs you.'

She slipped her arm through Kate's and, pinioned thus, Kate had no option but to return

75

and take prayer and hymn books from Mrs Bartholomew, who looked as though she'd sucked a lemon.

The vicar, now wearing his vestments, announced from the altar steps, 'Hymn number one hundred and ninety-six: "Guide me, O thou great Redeemer".'

The choir drowned out the wheezing discord of the organ, and it was Lizzy's voice that soared above all others as Kate listened, mesmerised. Mrs Summers nudged Kate, and against the grinding of the congregation's efforts she said, 'Now, do you see why I wanted you to stay. She is like you, my dear. Just listen to that voice. Now, sing up and help her.'

Kate found herself doing so, and around them voices grew quieter. In the choir stall Lizzy was gazing across the congregation, trying to find who was singing, just as the choir and vicar were doing. Mrs Summers waved to Lizzy, pointing to Kate, who was singing to Lizzy – and her alone. Within seconds Lizzy was doing the same, and it was as though there was no-one else.

The organ wheezed its last notes and the congregation rustled and sat down, craning round to see whose voice had melded with Lizzy's. They located Kate and stared, then shook their heads. Kate sighed.

'Let us pray,' said the vicar. More rustling as hassocks were arranged, knees plonked down; then they were standing again, and soon it was another hymn, 'There is a green hill far away'. This time the young female choir-leader looked out at the church, waiting for 'the voice'. Kate sang, but more quietly now, but still she and Lizzy sang for one another because, in Kate's world, there was no God.

The vicar took to the pulpit for the sermon, and Kate leaned back in the pew. It was at this point of the service that the Reverend Hastings had droned interminably on and on and she'd longed to be outside, playing with her friend Melanie, who had left the village soon after Topsy had died. Perhaps it was as well, because Melanie was a Roman Catholic and her father hadn't approved of their friendship, so it would have caused even more discord.

The vicar was clearing his throat and presenting as much of the good side of his face as possible. She supposed she might do the same, if her back had been visible, but maybe they both ought to brazen it out. She smiled at the thought of stripping off her clothes and revealing all. Her back had been perfect when she'd worked at the Burlesque Club, and if she'd known then what it was like to be pain-free, she would have appreciated every minute. The vicar was rustling his papers on the lectern. Oh, do get on with it, she thought, longing for a cigarette, and regretting her promise to donate the gin, because she'd need one after this.

The Reverend Thomas Rees at last began. 'I was going to talk to you today about suffering, but,' he tapped the papers he had before him, 'I have listened yesterday afternoon and this morning to my "flock" and will now read you Colossians three, verses twelve to thirteen.' He did so, then placed his Bible on the pulpit ledge and leaned forward, resting on his elbows. 'You will

77

see that we are asked to clothe ourselves with – amongst other virtues – compassion, kindness, humility. We are also advised that if, anyone has a complaint against another, forgiveness is every-thing, just as God is forgiveness personified. So, my friends, is this call for forgiveness reasonable, if we feel we have been slighted or our sense of decency has been outraged?'

There was a shuffling in the pews. Kate could see Mrs Bartholomew whispering to her neigh-bour, Mrs Fellows, as the vicar continued, 'You see, my friends, the Apostle Paul teaches that at the core of our Christian identity we are to become as one unified humanity. It is a humanity which, of course, he and perhaps we place our-selves firmly within. Do we realise, whilst trying to achieve this, that central to this humanity is forgiveness. Now, what stands in the way of forgiveness?'

He straightened, and looked at the congregation, and around at the choir. Kate wondered if they were to put up their hands or answer in writing. Forgiveness was sadly lacking, she wanted to say, in this village; and certainly in me too. In fact, the lack of it eats away at what was my heart until, quite honestly, there is just a husk left – not enough to make a silk purse, or even a sow's ear. The vicar was talking again, so clearly answers in writing were not required.

'Let us think of Matthew seven, verses one and two. Judgement is what frequently stands in the way of forgiveness. If you are pondering my words, let me help. Jesus tells us exactly what he meant: "judge not that ye be not judged". So, basically, he means that in the way you judge, you will be judged.

'I don't believe Jesus meant that we should never make a judgement about right and wrong, which is surely essential in our society. Think of Germany: had judgements been made by Hitler's people, perhaps the horrors in the making would never have been born. Yes, indeed, if someone kills, we can judge that this is wrong, but I believe he meant also that no-one is perfect, least of all ourselves. I have already said that I speak as someone who has listened to some discussions, so bring your compassion, your examination of yourself into the arena and move towards forgiveness of whatever you might feel has been a slight, or a wrong done to you or to a community.' He straightened and looked around.

'Beware of behaving in much the same way you have deemed wrong. Remember: we are at war, and for now that can't be changed, but in our own lives we have the power to open our hearts to kindness, acceptance and welcome. In Little Worthy, let kindness, inclusion and humanity reign. Now, may the peace of God, which passes all understanding, keep your hearts and minds, through Jesus Christ, our Lord, Amen.'

Mrs Summers pressed her arm against Kate's, murmuring as they rose to their feet, 'That's telling them.'

Kate replied, 'That's telling us all.' But for her, there were some things that couldn't be forgiven, and she couldn't sing the next hymn because her throat was too full. Yet again, as she had so often before, she felt the need to run free and make for the woods, to look up through the trees to the sky, to thoughts of her mother, and Topsy, and a time of safety and protection. But if she couldn't find it in her to forgive the unfairness of all that had happened, why should the village be kind to her?

As they left the church she shook Reverend Thomas Rees's hand. 'Interesting sermon, it was good of you.'

'As it was of you to stay here.'

'Yes, a bit above and beyond, I think, Vicar.'

'One day it might not be.'

She just smiled and waited at the side of the path for the choristers to be released. Mrs Summers joined her. 'Have the ticked-off come running to you in sackcloth and ashes, to embrace she who they wanted to cast out?'

'You can see the rush to embrace me with warmth and welcome.'

The two women laughed gently. Kate enjoyed the July heat, and tasted the dust in the air from the wheat that was beginning to ripen. She liked the August harvest time; it was then there was a faded fullness to the verges and gardens. In a few months it would be autumn, with its changing colours, and she must make a point of stepping out in the London parks. Then it would be winter and, when she lived here, before her mother died, the door would be shut, and chestnuts baked on the fire on shovels. She laughed at herself. Chestnuts on shovels had stopped for her, long ago.

Mrs Summers called, 'Hello, Lizzy.'

Lizzy was skipping out of the church and came to them. 'We sang, you and me,' she said. 'We sang and I didn't really hear anyone else while we

80

did. It was really strange, and Miss Easton, my teacher, says thank you for the offer of gin for the raffle. She teaches us church choir too, you see. I'm really quite hungry.' She set off along the path. Kate and Mrs Summers shared a look, laughed and then followed.

Mrs Summers said, 'You didn't really donate a whole bottle of gin?'

'What else could I do, or it would be all around the village that they could add being a drunk to my list of sins.'

They laughed together as they walked along the High Street. Just before Mrs Summers turned left, heading for her cottage at the end of Gosling Lane, she said, 'I hear you are in the ARP in London. Even though you're only here for a month, we do need you. Poor old Percy Evans is on his knees, toddling round after dark checking the blackouts and listening for planes. He's never had a real alarm, and I fear he'd have a heart attack if that ever happened. On the other hand, he might raise a cheer to have blown his whistle, just once. Anyway, he could do with a break. I've decided I'll sleep over on Tuesday nights to look after Lizzy, so that you can do a shift for him. I have a helmet you can use. My Jonty was a warden in '39. Then the old fool went and died on me.' Her voice broke, and after a moment Mrs Summers said her goodbyes and rushed off.

Kate looked after her, remembering Jonty. He was funny and always kind. Several women walked past. One stopped and said, 'Hello, I'm Fran, and I rent the end terrace, along from Melbury. I brought the children out of Ealing for the

81

Blitz, and think I'll stay on for a bit. I like the WI, apart from anything else. They'd like you to come to a meeting, I 'spect. Don't bother about the old sourpusses – they're just jealous. Imagine that lot stripping.' She grinned. 'If you need anything, let me know.' She hurried on.

Kate followed more slowly.

Lizzy was waiting at the gate into Melbury, 'I am really, really hungry. What did Mum put on the list for lunch?'

'Let's go in and see, shall we?' As she did so, Kate realised she hadn't actually said yes to the ARP shift, but that was Mrs Summers all over. She wondered what she thought of Ellie letting Sarah down and disappearing to the WAAF? She must remember to ask if there was any chance of the girl not liking it and returning.

Chapter Seven

Sarah stayed in a hotel in London on Saturday and Sunday, one that she and Derek had used on the first stage of their honeymoon almost ten years ago, but it wasn't the same. Well, obviously, what with the windows taped across, the blackout and the darkness of the streets. She shouldn't have come. She should have had longer with Lizzy, because this just spoiled what had been a precious memory.

All day on Sunday she walked along the Embankment, then up to Piccadilly and finally through Hyde Park, the look of which underlined how everything was on a war footing. Little Worthy seemed cosy and comfortable and a million miles from the world she would be entering tomorrow.

Sarah arrived at Portman Square promptly at nine on Monday and was admitted into a large flat buzzing with people; some other women were in FANY uniform too, and the men in the uniform of whatever corps they were nominally attached to. She sat in rows with them, wondering who they all were and why they had decided on this course of action: had some lost a lover, as she had, or were they here courtesy of purer motives?

Well, it didn't matter, because *she* was determined to find Derek. When she had seen the advertisement in the newspapers asking for photographs of France, it had been like a gift. She had sent hers, guessing that it might be some sort of intelligence department that needed them. They had called her in for an interview, and *voilà:* here she was and, if she completed her training, she'd be in France, on Derek's trail. Not that she'd told them that, of course.

A woman in a grey suit arrived and explained that the aims of SOE were to conduct espionage, sabotage and reconnaissance in occupied Europe, and for this they needed circuits set up, comprising small groups of Resistance personnel and agents. To this end, the recruits would commence training and, if they passed the first month, there would be a continuation of that training.

'You will be allocated a name by which you will be known for a while, but only a while. For however short a time, you must become that name Become it, own it – do you understand?'

They all nodded. How simple to become someone else, Sarah thought, as she was given the new name Amélie. Is this what Kate had thought, when she spent all that time in the woods? She beat down the rage she felt towards her sister, the trouble she had caused when she and Derek were newly married and renting a cottage down Gosling Lane. There had been no peace, with her father constantly knocking on the door, complaining about the girl and her wildness; and later the disgrace, and the lies she had told. And the way Kate had been able to leave, while she had to endure the burden of her father's fury, although at least she had felt repaid by the legacy of the cottage, and her father's shares. She felt no guilt, because Kate had received money that her father sent to start her off.

It occurred to her only now that he must have known Kate's address, though he had never said as much.

The woman had finished giving her instructions, and the other trainees were rising from their seats. Sarah focused. She must not drift in her thoughts ever again, because she could die if she did. She went with the six other girls, smiling at them. They travelled by coach to who-knew-where, arriving at a large house set in sweeping grounds, but with oaks and horse chestnuts shielding it from the road.

They didn't know the details of the training, but were told by an instructor on their arrival that it would be conducted in French. They

84

stood to attention in the hallway, their cases at their side. 'The food is good and off-ration, the beds comfortable. It is only the seven of you, and you are to talk to no-one about your lives, either here or in the outside world, not even one another. Your notes home are to be weekly, and you will not repeat anything of your experiences.'

Instructors sat with them after the evening meal, and as the evening darkened, the blackout was drawn across the windows, the table lamps switched on and they were given trays containing objects.

'Take a look and remember the articles,' one of their instructors said in French – always in French – his eyes cold, but his smile broad. It was disconcerting. He timed them for thirty seconds. He signalled. Other instructors who appeared from the shadows whisked the trays away. Then the girls had to describe what had been on the tray.

This was repeated twice, with different objects, until they all remembered correctly. 'Observation, alertness, memory: these will help you remember messages that you may well have to deliver, and could also save your lives,' the instructor said.

Later that evening one of the girls, Monique, laughed at a joke and said she'd tell her boyfriend before she went to bed. She was gone by the morning. It was then that Sarah realised she really was in an unforgiving parallel world. But if she was to be useful in France, it was a world whose rules she must obey.

They sat in classrooms and learned map-reading, and tapped out Morse code. Sarah was slower than the others and as the days passed, her panic caused the sweat to pour down her back in the July heat. What if one morning the others found her gone and, instead of working here, she was taking the train back to Little Worthy? The thought of seeing Lizzy meant nothing to her, because she would have failed Derek.

She was not sent away for her Morse-code limitations, but found herself with one less 'friend', as another girl disappeared at the end of the first week. They never knew why, and neither did they discuss it, as had been ordered. What they did realise was that people were watching and listening every minute of every day and any mistake was noted; any mistake that could cause harm to them or their companions. It was as though they were already behind the lines, in deadly peril.

For the first time she felt a flash of terror, but then it was gone. What did it matter what happened to her really, if Derek was dead? And in her heart, for just that moment, she allowed herself to admit the possibility.

Each day they increased their physical drill, rising early and running across fields before they had eaten, wrestling one another and the instructors, who smelled of sweat, but then she probably did too. Suddenly it didn't matter whether she had washed her hands before eating, whether hairs fell into her mess tin; nothing mattered, except lasting another day.

In the evening they added charades to their entertainment, but quite why no-one knew, and the articles on the observation trays increased. 'Enumerate them for me,' said the instructor.

'You *must* reach a point where it is second nature.'

In bed that night Sarah wrote a brief note to Kate, her second, and tried to sleep, but her head was full of facts about the revolvers they had handled, the rifles and hand grenades, the explosives they had learned how to manage, and the letter she had just written. Had she said anything about her life here? She put on the light and double-checked again and again; but no, she had only asked about life in Little Worthy, and told Kate about making tea at the canteen as part of her FANY duties, and sent her love to everyone, and hoped the choir was proceeding well.

The next morning she was called from the self-defence session and had to march at double time over to the supervisor's office on the ground floor. He had her letter on the desk in front of him.

She stood to attention. The supervisor let her, though there was a chair available. His desk was quite empty, except for the letter. She stared at it. What had she said? He looked up. His glasses glinted. The window was behind him and the sun blinded her as she faced him. He said, 'Amélie, who is Lizzy?'

She closed her eyes for a second, frozen. She had admitted to a sister called Kate, but that was all. She had double-checked last night that she had addressed the letter to Kate. How did they know about Lizzy? Should she say Lizzy was her sister, and perhaps pretend it was Kate's middle name? She said, 'A dependant.'

He replied, staring up at her. 'Your first letter was addressed to a person called Lizzy; this one is to Kate at the same address. You told us of a sister,

87

but not a daughter. Let me refresh your memory: Elizabeth Baxter, whom you call Lizzy, is at school in Little Worthy, being looked after by your previously estranged sister, Katherine, whom you call Kate. Sit down, Amélie.'

She did so, sitting bolt upright, her heart hammering. How could she have been so stupid? How had she not censored that first letter? How?

He said, 'We have come to understand that you lied to us.'

She shook her head. 'I didn't. She's not my biological child, therefore I didn't lie.'

'You're splitting hairs.'

'It's a fact.'

'Whose child is she then?'

'She has become mine. But you need me, because I know France and the French so well, and my language is fluent. You might not have taken me, if I had told you at the interview that I had a child. But I'm good, you must see that by now. You'll have to drag me out by the hair, whether it's split or not.'

'Don't lie to us again. Your sister will stay the course for as long as need be – perhaps for the rest of her life? We can't have your attention straying.'

'Yes, she will, without a doubt.'

It was as though he was waiting. And as Sarah watched him, watching her, she realised that this organisation probably knew exactly who was the real– No, not real, the *biological* mother of Lizzy. She lifted her chin. 'My sister is getting to know Lizzy, who is her biological child, but you probably know that through your investigations. So here I am, right now, confirming it. Yes, my sister will take on my child's care. My child who is also her child. You see how complicated it is. She is mine, but she is also Kate's. I repeat that my sister will, without a doubt, stay the course. If there's one person I know well, it's Kate.'

He looked at her long and hard and, at length, nodded, his expression grave, even sympathetic. 'Life presents us with hard decisions, does it not, Amélie?'

It was her turn to nod, hardly daring to breathe, her own words resonating, because she had never actually spoken of this to anyone outside the family circle: Sarah's child, Kate's child. It was like some sort of song chorus and, for a moment, doubt set in. Would Lizzy grow too fond of Kate? Would she herself really not return? In that case, Lizzy must love Kate. Would Kate...?

They sat in silence. It was all too difficult, and her thoughts were fragmenting, then swirling. What on earth was she doing here?

She waited, and into the silence came Derek's voice, his laugh. Of course, *that's* why she was here. Her hands balled into fists, and her resolve stiffened again with every passing second. Would she be sent away? No, she had meant it: they'd have to drag her out.

At last he nodded slightly and gave her the letter. 'If you are going to stay, you have to be consistent with your lies; in fact, you have to *be* a lie. Post this. Let me discuss the situation with others.'

The supervisor pulled a folder from his drawer. She left, shutting the door and walking away. She couldn't do anything wrong again, she knew that; and if it took a lie to remain, then so be it, because how on earth could she know Kate, after so much time, and all that the girl had done to the family in the past?

She passed a window and looked down to the back lawn. The self-defence session was over and just two instructors remained, practising on one another. She ached from the bruises she had collected during the week, but thought she could probably kill someone now without a second thought. How could the change in her be that quick? Well, perhaps because every second of every day and night was creating a different world in which to exist and survive.

She paused, nodding at the thought, then came back to the present, knowing that right now she needed to make her way to the start of the trek across the hills, which would begin in... She checked her watch. It would begin in ten minutes.

As she walked down the corridor in her plimsolls she heard a voice. Surely it was Victoire's, but she should be in the changing room, donning her already grubby civilian kit. She stopped and peered round the corner. Victoire was on the telephone. Sarah pressed herself back against the wall, her mouth quite dry. Phoning was a clear breach of the rules – forbidden and serious, for any outside contact apart from a weekly letter was prohibited. What should she do? Victoire was so nice, so desperately keen to help out behind the lines; and her knowledge, not just of French, but of Danish and German, was so good that she was invaluable.

Sarah almost crept past the corner and towards the changing rooms. How could she tell the supervisor, when she herself had perhaps been given a second chance? How could she be responsible for ruining a wonderful girl's chances and for breaking up the group, for they had all bonded so closely? Besides, everyone would hate her, and she wasn't used to that.

She checked her watch. They would be leaving soon for the trek up Morgan's Hill. She entered the changing rooms, and the others looked up. 'You all right?'

'I'm fine. Just an administration thing.'

They had learned that they didn't share anything. Victoire slipped into the changing room behind Sarah, and they both changed into their mufti, putting on ordinary shoes. It was like a dress rehearsal, because they'd not be wearing walking boots or plimsolls if they were being chased.

Sarah jogged out of the grounds, with Victoire ahead of her. Victoire was fitter than the rest of them, as though she'd been doing this for a lifetime, and she almost bounced as she ran. They had each been given a map and would separate, as the directions scribbled on their maps dictated. Sarah's map led her into a copse and then through the other side. She was slipping and sliding on the sodden ground; she carried a rucksack half filled with wood, and had slung an unloaded rifle over her shoulder.

The breath was heaving in her chest, and the rifle was banging against her side. She stopped running and walked thirty paces, then ran thirty;

91

the 'rifleman's progress', their instructor called it. It was energy-efficient. She checked her map, and last night's rain dropped onto it, from the canopy above. How on earth could Victoire run as she did? How was her Morse code so efficient? Some were just quicker at learning, she supposed.

She ran out of the woods and up, up to the crag. She breathed in the cool air, watching Victoire stride downwards. The girl was just too perfect. Sarah watched her for a moment longer and then realised the truth of it. She ran down, driven by desperation, because she had just realised why Victoire was so able. She was a plant, and it was a test. She tore down the hill, not even stopping when she reached the end, but hurtling past the check-in instructor and thrusting her map at him. 'I can't stop, I need to see the supervisor.'

The instructor nodded his consent. Sarah dumped her rifle on the table provided alongside him, ripped off her muddy shoes in the changing room and, in her stockinged feet and mud-splattered skirt, ran along the corridor, slowing as she arrived. Panting, she knocked.

The supervisor called, 'Enter.' He sat there, the sun still shining in through the window.

Sarah said, 'I have to tell you, though I don't like snitching, that Victoire used the telephone.'

He stared at her and reached into his drawer, pulling out a sheet of paper, not a folder, un-screwing his pen, checking the time and writing it on the paper. Reading upside-down was an-other skill that had been encouraged.

He asked, 'When did this occur?'

She told him. He wrote that down, then looked

92

up at her. 'Two hours between witnessing it and reporting the said infringement. Why was that?'

'I didn't want to tell on her, because Victoire offers so much that we need.'

'What changed your mind?'

'Suddenly she didn't add up. Her Morse is too good, she runs too well, she's too nice. I guessed she was a plant. I'm late, but I'm here, and I reported her in the end.'

He sighed. 'Sit down, Amélie. Now listen. Those two hours could have killed you, out in the field – and your group. The only reason I'm letting you stay is because of your powers of observation. You realised there was something wrong with Victoire, so you're learning. But you need to hone this, and we will be helping you do so. Now it's ever onwards; and if you pass each section, perhaps we'll get some sort of use out of you, but don't count on it. You've a long way to go. Dismissed!'

She about turned.

He said, 'Amélie, you've had your one chance, and you won't get even that out there. Don't muck up again.'

She spun back 'Yes, sir.' Then she doubled out of the room. She had almost three weeks to get through. She must make it.

Chapter Eight

The padre waded through the surf, knocking aside timber, bodies, helmets, clambering towards the beach, crouching low, hands to his ears; the noise, the terrible noise: shells, screams, groans, shouts: 'Padre, here.' 'Padre, over there.' 'Padre', bloody everywhere.

'I'm coming, coming, coming.' But he wasn't. His feet were sinking into the sand. He was being sucked down by demons coiling around his legs. 'Daniel, I'm coming. Daniel, wait.' But Daniel wasn't waiting. Instead he was on the sand, blown out of the trench the men had dug in the dunes. Yes, he was out and hurt by the bombs, but the padre couldn't hear what Daniel was saying because of the shouts. 'Padre, here.' 'Padre, over there.' 'Padre', bloody everywhere.

The sand was in Tom's mouth, as he called again, 'Daniel, I'm coming.' He kicked at the demons, and again, until he was free. He called, 'Stay there, I'm coming.' He didn't want to go, not out into the fire-storm, not out into the bombs. Not again. He stayed, breathing, just for a moment, only a moment. The sand was in his mouth, sharp and choking. It tasted of salt. 'Padre? Where are you, Padre?'

He ran now, crouching, weaving, medical bag over his shoulder. It banged against his side. Bang. Bang. Daniel was bleeding, and so too Fred, and Archie. 'Padre, here.' 'Tom, here.' 'Tom Rees, where are you?' Tom ran faster, each step sinking into the sand, but he'd paused too long. Bang. Bang. Boom went the

94

*bomb, on Daniel, Fred and Archie. The medical bag
burst. Shriek went his voice; the air was sucked from
his lungs, then a scream, then only pain. He fell,
crunching into the sand, tasting blood – his blood –
smelling cordite, and his flesh. He had been too late.
He had waited, paused, not come.*

Tom woke, the darkness cloaking him, choking
him, the sheets tangled around him. He struggled free, sweating. He swung out of bed and sat
upright, making himself breathe, making himself
return here, to this room, this village, this life.
'For God's sake,' he breathed. 'For God's sake –
if not my sake – leave me alone, let me go. I tried,
but I couldn't reach you. I paused, that's all. I
paused because I couldn't do it again, just at that
moment. I couldn't do it any more.'

He slumped and sank his head into his hands,
but that hurt his damaged eye and cheek. Rising,
he dragged on his dressing gown and inched his
way to the door in the darkness, making his way
down the stairs, feeling the bare boards beneath
his feet.

'Solid ground,' he muttered, longing to hear
some human voice in this creaking quietness of a
house. It was so big, so empty, but he was empty
too, his God as elusive as Miss Katherine Watson's.

He turned the light on in the sitting room and
sat in Hastings's favourite armchair. It was so old
that the cushions had acquired the old man's
shape, but it suited him too, so that was that.

'So, Tom, you're here, sitting as perhaps he sat.
Now what? You're alone. You're out of the army,

95

you've just been ditched by Pauline, who can't stand to look at you, so what now?'

Not that she'd said that; she had been too polite and merely handed him back his ring, saying, 'People change, Tom. I'm sorry.'

He had felt like saying, 'Yes, people tend to change when a bomb goes off in their face.'

He minded, of course he bloody did, he had said to his mother when he had telephoned her a few days ago. He then asked what it meant if a girl went away to stay with relatives for six months and was 'no better than she ought to be'.

His mother had said, 'It means someone has a vicious tongue, and you shouldn't pay them any mind. You're a vicar, for heaven's sake.'

He laughed now in the quiet of the vicarage. She was right, of course, but then his mother usually was. She'd asked about the nightmares. He had lied and said he was untroubled. She'd said, 'Don't talk nonsense, Thomas Edward Rees. But one day you will be as untroubled as most people, which means that you will always have something to mither you, but not as much as you have at the moment. Make sure you keep busy, do something constructive. I like to spring-clean if I have something on my mind.'

The thought of flicking a duster around Mrs B's domain, where not a mite of dust would dare settle, was a battle too far, but perhaps he could prepare his commentary for Farmer Fletcher's funeral? He turned away from that thought, unable to face more death at this precise moment. But in the annexe beyond the kitchen there was a load of furniture and boxes left over from

Hastings's time, which should be sorted. The old boy had no relatives, so his personal effects had been 'stored', as the bishop put it, when he had sent Tom here on his release from hospital and the army.

Perhaps clearing out the annexe equated to his mother's spring-cleaning?

Well, now was as good a time as any. He checked the clock. Yes, one thirty, as usual. It was amazing how little sleep one could manage on. He slipped through the hall to the kitchen, and then into the lion's den. There was electricity to all the rooms, which was a blessing in a village. The annexe smelled musty, undisturbed, and he should have put his eye-patch on, to keep the socket dust-free, but it was almost 100 per cent healed, just tender. Soon he'd get a glass eye put in.

He checked the blackout and heaved a load of yellowed newspapers off a small table. The dust rose. He placed them in a heap by the kitchen door. They, could go out in the morning, for collection by the Scouts and Guides tomorrow. For the next half hour he worked his way through all the scrap paper. Finally he reached a scratched and worn desk that he had spied within moments of starting his spring-clean. He needed one, so this could be a good night's work.

The top drawer was full of lists, addresses and minutes of the parish council dating back to 1908. The secretary would have copies, so they went on the scrap pile too. The bottom drawer held much the same, but there were also several hard-back notebooks, which he sat down to flick through, because on the front of each was written:

'Helpful aids to my failing memory, and those who come after me.' They were dated from 1930 onwards.

He heaved an old typewriter off an equally elderly armchair from which horsehair bulged through splits, and sat down. The annexe had a stone floor and his feet were freezing. Tomorrow he ought to see if there was a pair of slippers somewhere amongst the detritus. He opened one of the notebooks. The handwriting was almost copperplate and put his to shame. Reading was not his favourite occupation, with only one eye, but he read on, as the villagers and their lives were laid out before him. The whole exercise told Tom as much about Albert Hastings as it did about the local people and their difficulties. Slowly he relaxed back into the chair, understanding Hastings's frailties, doubts and his humanity in a way that made his own struggles to find his faith seem normal.

He had reached 1931 when there was a loud rapping at the annexe window. 'Hello, hello, anyone there? You're showing a light. Put it out or adjust your blackout, please.'

It was Kate Watson, who had been arm-twisted into helping Percy, the ARP warden, whilst she was here. Tom leapt to his feet and forced a way through to the window. The blackout was sound. He yelled, 'It seems all right.'

She knocked again. 'It most certainly isn't, Vicar.'

Perhaps there was another window. 'Hang on, hang on,' he called back. 'Keep knocking – I'll track you down.' He eased aside boxes balanced on top of one another, following the sound, until he reached a coat-stand hung with old mackintoshes. This almost hid a small shuttered window. Shrunken knot-holes in the wood let some light shine through. He moved a couple of pictures along the picture rail and hung a mackintosh from them, covering the window.

'How's that?' he yelled.

'You are forgiven, Vicar, without even having to pay the penance of a Hail Mary.'

'Wrong religion, but have you time for a cuppa?'

'Put the kettle on or find a gin, and I'll nip round to the kitchen door.'

He grinned at her nerve, her sheer ... well, what? She fizzed with energy, rather like little Lizzy, who in the space of these last ten days had come alive for the first time since her father had been reported missing.

He hurried towards the steps that led up into the kitchen, knocking into a pile of books and stubbing his toe on the top step. He swore as he felt his way through the kitchen, not daring to put on the light, or he'd get ticked off when he opened the door. He unlocked it, and in Kate stepped. He fumbled for the light switch and flicked it on. As he started to turn, he remembered he had no eye-patch and hesitated, aware not just of that, but of his old dressing gown and faded pyjamas, not to mention his bare feet – and the neighbours, who would be shocked at him entertaining a young woman in the dead of night. Thank heavens Mrs B didn't live in.

Kate wore her ARP helmet and huge blue overalls. She had rolled up the sleeves and trousers,

99

which made her look vulnerable, but there was something about her that made Tom feel she was that anyway. She was examining his face with no embarrassment, and he could think of nothing better to do than stand there and let her.

She said, 'It must have hurt like nothing on earth. Probably still does. Will you get a glass eye, and pop it out at the Sunday School Christmas beano, as your party piece? Let's get the kettle on, shall we? Mustn't shock the neighbours with gin on my breath, if I have to take them to task for showing a light. Though most are asleep. Not you, though?'

As she was talking, she was shaking the kettle to assess how much water it contained. She clearly decided there was enough and put the kettle on the gas hob. There was a plop as she lit it.

'We still have the solid-fuel range at Melbury Cottage, though there is gas to the house, so perhaps Sarah will get it connected one day. You get the cups. I'm not doing all the work.'

He did, grinning. What was it about this girl that was just so damned – well, what? He found he kept thinking this about her and couldn't quite put his finger on it.

The kettle was already boiling. 'Shall we use your precious ration or nip into the garden and pick mint? It makes a good soother and could help you sleep.'

He went to the windowsill, feeling unbearably smug. 'No need for the garden. Mrs B keeps mint here to add to salads. How much?'

Kate came to stand next to him. She smelled of a mixture of cigarettes and perfume. Where on earth did she get both from? She plucked a few of the mint heads from the plant. 'Do not tell Madam Bartholomew it was the Devil Incarnate herself who came and besmirched her mint and made herself at home. It would lead to an exorcising of the house. Is it war nightmares that keep you from sleep?' She nodded towards the annexe. 'Are you going to turn the light off? It's such a waste of money.'

He did, then came back and sat at the table with her. 'Talking of lack of sleep, how do you manage to do this ARP lark once a week, especially now it's school holidays and you're on duty all day?'

'It's not for long, and I used to do ARP shifts in London after my turn at the club. There's a war on, young man. We must all do our bit.' Her tone was ironic. 'So, what were you doing in the annexe? I remember old Hastings used to brew home-made wine in there down one end. He made it from elderflowers. The village would love you beyond all reason if you tried to, but perhaps you'd need sugar. I wonder if honey might do?'

Tom liked listening to her voice. It was as melodious and lilting as her singing. He would like to hear her at her club. 'Hymns aren't, are they?'

She looked surprised. 'Aren't what?'

He realised he had spoken aloud. 'I was just thinking of hymn-singing as opposed to other sorts, that's all. Has Miss Easton spoken to you?'

'Yes.' Kate sipped her mint tea. 'She's chasing me about her War Bond fund-raiser. You know she wants to put on the musical *Anything Goes* close to Christmas and will be auditioning the villagers to find talent at the end of the school

101

holidays. She'd like me alongside, and also thinks I could help with the dance routines, and with training the children in tap, and so on. Plus – and this is the worst bit – she needs me to nip into school to teach the young ones the three Rs: reading, writing and 'rithmetic. Fortunately, I will escape all of this and be back on my own turf within two or three weeks.'

Tom sipped his own tea, and liked it. 'Counting the days, eh? How many hours?'

She grinned. 'If I'm not counting them, then everyone else is, led by Mrs B.'

'Not everyone.' He swished the mint around and downed the last of the tea. He realised that he had spoken his thoughts aloud and hastened to add, 'Lizzy will miss you.'

'Not when her mother's back. Lizzy needs her more than she knows, especially now that her dad is who-knows-where. Perhaps your God has a direct line to the Pearly Gates and can do an audit of those who've entered?'

'Well, *you* could ask him.'

She checked her watch. 'Time to patrol the outskirts now.' She put her mug on the draining board. 'Better wash those up, Vic; or Mrs B will know, and then your life won't be worth living. Entertaining she-who-is-no-better-than-she-ought-to-be in the middle of the night – tut-tut. Will you be going back in the annexe, to dig about some more? If so, put the patch over your eye, because you don't need an infection. Trust me, I know.'

'How?'

'About infection, you mean? It happens with

102

burns, everyone knows that. So, why not give in gracefully and let the tea work its magic?' She was walking to the door.

Tom said, 'I should be working on the commentary for old Farmer Fletcher's funeral. Platitudes are tricky, when you don't know the person, and I hardly had time to get to know Graham Fletcher.' He was washing up the mugs.

Kate said, 'I'm going to flick the light switch, so you're about to be plunged into darkness, which is what should greet that bastard Fletcher, rather than an angelic choir. He was known to beat the living daylights out of his poor wife, Olive, on a regular basis. I dare say she is hugely relieved he's gone.'

In the darkness he heard her opening the door and, as her words resonated, he said, 'I can't comment on that.'

The moonlight flooded in through the door and for a moment there was silence, and neither moved. Kate's voice came, disembodied, but loud. 'Well, you damned well should. What are vicars there for, but to protect their flock? Maybe you don't need to stop old Graham Fletcher raising a hand to Olive, for that's sorted, but what about their son? Damnable thug, if ever I saw one, that Adrian Fletcher. You should keep your eye on him and the way he treats his lovely little wife, Susie. You've still got one good eye, so why not use it?'

The moonlight was cut off as Kate slammed the door. He didn't bother to put the light back on, but dried the mugs by feel, wanting to throw them at the wall and hear them break. Mrs B had said Kate was difficult, and how right she was. He flung the tea towel down on the draining board, put the mugs away and felt his way across to the annexe, too annoyed to sleep. Damn the girl!

He flicked on the light and settled back into the decrepit armchair, picking up the notebook. What gave her the right to give instructions on burns, anyway? It wasn't as though singing in a ruddy nightclub gave her medical expertise? She was just a little know-it-all.

Tom read for another half an hour.

The village turned out to the funeral the next day, Monday. Olive Fletcher, Graham's widow, wore grey, not black, but in contrast Adrian wore a black tie and a shirt that looked too tight for his bull-neck. Susie Fletcher, the son's wife, was thin, and pale. Tom greeted them at the door of the church, and Mr Fellows, the chairman of the parish council, showed them to their pew at the front. Farmer Graham Fletcher was already in place, in a casket with brass handles. There were no flowers.

Tom Rees began, 'We bring nothing into the world, and we take nothing out. The Lord gave, and the Lord taketh away; blessed be the name of the Lord.'

Olive Fletcher had been dry-eyed and com-posed when she came to see him last week, but he had supposed farmers and their wives were used to death – even sudden death, for Graham Fletcher had died in a tractor accident. It appeared he had fallen onto some sort of sharp-pronged machinery that he was towing, perhaps something to do with the harvest, which he was taking in at the time. Olive had asked Tom to do what one of her family could have done, and talk about Graham. She had said they would not be able to do her husband justice.

He stood in front of the altar and looked at Olive, and then out across the congregation. He began, 'We have come here today to remember...' As he moved on, he thought of all the good men and true who would not survive this war. He remembered those who had died around him, as he dashed from one wounded bloke to another, some of whom had called for their mother, others for water; some of whom he was too late for, like Daniel, his best friend.

He looked out across the casket, encompassing the congregation, and he saw Kate. She stared at him, her head unbowed. She looked very much as though she were there to assess Tom's per-formance. He didn't find her a reassuring pre-sence, merely an embarrassing reminder that she had been right about Graham Fletcher. Tom had read Albert Hastings's notebooks for some hours, and there it was: poor Olive's life with Graham Fletcher, explained in copperplate writ-ing. So what about Susie Fletcher? Was history being repeated?

As he read out the bare facts of Graham's life now, Tom emphasised the farmer's well-run dairy herd, his age, and added at the end, for it would no doubt be true, that his presence would leave a gap in the lives of his family, which they must strive to fill, with the help of the village. He said nothing more. He looked at Olive Fletcher and she nodded. The son was swallowing, tears streaming down his face. The daughter-in-law sat on Olive's right. The two women held hands. Tom found Kate again, and then looked at Olive. Usually he would have flannelled some more. Now he merely smiled at Olive. She nodded again. He had said nothing really, and Olive thought it enough.

Psalm 23 had been chosen by Adrian, the son, and he duly read it. The service droned on, and then it was time for the committal.

The funeral directors removed the brass handles; it was wartime, after all. They traipsed along past the meadow, as the left-hand side of the cemetery had been christened, in Tom's mind. They reached the grave, with soil heaped to one side, and lowered the casket. The committal began.

'Almighty God, you judge us with infinite mercy and justice...' He had chosen that, because he felt 'justice' was particularly apt, in this case. They continued with the committal as the wind stirred the yew tree, the bees buzzed, the pigeons cooed, and the distant sound of children playing on the recreation ground reached them. Children were ignorant of death, thank heavens; or were they? Some were evacuees from London.

He looked at the Fletchers. He had reached the home stretch.

'May God give you his comfort and his peace...'

It was over and time to sprinkle some soil onto the casket. He handed a trowel to Olive Fletcher. She dug it into the heap of soil. Many of the villagers were drifting away, eager for the ham tea that the Fletchers had arranged at the village hall. He reached out to reclaim the trowel, but

Olive was digging it into the pile of earth again, and this time she didn't sprinkle, but hurled it onto the casket, and again, and again. Mrs B was standing opposite, looking shocked. The funeral directors looked the other way.

Behind him he heard a whisper, 'Oh my, justice indeed. You did well, my reverend friend, very well – no embroidery or flannel. I would applaud, but the show isn't over. You really do need to take care of that poor little Susie, because like father, like son?'

It was a question that somehow Tom knew he must address, partially due to Kate's prompting, which had so annoyed him. Mrs B had left and was heading down the path and then out of the gate, making for the village hall, determined no doubt to share Olive's comments with her friends. So far Tom had read nothing of Albert Hastings's insight into Mrs B's life, but surely there was something that he could do to help.

Adrian Fletcher was staring at his mother, but now she handed the trowel to Susie, who took up where she had left off, tipping soil onto the casket, then again, and again. Olive turned to her son, whispering fiercely, 'You touch another hair of yon girl's head and you might have an accident, an' all. You're too like that father of yorn. Things happen on farms, so if you want to come into the farmhouse again, then it is with decency, because that is where Susie and I will be livin'. You think on, my son.'

Now she took the trowel from Susie's hand and returned it to Tom. Together the women walked away from the grave. Mrs Fletcher called over her

107

shoulder to Tom, 'You can let 'em fill him in now, Vicar, and I thank you.'

Adrian stared from the women to the vicar. 'You 'eard all that, Vicar; and you, Kate Watson. She bloody killed 'im.'

Tom froze, just for a moment, as he had frozen on the beach that terrible day, but then he saw movement at his side. It was Kate stepping towards Adrian, her mouth opening.

No, no, he was not going to be found wanting a second time. He said, cupping his hand to his ear, 'I have the most dreadful hearing, after the Dunkirk beaches. You too, I think, Miss Watson. It's all that drumming behind you on the stage. It does damage the ears, so they say.'

Kate slowed, closing her mouth. She frowned, looking puzzled, and glanced from Adrian to Tom. Then suddenly she caught on and said, 'Pardon, you'll have to speak up, Vicar. The clubs are so noisy, I find I miss a great deal. I thought I'd head off and pick up Lizzy.'

Tom said, 'Off you go then. I'll walk with Adrian to the village hall.' He gripped Adrian's arm and moved him along. 'You and I are going to have to work together to support the family now, you know, Adrian. The village will of course be keeping a very, very close eye on you too, just in case there is need of help.'

Kate called, 'I'll take the eastern gate then. Sleep well tonight, Vicar. Oh, I forgot: he's Mutt 'n' Jeff. Tell the vicar what I said, would you, Adrian? I'm so sorry for your loss. Please tell your mother.'

Tom felt Adrian gear himself up, as though to spring from his grasp, and said, 'You've been

108

given a chance, Adrian, to run your farm and your life, now your father has gone. Use that chance wisely. Better men than both of us are dying to protect their wives and families and allow our way of life to continue. To protect, Adrian – remember that.'

That night Tom slept until dawn. It was a natural awakening. Yes, he'd had the dreams, but the demons had not pulled him down so far, the sand hadn't clung to him. And although on that day in Dunkirk he had paused, he knew that had he gone immediately, he would have been killed too. Perhaps he had been saved for today, possibly to save a family who had suffered enough.

He rose and lifted the blackout at his bedroom window. He didn't really know, any more, what was right, what was the truth, so he just had to manage as best he could. After all, Kate would not be here much longer to act as a cattle-prod. He half laughed, knowing he would miss her, but also that life would be simpler with her gone.

It was as he turned from the window that he pictured Olive Fletcher throwing earth onto the coffin in a flurry of fury. Something had been nagging at him, and now he remembered the chip on the inscription on Reginald Watson's headstone. This evening he would continue to clear out the annexe, and as a reward to himself he would continue to read the notebooks. Perhaps, just perhaps, there would be some answers to the riddle of Kate Watson, which was buzzing inside his head.

Chapter Nine

The hammering on the front door startled Kate, who had been dozing since dawn. It was now Tuesday, and the funeral of yesterday was still playing on her mind. The hammering began again. She slung on her dressing gown and hurried down the attic ladder, meeting Lizzy on the landing.

'It's only seven, Aunt Kate. Is it the telegram boy? He banged like that when he brought the one about Dad being missing.'

Kate didn't stop, but took the stairs two at a time, calling over her shoulder, 'The only way to find out is to open the door.'

Lizzy followed. 'Coming, we're coming,' the child called. The hammering continued.

Kate yelled, 'You'll knock the door down in a moment, so give your knuckles a rest.' She yanked open the front door.

'Telegram, miss. Sign 'ere.' The boy thrust the buff envelope at her.

Kate signed for it. Lizzy leaned against her as they watched the boy hurry back down the path, leap on his bike and pedal off. Somewhere a dog barked and a cockerel crowed.

'It must be about Mum. She's in uniform now.' Lizzy clung to Kate, who stroked her tangled hair.

'You can see through an envelope, can you, my girl? Let's close the door and toddle to the kitchen, sit down and read it. Let me go; hold my

110

hand and pull me, so we get there more quickly.'
After all, what would it hurt to delay the inevit-
able, but how could it have happened? Had the
canteen been hit, or had Sarah been driving a
lorry? Kate's mouth was dry, her heart thumping.

Lizzy was tugging her along.

'Go on, give me a real pull.' She'd do anything
to distract the child, whose face had been taut
with fear, but was now just set with determination
as she hauled this lump of an aunt along the hallway. In the kitchen, Kate sat down at the table.
Lizzy came to stand by her. Kate said, 'Come
along, we'll read this – two girls together, eh?'

She opened it, but after all the fuss, it was only
from Brucie:

*You not telephoned for week Stop You said Mondays
Stop Get train today Stop Scout for New York Cock-
atoo today five Stop Red dress in dressing room Stop
Brucie*

'Who's Brucie? We were worried, weren't we? It
wasn't fair to do that.' Lizzy stood with hands on
hips, as though Kate was to blame for all the
anxieties of the world.

Kate leapt to her feet. 'Never mind that. Mrs
Summers is in Exeter today, so she can't look after
you. Quick, I must do something with my hair,
while I think about who else might manage it.'

Lizzy planted herself in front of Kate, refusing
to move. 'Who is Scout? We have them, but they
collect stuff for the war. What does this one want
with a bird? I think you are being naughty, like
Mummy said. If I'm worried, I must get help

111

from someone. What's more, it's the school holiday picnic, remember, and you said you would make sandwiches and come with us, to help Miss Easton and...'

Kate waved Lizzy to a hush and scooted around her. 'Look, I'll make sandwiches, like I said, and leave them with Fran at the end of the terrace, or Miss Easton, either of whom I'm sure will look after you until it's time for the picnic.' She wasn't sure at all, but it was worth a try.

Lizzy moved swiftly to block Kate as she tried to enter the hall. 'Or you could take me with you. I haven't been to London, and I'd like to go.'

'I can't take you – it's for grown-ups.'

She slipped past Lizzy, flew up the stairs and washed her hair, pinning it up so that it would bounce onto her shoulders, once it dried. She dressed in a straight skirt, stockings, high heels and a silk blouse, and then appeared again in the kitchen.

Lizzy was nursing a cut finger at the sink, counting the drops of blood that dripped into it. On the kitchen table was the loaf and the bread knife. Two doorstep slices had been cut; one was blood-stained. Lizzy said without looking round, 'I thought I'd help, by cutting the bread for the sandwiches, so all you had to do was boil the eggs and mash them. It would make you pleased with me, and you'd take me. Everyone leaves, and I'm never sure they will come back. How can we know anyone will come back? But now you'll be cross, and I'll have to go on the picnic.' She turned now, holding up her finger. The blood ran down her hand and then her arm. 'I'm sorry too, because you're not naughty... I know that. I don't ever need help when you are here.'

Kate tied on an apron and herded the child back to the sink, then ran the tap. 'We'll let the water wash it clean.' Lizzy leaned against her, and Kate stroked her hair. 'Cuts hurt, and of course I'm not cross.' How could she be, with this precious child, whom she was coming to care for far too much? 'Accidents happen, we all know that, and this was one born of good intentions, as our beloved vicar might say from his pulpit.'

Lizzy giggled.

Kate said, 'Now budge over, you dear little horror, I have to find medical supplies.'

She searched in the household cleaner cupboard and dug out the first-aid kit, while Lizzy said, 'I'd really like to come with you.'

'Let's sort out one thing at a time. Blood takes priority.' Kate patted the cut dry. It wasn't deep. She bandaged it with cotton wool and gauze. There was not one whimper from this dark-haired, dark-eyed child with the voice of an angel and a spirit that made Kate smile. 'Thank you, Miss Elizabeth Baxter, for trying to help me; let's boil the eggs. We'll have one each for breakfast, after which your job will be to mash them, because I'm hopeless at that sort of thing. How about it?'

'But you will take me, won't you?'

They arrived at Waterloo Station at four o'clock, after an interminable journey that took almost five hours. Lizzy had slept for some of it, but fretted about her hair, which kept escaping from her plaits. She wore her new deep-pink dress,

113

white socks and sandals. Miss Easton had accepted the sandwiches and the excuse of a meeting, which indeed there was, wishing them a lovely time. They had travelled on the bus with Mrs Bartholomew's friend, Mrs Whitehead, who was taking the train to Sherborne. Kate's heart sank, because Lizzy, with the excitement of London looming, shared every detail of the telegram with Mrs Whitehead, right down to the Cockatoo.

Mrs Whitehead had pursed her lips and said little. But as she left the train at Sherborne, she had mouthed to Kate, 'Shame on you, all dolled up and taking a child to a nightclub.'

They took the Underground from Waterloo, and Kate made a game of running through the streets, once they reached Leicester Square. They arrived at the Blue Cockatoo, panting. Kate's feet were killing her. She lifted Lizzy so that she could bang the brass knocker, lowering her to the ground and trying all the while to keep Lizzy's sandals from smudging her cream skirt. There was no answer, and Kate whacked the knocker. She heard Tony calling, 'Keep your 'air on.'

The door swung open. Tony grinned, leaned forward and gave her a smacking kiss. 'Brucie's about to burst a gasket; you've fifteen minutes to get your glad-rags on. Looking good, gal – got a bit of colour in yer cheeks.'

She slipped past him, pushing Lizzy before her. 'That's because we've been running, haven't we, Lizzy? Is Teresa here yet?'

He shook his head, pointing at Lizzy. 'The boss won't like that.'

'*That*, Tony, is my lovely niece, Lizzy. What

114

about Frankie?'

'Good idea; he'll take her off to the kitchens. 'Ang on a minute. I'll see if the coast is clear.' He stuck his head round the curtain into the club. 'Quick, now.'

Kate put her finger to her lips. She turned to Lizzy and said quietly, 'Remember I told you this place is for grown-ups, so I need to make sure that you are safe and sound somewhere else. We're finding Frankie to look after you, just while I meet this scout, because he might have some work for me, when your mum comes home.'

She slipped around Tony, leading Lizzy along the back of the tables, which were all laid up.

Lizzy whispered, 'It's really dark.'

'The lights come on when people start arriving, a bit like the theatre, which it is really, but with people eating and dancing. I expect Brucie has kept it closed while the audition takes place.'

'Mrs Bartholomew said you worked in a place where people drank and behaved badly. I heard her telling the old vicar. I think some man told her, because he'd seen you, but it wasn't called this. It was called the Burley Club, or something like that.'

They were hurrying into another corridor now, and Kate opened the door into the kitchen. It had a row of ovens, and bottles of wine stacked in boxes. Frankie was sorting out some pans with the chef. ''Allo, lovely gal,' he shouted, almost running towards Kate and folding her in his arms.

For a moment she rested her head on his shoulder. 'It's good to be home,' she said.

'So good to 'ave yer – ain't 'alf missed you. But

115

you're almost late. He's in one of his baits, cos the big cheese is 'ere and you ain't.' He looked at Lizzy. 'Babysitting problems?'

Kate nodded. 'I feel bad bringing her, but can you keep Lizzy in the kitchens? She's great at mixing things, Alfredo.' Alfredo, the chef, was chopping vegetables at the large table and nodded, unimpressed.

Frankie squeezed Kate's arm. 'I'll look after her. She can dust the bottles with me. 'Ow about that, little lady?'

Lizzy was looking from one to the other, wide-eyed.

'I'll be back soon, all of you. Be good, Lizzy.' Kate left, half running along the back of the tables again, down the other side and through the curtain to the right of the stage, where Roberto, Stan and Elliot were now tuning up. They waved and winked, but she didn't stop, just rushed into the dressing room.

Cheryl was there, stripped to her underwear, about to put on Kate's red dress.

'What on earth are you doing?' Kate demanded.

Cheryl flushed. 'Well, you weren't here, so I'm grabbing my chance.'

'Well, back off, get in line and wear your own damned dress.' All Kate's pent-up frustration at the day spilled out onto this girl, who bit back.

'Brucie said I should.' Cheryl flung the dress at Kate and stalked out, slamming the door.

Kate changed in just a few seconds, brushed her hair, added more lipstick, then strolled onto the stage as though she'd been here all day. Brucie

116

was standing on the dance floor, introducing Cheryl to a man smoking a cigar, his waistcoat stretched across his massive girth. None of them had noticed her. She leaned against the piano, where Roberto was warming up, playing 'Top Hat, White Tie and Tails'.

He whispered, 'Give 'em hell, darlin'. That Cheryl would dance on your grave, if you gave her half the chance. We can't wait to have you back. No nanny yet, then?'

When she shook her head, he crashed his hands on the keys, bounding into the song. The scout turned round. Kate began to sing and dance, because it was what she was born for. As she did so, she could almost smell the wood-smoke of the fire, see the darkness of Andrei's eyes and the dark hair that he would fling back before he danced, and feel the warmth of his hand as he pulled her from where she sat on the log. She felt the strength of his body as he held her to him, spun her away, dancing as others were doing. It was a lifetime ago, but the memory still kept her breathing, kept her feeling alive, made her rise in the morning.

Stan brought his saxophone to the microphone, Elliot thumped on the bass, Kate flung back her hair and then they rolled into 'Begin the Beguine'. As they finished, she saw that Cheryl had gone, and that Brucie was leading the scout through the curtained doorway. She checked behind her, and the boys shrugged.

'We don't like the look of that scout, Kate,' Stan said. 'You can do better than go across to the States with that one, but it's up to you.'

117

Brucie had re-emerged and beckoned to her. She thanked the lads and joined Brucie, who hugged and kissed her. He'd been drinking, and she could smell cigars on his breath too. 'You go on in, sweetie. Teddy McManus wants to talk to you. Handle him well and we could be on our way to the big time.'

She gave a quick glance towards the kitchen corridor. No sign of Lizzy. 'Thank you, Frankie,' she whispered to herself as she slipped behind the curtain and along to the half-glazed office door. It was ajar.

McManus was half sitting on Brucie's desk; his waistcoat unbuttoned, his jacket folded on the chair behind the desk He waved her in, and the cigar he was holding left a trail of smoke.

'Ya knocked me over, darlin',' McManus said in his American drawl. 'I have a place for you, too damned right. And that dress... Phew, makes me feel hot just to look at ya.' He reached over and picked up his glass, containing a double Scotch, perhaps even a triple. He gulped, then replaced it on the desk, wiping his mouth with the back of his hand. 'I got a cute little contract here. Come on over and let's take a look together. Then I can put ya right on any points ya don't like. I have to tell ya, Brucie boy thought it a damned good deal. Come on over – don't be shy.'

Kate had been here before and wasn't going to pore over a contract in close proximity to this man today, or any day. 'I'm pleased you liked my act. Why not pass the contract over, then I can sit right down here and take my time.' She gestured to the sofa that Brucie kept in his study because

118

he felt it made him look like a big-businessman.

'Well, why not, little lady.' McManus held the contract out to her, resting his cigar on the edge of the ashtray. She reached over, but instead of handing her the contract, he grabbed her arm, pulling her to him, his mouth opening on hers. It tasted like the bottom of an ashtray. Kate was off-balance and fell against him; he kneaded her breast and trapped her between his legs.

She pushed away, but he was too strong – her legs were pinioned, but her arms were free as he pawed her body, pulling the top of her dress down, baring her breasts and bending his head, his mouth open. She beat at his face, going for the eyes and, as he cursed and released her, she tore away, holding her dress up. He grabbed her back, slapping her full across the face, splitting her lip and yanking her hair, wrenching her head back and ripping her dress away. Once more she hit him, and kicked. He hit her back. She stabbed at him with her high heel, catching his shin. McManus recoiled and Kate staggered away, turning from him and heading for the door, clasping what was left of her dress.

She heard him coming after her. Then he stopped, saying, 'What the hell are those scars on your back? They're bloody disgusting. If I'd seen them, I'd have left you alone.'

She reached the door, opened it and, forcing herself to keep her voice level, said, 'It's collateral damage. Try it sometime. But no, you spend your time over the pond, away from the bombs, you bastard.'

She closed the door quietly behind her and

looked both ways, tasting blood, feeling her lip swelling and her nose bleeding. Her eye hurt too, but not as much as having some fat old bastard saying that she disgusted him. And what's more, her back was hurting from the struggle.

Once in the dressing room, she locked the door and leaned back against it, letting the torn dress fall off her to the floor. She wiped her hand across her face. It came away red. Blood or lipstick? She checked her watch. Lizzy? She must hurry. The dressing room smelled of Cheryl's perfume, though that was preferable to cigar smoke and sweat, but only just. Furiously Kate dressed, dabbing at her face with water from the sink in the corner. She stuffed cotton wool up her bleeding nose, patted her lip, brushed her hair. Someone banged on the door. She froze.

'Kate, it's me, Brucie.' He was almost whispering. 'Come on, open the door – we can put this right.' She opened it and he stared, then said, 'What the hell have you done? What 'arm is there in a bit of a grope? Doesn't "casting couch" mean anything to you, babe? Come on now, play along; it's just business.'

She listened to the words, then reached for her handbag. 'I need to catch the train. I don't know if I'll be back.'

He held out his hand. Kate side-stepped him. She had always known that Brucie was hardly the perfect boyfriend, but this treatment of her now was something she'd never expected. 'You're a bastard too, you know, Brucie. We've been together for too long for you not to know that I don't do casting couches. Besides, I'm damaged goods – didn't McManus tell you? He doesn't care for my scars.'

'He likes your front, though, and he likes your voice and the way you move. We can still swing it; we can still make this work.'

She pondered him, head on one side, eye throbbing. But what wasn't throbbing? 'We? You're up for a bit of a grope, are you? You like having your clothes ripped off you, do you?'

Brucie put up his hands, as though in submission. 'It's just a game, sweetie, a damned game. I'm sorry he hurt you, but it will heal. I'll try to fix it. It's not all lost.'

She pushed past him, clipping along the corridor in her high heels and into the club. The band sat round a table, smoking. Stan half rose when he saw her, but then, at Kate's gesture, sank back down. 'All these doors I walk into,' she said. 'Maybe see you in a couple of weeks, lads.'

They just narrowed their eyes against the smoke, nodding. Roberto said, 'No trip to the States then?'

She laughed. 'You should see the other guy.' She walked on and into the kitchen, where Alfredo was working alongside Lizzy, and both were whisking something in bowls. Lizzy wore a high white hat and was listening as Alfredo explained the intricacies of the clientele's needs.

Frankie came to stand beside Kate. 'I won't ask.'

She nodded, suddenly exhausted. 'I don't know,' she said in a loud voice. Lizzy looked up. Kate continued, 'I had completely forgotten that the step was there, and down I went, into the door.'

Lizzy gasped. 'Holy moly – have I said that

right, Alfredo? You look awful. What have you got up your nose?' She laid the whisk beside the bowl, and Alfredo undid her apron as Kate explained about the cotton wool, and that her nose had probably stopped bleeding now.

Alfredo wagged his dripping whisk at her. 'You remove it outside my kitchen, then you may take this child for a meal. I have a friend in Leicester Square.' He gave Lizzy a business card. 'He will know I sent you, and will have something to delight the tastebuds.'

It was the last thing Kate needed, but she smiled, making her lip bleed again. She dabbed it. 'Come along then, and thank Frankie and Alfredo very much, Lizzy. See you soon, lads, I'm grateful.'

It was seven o'clock before they were on the train, but it was an uninterrupted run, a mere two and a half hours this time before they arrived at Yeovil. A taxi was there, which they shared with another family. Lizzy told them the tale of the forgotten step, the door, but also included the wonderful singing and dancing at the theatre, confessing that she had peeped. Kate smiled and said nothing.

The family were going on to their farm, well past Little Worthy, so Kate and Lizzy were dropped at the bus stop at the village turn-off. They paid their share and walked through the village, lighting their way with a filtered torch.

Lizzy said, 'The roses smell stronger at night, don't they, Aunt Kate?'

'If it's been a hot day.'

They were passing the village hall just as the WI members left. Leading the charge was Mrs

Bartholomew, who turned as she heard Lizzy's voice calling to Fran Billings.

'Mrs Billings, hey, Mrs Billings, we had a lovely time. And we're home so late, and I'm not a bit tired. Aunt Kate did a lovely song and dance at the theatre. It had lights and a band, but she's not going to America. She had a fall too. She forgot a step was there and bashed her face against a door.'

Deliberately, so that Kate could hear, Mrs Bartholomew said loudly and disapprovingly to Mrs Whitehead, 'You met them on the train, didn't you, Mrs Whitehead? It was a nightclub surely – not at all the place for a child. I can't think what her mother will say. Tripped on a step, indeed. Too much alcohol, I expect.'

Lizzy looked up at Kate, who had not faltered at Mrs B's jibe, but had kept on walking. 'But it was a step, wasn't it?' Lizzy asked.

'Of course it was,' lied Kate. It was a decent lie, one that saved others from the truth. Perhaps that's what she should have done all those years ago.

Fran Billings and Miss Easton caught up with Kate and Lizzy, leaving sour Mrs B and Mrs Whitehead behind. Soon Mrs Martin, the butcher's wife, and Mrs Woolton, the haberdashery owner, caught up with the foursome too.

'How exciting,' Miss Easton said to Kate. 'What a shame it had to end like that. I can't smell any alcohol on your breath, Kate, so what on earth is all this about drinking?' She had raised her voice. Mrs Whitehead carried on past, rather like a galleon in full sail, with Mrs Bartholomew at her side.

Kate whispered, 'Oh, Miss Easton, don't worry.

123

You're new to the village and will find that Mrs B's bark is worse than her bite, and besides life hasn't been easy for her.'

Mrs Woolton peeled off at the haberdashery, picking her way carefully with her limited torch-light, but called back, 'Yes, I will do the costumes for the fund-raiser, Miss Easton. It's just a shame Miss Watson won't be here, but I'm sure the vicar will do the honours, weeding out those who come to the auditions.'

'Well, good luck with that,' Fran muttered. 'It will be as bad as choosing one load of leeks over another at the village show.' They all laughed, including Kate, who wished she hadn't, as she tasted blood again.

Mrs Martin waved and walked across to her shop. Fran Billings headed off to her end of the terrace. Her eldest child, Sandra, was old enough to look after the other two, it had been decreed. Finally, at last, there was Melbury Cottage.

Kate said to the teacher, 'Surely you don't live down this way?'

Miss Easton touched Kate's arm and leaned close. 'I am enjoying the walk. I'll turn now, but put something cool on that face – and all thoughts of spiteful words out of your mind. I, for one, will miss you on your return to London. You make me laugh, you are so strong and vibrant, and you seem to have made our vicar smell the roses again.'

Kate said, 'If I was staying, I'd be in there help-ing you, doing all I can. Good luck anyway. And thank you.' The two women smiled.

Miss Easton replied, 'You are easy to help, and deserve better than this gossipy lot.'

'Ah well, you weren't here then. I'm sure it didn't appear to be my finest hour.'

That night Kate lay in bed, the blackout curtains wide open, the moon lighting the trunks full of the memorabilia of Sarah's childhood. There was none belonging to her. Lizzy had asked where Kate's things had gone. She had thought for a moment, then merely told Lizzy that mistakes happened, things got thrown or given away when perhaps they shouldn't.

She stared at the ceiling. Here there were just eaves – no damp stain to watch, while your world was ripped from you, and you knew you would never be the same again. In two weeks she must leave yet again, as she had done all those years ago. At least she had someone to go to, because, when all was said and done, Brucie only wanted the best for her; and he loved her, even though she was scarred. There weren't many men who would.

The next day Yeovil was bombed and three were killed, and many injured. For a while Mrs Bartholomew and Mrs Whitehead had other things to talk about.

Chapter Ten

The Reverend Thomas Rees arrived back from Portsmouth at Little Worthy vicarage on Tuesday evening, as July was about to fade into August. Mrs B had headed home some while before, to her bungalow. She had left a note directing him to a grated-cheese salad left in the meat safe, and mentioned that his stand-in, the Reverend Bob Sylvester, had performed the morning service competently, but had done little else. She added that she hoped his check-up had gone well.

Well, it had, and after being poked and prodded at the military hospital in Portsmouth, Tom had been pronounced as close to perfection as he would ever be. His new glass eye had been fitted; the absence of a spleen was not proving onerous; and although his leg, which had been broken in two places in the blast, would ache from time to time, he was signed off.

He unpacked, placing his mother's birthday gift of new pyjamas in the second drawer in his bedroom. He could hardly tell her that he went to bed naked in the summer heat, after she'd searched the shops for them. Probably he'd change his mind when the winter winds blew, but so be it. He knew where the pyjamas were.

He seemed to be thinking 'So be it' a great deal these days, now that his sleep was so much better and his work less intimidating. In fact he felt that at last he was doing some good, and the villagers Tom had met as he walked down the High Street seemed pleased to see him. As he sauntered along, he had smelled the roses and heard the owls. In a month or so the countryside would look shorn, and then ploughing and sowing would begin.

There was a relentless predictability to the country year that he found comforting; he hadn't thought of it until Kate had mentioned it after church a couple of Sundays ago. She'd also reminded him about mending the church clock – in that voice, as only she could. He sighed and ate at the kitchen table as the clock chimed ten.

He washed and dried his plate and cutlery, then was at last free to slip into the annexe, which now looked much more like a snug than a study. He had brought in Hastings's old armchair from the sitting room, but kept the other in here too, still oozing horsehair. A couple of bookcases had been hidden behind trunks laid on top of one another and were now filled with his books, but the *pièce de résistance* remained the writing desk.

He had even discovered a fireplace, behind boxes of *National Geographic* magazines that he had donated to the local grammar school. Finally he had resurrected Hastings's typewriter, and it was on this that he stabbed out his sermons and other parish business; importantly, Mrs B and her duster were banned from the desk, and in that way the papers on it stayed where he put them.

He loved his mother, but as he settled into Bertie Hastings's armchair – the one that suited his predecessor's shape – he relaxed. It was good to be home, and this feeling had been growing as he neared Little Worthy. Yes, good to be home and to have a chance to catch up on the notebooks, knowing that already the old man's insights had enhanced his understanding and had created a desire in him to be alert to his parishioners' needs, and to be active in helping them, when possible.

He picked up the second of the notebooks, but as he opened it at the bookmark he paused, recapping on all that he had learned, both from the notebook and from village happenings. How would he cope, for example, if he lost his two children from diphtheria, as Mrs B had, only to suffer another blow when her husband left her for a younger woman, some two years later. It made him more tolerant of her meanness of spirit, but did not stop him in his intention to curb it.

Then there were the Fletchers. Had Olive really killed her husband, as she had insinuated? He suspected she had, but they would never know, and did it really matter? It was over and done with, and the son seemed lighter, more in tune with his young wife, without the tyranny of his father leading him astray. Adrian was certainly less combative now, when Tom called. What's more, he knew that a certain Kate Watson dropped in on them from time to time too.

Tom checked his watch. At midnight he would push aside the blackout curtain so that Kate would be forced to tick him off for showing a light. Naturally he would ask her in for a cup of tea, after all he had no time to waste in his new campaign to help where he could – and Miss Kate Watson could do with his ministering, if the notebook was anything to go by. For now, though, he would bury himself in Hastings's thoughts, but before he did, he wondered briefly, as he had before, whether this was an invasion of privacy? But any information would remain with him and, as he had told his mother, he would destroy the notebooks when he had completed his reading, just to be on the safe side. Perhaps he, in his time, would leave a history for his successor, or some

128

words of wisdom, if he ever managed to acquire any. 'At the moment, I don't know my arse from my elbow,' he had said.

His mother had agreed, which he felt was not altogether supportive.

He opened the book, crossed his legs and began to read. At two, Kate's knock came, as he had hoped. He adjusted the blackout. 'I'm putting the kettle on.'

'I'll be at the back door any second.' She sounded tired, but that was hardly surprising when she'd been up all day, and sleep wouldn't be forthcoming until Lizzy was in bed tomorrow evening.

He opened the back door. Kate stepped into the darkness of the kitchen and he shut the door behind her, switching on the light.

'How did it go?' she asked. He turned and she said, 'Ah, my word, young man, you have an eye, and it's the same colour as the other one. The church's blue-eyed boy, eh?'

He grinned. 'Mint?'

'Please.' But first she caught at his sleeve, examining his face carefully, which even his mother couldn't do.

He said, 'I heard last week that you'd been away yourself. Well, for a day at least. I can still see the remains of the black eye. I don't know: here I am, almost presentable, and there you are... Quite a pair, eh?'

'Indeed,' she said, nodding. 'And those eyes are, too. They've matched the colour very well. Does it hurt?' She reached up, and touched his scar.

He said, 'The scar or the eye?'

129

'The eye.' She dropped her hand. 'The scar too.'

'Neither, not really, except for the corner of my lip, where the good meets the bad.' He turned now, and made the tea.

Kate said, 'There's no bad – it's all still you, and I do think the scar is less obvious, don't you?'

He could still feel where her fingers had touched his cheek and for a moment he couldn't speak. No-one had done that; no-one had ever looked so closely or had ever said, 'It's still you.'

This wasn't the daughter he had read about, the one who had run wild with the gypsies, causing her father, the verger, untold outrage, and Hastings so much concern. No, this was a young girl who had lost her mother, her dog and Melanie, her school friend, all within a short space of time, and who had reacted to her loneliness by seeking out companionship and life.

They took their tea into the annexe and Kate responded as Tom had thought she would. 'This is excellent; it's your own private space. I can picture old Hastings here.' She paused. 'I used to like him.' She blurted out the words with a savagery that took him aback.

He said nothing, but gestured to one of the armchairs, determined to pursue his agenda.

Kate sat. 'Your sermon when I first arrived was kind, and I think it was directed partly at Mrs B. I wasn't sure whether to tell you why she is as she is, but by now you probably know. After all, the village has a way of getting the past across to incomers. Just don't think ill of her, but perhaps work out a way that you can help her emerge from her disaster. She can't seem to take even a few steps towards something better.'

He looked into his mug, then nodded, pleased that she had given him an opening. He leaned forward, glancing at her. 'You're right, but what makes you think it's easy to take such steps? It isn't, you know, and anyone who thinks it is is lying to themselves.'

She said nothing, but seemed to be thinking of other things. She gulped her tea down to the dregs, then stood, thrusting her mug at him and glaring at the floor. 'I didn't say it was easy, but it has to be done. But you're a vicar, so what do you lot know about life? And who the hell are you calling a liar?'

She spun from the annexe into the kitchen darkness.

'For heaven's sake, check your blackout more carefully. Poor old Percy won't be able to keep spending time with you, when I go, just because you can't damned well sleep.'

Tom struggled to his feet with both mugs, his own tea slopping as he followed her into the dark kitchen, bumping into the table. There was a draught, then the door slammed behind her. He placed the mugs on the table and felt his way to the light switch, flicking it on and staring at the door. 'Damn the girl, and damn me.' He spoke aloud because he was so furious with his clumsiness, when all he wanted was to give Kate an opening to talk. But why on earth should she spin off into a fizz about lying, when that wasn't his point at all?

He washed up the mugs in the sink, picking up the tea towel and drying them. He put them back in the cupboard, wanting to groan with a frustration that seemed familiar, whenever he had anything to do with Kate. That would teach him, for being cocky enough to decide that he was more than ready to do his 'good vicar' bit, and proceeding to dive in with his boots on. Well, she'd shown him that he still didn't know his arse from his elbow, so it was back to the drawing board. And who knew what Kate thought of him now? That thought hurt.

He was hanging the tea towel back on the hook when there was a tap on the door and he heard her voice. 'Thank you for the tea, and I'm sorry. I know you have experienced a lot of awful things, but... Oh, nothing. Anyway, I'll be gone in a few days, and you won't see me again. It's good news, isn't it, about El Alamein? Perhaps things are really on the turn, now we've halted their advance.'

Tom heard Kate's footsteps as she walked away, and again felt the touch of her fingers tracing the ridges of his scar. She was leaving again soon, for ever. Now a strange anger flared, to push the hurt away, and he wanted to shout, 'So you're running away yet again, Kate Watson, in spite of all your fine talk of putting one foot in front of the other. Come back, let me help you. And forgive me. I don't know why you think I accused you of being a liar. I just wanted to help.'

His heart ached for her, just as it had for Mrs B, because although he had at first thought the house-keeper's insinuation about the two Watson girls going away – one to give birth, the other to adopt – had been tittle-tattle, he had since come to realise, after further thought, that in all probability it was true. A tidy little solution, it might be said. But no, there was nothing tidy about it. It must have torn the heart out of Kate, just as it had with Mrs B. To be pregnant at fifteen, by a gypsy who probably would not marry her, or had perhaps already left the area, must have been appalling, and Kate must have felt so frightened and alone.

He switched off all the lights and headed for bed, but barely slept, thinking of her, feeling exasperated and then tender. 'Damn you, poor little Kate Watson. And damn me, for being a great clod,' he said, as night became day.

A few days later, Kate and Lizzy waited in the kitchen for the sound of Sarah's key in the lock. Kate's case was packed and parked in the hall. The red rose that Brucie had sent, by way of apology, would remain in the vase in the kitchen, because Lizzy liked it. In her pocket, though, Kate kept his note bearing words of love more fulsome than ever before, as Brucie begged her to return.

She had spoken to him yesterday, Friday, standing in the village telephone box, slipping in extra money as the pips sounded. She listened to his escalating pleading, until she finally confirmed that she would be returning, probably on Sunday. Kate had always known that she would, for what choice did she have? And she loved him, she supposed, though she wasn't sure quite what love was. What she was sure about, when she woke this morning, was her inability to stay here, feeling excluded, while Sarah and Lizzy rebonded.

Lizzy was sitting at the table, opposite her. 'You

133

will come again, promise you will?'

'Your mum will be here, having sorted out a new, and lovely, nanny, should she have to go away again.' Kate was apparently reading the newspaper, staring at words that didn't register, but in reality she was watching Lizzy doodling with her finger on the oilcloth. She closed the paper and moved to the window. She had never hugged this child; how could she, because then she would have to acknowledge that she cared too much? And she'd had enough of misery.

Lizzy was sliding off her chair. She came and stood close, her hand resting on the edge of the sink. Her fingers were long, like his. Kate walked away, to stand at the back door, looking out towards the woods. She should have gone with Andrei when the gypsies left the village, but she had been scared of the unknown. She didn't know then what the future had in store.

She checked her watch and, as she did so, she heard the key in the lock.

Lizzy tore down the hallway and flung her arms round her mother. Kate watched from the kitchen. Yes, Lizzy's mother – one who was fit and suntanned, and moved with fluidity and ease, and was indefinably different from the Sarah who had left. Sarah who was hugging Lizzy and kissing her hair, which was neat in plaits and kirby grips.

'Mum, I'm so glad you're back. Yeovil was bombed, but not us. We are raising money for War Bonds. The vicar and Miss Easton are holding auditions. Can I sing? Please, please, and will you? I expect you have a nice voice, like Aunt Kate. She sings in church with me now.'

134

She was dragging Sarah towards Kate. 'Tell her, Aunt Kate.'

Kate laughed. 'I think you'll have lots of time to tell your mum everything. When is the nanny coming, Sarah?'

Sarah said, 'I'm not quite sure. Are you off to catch your bus?'

'Indeed I am. I think you'll find everything in order. I've been sleeping in the attic room, so all is ready for the new girl. I have washed my sheets and they're on the line. You look so well – obviously being a FANY suits you. I'm really pleased. You've succeeded in your training?'

Sarah was holding Lizzy's hand. 'They'll let me know within the week. And yes, it does suit me, Kate. It's doing something useful.'

'Aunt Kate's been useful too; she's in the ARP. Mrs Summers comes and sleeps over. Not in the attic room, though, in the nanny's room, but she brings her own sheets. And Aunt Kate took me to London. She had to sing for Scout and had a fall. She had a black eye, and her lip was like a balloon...'

'I've got to go.' Kate almost ran down the hall, snatching up her case. Sarah followed, dragging her child and hissing at them both, 'What did you say? You went to the club? How could you, Lizzy, after my warnings? How could you take her, Kate?'

Kate stopped. 'For goodness' sake, Sarah, it wasn't a trip into hell's mouth. I couldn't find a babysitter, and I had the chance of a step up. The FANYs is your life, and mine is different. Lizzy was in the kitchen all the time, never in the club.

Rest assured, she didn't want to come. I insisted.'

Lizzy smiled at her, and the warmth in it stirred something that Kate couldn't afford to feel. She left, calling, 'I'm glad I could help you both out.' She hurried down the path, and through the village, looking neither to left nor right.

Once in London, just after lunch, Kate took the Tube, then hurried to the club. There were posters pasted on the wall, featuring Cheryl as the star. Well, they could come down, right now. She knocked. Tony opened up and hesitated. 'Kate, we weren't expecting you until tomorrow. Come on in, sweetheart, so good to see you. I really mean that. We'll have a bit of class onstage again.' He took hold of her chin and searched her face. 'Bastard,' he said, 'but the bruises are all gone, and you look as good as new.'

'Brucie's in the office, is he?'

'I've just arrived for my shift, so I'm not sure.'

She left her suitcase in the corridor. 'Guard it with your life, my lovely friend.'

Tony laughed. Was it her imagination or did he sound a bit odd? 'You bet.'

'Everything all right?' she asked.

'Always, darling, just missed you.'

Kate swept aside the curtain. Once in the club, she skirted around the tables, heading to the kitchen with the runner beans she and Lizzy had picked yesterday and had wrapped in newspaper for Alfredo. He was chopping vegetables, as usual at this time, prepping for the evening. He too looked surprised. 'Tomorrow. It was tomorrow.'

'Well, like a bad penny, here I am.' She placed

the beans on the table. 'From your apprentice chef; she wrote you a little card too.' Kate had kept it in her pocket and it was crumpled.

Alfredo seemed not to mind, but said, 'You stay here, in the club. I will make a nice cake. I have sugar, and butter.' He put his finger to his nose.

She laughed, 'Thanks, Alfredo. I'll be back when I've seen Brucie.'

He called after her, 'He is not here. He shops. Yes, that's right. He shops for you, for your return.'

She grinned. 'He's a big softie really.'

Frankie met her as she headed back to the corridor, to pick up her suitcase. 'Tony just told me you was 'ere. Stay for some food, babe. I haven't seen you for too long.'

'I might as well nip to the flat and unpack.'

Tony loomed in the doorway. 'Or you could leave your suitcase and see if you can catch up with Brucie in Oxford Street.'

She laughed at the men. 'That shows how little you know about shopping. How on earth would I find him, amongst all the other people? There might be a war on, but the Oxford Street shoppers remain. Besides, you know how Brucie drifts about. He'll end up doing a bit of business, and then a bit more. No, I could do with putting my feet up. Don't worry, I'll be back later.'

Frankie said, 'I wish you'd stay, you–'

Tony interrupted, 'We'll see you later, petal. You're always welcome here; just you remember that. You are the one with the talent. Everyone else just trails along as a passenger.'

She laughed. 'You're forgetting I'm not leaving, Frankie. I'll see you this evening.' Her flat was a short walk, thank heavens, because her feet were hot and her suitcase too heavy, but she hadn't wanted to leave any clothes at Little Worthy.

She would never return there. It was too painful.

Kate carried on and opened the front door to the house, which had been converted into small flats, and climbed the stairs. She'd never know how Lizzy performed in the fund-raiser, or how well she did at school, but it was just as well. Lizzy had a mother, and her father might come home. Her own child was part of the fabric of the community and, most importantly, Lizzy was safe, because he, the child's father, had gone from the village.

She paused at the top of the stairs, suddenly exhausted. She should be pleased to be back, but, as on every other morning, afternoon and night, the pleasure only went so far. She almost dragged the case to flat number ten. She had painted the door a cheerful red. At the end of the landing was a stained-glass window and the sun was shining: red, blue and ochre stained the floorboards. She inserted her key and turned it. Soon she would be inside and could shut the door, and stop pretending.

She opened the door, then closed it, put her case by the sofa and slumped down, stretching out her legs. 'Here we are again,' she breathed, leaning back, resting her head. Would Brucie come here, when Tony told him on his return from shopping? She smiled. Brucie wasn't perfect, any more than she was, but they made some sort of a couple, and what did it matter? He hadn't had to shop for anything else for her; he had sent the rose, which was at least something she could leave for Lizzy. Because the child had wanted it.

She looked around. The room seemed small and dark, but she could smell Brucie's Brylcreem, which was comforting, because all she needed was undemanding sameness. She ran her hands through her hair. She was tired, but she would sing tonight and soak in the applause, and feel real, for a while. But... She sat forward, puzzled. There was something else, over and above the Brylcreem. Then it came to her: it was perfume. She breathed deeply. Surely it was L'Air du Temps by Nina Ricci, the same perfume that she had smelled in the dressing room on the night of the McManus audition.

She rose, looking around, expecting to see a bottle that Steve, the toerag, had left for her at the club. Perhaps Brucie, the old softie, had thought to spray some perfume in welcome. But why, when she was due home tomorrow, not today? There was no bottle of perfume on the mantelpiece, or the small table by the sofa. It was then that she saw it, a handbag on the easy chair by the electric fire: Cheryl's.

Of course, that's why the boys at the club had wanted her to stay put.

Kate crept to the bedroom door and took hold of the handle. She turned it slowly and then, scarcely breathing, because she didn't want to see what she was sure she would, flung it open.

Brucie lay in her double bed – *their* double bed – his arm around Cheryl; both were naked. Kate wouldn't think, not yet. She coiled her courage

139

together and said, 'Get out, right now! This minute.' She made her voice sound quite calm.

Brucie said, sitting up and letting Cheryl fall back onto the mattress, 'Sweetie. It's not what it looks like.'

Cheryl said, 'It is what it looks like, you daft bitch. It has been for months – just not here.'

Kate left the room, went to the kitchen and found her largest pan, filled it with cold water and returned. Brucie was scrambling towards his clothes, draped on the wicker chair, but Cheryl lounged on the bed, lighting a cigarette. Kate tipped the cold water over her, drenching her hair, face and as much of her body as she could manage. It didn't matter that it soaked the sheets and mattress. She ignored Cheryl's screeching, but brought the pan back over her shoulder, getting ready to swing it down.

'You have ten seconds to leave this bed, get dressed and get the hell out of this flat.'

Brucie came towards Kate, his hands out. 'Babe, she's lying. It's a mistake.'

'No, she's not lying. And yes, it's all been a mistake.'

Cheryl was scrambling out of the other side of the bed, screeching, 'You're mad, you are.'

'No, not mad. Eight seconds.' She dangled the pan from one hand and moved to the wardrobe. 'You, Bruce Turnbull, must get out too.'

Kate dropped the pan, opened the window and then the wardrobe door, and threw Brucie's clothes down to the street, hangers and all.

Bruce was hopping into his trousers, but stopped and grabbed at Kate, shoving her into the wardrobe door. 'What the hell are you doing?'

'Helping you move out.'

She picked up the pan again, her cheek hurting, and looked from one to the other. 'Four seconds.' Cheryl, half dressed, picked up her dress and shoes, running in her pants and suspender belt out of the bedroom.

Kate called after her. 'Don't forget your handbag. Anything left, I keep.'

Brucie followed, holding up his trousers, his shirt in his hand, trying not to look as though he was hurrying. She chased them into the sitting room and he scuttled to the front door in his bare feet, yelling at Kate, 'It's your own damned fault – you're frigid. And those scars... Who the hell else will give you the time of day, if not me? Well, you've blown it with me and the Cockatoo, so you've got nothing. You got that?'

He slammed the door behind him. Kate threw the pan, which dented the door and crashed to the ground. 'Well, all the scarred brigade together, eh?'

She opened the kitchen window to listen to the world on her doorstep. London, her world, continuing its wartime existence; one that was bigger than her, braver, and one in which she had found she could become lost. She dragged out the bottle of gin from beneath the sink and drank a glass, with water. Then another. Her cheek ached, her eye socket too. Not another black eye? She didn't eat. She dozed on the sofa. She paced the sitting room, fingering the door. It was scarred, like Tom's face, but her back was much more hideous than either of those. Hideous, disgusting.

141

Well, the outside was like the inside, then.

Night turned into day. Kate heard London carried on the breeze.

Frankie knocked on the door. 'You all right, cookie?'

'I'm fine. I'm always fine. I just need time.'

Stan, Roberto and Elliot came, and Kate called through the door, 'I'm fine. I need time.' They went away.

The days passed. The nights passed. She didn't eat. She didn't sleep. She drank until the bottle was empty. She had another, but where was it? She hunted until she found it, at the back of a shelf in the pantry cupboard.

Brucie knocked on the door. His voice was low and urgent. 'Come on, darlin', the club needs you. I need you. That GI came good; his dad really is a scout and is coming over in December. Come on, sweetie. This'll all pass. I was a fool.'

She didn't answer.

Tony knocked. 'Come on, doll, I don't want to break down the door. I have to know you're all right. We're sorry. Should we have told you? Was it a mistake?'

She answered, 'No, not your mistake – just another of mine. I'm all right. Go back to the club, you'll lose your job.'

Manuel and Teresa knocked. They called through the door, 'We miss you. Come back; steer clear of Brucie, if it helps. People are staying away, because it's Cheryl. It's you they like. Just like we do. We'll leave a rose here, on the floor. Don't let it die.'

142

She answered, 'Thank you.'

That day the tears rolled down her cheeks. She was so dreadfully lonely. 'Mummy,' she whispered. 'Oh, Mummy, I miss you. Every day I miss you.'

She poured more gin. There was only a dribble. She dropped the bottle on the carpet and lay on the settee, her head swimming, hurting; beating in time with her pulse.

No-one else knocked until the ninth day. 'Aunt Kate, Aunt Kate, it's me, Lizzy. There's a dead rose here. Did you know? It's gone quite brown, and it should be red. We called at the club, and Tony said you were here.'

Kate could barely lift herself into a sitting position. Her mouth was sour, and she smelled of sweat. She thought she was hearing things. She stood and her legs buckled. She fell, forcing herself onto all fours.

Sarah said, 'Come along, Kate, do please answer the door. I know you've had a bit of bad luck, but time to pull yourself together. There's a war on, after all.'

Kate stood again and tried to speak. Her throat was so dry. She struggled to the sink, ran the tap and caught cool water in her cupped hands. She drank. 'Wait a moment. I'm in the middle of changing. I am off to an interview.'

She struggled to the bathroom, ripping off her clothes and washing her face and armpits. She cleaned her teeth, slapped on perfume. It was Cheryl's. Well, she'd said that anything left was hers. She coiled her hair into a pleat. In the bedroom, where the bed was still unmade, the window open and the wardrobe door swinging in

143

the wind, she dragged on a pencil skirt. It hung loosely on her, and she added a pale-pink blouse. Without renewing her make-up, the new bruise was visible, but there was no time.

Back in the sitting room again, she kicked the gin bottles under the table, thankful that the open window had seen to it that there was no smell. She hadn't even unpacked her suitcase, which was still there, by the door.

She ran her hands down her clothes. She didn't have to wear shoes; she was at home, for heaven's sake. She walked across and opened the door, her head thumping.

Lizzy gasped. 'You look so poorly.'

Sarah looked startled too. 'They didn't say you'd been ill, just that you and Bruce had broken up. And what's that bruise?'

Lizzy said, 'I expect she's walked into another door. Did you, Aunt Kate? You should look where you're going.'

'Yes, I caught it on the wardrobe door, but I'll be fine. What are you doing here?'

Sarah put both hands on Lizzy's shoulders, keeping the child still. 'May we come in?'

Kate stood aside as they passed into the sitting room.

'Father would be pleased. It's nicer than I thought it would be,' Sarah said.

'Every one a gem, Sarah,' Kate murmured.

Sarah flushed, 'Oh, Kate, I didn't mean it like that. It's just that this flat looks as though it belongs in the country. Such lovely wallpaper, and the dresser over there.'

Kate looked at her curiously. Her sister really

144

seemed to mean it.

'What can I do for you both?' That was as much as she could manage, but before Sarah could speak, Lizzy almost shouted, 'Please, please come back. Mum has to go away, and I won't mind her going, if you come and look after me. It will be for ages, and Tony said you weren't working there any more, so please come.'

Sarah was holding her daughter's shoulders again. *Her* daughter, Kate reminded herself, and shook her head. It was too much for Sarah to ask this of her, as it had been right from the start. She allowed herself to remember how the pain of giving birth had been nothing, compared to the pain of seeing her child taken away by the nurse the moment the midwife cut the cord, saying, 'It's best for the child, and for you. Then you can forget.'

Sarah had brought the baby into the room the following morning and had allowed Kate to hold her, just once. Her baby had snuffled and turned her head, searching for Kate's breast, but it was then that Sarah had snatched her back. Lizzy, as yet unnamed, had cried as they left the room, leaving Kate with a pain far worse than any fallen beam across her back.

Lizzy whispered now, 'Please, please come back.'

Kate said, 'Absolutely not. I must find another job. I still have a chance at a break when a producer comes over from America in December, so I have to keep up my professional status, and that's that. But let me make you a cup of tea before you leave.' It was all she could do to speak without weeping. She was saying goodbye once more to her daughter. But she must, in order to survive.

The sink was in front of the window. The kettle stood on the draining board. The water in it would be too old. She poured it away and filled it, switching it on. Her sister gripped Kate's arm and whispered, 'Listen to me, Kate. I am a FANY, but I am more than that. I can't tell you what, but let me just say that I will need my French language and my knowledge of France – or I will, if I get through the second stage of my training. It's something the country needs, and it's what I can do to try and find Derek. If I don't come back from wherever it is I'm going, our child – yours and mine – will need a mother. Now, will you agree that it has to be you?'

The two women stared out of the window while the kettle hissed and hawed on its journey towards boiling. Somewhere a policeman blew his whistle. Kate hoped he wasn't chasing after Stevie, the toerag whose life she had saved, because it would be a waste of her efforts. Suddenly she wondered who had been receiving the monthly gift that Stevie usually brought to the club. Well, what did it matter?

The kettle was boiling. She scooped tea into the teapot. The caddy was almost full. Ah, so Brucie had brought the toerag's gift here. Stevie sometimes managed to acquire tea, but would never say from where. She should refuse it, but she didn't.

Sarah said, 'Did you hear me?'

'Yes, I heard you, but you have no right to go into danger, when you have taken on the responsibility for a child. No right, do you hear?'

They were both whispering. 'It's too late. I've done it, and it's necessary. And I knew that Lizzy

146

would never be alone because you exist.'

Kate poured tea for them both, and a glass of water for Lizzy, who was sitting on the sofa, swinging her legs. 'You'll have to have it black, I haven't any milk.'

'Aren't you going to answer?' Sarah asked.

'Just tell me one thing. You promised you were definitely going to find a nanny. Did you even try?'

Sarah looked at Kate, then out of the window. 'No.'

Kate nodded. 'You'll do well at a job that depends on you living a lie, but at least you have, for a moment, been honest. Highly ironic, don't you think, sister dear? You, the apple of Father's eye, his mirror image; rectitude personified, someone who despises those who lie – or so you both declared eight years ago. For God's sake, Derek's a big boy; let him defend himself, and you stay and look after that wonderful child you chose, and have loved. The child you have brought up, protected. You can't walk away from Lizzy now, it's not fair on her. She loves you so much.'

'I know, and I love her, but life is not simple at the moment, not for anyone. Look, Kate, there is work that must be done by those who can do it, and that includes me. What *is* simple is that I know now that you will love her; in fact, that you do love her. So will you come back, or will I have to find a stranger to take over my role, if I don't return? Don't make this any harder than it already is for me, please, Kate.'

In that moment Kate hated Sarah more than she had ever done, but at the same time, and for

147

the first time, she admired her. This woman had chosen a role that required residues of courage and commitment the like of which most people could only dream of. They were attributes that Kate, for one, had never guessed her sister possessed. The words of 'A Foggy Day in London Town' ran through her mind, even as her emotions raged: 'What to do? What to do?'

Chapter Eleven

The train journey to Scotland was full of stops and starts. A condition of Sarah and the other remaining trainees embarking on this next stage of their training was that they had been given new identities. The utmost secrecy was imperative, even in training. Sarah – now Gabrielle to her fellow operatives – slept most of the way. They should have continued with the commando side of the course in the final week of their first month of training, but something had intervened, although no-one knew what. So here they were, a small group, an amalgamation of those who had passed the training thus far.

It had been strange to change over to her own language in Little Worthy, and for the first few days Sarah had to consciously remember to alter her inflection; and it was strange to talk English to these others now.

At Glasgow they transferred to a smaller train, and then a lorry. Before they were driven off, they were instructed to revert to French. Only one other girl had survived the first month, and now she was known as Darcel. They sat opposite one another amongst three men, all British. The Norwegians, Dutch, Poles and others were trained separately. Sarah saw the sense of this as they jolted along. If, in due course, any were captured, they would know fewer agents to betray.

As she arrived, she allowed herself to think of Lizzy, just this once. One day she would bring Lizzy here, to these heather-covered moors. They would gaze at the raptors gliding on the thermals, and paddle in streams hurtling off the high hills. One day she, Derek and Lizzy would go on to live the life they should.

As they jumped down from the back of the covered lorry she thought of Kate. Mrs Summers had assured her that Kate had grown into a wonderful girl, that she had handled Lizzy beautifully, that there had been no alternative but for her to take Lizzy to London; and the child had never been allowed into the nightclub proper. Instead Lizzy had learned how to make a batter with very few eggs. Mrs Summers had added that many in the village liked Kate, and more would, as the insanely ambitious village show *Anything Goes* got under way.

Sarah gritted her teeth as the instructor had them running into the grand house, which seemed more of a castle on the edge of the loch, their baggage clunking against their sides. She stampeded with the others into a vast changing room, where they marked time as two instructors looked them up and down. Had her father been alive, there would have been no problem, because he could have overseen any nanny; but he wasn't. So there was nothing she could do about things now except forge ahead.

She and Darcel shared a room, crashing to sleep at the end of each day. There was practice, practice, practice with Sten guns, tommy guns, revolvers and rifles. After two days they changed from blanks to bullets, which thudded into stuffed straw targets that she imagined as the enemy, as men who would do her harm, do her country harm. Increasingly Sarah pulled the trigger with venom, because these people were stopping her from living the life she had dreamed of. She supposed she was slightly off her head, because nothing was real any more, except France, except doing something, except winning this war and bringing her family back together.

The days sped by in a blur of exhaustion, concentration and appalling noise as they hurled hand grenades and bombs. Sarah thought of the vicar and his hideous scarring, the false eye. Could that be her? She shut her mind. There could be no flinching, no recalling of the past, for soon who knew how many seconds, hours, days or – the greatest prize, weeks – they would survive in France. Did the other trainees, Bernard, Javier, Carel and Darcel, think these thoughts? She'd never know. Neither would she know if they thought about the three-month or so life-expectancy of an agent and the six-week life-expectancy of wireless operators.

From weapon instruction, they moved on to assault courses, then to crawling through bogs and burns, cycling across fields and along tracks at speed, hurling the bikes over gates, hiding beneath hedges – anything to escape, anything to prevent capture and possible betrayal of your comrades, by you.

As time wore on, the five of them stalked a copse on the trail of an enemy, all of them trying to remember the instructor's advice, all of them swallowing midges as they breathed through their mouths to restrict any noise. They were so alert that their heads ached, as they strained every fibre to listen and look, but were nonetheless captured by their 'enemy' instructors, who rose from beneath layers of leaves and branches to ensnare them. 'You should have noticed the broken twigs, the stub of a cigarette, the footprint.' The trainees would have been dead or captured.

The next day they spread out and went hunting again, heading for the river, knowing that somewhere the 'enemy' lurked. They used cover, speed and silence, employing their ears and eyes. They smelled cigarette smoke and froze. They signalled one another and flanked the prey. They waited; the instructor moved and they sprayed him with blanks. They were lacerated by his words: 'Take me alive, if at all possible. Question me, you bastard idiots. Don't ever, ever kill me unless it's a last resort, because you don't want hostages taken in revenge for the death of one of the bastards. We are teaching you to fight, and kill, in order to hone your focus and determination, but use that skill sparingly.'

Their pride turned to chagrin.

They trudged back, absorbing the instructor's

words. But they examined them in French, they dreamed in French, they were French; and hoped they would never be responsible for hostages being shot in reprisal. Every spare moment Sarah reminded herself she *was* Gabrielle. She did not remind herself that she liked Bernard, or his deep-set eyes, though he reminded her of Derek. It was probably a good thing that he reminded Sarah of Derek, because somehow her husband was fading from her memory. Try as she might, after so long it was hard to keep him alive. It had been *so* long. And even though Sarah was searching for Derek, she was also finding herself along the way.

The next day Sarah followed Bernard as they made their way along the lee of the ridge on a hill, which was so high it was almost a mountain. The hair curled on his collar. He turned. 'Gabrielle, your turn to take the lead.'

The wind tore at them. Darcel closed up as Sarah took her place, panting as she drove forward, her grip on her machine gun never faltering. They had lost Javier, who had been able to keep up and cope with sleeping out overnight in the wet and cold; when 'attacked' by instructors, he had shouted in English. He'd already had his one chance. So too Carel, who had passed the twenty-five-mile trek, but foundered twice on the canoe course.

The following day Sarah, Bernard and Darcel were taught how to gauge the charge needed for demolition, and were tasked to explode some derelict bridges. That same day, as day became night, they blacked up and crept out wearing balaclavas, heading across to the Norwegian centre. They jemmied their way in and relieved the mess of its gin, then arrived back to find the Norwegians just leaving the British premises. They passed, like silent ships in the night, unwilling to acknowledge one another. The three of them sat in the mess and toasted to the success of their mission – in French of course.

Bernard grinned. 'I am enjoying this drink all the more because I saw an interloper over by the rhododendrons yesterday at dusk. I sneaked up, heard his Norwegian. I happen to speak a little and knew they were on the way this evening, so I watered our gin and left the bottles visible.'

'Of course you just happen to speak Norwegian,' Sarah said drily, raising an eyebrow at Darcel, who commented, 'Of course you watered it, but just remember: no-one likes a smart-arse.' The girls sipped the gin. Together they said, 'Except someone who gets it right.' They finished the bottle. Sarah staggered to bed, happy with her persona, because as *Gabrielle* she could misbehave, whereas *Sarah* didn't know how to.

The next day their heads ached, and the ground seemed to move beneath Sarah's legs as she eyed the horizontal ropes slung high up, one above the other, between two trees; they were swaying in the breeze. 'Climb up, go across, then climb down,' the instructor ordered.

Darcel screwed up her face. 'I hate heights.'

'Not as much as you'll hate me, if you don't shift your arse and get up those trees. And I hear that the Norwegians got the worst of it last night.'

Sarah said, 'Actually, Sergeant, I think it's evens.

I have a head fit to burst.'

Sergeant Alton shouted, making them all wince, even clever-clogs Bernard, 'Do you think I care? Do you think the bastards who are chasing you will care? All they want to do is catch you. Gabrielle, you can stop looking as though you're going to be sick, and get yourself up there first, and don't bloody dawdle. Just imagine I'm a big Hun on your tail, breathing fire and about to do more than eat you.'

She started to climb, seeing the short metal rods that had been banged into the sides to give them a bit of help, but only every so often. Her rifle was slung over her head and shoulder, safety on. It was like a third arm that wouldn't do as it was told. 'Get a bloody move on, we haven't all day. I'd have grabbed you by now.'

'Yes, Sarge.' She didn't get a bloody move on, but just kept going, which was a miracle, as she felt as though she would vomit any minute, hopefully over the sergeant. She breathed deeply. It was what her father had told her when they had taken the ferry across to France, to start her time as a nanny. At Calais they had met Monsieur Arnaud, whose children would be in her care. Her father had kissed her cheek in farewell. 'We will see you when we see you,' he had said. Now, as she reached for another branch, using her body to swing the rifle clear, she remembered that Kate and her mother had been there too. Kate had clung to Sarah, saying, 'I don't want you to leave us.'

Her mother had died while she had been in France. She paused as she reached the rope.

Paused as she looked along the two ropes to the other tree. She hadn't returned for her mother's funeral, as her father felt there was no need. She hadn't felt there was, either, because she was happy in France and had only a few months until she was to return for her wedding.

As she placed her foot on the rope, she felt it give and sway. The vomit rose. She swallowed. The ground blurred as tears brewed. She hadn't gone back for her mother's funeral: how? Why? What sort of a daughter was she, what sort of a sister? She had been happy, but Kate wasn't, after their mother's death. Sarah had written, but still she hadn't returned. What about Derek? Had she missed him when she was away? Of course she hadn't, because he had come across often to see her. Kate had begged Sarah to let her come to France too, just once, because she was even more lonely after Topsy died. They had said no, because they didn't want a gooseberry.

She gripped the top rope now; it swayed. She took the first sideways step. In France her life had been perfect, free of her family, in charge of two small children. Derek and she had stayed together in the cottage, her quarters in the grounds of the chateau. There had been no sex of course, just in case. But after the wedding, children had never happened, which is why they had taken Lizzy.

She shook her head. She must focus. She must concentrate on the important things. She had to remember to be Gabrielle, not Sarah. The sergeant bawled, 'Do I have to come up there and push you off?'

'No, Sarge.' She slid her hands along the top

155

rope and side-stepped along the bottom one, her mind emptied of everything but survival. There were no safety nets, just as in life. The top rope swung one way, the bottom another. She gripped tightly, kept going, reached the other tree and climbed down. At the bottom she bent over and vomited, again and again, and while she did so, Darcel climbed and reached the rope, but couldn't move; she returned down the same tree. Bernard, however, almost ran up, and slid along the rope and down the other tree. He passed Sarah, slapping her on the back just as she was thinking she couldn't possibly be sick again. She was.

They had to run up the next hill and, as dusk settled, they had to sleep out under the non-existent stars, without blankets or food. They had been shown how to catch and gut rabbits, but food was not on their agenda; just sleeping off the gin, and the worry about Darcel. Would she be flung off the course?

The next day they were taken to some old buildings. Their task was to jump from one roof onto the other. Bernard jumped first, and Sarah stood with Darcel. 'I will, if you will,' Sarah said. 'I don't want to go on without you.'

Darcel looked at her, the light Scottish summer night showing her fear. 'I can't,' she said.

'Yes, you can. You need to.' Somewhere she had heard an echo of those words. She couldn't remember where...

'Please, Darcel. You look so lovely.' She stopped. Darcel looked at her, puzzled, as well she might. Sarah said, 'I'm sorry, I don't know where that came from.' Then she remembered. Kate had said, 'Yes, you can, you need to. Please, for me, for Derek. You look so lovely.'

It was when she was to be married, and her father told her the neckline of her wedding dress was too low and she looked like a trollop. She had faltered until Kate said those words. They had made Sarah draw herself up and walk down the aisle towards her love.

Darcel still paused. Sarah said, 'Someone said something like that to me – "Please, you look so lovely" – because I was hesitating about doing something. I can't tell you what, because I am not my true self, I am Gabrielle.'

Darcel half laughed. 'Well, I will pretend I look lovely.'

'Don't pretend. You do.'

Darcel ran and jumped. The instructor bawled, 'Welcome to the party, Darcel.'

Sarah followed, landing on all fours like a cat, not even winded. Darcel patted her shoulder, but Sarah backed away, feeling ashamed of her old self. They leapt back over to the other building but, as she landed, she remembered Kate's dreadful self-serving lie, just to protect herself and the father of her child, who had left with his tribe. It was a lie that could have ruined the best of men. Sarah's shame faded as they jumped down to the ground and sprinted off onto the moor, and she was grateful for the exercise and tried to pound away the anger that she still felt towards her sister and the whole sordid business.

All three trainees were passed through to the next stage and took the train to Manchester, where they clambered into yet another lorry,

157

which would, take them to the parachute school.

Once there, Sarah examined her pigeonhole. Yes, there was a letter from Lizzy, with a footnote from Kate. In her room, she tore open the envelope.

Hello Mum

When Aunt Kate writes the envelope, it makes me laugh that you have a PO Box address. It makes me think you live in that little box. We are very well. We went to the river to play Poohsticks, and Fran Billings came too (she lets me call her Fran because the children in her street in London do) with Sandra, Milly and Tim. Sandra had a birthday party and so I had mine with her. I'm nine now, but you know that. Thank you for the present you left. I like the doll.

Mrs Whitehead gave Aunt Kate an egg from her hens, so we could bake a cake. We were very surprised because she hasn't been friendly to Aunt Kate; but now she is. The cake was all right, but not very sweet. Mrs Whitehead came to the party because she had given us the egg. Mrs B didn't. She said she was busy. I don't think she was, but she just seems very cross all the time, doesn't she? Aunt Kate said I had to think of her with kindness because life isn't always as it seems.

The vicar is still leaving the long grass and the flowers in the cemetery. Perhaps that's why Mrs B is cross. She thinks it's a bad idea. He says bees are important. He told us a story about bees in Sunday School. Miss Easton's fiancé is missing. She had one of those telegrams, like ours. She's very sad, but thinks he's a prisoner, like Dad.

I'm glad you are in the FANYs and will be safe. I

158

suppose it is safe, because the bombing is getting better. I love you, Mummy.

Your daughter, Lizzy.

Hello, Sarah. Everything is fine here. The harvest is in. The Fletcher boy has started coming to church. Mrs Whitehead has softened. Lizzy is being a very good girl. I am too. Be careful, and I say that from the bottom of my heart.

Sarah folded the letter. On the other bed, Darcel was reading hers. Darcel's mother also thought she was dishing out teas on station platforms, in her smart FANY uniform. Lies, damned lies. Who had said that? She didn't care, because her lies were for the good of the country.

Sarah wrote a letter full of nothing, because it had to be. She would find the time to write other letters, which were equally bland and date-unattributable. They would be posted in her absence. In the meantime she had to continue to try and leave her own life behind and focus on being Gabrielle.

The next day they were tasked to learn to fall, as though from an aeroplane. They had done some preparation in Scotland, but this training was urgent and focused. 'Keep yer 'ands in yer pockets,' roared the instructor, who always wore singlet and shorts.

Darcel murmured, 'With legs like that, who needs hands?'

'For that observation you will show us, Ma-

159

demoiselle Darcel, how to do it properly.'

She did, but Sarah felt anxious, because this was very much on terra firma. What would happen to Darcel from any sort of height?

The next day they strapped on a parachute harness and practised falling again. Finally they climbed up to the gallery, erected high in the hangar. A cable was attached to them. Darcel was pale but composed as she handled the harness and landed, knees bent and together. Sarah did too.

The next day they were promoted to a tower, and then to a platform attached to a barrage balloon 900 feet up. Sarah expected Bernard to yell 'Geronimo', which was what some of the American parachutists shouted as they left an aircraft, their instructor had told them. He'd added that he'd have their guts for garters, if he heard even a whisper of the word. Darcel said nothing, but landed neatly.

Finally it was the Whitley bomber that awaited them one morning. They clambered in and Sarah's stomach turned somersaults, not just at the thought of jumping out of a real moving plane, but at the smell of oil, metal and something indefinable; perhaps it was just the fuselage. There were other parachutists there that she didn't know. No-one spoke. She kept her gaze fixed on Bernard's hands as he sat next to her. They were strong and absolutely still on his lap. This man had no nerves. Sarah saw that Darcel, who sat opposite, was also watching, her lips set in a thin line, sweat beading her forehead.

The first to jump made his way to the hatch. He swung his legs over, staring down at the countryside, knowing that he was to land in a field marked with sheets spread on the ground. He hesitated, and the RAF sergeant despatcher patted him on the back and gave a push. Out he went. It was now Sarah's turn. She felt and heard the wind, seeing the tiny fields and the one with white patches. Legs down, head down. She steeled herself, took a deep breath and thought, 'I can do this. I am Gabrielle, not Sarah, and Gabrielle is brave.' A tap, and out she went.

She turned a somersault, a static line tugged the 'chute open and she felt the jerk switch her from a tumble into a descent. Down, down, she was floating; the wind was light and there was a slight drizzle. She drew closer to the earth, closer, and then it was rushing up. 'Bend the knees,' the instructor's voice echoed in her head. She did; the thwack as she hit the ground ricocheted throughout her body. She rolled, before struggling to her feet, tugging at the parachute, which was threatening to drag her along the ground.

She dug in her heels, but over she went, the parachute billowing and pulling her along. She twisted and turned until she was rescued by an instructor. By then she was covered from head to foot in dirt, her cheek was grazed and sheep-poo stained her uniform. She stank.

Bernard was waiting. 'Fragrant? I don't think so.'

Darcel was nowhere to be seen. 'She's safe,' the instructor said. 'But you won't see her again.'

Soon those who were left went on to the more psychological aspect of their training. Again, they were grouped together by nationality. Their group contained seven men and Sarah. Bernard and she sat together, bound by joint experiences. They were inducted into the rules of the German occupation of France; the differences between the military police and the Gestapo; the need to remain vigilant but unnoticed, because there was no way of knowing who was friendly and who would sell you for a bar of soap. They also learned about Vichy France, which was established after France surrendered to Germany on 22 June 1940 and took its name from the government's administrative centre in Vichy, south-east of Paris. While officially neutral, Vichy actively collaborated with the Nazis, and the trainees had to beware of its officials, and also some of its civilians.

They examined bus timetables, destinations, what was on ration, what was not, and how to avoid ordering the wrong thing, in the wrong way.

They were given yet another identity. Sarah now became Cécile Lamont and was given her new background, including job experience. They were taught to act convincingly so that, if questioned, information could be given realistically. She remembered how Kate had loved to act and always wanted to go on the stage, and how their mother had helped her learn her lines for the school Christmas play, sighing and confessing that she had always wanted that life for herself.

Sarah's instructor called her back to the task in hand, testing her and coming at the subject of her past from other angles. She was Cécile Lamont from Limoges and had worked in a butcher's shop, a *boucherie*, in Poitiers. She had to learn

162

cuts of meat, and the cooking of them. Soon Sarah became Cécile, in her innermost core and, at night, as she fell asleep, she wondered if this was what Kate had been seeking after their mother's death? Was the wildness just some escape from being Kate Watson, daughter of a dead mother and a strict father, owner of a dead dog, friend of a missing Melanie, and sister?

Sarah opened her eyes wide. Had Kate lived so much in another world that she had forgotten what was true and false? She could see how that could happen. Sarah willed herself to sleep, because she refused to go over the same ground again. She was now Cécile from Limoges. Limoges is known for its medieval and Renaissance enamels on copper. Limoges is known for its nineteenth-century porcelain. It is known for its oak barrels, which are used for Cognac and Bordeaux production.

She was Cécile walking along the lanes in the countryside outside Limoges to which her parents had moved, living in a small hamlet. She was stopping to look at the orchids growing in the grass verges sheltered by the hedgerows. Perhaps she was taking just one back to her mother and father, who was a cobbler. Her mother made excellent *boeuf bourguignon*. The clouds were scudding and the geese were squawking in Monsieur Hollande's wired pen. They were bred for the Christmas trade, sadly depleted now that they were occupied, but the Germans still liked a good Christmas Eve dinner.

Limoges, yes, she loved Limoges, but she had to go to Poitiers to work in a new *boucherie,*

163

because Madame Broussard had to close hers when she became too old. She was waving good-bye, and rode her bicycle to her parents' home, along a rough track. It rattled the handlebars; her grip tightened, but she was being shaken and tossed from side to side. She woke, shouting in French, 'What is it? What?'

The men shaking her were in uniform. It was the Gestapo; but she wasn't in France, she was training. How? Who? What?

They were shouting at her in German. She responded in French.

How?

Then Sarah woke completely. They were not Gestapo; they were acting, and she must be Cécile. She was hauled from bed and dragged, pushed and prodded into a dark room, then flung onto a chair. Her feet were cold.

'What?' she said. 'Why am I here? I need to work, I need some sleep.'

'Where do you work?' She gave the name of the Poitiers *boucherie*, because a Cécile Lamont had indeed worked there. That Cécile had left on the outbreak of war, after breaking her leg in a fall, and had lived in England. 'Why there?'

'Because that is where I found a job; there were none near my home.'

'Where is this butcher? Describe the street.' Sarah did. In reality Cécile Lamont had died in a car accident after she had moved to Sussex.

On and on the interrogation went. Sarah grew tired, but she was always Cécile.

'You can relax now,' one of the Gestapo said in English.

'Thanks,' she replied in English.

He said, 'Bang, you're dead.' He cocked his finger and shot her.

Again and again they were tested in this way. Often they failed, but then, slowly, they began to get it right. Bernard, of course, got it quicker than anyone. She and he would sit in the mess in the evening, playing observation games, testing one another, just as the other three who remained were doing. It was relentless, but it would save their lives.

Only when they returned to their beds in the small hours did Sarah think that soon this would be real. Soon they could be in a Gestapo cell under torture. Soon, on the other hand, they could be doing some good, as long as they stayed insignificant, checked for people shadowing them, double-backed when walking, jumped off buses to shake a tail, stared in shop windows to study the reflections of those around them. Yes, they might do some good, as long as they remembered to shoot straight and hit someone only when strictly necessary; to trust no-one – no-one at all – and never relax. Never. Yes, they might do some good, as long as she took part in exercise after exercise that showed her how to make contact with those who would help set up groups within circuits; circuits that would operate now or that would sleep, to be activated when, not if, the allied invasion actually took place.

As long as she learned, by heart, messages that needed passing, and diagrams that could be transcribed for a group. As long as she could leave a written coded message in a drop, or perhaps handed to a shopkeeper or waiter, or written on the margin of a newspaper. As long as, as long as...

Chapter Twelve

At Little Worthy the fields had been ploughed, and some sown, and Kate sat at the kitchen table in the waning evening light on a Sunday evening in September, darning a pair of Lizzy's winter socks. She had found her mother's green wooden darning mushroom and her pincushion in Sarah's workbox. She remembered pushing the pins down into the soft cushion, and her mother would tap Kate's hand. 'Leave that, darling,' she would say. 'Watch while I show you how to darn.'

Kate had thought darning was just like weaving, and had said as much to her mother. It was something Lizzy had said too, the previous evening, her finger pointing to the interwoven wool. Kate just managed to stop herself from saying that Lizzy was so like her. Instead, as Lizzy swished her hair over her shoulder, Kate had said, 'My word, you smell of lavender.'

'That's because you rinsed it with Mum's special conditioner, don't you remember? But then old people don't, do they?' Lizzy's look was the height of innocence, but her giggle gave her away. Kate had wanted to kiss her, like her mother had done to her that day so long ago, but Lizzy had danced away, her thoughts already on other things. It was best because, one day, Kate would leave to take up her place onstage somewhere, and Lizzy would remain here, with her mother.

Kate forced herself back into the moment, here, this evening, the darning mushroom in her hand, with only her memories of her mother to the fore, as she had said, 'You notice so much, little Katie.' But then Kate had remembered her father snapping, 'Time she was doing it herself. And sit up, child. Stop wriggling.' Her mother had squeezed her hand and murmured, 'It's a lovely evening, Reggie. She'd be better outside.'

Instead, her father had taken up his golf clubs and headed out, picking up Dr Bates as he went. Somehow the house relaxed when he was absent. Kate looked out of the open back door into the garden, where Lizzy was now swinging herself high on the seat they had cleaned up last week. The swing hadn't been used for years and had had all sorts of wooden planks resting against it. Kate had carted them to the end of the garden, insisting that Lizzy took one end of the lighter ones.

'If you want something badly enough, you must make it happen,' she had nagged. It's what her mother had often said.

They had used a wire brush on the rust from the chains that held the seat, and then on the uprights. 'I need to see if it's sound,' Kate had said. 'I can't have you hurting yourself unnecessarily. What on earth would your mum and dad say when they come home?'

She tested the seat by sitting on it and bouncing up and down. 'If it will take my great weight,

167

it will take yours.'

Lizzy watched closely. 'It's all right, Aunt Kate. I can't even hear it creak.'

'I'll give it a go, just to make sure.' Kate had pushed with her legs, taking the swing back and letting herself go, swinging higher and higher, feeling the air rushing through her. Higher, flying up and back, up again, looking over the gardens. Fran was clipping the hedge with the shears. 'Send the children round,' Kate called, before she swung down.

She heard Fran say, 'Where are you?'

She swung up again. 'Here,' she laughed, dipping down again. Lizzy was screaming with laughter.

Kate heard Fran's guffaw, then her shout, 'You're nothing but a big child.'

Up she had swung again. 'Come on, Fran, send the children, and come too.' She was whizzing back down.

Lizzy was jumping up and down. 'It's safe. You can see it's safe for me. Stop now, let me have a go.'

The music of their laughter in their garden drowned out the early owl, and the faint shouts of support from the bowling team as they played their latest league match. Fran and the children had arrived, and it had been fun. Milly, Sandra and Tim were round here again this evening, and their laughter drowned the poor old owl, yet again.

Kate returned to her darning, weaving the needle in and out. 'Well, Mum, who'd have thought I'd be here, at the same kitchen table, darning your granddaughter's socks.' She found that she talked to herself rather too much these days, but it was so strange, finding little bits of her past in the simplest of things. Behind her, the wireless muttered. At nine the news might carry details of the bombing of Bristol yesterday. They'd heard the planes flying over and, as Percy's ARP underling, Kate had stood, as ordered, in the streets blowing her whistle while Percy shouted, 'To the shelters.' Everyone ignored them.

'The planes are too high; they're on their way to some other poor people, Percy,' Mrs Martin had muttered, while Stella Easton had just stood, staring at the sky, despair on her face. Poor girl. Was her fiancé Bradley safe in a POW camp?

The sock was finished. Kate held it to her face. This was her child's; somehow the shape of Lizzy was in the sock, in her shoes. To hug them to her was the closest she allowed herself to get to Lizzy, because she was no longer her child, and there was only so much she could bear. One day all this would come to an end, when Sarah returned, or Derek, because two in the same family couldn't die. Tom Rees's God wouldn't be so cruel. Or would he?

There was a knock at the door. She checked the clock: eight twenty-five. Was it Fran? But she'd just walked round the side, into the garden. Kate replaced the sock in the mending box and headed for the front door. She opened it, and there was Tom Rees.

'I thought of you – or your God, actually – and here you are. Does this make me a witch, or some sort of pagan? Are you going to duck me in the village pond?'

169

He stepped back off the step. 'Are you cross with me, or just cross?'

He looked better these days. His skin was tanned, and his sermons were lively and shorter, which was always a good thing, when Kate was there under sufferance.

She smiled. 'Neither, or perhaps a little bit of – just cross.'

'Can I help?'

'Good with a mangle, are you? I have a pile of washing to finish tomorrow, as Little Worthy only likes washing out on a Monday, or so I was reminded by Mrs B yesterday.' She crossed her arms. What did Tom want?

'Ah, Mrs B. Should I have a word with her on your behalf?'

'What, and tell her that she has nothing to be bitter about? That two children dead and a bolter of a husband are no cause for complaint?' There it was again, the sharpness that somehow came to the fore with this man, and she didn't know why, except that today her back hurt even more than usual and she was, sure the damned mangle was implicated. 'Her children would be eighteen and nineteen now, old enough to be in the army, so perhaps they would have died anyway, but that won't help her.'

He was looking at the rose that grew in the centre of the front garden. The darkness was falling fast, and the colour could only be imagined if you didn't already know it was red.

Kate said, 'Mum would not allow red and white flowers in the same vase. Bandages and blood, so therefore bad luck.'

'You miss her?'

He was bending slightly, and running his hand through the lavender that grew along the path, right up to the porch. The scent was released into the warm evening. Kate murmured, 'I miss her. She loved me.'

Tom Rees, his dog collar clearly visible in the dusk, said, 'Most parents do.'

She did not answer, but said, 'I reckon that dog collar is a breach of blackout, Vicar.'

Fran called from the front gate. 'Send 'em back, would you?'

To Tom's raised eyebrows, Kate said, 'Not your collars – the children. They're in the garden playing on the swing. I suppose I have to ask you in, because you're not going to go away, are you?'

He laughed and shook his head.

Kate said, 'Follow me then.' She waved to Fran. 'I'll prise them off and send 'em packing. I'll watch until they reach your gate, and you can herd them in from there. Come along, Vicar, your collar can light the way. Go on through to the kitchen.'

She stood to one side. Tom headed for the kitchen where she indicated one of the kitchen chairs, before hurrying into the garden. 'Bedtime for Mrs Billings's bunch, now, if you please; not in a minute. Lizzy, you'd better come in too and head for bed.'

The children knew better than to argue and ran through the house, with Kate in hot pursuit. They dashed out of the gate, leaving it swinging.

'Not so fast – were you born in a barn? Come and shut this, one of you, if you please.'

Milly did, before taking off after the others, who

171

were haring into their own front garden. How on earth would they feel when they returned to London? Kate shook her head. She didn't allow herself to think of London, now that she had Brucie's key to her flat safely back in her possession. She had read his accompanying letter, full of protestations and apologies, and had torn it up, letting the pieces flutter into the waste bin. After a moment she had grabbed them out and burned them in the sink. Lizzy had watched the smoke spiralling up and said, 'He's made you cross, hasn't he?'

'It will pass,' she had said, knowing that if it didn't pass, it would fade. Things did.

She looked up at the sky; the moon was hidden by scurrying clouds. Was rain on the way? The gardens could do with it, or she'd have to raid the water butt again. She hurried inside. Lizzy was talking to the vicar, who was pouring water into the kettle. He waggled a little screw of paper at Kate. 'I've brought unused tea leaves: better than gold dust, nicer than diamonds.'

'Indeed, and this sounds like a potential bribe. What do you want? It must be something big.' She placed the teapot on the draining board. 'You started, so you can finish while I chase Lizzy up the wooden hill.' Lizzy grumbled, but ran up the stairs. They ran two inches of warm water, not hot. It was not cold enough to have the range on full blast and, besides, Kate wanted to preserve their logs. She had collected a load of fallen branches from the woods and sawn them up, but many villagers had similar ideas, so it was definitely the early bird that caught the worm.

It was time for teeth, then into bed. Kate listened as Lizzy read a story. It must help her reading, surely? She thought of Tom in the kitchen. They hadn't really talked since she had flounced out of the annexe, and the memory of her overreaction to his comment about lying embarrassed her.

She gave this enchanting child a swift kiss. Not quick enough, for Lizzy caught her in a hug, her arms around her neck, pulling her close. Kate did nothing, unable to bear it. After a moment Lizzy released her, disappointed, turning on her side. 'Goodnight, Aunt Kate.'

'Sleep well.' Kate left. She shut the door and leaned back, smelling Lizzy's hair, feeling the pressure of those arms.

She hurried downstairs and into the kitchen, pulling out a chair. The back door was shut, the blackout drawn, a light on. She said, 'Not a chink. But dear old Percy is disappointed, because everyone is so good these days. Even you.'

Tom grinned. 'Well, I put my foot in it last time, without in any way meaning it, so I thought I must improve.'

She ignored his words, because she didn't want to have to comment. Instead she toasted him with her cup of tea and sipped. 'Ambrosia. Now what's the going payment for tea?'

The clock on the wall was ticking. The range gurgled; it needed feeding. She found a log from the basket and tossed it into the furnace, and then a second, because it really was very low. She slammed the range door shut and returned.

Tom was drawing a couple of sheets of paper from his pocket, and a pen, the top of which he

173

unscrewed. He laid both on the table.

She said, 'Today's reading is from ... what, Tom?'

He cleared his throat. She almost blanched. It surely wasn't going to be a sermon, because this is what he did when he was about to launch into his message for the week. Last Sunday it had been on sorrow: Psalm 77. 'Will the Lord cast us off for ever? Is his mercy clean gone for ever? Hath God forgotten to be gracious?' She had been sitting at the back of the church, wishing that Stella Easton had come to sit with her and had not closed herself off in her sadness. Kate feared she would one day break completely in half, so rigidly did she hold her body.

Tom had then discussed one of John Donne's devotions, droning on about how Donne had lost all that he held dear. She had been annoyed because Donne suggested that suffering makes people pay attention, forcing them to look to God, who might seem the only source of comfort. Tom had leaned on the pulpit. 'Perhaps, even when we cry out in our suffering that God isn't here, we reveal our longing for Him.'

He had looked around the congregation, and did she imagine it or did his gaze linger on Mrs B, on Stella, on Adrian Fletcher, who sat at the back with his mother and wife. Lastly Tom had looked right at her, for goodness' sake. He boomed, 'But let us not forget that mere mortals – in other words, people – can be here to soothe, love and support, and surely that's an example of God at work. Yes, let us not forget that.'

He was fiddling with his dog collar now, picking up his pen, twiddling, replacing it. Finally she

174

said, 'Look, Vicar, do get on with it, there are only so many hours in the day, and I'm growing older and more wrinkled by the minute.'

He threw back his head and laughed. 'You, Katie Watson, will never be old or wrinkled. Someone will strangle you long before that.'

'Not a suitable remark from a man of the cloth, methinks.' She finished her tea and refilled both their cups. 'You or me to have the tea leaves?'

He said, 'You.'

'Good, then you may have some milk.'

He laughed again and drank, before replacing his cup carefully in the saucer. 'My mother always likes to drink tea from a bone-china cup.'

'Well, that's enormously interesting, and I will bear it in mind if she ever comes knocking, but why are you here?'

'I'll get to the point.' He moved his pen from the sheets of closely written paper. 'I have concerns.' He paused and looked up at her.

Kate swallowed. What had Lizzy said? Where had she been going wrong? Would the child be taken from her?

He continued, 'Stella Easton is, I believe, in the midst of great misery and lack of direction. She saw me today to tell me she feels she cannot continue at the school, let alone bring the fund-raising *Anything Goes* into even the first stages of production. We have, as you know, already started auditions and are some weeks into the school term, so it will be disastrous. Added to that, we have, as you well know from our similarly disastrous discussion not so long ago, Mrs B, who seems unable to move into any sort of light. And

175

then there is Adrian Fletcher, who is similarly mourning, though possibly in a confused way, and needs ... something.' He waved his pen in the air. The gold nib was ink-stained. 'Finally, we come to Miss Kate Watson.'

She put up her hand. 'I am perfectly all right, thank you very much, and Lizzy is–'

This time it was Tom who put up his hand. 'Exactly, and you are the only one who can work a miracle for Little Worthy. Don't you see, this show is the answer to everything? Mrs B plays the piano and can accompany any songs. Adrian Fletcher? Well, we can find him a role, even if it's only helping to make scene sets. And Miss Easton... Now, Kate, if the wind changes, you'll stay looking like that, and it will make you more of a gargoyle than me. Now, I say again: you are the only one who can get to work and save Stella, who must continue with the school and the production, for her own well-being.'

She said nothing.

Tom was running his finger down the page. 'Yes, what I need from you is to convince Stella that we need her to keep both the school and the production going. After yesterday's bombing of Bristol and the earlier bombing of Yeovil, the villagers don't know if they could be next. They are hungry and sugar-starved; their menfolk and some of their daughters are heaven knows where; and some are already dealing with loss. Nonetheless they collect paper, metal. The WI grubs in rubbish tips for Kilner jars, or whatever jars they can find. Winter is coming, and Christmas will be without much ruddy cheer.'

She smiled. 'Heavens, Vicar, you'd best wash your mouth out with soap, swearing like that.'

His smile was broad. Was it her imagination or was his lip becoming more flexible at the corner? He continued, 'You must convince Stella that she has a duty to stick with it, rather than turning tail and running away. After all, surely we all need something to work towards, other than war. Through her efforts she will help to bring light to our darkness, and money into the coffers.' He sat back, his finger having reached the bottom of the page.

'I thought you were going to say "money into the coffins",' Kate said.

He laughed, patting the sweat from his forehead. 'I do find you infuriating. Would you just answer me with a "yes"? Please.'

She shook her head. 'Sorry, but it's a "no". I will talk to Stella by all means, but I have no clout in the village, so I can't persuade her – or anyone – to do anything.'

He sighed, and now he looked at his second sheet. 'I thought you might say that, so on I go. We have children in the village who have had to leave their homes and live with strangers. Are they to lose their school, and a loved teacher as well?'

She reached across and snatched the paper from beneath his finger and waved it at him. 'You should be talking to Stella, for heaven's sake.'

Tom Rees snatched it back. It tore, leaving a corner in Kate's hand. He said, 'Now look what you've done.' He gave her no chance to reply, but sped on. 'You did tell her you would do whatever you could for the school and the show.'

177

She raised her hand again. 'I did, several times. She turned me down each time, saying she could manage.'

He shook his head. 'She patently can't. She's been in this adrenalin panic, keeping frantically busy, and inevitably she's crashed. I can't do more than help with Religious Studies at the school, such is my pastoral work, but with Lizzy at school, you have the time to take on the three Rs, at least for the small ones. But most importantly, you are the only one with the experience to help steer the all-important show.' He checked the page again, then threw it to one side, looking up at her.

Kate shook her head again. 'No.'

'Oh, for goodness' sake, woman, don't be so bloody difficult. I need you to shove your way in to Stella's side, because she likes you – heaven knows why.' He folded the paper. 'The village needs her, and I need you, and I'm not going until you agree.'

Kate stared at his pen, which was rolling very slowly towards the edge of the table. Tom scooped it up.

She stood. 'Turn out the light when you go. I'm off to bed.'

She turned towards the door. Lizzy stood there, her teddy under her arm. 'You have to do it, Aunt Kate. You're so good. I saw her at the club, Vicar. I peeped round the corner and watched; she made me want to cry, but I don't know why, and I never wanted it to end. Poor Miss Easton. You should help, because I think you're the only one who can. And besides, I don't want to go to another school if she leaves. I didn't know her name is Stella.'

Kate sighed and said, 'You mustn't call her that. Now go to bed.'

Tom Rees made his way back to the vicarage in the dark, smiling. Would he have swung it on his own? He doubted it, and blessed Lizzy, because the reason he had to involve Kate was that he was sure sorrow and confusion were buried deep inside her, and he was determined that she must be helped. Therefore Kate had to have another role in the village – something that would not only use her skills, but would gain her the support and liking of everyone. Yes, there had been improvements in the attitude of some, but this was his village and he was intent on helping where he could.

He whistled as he walked, his hands in his pockets. He would create a pool of healing, all being well, and Hastings would be proud of him. He looked ahead and saw the slit headlights of a car drawing to a halt outside the vicarage. He lengthened his stride. It was past ten o'clock, so who on earth?

He saw a figure emerge from the car, with a suitcase. He heard the voice that thanked the taxi driver. It was Pauline, his ex-fiancée. He waited for his heart to leap, but it did not. She saw him and ran, flinging her arms around his neck. 'Darling, say you forgive me. I made a terrible mistake and I have come back to you.'

Still he felt nothing, but that was absurd. He held Pauline close and kissed her cheek, searching for words, trying to accommodate his surprise.

179

She said, 'Cat got your tongue?' She pulled away, and he could hear the hurt in her voice. He had to say something.

'It's just such a shock; well, a wonderful one. How wonderful to see you. Wonderful.' For heaven's sake, he had to think of something other than 'wonderful', because it wasn't. 'Let me take your case. I'm sorry, I can't quite get my thoughts together. I thought you had left me for good?'

'Perhaps I should have telephoned, but having made the decision to see you, I just jumped on a train, which took ages. You surely knew in your heart that I just needed a bit of time to sort myself out, darling silly one, to see a path ahead.' She stepped back. 'Oh dear, I need to pay the taxi. Would you, darling? I was in such a hurry I didn't have time to get to the bank.'

They returned to the taxi together and, still dazed, Tom paid what seemed like a fortune for one on his stipend, tipped the driver and watched the car drive away.

Pauline was tugging at his arm. 'Shall we go in?'

'Well, of course, but I need to find you somewhere to stay. After all, it just wouldn't do to share the vicarage without a chaperone. I know, I'll telephone the Cat and Fiddle, they have rooms. Meanwhile, I have mint tea to keep you going.'

Pauline linked her arm in his, and as they walked up the path she chattered about her journey from Swindon. Tom couldn't give a damn about it, but that must be because he was still in shock, because he should be pleased to see her, although he wasn't. And she'd never before called him her 'darling silly one'. And he wasn't, anyway.

Not silly, and not her darling one; not recently anyway. He wondered if Dunkirk's legacy of trauma had confused him, but he was too shaken to think of much more than putting one foot in front of the other.

The next morning, at eight, when the baker opened for business, Kate lay in wait for Stella by the telephone box, pushing open the door as she passed. 'Well, Stella, just who I wanted to see.'

Stella Easton stopped. The energy had indeed fled from this young woman, leaving her uncertainty and grief increasingly obvious, but Kate hadn't needed Tom Rees to spell it out to her. Or perhaps she had, because she hadn't done much about it, had she?

Kate drew in a deep breath. She had rehearsed in the privacy of the attic, trying all sorts of approaches, and deciding on this. 'I need your help. You see, the man I thought I loved has left me for someone else. I just feel I will go quite mad unless I find something to do. May I please help at the school? I know I've asked before, and I haven't many skills, but it would help me so much to feel needed. Perhaps I could help with teaching the three Rs? I thought we could also work together on the fundraiser. I need to put whatever inadequate skills I have to good use, just to keep myself going.'

She linked her arm in Stella's, taking her basket from her and carrying it as she led her, not to the shops, but to Melbury Cottage.

'We could sit down and plan it all. It seems such a shame to let down those who've attended the audition, don't you think? You know, I have lots of tap shoes upstairs. Mum replaced mine whenever I grew out of a pair.'

Stella was silent, but let herself be led through the gate and round into the back garden, which was empty, because Mrs Summers had said she'd keep Lizzy until the deed was done, taking her to school if need be.

Kate led Stella through the kitchen. 'Come with me to the attic where the trunk is, then you can see what we have.'

She gripped the woman's hand and led her up the stairs, talking all the time about Brucie, about *Anything Goes*, about Tom's sermon. She felt that was pushing it, but it was worth a bash.

Still Stella said nothing, but just seemed in a daze. Tom was right; she had crashed, as Kate herself had once done. They reached the attic ladder.

Kate gestured upwards. 'You go first. This is the attic where I sleep. I like the view, you see. Come on now, Stella. Just put one foot in front of the other. It's not Everest.'

Stella was standing, looking up. Tears had begun to stream down her face, though she made not a sound.

Softly Kate murmured, 'One step at a time, my dearest girl. You have to go forward, you know that, and while you're doing so, you might as well do something useful.'

Slowly Stella climbed the ladder and walked to the window. Kate was close behind. Stella's tears were still falling. Finally she said, 'So, will it really help us both?'

The two women stood together. Kate said, 'It will.'

'I'm so alone.'

'No, we will be in this together, and you have other friends. Together we'll keep the school open, and raise money with a show that will also bring the village together. We'll get Mrs B to play the piano for us, and maybe move her forward too. Perhaps even Adrian Fletcher will join us.'

Stella turned to her, her tears finished now. 'I can't hope.'

Kate gripped her hand. 'Bradley is missing. Why not believe that he will be found, until you know differently. Show the children they have an example before them that they can follow.' Kate stared again out of the window. She could smell the wood-smoke and the trodden grass, and knew she should have left with Andrei. If she had, her life would still be intact and she would be alive inside. She shuddered, then drew a deep breath. Enough. One day at a time was all it could be. 'Now, tap shoes.'

She pointed to the trunk in which she'd found them. She hadn't known her mother had kept them, but this trunk had been hidden from sight in the cupboard under the eaves and had escaped the clear-out. She had dragged it out when she was after what she thought was a mouse one night. It had proved to be a trapped starling, which she had released into the air, watching it soar free.

'Come on, Stella, we have work to do, and plans to make. I will come into school at lunch-time and we can think more about it.' She knelt in front of the trunk, lifted the lid and picked up

183

a pair of red tap shoes that she had worn at the age of five, when her mother enrolled her in Mrs Major's dancing class. Her father hadn't liked it, but as most of the village five-year-olds pounded away in the hall, what could he say?

She pulled out another pair, also red. Would Stella help? Would Tom be pleased? She caught the thought. How absurd; what did it matter what the vicar thought? There was a movement and then Stella was kneeling by her side.

'We could ask other mothers if they have kept any of their children's ballet shoes or taps,' Kate said, handing her a pair. 'Practically all the girls, and a few of the boys, went to Mrs Major's classes. Oh my, we thought we were the bee's knees.'

She heard Stella take a deep breath, then say, 'Yes, Kate, I'll put a notice on the board at school, and follow it with a note to take home. Or you could get the children to do that, as part of a writing exercise.'

Kate groaned. Stella laughed, and though it sounded strained, it was an improvement. Kate said, 'We'll need a schedule for the auditions and must really crack on with it. We'll need a meeting to gather backstage helpers together, and costume-makers. It should be soon.' She didn't want to give Stella time for second thoughts.

Stella smiled wearily, but it was a smile. 'You, Tom and I will meet after school tomorrow, at five, in the vicarage. I expect Tom has had a hand in all of this, so he can accommodate us. How about that?' She rose from her knees.

Kate said, 'It would be better to have it today at five.'

184

Stella raised her eyebrows. 'You really have got the bit between your teeth, haven't you? All right then, and now I must dash. I have the school to open and will tell them all that we have a new teaching assistant.' She followed Kate down the ladder and, at the front door, Stella hesitated, turned and kissed Kate on the cheek. 'Thank you, my friend, you carried out your mission well. I'm right, Tom Rees is involved somewhere?'

The two looked at one another and laughed. As Stella hurried down the path, Kate called, 'One step at a time.'

Stella waved. 'I understand, and again, I thank you both.'

After Kate had cleared up Lizzy's earlier breakfast things and Mrs Summers had taken her to school, she headed for the vicarage to inform Tom of the arrangements. She knocked at the front door and smiled as Mrs B opened it. Mrs B did not smile back. Well, why would she break the habit of a lifetime?

'Is Reverend Rees able to see me, please, Mrs Bartholomew?'

'He has someone with him.' She blocked the doorway in her long, dark-green pleated skirt and cardigan over a white blouse.

Kate asked, 'May I leave a message then?'

Tom called from the sitting-room doorway, 'Who is it, Mrs B?'

'The Watson girl.' There was still a flicker of distrust and dislike in Mrs B's eyes, but far less so than on Kate's first day back in Little Worthy. Perhaps the old bag was warming to her?

185

'Oh.' Tom sounded strange.

Kate slipped past the doorkeeper and approached him. Tom stood aside almost reluctantly and gestured her into the room. A red-haired young woman sat on the sofa, flipping through a magazine. She looked up, saying, 'Oh, shall I leave you in peace, darling?'

Kate smiled, but it was an effort. 'Darling?' Who was this woman? And what was she doing in the vicarage at this time in the morning? Surely she hadn't been here all night? No, she wouldn't jump to any conclusions, but for a moment she forgot why she was here. She took a moment and then, keeping her smile, said, 'I won't be intruding for long. Stella is willing, Tom. She'd like a meeting with you and me today, here at five. But I can see...'

Tom looked embarrassed and dithered. 'Oh yes, I'd forgotten all about that.' He came to stand between Kate and Pauline, as though to block Kate's view of 'darling'. She looked at him instead, and felt shaky and confused as he said to her, 'Don't go, Kate. I'm sure Pauline has things to do and might even perhaps be on her way?'

'Of course I won't, darling. Not yet. I've only just arrived.' Pauline came to stand beside Tom, taking his hand. She smiled at Kate, but the smile didn't reach her eyes. She said, 'Do introduce me to your little friend – the Watson girl, as Mrs B so delicately put it, Tom.'

Kate's confusion cleared and in its place came irritation. She snapped, 'I'm not little, and I'm not his friend. I'm one of his flock. A meeting here at five o'clock then, Tom?' She turned on

186

her heel, and strode out of the room, past a startled Mrs B. Kate wanted to say, 'My word, it looks as though you have a sharp-tongued ally, Mrs B. You'd better get right in there and make a "get rid of Kate Watson" plan of campaign.'

Instead she held her tongue and stormed down the path, slamming the gate behind her. 'Little friend' indeed; and if that hair was red, then she was a brunette.

Chapter Thirteen

In the last week of September, Sarah was driven in a car with drawn blinds to a secret airfield, her mind carefully blank. She had been checked at the manor house nearby for clothing inaccuracies that could expose her, not just to the Gestapo, but to anyone who happened to look at her. Everything she wore was French, and old.

They entered the airfield, though she only knew because the tarmac road had been smooth, and now they swung this way and that over bumpy, spongy ground, their speed slowed to a crawl. She wore a flying suit, with what seemed like a hundred pockets. Lizzy would have found them intriguing. It was only now that Sarah allowed herself last thoughts of her child.

She had been given five days' 'embarkation leave'. Kate had brought Lizzy to her in Ringwood, and had returned to Little Worthy on the next train. Sarah and Lizzy had stayed in a small

187

cottage in the New Forest. They had walked on the moors, seen the ponies, spent evenings in front of a log fire while Lizzy told her of school, and how Miss Easton was smiling again because she believed that Bradley might come home after all. Or that's what Aunt Kate – had told her.

They had toasted bread on a fork in front of the fire, and Lizzy had mentioned the auditions, which had begun again. 'Some people think they can sing, but the noise they make isn't singing. The vicar is on the panel, or that's what they call it. It's Mr Sims's wallpaper table. Aunt Kate, Miss Easton and the vicar sit at it, and I can see they are swallowing laughs.'

Sarah had frowned. 'I don't think it's nice to laugh at people.'

'Oh, Mum,' her daughter had said. 'You're always so ... well, so serious. The people can't see the laughs, but I can, because I know Aunt Kate so well. She's kind, Mum. She gets them to try another key and, you know, sometimes it works. If it doesn't, she thinks of something they are good at. Even Mrs B smiles; she plays the piano for the show. I didn't know she could – no-one did. Aunt Kate teaches in school too, helping Miss Easton. The "three Rs" they call it. It's nice having her there.'

The car had now stopped. Sarah touched the revolver in one of her pockets, the knife in another, the flask, emergency rations, maps, compass, shovel. She could feel the money belt against her skin, holding thousands of pounds worth of francs, to be delivered to a contact in Vichy France. Last of all, she carried the pill that would kill her, if she was cornered and couldn't bear the thought of capture.

She carried French cigarettes in a case, which would be her means of contact in one of her destinations. She would offer the cigarettes to someone in Vichy France. Her mind clicked over the ration card, identity card, clothing coupons. Her suitcase was by her side. That had also been checked, and so too the false bottom.

At the end of their time in the New Forest, she and Lizzy had taken the bus to the station. Kate was waiting on the platform and held out her hand for Lizzy's suitcase. Lizzy said, 'Who else has got parts, Aunt Kate? Have you started teaching tap-dancing yet? I told Mum I'm going to be one of the dancers. Miss Easton said I shone, didn't she, Aunt Kate? Did I tell you that, Mum? Miss Easton said I was quite exceptional, didn't she, Aunt Kate?'

Lizzy was jigging about, as Kate used to, skipping from one foot to another, fizzing with energy. Sarah had stopped herself from saying as she usually did, 'For goodness' sake, stand still.' For those, she realised at last, were the words of their father, and just look where they had led? So, no; instead she had said, 'I will miss you, but you must have a wonderful fund-raising show, and I will try to be here for it. I'm sure you will be marvellous. I will write.' Her London train had arrived as she hugged her daughter. 'I love you,' she said.

She had looked up at Kate, who murmured, 'She will be safe with me, but you stay safe too, do you hear me, Sarah? Do you?' They had waved her off. Sarah had responded, leaning out

189

of the train until they both headed for their own platform.

Now she stood in the light of the full moon, which was when agents were dropped and picked up. Behind her the car's engine was humming, the airfield empty but for the looming bulk of the Whitley bomber, and she allowed herself one final thought of Lizzy, one more thought of Derek. And although she couldn't quite remember the details of his face, she could hear his voice saying, 'I love you.'

Then Sarah was back in Cécile's world, which she had made her own. She nodded into the night, as she was fitted with a parachute harness. Her suitcase was given its own parachute and contained supplies for the reception committee and her clothes. Its false bottom contained her revolver and was suitably shabby. There were two people waiting in the shadow of the Whitley, and now she saw that one was Bernard. Sarah smiled, as he did; yes, this was her world, one she was trained for, one in which she felt at home, as she had never done anywhere before. She was Cécile Lamont from Limoges and had worked in a butcher's shop in Poitiers; and she would be here, in this plane, with her friend Bernard.

It had begun.

They were helped into the bomber and clambered to the positions indicated by the RAF despatchers. Sarah sat on the floor, breathing in the familiar oily, metallic smell. It made her think of Darcel. Where was she? A wireless transmitter hung in a foam-rubber-lined bag from the fuselage, above the hatch through which they'd

190

tumble, when the time came. She knew the transmitter would be attached to its owner's parachute and that they'd go down together. Well, rather him than her. She didn't know the wireless operator; she only knew that she was to travel with one other person as far as... She stopped. No, don't think of details. It was best, just in case.

At least it wasn't going to be a blind drop; instead they'd fall into the arms of a reception committee, or that was the plan. There was another dropping zone, if that failed. There was always another. Plan A, plan B, even plan C. The engines started, the fuselage shuddered, they bumped and lurched as the Whitley accelerated and then there was the thrust, which always felt as though it was stretching her face into a grotesque mask. Poor Tom Rees; how could he live with that scar? No wonder his girlfriend had left, and how amazing it was that she was back, or so Lizzy had said. No. Not that world. Sarah had to drag herself away from it. It didn't exist, couldn't exist in her head, if she was to survive. She was Cécile Lamont.

The RAF sergeant brought them water. She drank, before lying down, as the wireless operator was doing. It might be her last chance for a while. Bernard inched towards her. 'Ça va?'

'Ça va. Et vous?'

'Et tu, surely?' The familiar voice was low.

She smiled and continued in French. 'Of course – the familiar.'

He said, 'We drop together, then you and I set off for the same destination.' No names, always no names, just in case. 'Like old times,' he said.

She clung to that thought. It was an exercise,

191

that's all, like it had always been. Because now, despite the drink, her mouth was dry. The wireless operator lay nearer the hatch. He would be a George. All operators seemed to be George, like the king. Which George, though? George the first, second, third?

He edged towards them. 'I'm George,' he said. 'I already know who you are. I go first, once we reach the dropping zone, then Bernard, then you, Cécile. After which I go my way, and you go yours. The Whitley will drop us on the first run; no need for a second, as there are just three of us to hit the dropping zone.'

Bernard and Sarah nodded. George had obviously done this before, and survived, which was encouraging. The dim lighting was switched off over the Channel. She couldn't see Bernard, but she sensed him. The torches of the despatchers created a pattern, as they did whatever it was they did. The disembodied voice of an RAF sergeant said, 'If you hear firing, we're probably not going down into the drink. It'll be the machine-gunner test-firing.'

They flew on, the flight longer than any she had experienced before. During practice it was up, up and then out of the hatch, and down. Sarah swallowed. She was Cécile, who had worked at a butcher's in Poitiers. She was French, she had papers, the correct clothes. She would stay alert, she would live and find Derek. She listened to the drone of the engine, felt the buffeting of the wind. She dozed, woke, looked to the side. Bernard was awake. He smiled, reached out and touched her hand. She gripped his. For a moment it was as though they clung to one another. She dozed again.

Sarah felt a hand on her shoulder. 'Comment?'

The RAF sergeant said, in English, 'We're over Tours, which is in occupied France. Not long now.'

She sat up, rubbing her face. George and Bernard were already leaning back on the fuselage, chatting quietly in French.

A despatcher opened the exit hatch. Sarah moved close and looked down at the moonlit Vichy ground, where there were a few street lights. It seemed for ever since she had seen lights at night. Bernard was close beside her, his arm touching hers as the ground seemed to streak away.

On they droned, losing height. It would be soon. Her throat was too parched to swallow or speak. A sergeant came close. 'Ground signal spotted.' A small red light appeared on the wall.

Plan A then, Derek, Sarah thought. Yes, Plan A, Lizzy. And all she wanted was to be safe at Little Worthy, as the three of them had been, with no war, and none of this. She tried to swallow, tried to smile at Bernard, but couldn't. George had moved with his wireless to the hatch. He swung his feet down, his flying suit was plucked by the wind. The despatcher raised his arm, the aircraft seemed to lurch, then levelled. The despatcher murmured, 'Five hundred feet – stand by.'

The red light changed to green. The despatcher dropped his arm. George was gone, and all that was left was the strop of the static line, hanging down through the hole. Sarah moved across and swung out her legs. The wind snatched at them. Her heart was beating too fast, much faster than it had ever done before. The moonlit ground seemed too close. The strop would yank open her parachute. She breathed in, pushed off with her hands and the wind caught her and tossed her into a somersault.

The canopy opened and she was spreadeagled, lying on the wind. She straightened and swung in ever-decreasing circles. She made herself breathe out, and then in, out; in, out. The signal torches on the ground were pinpricks. The swinging stopped. She was dropping like a pencil through the air, and the ground came up and whacked the air from her body, and too late she bent her knees. She fell to one side, jarred, but alive, her legs miraculously unhurt.

The 'chute dragged her. She punched the disc to loosen the harness and the 'chute dragged it free of her. Sarah stood there panting, as though she'd run a mile. A man was heading towards her. Another was catching up with the 'chute. There was a second parachute, which crashed to the ground with her suitcase. This too was captured. It was so white in the moonlight. Surely it had been seen? Surely the Whitley had been heard?

The man reached her. 'Comrade, welcome to the soil of France. Welcome. I am Jean. Ah, a woman. Even more welcome. Come, quickly.'

Sarah doubted that was his real name. Jean pulled at her arm and gathered up her suitcase. Further into the field Bernard was being welcomed. Sarah let herself be hurried to the edge of the field. Another man was there, with a shovel.

194

There was a grave dug for the parachutes, and in they went. As she left the field, with Jean carrying her suitcase, she heard the clink of stones on shovel. If she had heard it, surely someone else could?

She must have spoken aloud, for Jean replied, 'Perhaps the goats, but that is all. The police are not around here tonight. We get warning. Not all are German-lovers or Pétain-lovers.' He let go of her arm and led the party across the track, through a gate and over two fields. She could see a farmhouse. A dog barked, just once, and then tore towards them, curving at the last minute. It tucked in at Jean's heel. Somewhere a train hooted and there was the sound of a car.

They hurried around the edge of a farmyard and into the kitchen. 'Brigitte, here are our guests,' Jean said in French, always in French – always.

She was here, in Vichy France; it wasn't an exercise. It was real and dangerous, but vital. Sarah hoped Brigitte was really called something else, just in case Sarah fell foul of ... in case *they* hurt her too badly. They: the monsters of her dreams.

Jean brought them up to date on recent developments: the availability of food; the drastic rationing of tobacco. Clandestine crossings over the demarcation line into the occupied zone were possible, but not easy.' He wagged his fingers at the pair of them as they ate their omelettes and bread. 'Some funerals work well for us. Go as a mourner: one side of the demarcation line is the church and the coffin, and the other is the cemetery.' They nodded, but they already knew this. It was how Sarah intended to move across into

195

occupied territory when the time came, but she had no idea about Bernard. It was best not to know.

The following morning Sarah left the farmhouse with Bernard. They walked along tracks edged with wild flowers and came to a hamlet. No-one noticed them in their well-worn clothes and shoes, though some of the villagers clumped along on wooden soles. They kept on walking into Clermont-Ferrand, where they forced themselves to stop at a café, taking seats at a pavement table. They waited to be served. Was it still right to do so? So much had changed, Jean had said.

A waiter came to take their order of coffee. Ersatz coffee arrived, bitter and awful, though it was sweetened with something. 'Saccharine pellets,' breathed Bernard. They paid and walked on, looking into virtually empty shop windows, and Bernard insisted that together they tried lunch in a hotel. Would their ration cards work? The coupons were clipped without comment. The small portions stuck in Sarah's throat as she listened and watched, and slowly remembered to relax, to smile and chat. They moved on and parted at the railway station.

Sarah felt bereft to see Bernard take his place in the ticket-office queue whilst she looked at her watch and pretended to wait for someone. Would he pass examination at the ticket office? She looked around. Why didn't everyone know she wasn't French? Why weren't they all staring? Two *gendarmes* stood by a doorway. Were they looking? Yes. One stared at her and nudged his companion, pointing towards her. She wanted to run, but then a voice hailed them from behind her. 'Hello, Quentin, it's time we met again. Come one evening.'

The *gendarmes* saluted an old man who came from behind and walked towards them. The three of them shook hands and talked, and Sarah breathed a sigh of relief as Bernard walked towards her, looking at his watch and bumping into her. He raised his hat in apology. 'Dearest Cécile, we'll meet again, but keep safe, for if you are not, I would miss you. You must know that.'

He walked on, looking for his platform, taking the train north. Sarah queued to buy a ticket. Would she be as inconspicuous? 'A single to Toulouse, if you please.' There was not a flicker of doubt as the ticket was handed over.

She took the train, recognising the countryside from her time here before the war. It seemed a world away. Well, it was, just like Little Worthy. No, she was Cécile from Limoges, and if she was stopped and questioned, well, she had come to have a brief holiday, after a bout of influenza. She sat upright as the train rocked and clicked over the points. Stay alert.

Leaving the station, Sarah saw ancient horse-carriages, which looked as though they would fall apart if they lurched over a bump. That's if the thin horses didn't just give up, lie down and die. Would the shafts permit that? There were cycles that pulled passenger-trailers, and trams, but hardly any motor cars. Her instructions were to stay in the station hotel, which was opposite the station.

Sarah banged the bell on the reception counter,

and filled in her name on the registration card: Cécile Lamont. The room was shabby, though the bed was comfortable. She lay down, but couldn't rest. She was jigging about like Lizzy. Her father would say, 'For heaven's sake, stand still.' He had never needed to, because Sarah didn't jig. She hadn't done anything very much, she realised.

She rose, leaving her suitcase unpacked. It held little, now that she had given Jean the money and the forged documents for his group. All that remained were a handful of clothes and her revolver, still packed in the false bottom. She was to head for Le Petit Chat café for instructions and had memorised the route. She struck out to the east. The people were as grey as she, the town as weary. Everywhere there were photographs of Marshal Pétain. Also, stuck on a shop window, she saw instructions for sending parcels to the thousands of French prisoners-of-war stuck in Germany, probably being used as labourers. Was Derek in a British POW camp?

Sarah sat at a table outside Le Petit Chat and ordered a coffee, ersatz again. She sipped it as the day drew to a close. People passed, returning from work, shoulders slumped. Across the street, walking slowly but firmly, were what she felt were two Vichy Gestapo. She sipped again, but the coffee was still foul. An old man came out of the café and walked past her table, blocking her view of a horse-drawn taxi-carriage. She craned her neck past him, watching and listening to the clip-clop, keeping an eye on the Vichy Gestapo as they turned down a side-street. She felt the thudding of her heart. She concentrated on the horse; the ponies in the New Forest had been smaller.

Sarah sipped again at her coffee, and only then did she see the folded newspaper on her table and closed her eyes. She had missed the drop. Whoever was responsible was a professional, whilst she, clearly, was not. She beckoned to the waiter and paid, picked up her handbag and her newspaper. She tucked it under her arm and strolled back to the hotel, looking in shop windows, checking reflections, alert to the activity around her.

She diverted down an alley, knowing it would come out to a parallel street where she would turn towards the east. She looked both ways before crossing the road. No-one stopped to tie a shoelace, or hid behind a newspaper. She eventually found her way back to her hotel room. She checked her suitcase. The hair that she had stuck on with spittle was still there, so no-one had breached it. She read the coded message written on the edge of the front page of the newspaper, which used the last verse of her chosen poem, 'Stopping by Woods on a Snowy Evening' by Robert Frost, as a key.

It gave Sarah a route to follow tomorrow. It was then that she would receive a message to take on to somewhere she didn't yet know of. She slept, exhausted, and not hungry. In the morning she tucked the revolver into her jacket pocket and found a café for a bread roll for breakfast, and took barely a sip of ersatz. She made her way to where her bicycle would be and cycled along the route she had memorised. After two hours she had met no *gendarmes*, no challenges, and pulled up at the opening to a track where a fallen tree lay. She sat on it and waited, her bicycle upended as though it had a puncture – just in case anyone became curious. If they did, she would say that she was waiting for a friend who would help.

Eventually a girl appeared on a bike, hurtling past without a second look. Sarah continued to wait. She checked her watch... She might be well south of the occupation line, but she was still in danger, and there were still allied agents at work; and others who were the enemy. It was cat-and-mouse, and she was the mouse. After another ten minutes she would leave, in case the contact was blown. If compromised, she would head for Paris immediately. There she would use the emergency drop, and might be of use to another circuit.

Sarah caught a glimpse of a bicycle approaching from the other direction and ignored it, continuing to act as though she was waiting for help. The rider stopped just behind her. The hairs rose on the back of her neck. She reached for her revolver in her jacket pocket.

A girl said, *'Bonjour.* I feel the rain could make things dark, but I have promises to keep.' She had included the three words: dark, promises and keep.

Sarah kept her hand on her revolver as she pushed herself up from the verge, brushing her hair back and tucking it behind her ear. 'The wind sounds worse in the woods, which is where I'm headed. I wish I could stay on the road, if I'm honest.'

The girl nodded and turned down the lane. Sarah followed her, bumping and rattling around and over the ruts until they reached a copse. The girl headed into it, so Sarah followed, only drawing to a halt at a charcoal-burner's kiln set up in a clearing. The heat was comforting. They stopped. All around the grass was flattened. An old man came from the trees, a rake over his shoulder. He must be the charcoal-burner. He ignored them. The girl gestured to Sarah to dismount. She did so, leaning the cycle against her hip.

The girl cycled away, crunching over the twigs, and at the same time a man's voice behind her said, 'Take your hand out of your pocket.' Sarah hadn't heard him approach, and fear clutched at her. The charcoal-burner began raking. Sarah removed her hand from her pocket. She was patted down, and her revolver removed. 'Welcome,' said the man, still standing behind her out of sight. 'Now, read this message, memorise the map and deliver it to Renaud tomorrow.' Over her shoulder, the man handed her a scrap of paper. 'You can cycle from Toulouse; the meeting point is halfway to Revel, the map shows precisely where. It is there that you will be told what it is you must do.'

Sarah read the note again and again, making sure she had it fully memorised. She held it up. The man reached over her shoulder and took it.

Sarah's revolver was replaced in her pocket. The girl who had led her to the clearing reappeared. Sarah, sensing what was expected of her, mounted her bicycle and followed the girl out of the clearing. At the edge of the wood the girl stopped and, without a word, pointed down the lane, before riding back through the trees.

All week Sarah worked in her designated role as courier, cycling first to one place and then another. She felt the bike could do it all without her, for it knew the feel of her hands on the handlebars, and of her bottom on the saddle, so well. She knew nothing of the bigger picture, but a circuit was clearly being formed. Perhaps Vichy would one day be occupied? There was already a sense of menace, reinforced by the French *gendarmes* and ersatz Gestapo, though so far she had seen no German troops.

Each evening she returned to the hotel, and one night as she finished cleaning her revolver, she heard *gendarmes* pounding up the stairs. She waited with her gun just behind the door, fear gripping her throat. They pounded past and hammered on a door at the end of the corridor, taking someone other than her away.

The next day two *gendarmes* stopped her outside a small town, but they were young and gave her documents just a cursory look. The following day, there were several ersatz Gestapo at a roadblock. Sarah was with many other cyclists, one of whom had a dog, which, when his master was pulled to one side, rushed around, barking and biting. The Vichy Gestapo shot it. In the uproar, three cyclists wove at speed through the melee and continued, turning off at the first opportunity. They were not challenged. Sarah was amongst them.

The weeks merged, one into the other, until October drew to a close and at last Sarah was given orders, via a newspaper drop at a café, to head for a hamlet abutting the demarcation zone, at which there was to be a funeral the next day. She took the train and, following her memorised instructions, walked to the hamlet in the cold, pouring rain. What an appalling day for a funeral, she thought, but a wonderful day for her, because the rain made it difficult for any border guards to see what was what. She joined the mourners, who said nothing, but just closed ranks around her, their umbrellas hiding her as they passed over the border to the cemetery. There, one of the mourners came to her side and pulled at her arm. He muttered, 'Such a sad day for a friendly and debonair gentleman.'

'Debonair' was the password. She relaxed. He led her to a farm, where she stayed until he collected her in the morning, when they caught a bus into the nearest town. Here, she made herself behave as though she had been walking amongst the German soldiers, and Luftwaffe pilots, for the last two years.

The guide left, ignoring Sarah as he walked back to whatever life he lived; and heaven keep you safe, she called silently. She felt abandoned as she made her way to the station, where the announcements were being made in French and German. She stood amongst the weary crowd, waiting for the Paris announcement. Everyone seemed to be avoiding eye contact. Did they wonder who their neighbours really were? Was this fear something you ever became used to? Would she? At last the train to Paris was announced, and soon she might be with a team. At last she might see Bernard again. At last she might hear on the grapevine of British escapees, for so far no-one had let anything slip, and of course she couldn't ask, or that personal information might identify her, if she was captured.

Chapter Fourteen

The Reverend Tom Rees breathed a sigh of relief. It was ten thirty on Sunday evening in early November, and Pauline had agreed that it was time for bed, saying, 'I was thinking the same, darling, and it's raining outside, so perhaps we should...' She meant only one thing.

He said, turning off the wireless and almost running into the hall, 'All is well, I have an umbrella.' Pauline followed, her face taking on the petulance that came and went, depending on whether or not people agreed with her.

He snatched her raincoat from the coat-stand, jiggling it to encourage her to hurry and slip her arms into the sleeves. Then he grabbed his umbrella and practically ran her to the pub, using the excuse of the weather. When they stood together outside the rear door, she said, 'I suppose there's another audition tomorrow after school, followed by interminable discussions about the actual make-up of this dreary little show?'

'You don't have to come. Besides, the office must be wondering why the trains are always such a problem on a Monday. I mean, you stayed on last Monday as well. What must they be thinking?'

'Work at the solicitor's is rather slow, and

they've said I can have this time off as compassionate leave, to help your recovery, so it's not a problem.'

He tried to look pleased, but went on, 'There's really no need. I'm as recovered as I'm going to be. The time I needed help was months ago.'

Pauline pouted.

He shouldn't have said anything, and he did hope there wasn't going to be a 'do', as there seemed to be rather often. He kissed her, aiming for her cheek, but she turned her head and met his lips. She pulled him close, which Tom would have given his right arm for once, but for him everything had changed.

Anyway, Sunday was a day that left him exhausted at the best of times, and it seemed so much worse since she had been insisting on cooking Sunday lunch, because, sadly, she couldn't cook. Sadly, also, she upset Mrs B, whose prerogative it was.

Pauline stood on her tiptoes to kiss him again, but he stepped back, laughing slightly. 'I have to remember I'm the vicar. Public kissing is perhaps not such a good thing.'

'Private kissing seems to have its problems too,' she snapped, turning on her heel. Then, as she opened the door, she stopped, saying over her shoulder, 'I'm sorry, I shouldn't have been cross. I find Sundays rather tiring, what with all the services, and lunch. But I like to look after you. It's what a fiancée should do.'

There was a pause. He said, 'Goodnight, sleep well.'

The rain was falling hard, darkness cloaked the

puddles and he lost count of the number that he inadvertently walked through. His trousers were quite sodden on his return, which made him cross. He slammed the door behind him, shook out his umbrella and left it in the hall-stand. He should tackle Pauline about this fiancée business, but somehow every time he started, she distracted him. And it then became too difficult, and he simply couldn't bear the thought of a scene. He'd have a bath and try to clear his head.

He padded up to his bedroom, bathed quickly, hung up his trousers to drip into the bath and dug out the pyjamas that his mother had bought for his birthday. He needed some comfort, damn it. He sat on the bed, acknowledging to himself that he simply didn't know what to think, and what to do about 'things'. His mother had telephoned him last week, warning him about Pauline and sure that, having been dumped by the policeman she had left Tom for, she was looking not just for a husband, but for a child.

'She wants to avoid war work at all costs, or so the girls at the hairdresser's said, and a baby is as good a way as any.'

He thought about his mother's words as the rain beat on the windows; but really he should ignore them, because he was a man of God, and gossip was harmful, as had been obvious where Kate was concerned. It would, after all, be hypocritical to work towards repairing the damage done to Kate, whilst listening and being swayed by tittle-tattle from a hairdressing salon. Anyway, what could he do, when it was he – not Pauline – who had changed? They had a past, after all, and perhaps he was in fact honour-bound to marry her, as she had said when she returned; she'd just needed time to sort herself out, and he knew all about that.

He couldn't settle and paced to the bedroom window, then found himself making for the stairs, and finally fiddling about in the kitchen. Should he drink a gin or a Scotch? He discovered there was no gin, which he'd prefer, but an inch of malt whisky remained. He was also bloody hungry, because he'd visited Sadie Jenks, one of Stella Easton's schoolchildren, after morning service. Her father, a merchant seaman, had been killed, so he had sat with the family as their grief and anger ebbed and flowed.

On his way back from visiting Sadie Jenks, he had called on Mrs Martin, the chairwoman of the WI, whose father-in-law was dying of old age. He had sat with elderly James Martin and chatted about seagulls following the plough. He had moved on to the success of the bowling club, which had brought them close to the top of the league table; then to the American attack on the Solomon Islands, and the arrival of more and more GIs in Britain, until James had held up his hand. 'Bugger off now, Vicar. I need me sleep, in case I have to go down below and stoke the furnaces, instead of going up to bang on the Pearly Gates while listening to some ruddy choir.'

Tom had returned to the vicarage for lunch, only to find Pauline's roasted neck of lamb was now a charred blob. They had eaten National wholemeal bread with gravy and overcooked vegetables. Mrs B had left a pudding of spotted dog, for which he had blessed her crusty old soul, until Pauline realised she had forgotten it was still in the oven and it was now burnt to oblivion.

He remembered the burnt smell as he stared at the Scotch, and his stomach rumbled. Damn it; he poured a small one, and slip-slopped in his slippers to the annexe, which he had begun to call the 'snug', lighting the paper beneath the kindling and dried logs. It was an extravagance, but tonight he deserved it. He settled himself in his chair and sipped his drink, feeling its warm comfort slip down his throat.

But he couldn't keep his mind away from his dilemma, because he suspected Pauline would never fit into the life of a vicar's wife, if they did marry. She came to the auditions, granted, but sat reading a book at the side, as one person and then another gave it a go. She sighed frequently, and when the plumber had taken to the stage and gave a fairly dreadful rendition of 'Keep the Home Fires Burning' on a comb, she put her fingers in her ears. Arthur had seen this and flushed, and so had Stella and Kate. Stella opened her mouth and then closed it again. Not Kate, though. But when was she ever stuck for something to say?

The fire was crackling now as the logs caught alight.

He grinned at the memory of Kate stabbing her pencil at Arthur. 'Do you know, those of us with taste think having that song in the concert is inspired, Arthur, thank you so much. We're really pleased, aren't we?' She looked at Tom and Stella. They both nodded, wondering where this was leading. 'I think you'll make a wonderful addition to our band.'

It was a perfect solution, because Arthur could be merged in amongst the other instruments and his feelings would be spared.

Kate had scribbled on one of the cut-up pieces of paper that Stella brought to every audition, and now beckoned Arthur over. 'I've written "Band" on this. Bring it to the first rehearsal, but not to worry if you lose it. Miss Easton has you written down on our list. Also, Arthur, we've a problematic ballcock in the village-hall toilets. Any chance of slipping in with your tools as soon as possible – tomorrow would be good? I know it's the Home Guard's evening, but perhaps they won't mind.'

What could Arthur say? Without a pause, Kate had called the next act on. They were jugglers from Stickhollow, a village along from Little Worthy, near a bend in the river. There were three of them, aged eleven. Their parents sat on the chairs set up at the back of the hall.

Stella had passed along a note: 'Whatever the reaction – fingers in ears or whatever – these children must have a place.' Kate had nodded. Tom remembered that he had flushed at this, but hadn't leapt to Pauline's defence. Perhaps he should have done.

Here, in his sanctuary, he closed his eyes for a moment, listening to the logs crackling, and feeling the heat on legs still stinging from the slapping of his wet trousers. Life so often seemed to steer him towards such a muddle.

He withdrew Hastings's notebook from the drawer, with a sigh of relief. He hadn't been able to get to it for a couple of weeks and he had missed meeting his mentor, as he increasingly thought of

Bertie Hastings. He settled back. Hastings was up to 1933, nine years ago. He sipped his Scotch, feeling the day's pressures ease, and began to read about the new baby born to the Fellows's maid, following her marriage to the chauffeur, and the couple's subsequent dismissal, for it was not in Mrs Fellows's remit to house a child. It didn't surprise Tom, knowing the woman and her husband, who was the leader of the parish council and so enjoyed his status. Fortunately, Hastings had known of a more generous employer in Preston Road, Yeovil, who had taken on the couple.

Tom smiled. This village was why he was beginning to love his calling and inch towards God. But even as he thought it, he felt that awful frisson that presaged the remembered sound of the guns. And here they were, along with the blast, the heat, the pain ... and Daniel's call. He buried his head in his hands and rocked, rocked, until – much quicker than in the past – it faded. He pressed his head hard, until the images were finally gone. He breathed deeply, sat back and gripped the notebook as though it was a liferaft. He was here, in this snug, in front of the modest fire, his shabby slippers on his feet as protection against the stone floor. There was no sand, no dunes, no bombers. Dunkirk was over. It was finished, *all* of it.

He opened the notebook and flicked over the page, where Kate's name seemed to jump out at him. It was as though Hastings had leaned more heavily on his pen, almost gouging the paper. He read on, absorbing Hastings's distress as he recounted a visit from his verger, Reginald Watson, who had begun by sitting opposite Hastings

210

in the sitting room. He wrote of the man's uproar of spirit as he pushed himself from the chair and paced backwards and forwards, telling of how he had followed and seen his daughter – Katherine, Kate – in the woods.

She was dancing like a wild thing, with a gypsy, Hastings wrote, clearly noting Reginald's words, perhaps almost to the letter. Reginald had heard the others call this boy 'Andrei'. It was a tango: the abandonment, the wildness, he had almost wailed, or so Hastings wrote. He had dragged Kate home, in disgrace.

Tom laughed to himself. Wild child indeed, our Kate, and to some extent she still was, but it was only a tango, for heaven's sake. He had been taught to tango at a dance academy, along with the waltz, the quickstep and the list of usual suspects, because his mother felt that in the army he would need social skills. He couldn't imagine Kate pacing backwards and forwards like Reginald Watson, but perhaps if he'd been in the woods with a gypsy girl, she... He nodded. Yes, perhaps she would have some concerns, but wailing. Oh, come on.

He flicked over the page, then checked his watch. Yes, time for a bit more. He was still smiling as he read on. Kate went back to the woods, climbing out of the attic window, he now read. What's more, she's pregnant, Reginald Watson had finally said, sitting again and burying his head in his hands. She's pregnant, Vicar, and she's only fifteen. He had wept.

Well, Tom thought, drawing in a deep breath, that had been increasingly clear from the continuing gossip, and here it was, in black-and-white. He paused in his reading, feeling – what? Sad, worried, but also, good grief, a sort of... He couldn't put his finger on exactly what he was feeling, but it was almost – well, he didn't know.

He metaphorically shook himself. His feelings, whatever they might be, had no bearing on the revelation. What did matter was how dreadful it must have been for Kate to give up her child, give up her life in the village. How empty she must have felt: her mother dead, her child gone; how scared, how alone.

He read on as Hastings described how he had risen from his own chair and patted his verger, a dry and unapproachable man who, he wrote, had been left a widower in charge of two girls: one of whom could only be held up as an example to follow; and Kate, who had always been a challenge. What's more, Reginald Watson was a pillar of respectability, on a par with his close friend, Dr Bates.

Together they had built the local golf club into something of which to be proud, and although Bates wasn't a regular churchgoer, he too was an exemplary character and a medical doctor. The villagers depended on him and he never failed them, turning out at all hours to tend to their illnesses, and travelling to the other villages too. As for Reginald, never had the church been run so efficiently.

Tom yawned. This was all beginning to read like a reference for a job, or even an obituary for the two men. So what had this to do with a girl who had made a mistake, probably because she was still grief-stricken over the death of her mother? Yes, she had her sister back from France, but Sarah was married with her own life and probably not involved.

He thought of himself at fifteen. The confusion, the boredom, the frightening thought of life as an adult. And all right, Kate had broken the bounds of her father's precious respectability, but where was the compassion for her from Hastings? Why all this talking up of her father, and Hastings's friend, instead of care for this young motherless girl? He felt disturbed, and distressed at this virtual dismissal of someone who had become his friend.

Tom finished his Scotch and chucked another log on the fire, staring at the sparks that shot up, and then the flames that sneaked around the sides. Where was the gypsy, Andrei, now? Did he even know he had fathered a child? For a moment he thought of the two of them together, by a camp fire or in the shadows, and there it was again, that feeling... Yes, a sort of pain. He stood up, then sat down.

He poked the fire. It was time he let it die and headed to bed, but he couldn't. Well, it had been a difficult day. Yes, that's all it was. He leaned back, shut his eyes and sought some calm, but all he could see was Kate – her beauty, her energy, with this wretched Andrei. Damn it. How could Andrei have taken advantage of her? How could she have got herself into such a mess? For a moment he pictured them together again, and the deepening pain took him by surprise and he simply couldn't understand himself.

213

Unable to sit still any longer, he paced the tiny study, and then it came to him. He was damned well hungry. Yes, that's what it was. He stormed into the kitchen, searching the cupboards for something, anything. There was some jam, but no, he couldn't stand bread again. He slammed the cupboard door shut, then saw the cake tin on the shelf and eased off the lid. Was there any chance? Yes, yes, a sponge cake. God in his heaven, bless Mrs B.

He cut a slice, and then another. Mrs B would sniff, but perhaps she'd be pleased that he'd liked it enough; or would she think Pauline had eaten a slice too? Lord, even eating a piece of cake was complicated. He boiled the kettle and made mint tea, which had been Kate's idea. She was as much of an example as her sister – couldn't her father see that? She'd made a success of her life and was kind. Kind enough to draw Stella Easton out of her misery, and to make Mrs B feel as though no-one else could accompany the auditioning singers.

As he finished the second slice of cake he felt so much better that he thought he'd just read a few more pages while he finished his tea, then up the wooden hill, as... Yes, as Kate said. He took his tea into the warmth of the snug again and sat with the notebook in one hand, his mug in the other. Hastings had moved on from the men, and was back to the actual event:

Reginald sat there, disbelief in his voice, and told me of Kate's dreadful lie, and her accusation. With the discovery of her pregnancy, you see, her father had stormed to the woods, dragging her with him, hunting for–' as he described him – 'the beggar of a gypo'. But he, and they, had moved on. All that remained was the flattened grass, and the scorched earth where the communal fire had been.

Kate told her father, 'They left two weeks ago. Andrei asked me to go with him, but I was too scared. I don't really know him. He taught me to dance, and he was kind. I didn't know I was pregnant then, or I would have gone.'

Reginald told me he'd lost control and slapped her; she had fallen, shielding herself as he slapped her again and again, at which point he had been filled with shame. But then, as he pulled her up and hurried her through the woods, she had said, 'It's not his baby; it's Dr Bates's, Father. He came when you were doing something at the church and I had flu, don't you remember? He took my nightie off. I thought he was going to listen to my chest, because he wore his stethoscope round his neck, but he didn't. He didn't do anything of the sort; he climbed on top of me instead. He did, Father. He said I must never tell, or he'd hurt you. But now I have to tell, don't you see that? But how can we keep ourselves safe, and the baby, now that I have?'

Reginald told me that Kate had said to Dr Bates, 'Please don't, Dr Bates, you're hurting me.'

It was all a fabrication, we felt sure. The idea that Dr Bates would do something like this was absolutely preposterous. Dr Bates is an upstanding and respected member of Little Worthy's community. He is known by every family in the village, and I have never heard a bad word said about him. Did this flighty young girl, who'd given her widowed father so much trouble over

215

the years, really expect anyone to believe her tall story? Did Kate know the damage she would cause to an innocent man's reputation? Just to make doubly sure, we telephoned the nursing home where Dr Bates would have been on his regular calls at the time this event was supposed to have happened. As we thought, his visit showed up in their diary. It was a lie, such an awful lie, because Dr Bates could not possibly have been at the two places at once. She could so easily have destroyed a wonderful man.

Tom was reading fast now, drinking in the words, drawn on, but wanting to stop.

Hastings hadn't finished:

Kate came to see me two days after her father. She knocked on the door and brushed past Mrs B, as though she was a block of wood. She barged into my sitting room, while I sat at my desk, working on correspondence. She said, 'It's not Andrei's baby. I had flu. I thought Dr Bates had come to see how I was, but he hadn't come for that. He can't have been at the nursing home – he can't.'

I couldn't believe my ears. Then she went on to say, 'You're a vicar, it's your job to believe me.'

I replied, 'It's my job to endeavour to reveal the truth. I have investigated, and it can't have been the doctor. He was elsewhere at the time. I have proof. Your accusation can only be termed wicked and destructive. You must withdraw it immediately, before it spreads beyond we three.'

I thought she would strike me, such was her anger. Instead she picked up a vase and threw it into the fireplace. The flowers, I can see them now, delphiniums;

and then she rushed from the room, almost into Mrs B.

Kate tore back in, shouting, 'All right, believe what you like. Andrei didn't want me, and ran away – that's what happened, because that's what you all want to hear, so there you are. Tuck that into your prayers and tell your God, and may you all burn in hell.'

She was gone the next day, with Sarah, leaving her father a broken man, with a fractured friendship, because of course Dr Bates knew we had asked questions of the nursing home. He moved soon afterwards, to a different parish. We didn't see much of him, and I can't say I blame him.

Tom realised he still held his mug of mint tea in his hand. It was cold, and he couldn't face it now. He looked again at the fire, which was dying gradually, and slowly a great disappointment enveloped him. He knew of Dr Bates's reputation, which was above reproach, so how could Kate have...?

Well, of course she was young, and scared, so perhaps a lie was a way out, in her desperation? He sat up, a thought flashing through his mind. But what if it hadn't been a lie, because the Kate he knew was so utterly straightforward? He settled back, exhaustion overcoming him, because Hastings had checked the doctor's whereabouts, so that was that.

He gripped his mug, feeling cheated, just as Kate's father, sister and Hastings himself must have felt. No wonder she had to leave the village. Just imagine if she had repeated the slander to someone else? Just imagine if it had been believed, and Bates had been ruined?

217

What a bloody mess, and a perfect end to a totally miserable bloody day, and he found that at last he was relieved that Pauline had returned. At least she was familiar, and made no bones about who she was and how she felt.

He shoved the notebook back in the drawer, took the mug to the sink and poured the tea down the plughole. The mint leaves clung to the grille. He picked them up, wet and limp, and put them into the waste bucket. This must be why Mrs Summers had been asked to keep an eye on Kate, as Mrs B had explained to him. Did Mrs B know about the lie, or had she merely heard the confession about the gypsy?

Tom climbed the stairs, his mind racing, darting down alleys and backtracking, and finally decided that if Mrs B had heard, she would have mentioned it. She hadn't. The perceived wisdom was that Kate Watson had run wild with the gypsies, and so let that remain the case. But how the hell was he going to face her tomorrow, and yet another audition? Then there would be the rehearsals, not to mention the show. He wasn't sure how he'd react, when he saw Kate again.

He opened his bedroom door, moved to the blackout blind and, before he pulled it down, said, 'Oh God, help me. It's in the past. Everyone has moved on, and Kate has her strengths and is proving a good aunt to Lizzy, so far. Let me treat her the same; let me hate the sin, but not the sinner. Please let me not show my innermost feelings, my hurt.'

He pulled the blind down and drew the curtains, feeling his way to the bed, and wondering why on earth he had said 'my hurt'. It was Kate's family who had experienced that, for pity's sake. He clambered in, pulling up the blankets and staring at the ceiling. He tossed and turned. What a mess, an awful bloody mess.

It was only in the morning that he realised it was the first time he had really prayed since before Dunkirk.

After supper the next day Kate hurried in Lizzy's wake, remembering a time when she too had skipped, just as this lovely child was doing. She carried all her class's reading and arithmetic books, so that she could mark their work in idle moments during the evening.

She would spend a little time at the start of the evening with the children who had surrounded her on Sunday, explaining that they were frightened to sing in the show because they only knew hymns. She would tell them that, with Mrs B playing, they would be in safe hands; and either she or Miss Easton would be leading them anyway. The important thing was that, by the time of the show, they were well rehearsed and ready.

She and Lizzy hurried into the hall, and while Lizzy sat at the back with the other schoolchildren, Kate had a quick word with them all and left them smiling. She and Stella Easton waited for Tom Rees to appear. He came with just a minute to spare, his arm around Pauline. As he reached them, he kissed Pauline's cheek and asked her to draw up a chair and join them, if she would like. She did like.

Stella nudged Kate. They shared a look. Something had changed between Tom and Pauline, and Tom seemed to be ignoring them. At last he nodded to them, taking out his pencil. 'Shall we begin.' It wasn't a question.

They listened to various acts and singers, and Stella whispered to Kate at one of the changeovers, 'I know we've talked of tap for some of the songs, but surely we need ballroom too? And Adrian Fletcher, would you believe, was talking of a tango. He can, apparently. I've been thinking of using "Jealousy". I think you should also dance it, because Lizzy was saying you were really good at the audition at the club.' Stella nudged her, laughing. 'Stop pulling that face.'

She was much happier today because she had heard that Bradley was a prisoner-of-war in Germany, and quite safe.

'Come on, Miss Kate Watson, you know we need some stars for the show, and you're definitely one. We'll need your voice too. Oh, Kate, we are unearthing so much talent, I don't know quite where to start.'

Kate murmured back, 'Maybe we should include our lovebird vicar in the discussion.' She didn't know why she was annoyed, but she was, and she sensed the same in Stella. Pauline had no place on the panel, surely; what's more, she was clearly longing to be gone.

Kate and Stella craned forward. Pauline was reading a newspaper, while Tom was busily doodling on his pad. Kate nudged him. 'Stella has a proposal. Do listen, while I check whether Mrs B has the music for "Jealousy".'

Pauline stood too. 'I could do with stretching my

legs to get my circulation going.' She walked with Kate over towards the piano and Mrs B, uninvited. 'I'm thinking of moving down here, Kate. Poor Tom isn't being looked after well enough.' They had reached the piano, and Mrs B had heard.

Kate said, 'Mrs Bartholomew has been a staunch support, first to the Reverend Hastings, and now to Tom. She knows how things run and has helped him settle into the routine. Now, Mrs Bartholomew, have you the music to "Begin the Beguine"? Mrs Martin and the WI committee have been practising and want to give it a shot. And our leader insists on a tango danced to "Jealousy".'

Mrs Bartholomew nodded. She stood up, her face grim, and checked through the pile of music on top of the piano.

Pauline hadn't finished yet. 'You see, I can play the piano too, and because I'm young, I won't get so tired and hit so many wrong notes. I think I could come up with some creative ideas for food at the vicarage too.'

Mrs Bartholomew let the sheet music drop. She turned, but Kate was dragging Pauline away. 'Mrs Bartholomew is a loyal member of the village. She has looked after all the vicars extremely well. We do have rationing, so cooking is difficult, and we don't need you to play for us. I think, Pauline, that you need to watch your tongue, or I will have to tie it in a knot and sling it round your neck. I would then pull it tight.'

They were heading back towards the table and Pauline stared at Kate, outraged. She said, clearly and distinctly, looking at Tom, 'I don't think that's any way to talk to the vicar's fiancée. I really don't. I was merely making an observation and, as I'm not welcome here, I will wait for you, Tom, at the vicarage.'

She stormed out of the hall, and Kate felt as though she had been slapped across the face. Fiancée? Tom had never mentioned anything of the sort. Kate had assumed there was more than met the eye, when she first met Pauline, but why had Tom kept Pauline a secret from her – well, from them all?

Drawing herself up, she turned to Tom. 'You must have heard how Pauline spoke to Mrs B, Tom. If you didn't, you must really be deaf, not just using your hearing selectively, as you did at a particular funeral, if I remember rightly. That poor woman has looked after you well, you know she has, and Pauline has no right.'

'Oh, do be quiet, Kate. Pauline doesn't mean any harm, so stop making such a fuss.' Tom moved onto Kate's empty seat and showed his list to Stella, who wasn't ready to be so easily distracted and jumped to her friend's defence.

'Kate's right. Please don't bring her again, she's a disruptive influence.'

Tom sighed and closed his eyes.

Kate composed herself and said very quietly, 'You are the vicar. I know you want to get up and stalk out after "fancy pants", but if you do, you will lose all authority. I don't know what's bothering you today and why you're being so vile, but I suggest you talk to Mrs B at the very least. Go and reassure her that she is valued.'

'Why don't you do that, Kate? You seem so good with words and aren't unduly bothered by the truth.'

Kate stared at this man, who had been her friend. His eyes were so cold, where previously they had been full of warmth and laughter. She turned on her heel, feeling abandoned and uncertain. She walked back to Mrs B, who was putting her music into her case and closing the piano lid. Kate was playing with those last three words – 'by the truth' – and now she understood. Her heart sank. Tom knew that her father thought she'd lied. But how? It can't have been Sarah, or Tom would have been like this from the start. His remarks played again in her mind, and then she saw beyond the rudeness. Was he also saying that Mrs B was not of value? Had he lost his mind?

Mrs B had put on her jacket, though the next person to audition was onstage, waiting. There was no more time to mull it further. Kate reached her and said, 'We're all mortified. Pauline is not herself at the moment, and of course she didn't mean what she said. Everyone knows that you are essential to the smooth running of the vicarage. Not only that, Mrs Bartholomew, but what would we do without you here? Please, I beg of you, don't go.'

Mrs B said as she picked up her music case, '"Mrs B" to you, young lady.'

Kate was so surprised that for a moment she smiled: at this moment, when it felt as though she had almost been destroyed by Tom, Mrs Bartholomew had caught her and helped her up. Kate said, 'Please, Mrs B, please don't leave us to

Pauline's tender mercies. It's not fair on the children or the other performers, or us. And I suspect I know what her piano-playing is like. Stay with us – we're all part of the same gang.'

Mrs B stood there, then looked towards the panel table.

'Did the vicar send you?'

'Why on earth wouldn't he? But I would have come anyway, because only the panel decides who plays for our concert, and that's that. We desperately need someone as reliable and good as you, but you know that very well.'

Mrs B removed her coat and unpacked her music.

Kate nodded. 'Thank you.'

She walked away, but Mrs B called after her. 'Thank you, Kate, I'm glad someone came to make it right, and I'm happy it was you. You fudged when I asked if the vicar had sent you, which I think is rather splendid. We are going to make this show a success, you know. By the way, I have located more tap shoes, from a family in Preston Road. The mother used to work for Mrs Fellows, until she became pregnant. She and her husband now chauffeur and house-keep for that family. The pay is better too.'

Mrs Fellows, who was waiting to play 'Mood Indigo' on the violin, flushed. She called, 'We all make mistakes, Mrs Bartholomew.'

Mrs B laughed. 'Indeed we do. Did you hear that, Vicar?'

Kate stared. She had never seen or heard Mrs B laugh. She walked back to the panel and, as Tom made no effort to vacate her seat, she took

224

his place. Stella leaned forward and said to Kate, 'You worked your magic then.'

Kate shook her head, barely able to speak. 'No, the show is doing that quite well on its own.'

She didn't talk to Tom for the rest of the evening, because why would she bother? If he was in a mood, let him get on with it. She was too busy and the world was turning, so he'd just have to try and jump on when he was ready. If there was no-one there to catch him, that was his own fault. The thought felt strong, but she was in fact crumbling, in spite of Mrs B's kindness. She gripped her pencil as she listened to the last singer, Mrs Williams from Down End. Her voice was surprisingly good, an alto.

Kate wrote down her name, checking with Stella, who had done the same. They shared a smile. Mrs B looked over and nodded. Kate reciprocated, hiding the hollowness and sense of abandonment that was setting up home within her again.

Chapter Fifteen

Sarah arrived at the Gare d'Austerlitz in the early morning. The leaves had been falling in the early November wind as they chugged through the countryside, which reminded her for a moment of Little Worthy. She blanked this from her mind.

As she disembarked onto the platform, the wind was as keen as it had seemed from the train window. Without hesitation she strode into the centre of Paris, to walk the boulevards, as though it was not years since she and Derek had been here. She struggled to see his face, hear his voice as she walked, stunned at the change in this most beautiful of cities. There was so little noise, so few cars. Instead there were bicycles bearing number-plates, gloomy shop windows; and women – even here, in this bastion of fashion – wearing wooden-soled shoes.

Sarah stopped every so often to look in shop windows and check the reflection. Was it still the same man following? No. She turned right down a street, then left, walking parallel to the boule-vard, then right, but there was no shadow. She passed a hotel for Germans only. The Luftwaffe pilots and the Wehrmacht officers swaggering in and out chilled her, but the men in suits, with hats pulled down low, were even more forbidding. Gestapo? And, of course, there was the Abwehr, the military intelligence organisation. She didn't falter, just kept on walking as though it was her normal route. She crossed the Seine. Last time she was here, she and Derek took a boat to Mont-martre. Sarah still couldn't remember his face.

She checked her watch. Ten o'clock, so she had been walking for about two hours, just right. She located the hotel where she was to stay, registered and left her suitcase. She found the café near the rue Vernet where she was to wait. She sat at an outside table and eased off her faded and torn leather gloves, ordering coffee, longing for the real thing. It was not forthcoming. They were sheltered here from the wind, but it was still cold, though that didn't seem to put off the clientele who sat at other tables, reading newspapers or chatting with friends. An armoured car passed, driven by Germans. Well, of course.

Sarah sipped her ersatz with a mounting sense of relief, because she was to meet someone here with whom she would be working, rather than being directed here and there by a phantom. She had not thought, whilst training, of the dreadful loneliness, which she found increasingly hard to endure.

She sipped again, diverting herself with thoughts of finer things, like shoes. Into her mind leapt lines from Lewis Carroll's poem 'The Walrus and the Carpenter': of shoes, and ships, and sealing wax, of cabbages and kings. Her mother would recite the poem to her, and later to Kate too. She ached to be young again, sitting with her mother and sister. What had happened to that Sarah? Why had she allowed herself to become so dull, so hard, so like her father? Ah, was that it? Was it perhaps because it pleased him, made him nicer, and life was therefore easier for her? But not for Kate; she had remained who she was and wouldn't bend, no matter how he had shouted. Sarah drank the ersatz to the dregs, ashamed of herself.

The time passed, and the sun glimmered between shifting clouds. She ordered a second coffee, checking her watch. Eleven thirty. She raised her face, closed her eyes, but a shadow fell, blocking out the slight warmth. She shielded her eyes, squinting. A man stood there; he tipped his hat. 'Cécile, how lovely to see you here. You look as though you were about to fall into an easy sleep.'

227

It was Bernard, with three words from Frost's poem in place: lovely, easy, sleep.

'What a surprise, Bernard. I arrived in Paris early, my business is complete.' Surprise, business, complete: the code words.

He sat, reached out and grasped her hand. 'Thank God you're here. I gather you did well?'

Sarah laughed. 'I have thighs like a stevedore's, with all that cycling, but my mother always said cycling gave people good ankles.'

Bernard raised her hand to his mouth. 'Enough about your thighs – it does my blood pressure little good. Have you finished? I have a place where the coffee is ... well,' he whispered, 'coffee.'

Sarah gestured to the waiter, paid him and left with Bernard. They walked towards the boulevard Haussmann as though they had all the time in the world, when they only had this moment for certain. Finally they turned down a street, and then another, until Bernard gestured towards a small restaurant just as a German patrol strode along the street. She didn't falter, but laughed up at Bernard. 'My word,' she said, 'a reception committee.'

'No, no, my little cabbage, just a normal patrol.'

The patrol was fast approaching, but now, the soldiers hesitated. Were they going to check their papers?

Bernard bent and kissed her, full on the lips, wrapping his arms around her. Sarah responded, listening all the time. The patrol passed. He released her. 'Sorry, but needs must.' They continued, then he stopped. 'Actually, I'm not in the least sorry. It was quite delightful, just the thing to lift a cold morning. It stokes the inner furnace.'

He held open the door of the restaurant, ushering Sarah in. She murmured, 'Better than coal then?'

His laugh followed her. She kept her smile as she saw two Wehrmacht officers sitting near the back. To the left of the window a man waved, pointing to a chair. 'You two lovebirds, you are late.'

It was George. He stood, his knitted scarf dangling, his tattered jacket unbuttoned. He kissed her hand. 'Too long, Cécile, too long indeed. Sit, I can recommend the mutton.'

She sat, as did Bernard. The patron came, with a scribbled menu. Most of it was crossed out. 'Mutton is all,' he shrugged. 'Good, not plentiful.' His fingers were nicotine-stained.

Bernard ordered for them both, saying, 'It's best to be here early or it is all gone.' It was midday. George was halfway through his meal. There were others, men and women, eating.

George said quietly, 'Good use is made of the black market, thank the Lord.'

Bernard nodded, easing off his coat and letting it fall onto the back of the chair, as Sarah had done. He muttered, leaning forward so that his lips could not be read, 'Welcome to Paris. We have a safe house for you, Cécile. I will lead you.' The two men laughed, and Sarah joined in. It must look as though their conversation was that of old friends, which of course they were, but even these friends were treated with reservation, for who knew if they had been turned by the enemy?

Sarah listened to the two men, but thought of the Resistance worker she had heard of who had

229

been captured, unknown to their group, and subsequently released back into the fold. From this tightly knit world he had reported on his fellow agents and activities, until suspicions had been aroused. It transpired that a member of his family had been taken hostage, and how could you choose between a mission and the life of a loved one?

It was difficult to spot a traitor in a hostage situation, because there was no need for the Gestapo to shadow them. Why bother, when to run or disobey would bring about the death of a relative? So, if there are no suspicious shadows, there was no suspicion. It was simpler when someone was doing it for thirty pieces of silver; then Gestapo tabs would be kept on them, and sometimes, just sometimes, it was possible for the betrayed to catch the betrayer.

Bernard spoke, his lips barely moving. 'Cécile, we are in this area to organise the sabotage of selected targets. For, this we need to receive explosives, incendiary devices and weapons, and deliver them on to others.' He lit a cigarette.

George raised his voice. 'Ah, here comes your mutton. I am about to finish, but if you have a poor appetite, I will help.'

As the patron placed the mutton before them, Sarah said to George, 'I understand what you say about the cold, but I like the seasons. If you want sun, you should have been living in Nice.' The patron stood beside the table, his apron smeared with gravy. Steam rose from the plates.

'Nice? With those Vichy swine.' George raised his voice again, as though he wanted the Germans to hear.

They thanked the patron for the mutton, their expressions unchanging and no acknowledgement being given. He could be a plant. He nodded as though he understood, and left.

Bernard said, 'We think he's all right, but we're not sure.' He inhaled, carefully pinched out his cigarette and left it on the ashtray for later. 'Our task, Cécile, is – as always – to find the right people for each group. Ones who are prepared to take risks and become a part of the quiet army of those who are fighting back. We have to make them aware that we need to create damage with carefully placed explosives and, if possible, without the enemy realising the cause, to prevent retribution.'

She knew this, of course she did. So what was her role?

He was shovelling the mutton into his mouth as though he hadn't eaten in days. He was so drawn and thin that perhaps he hadn't. Her heart twisted. She ate hers, but hadn't felt hungry since she had arrived in France, so she took it steadily, eating only because she needed fuel.

He said, through his chewing, 'We need to find grounds suitable for drops, and places to hide the equipment when it is dropped. We need to find people to train to use it. Simple.'

George laughed. 'I have to go, as others are reminding me.' He was warning them that the Germans were passing nearby, on their way to the door.

Sarah said, 'So, shall we be together for Christmas? Mama would be so pleased.' There was a draught as the door opened, then slammed shut.

231

She said, 'My task?'

'To work with me, Cécile – that is your task. I need a courier and trainer.' Bernard would say no more, because no detail must be passed in front of George.

They ordered coffee, real coffee. This she savoured, holding the cup between her hands and breathing in the scent of it, sipping slowly. Work with Bernard? Thank heavens.

He said, 'I have a contact; and from him will come others. George, we will come to you to pass on information of the drops needed, or leave messages at the safe drop. You know where I mean, and soon so will Cécile. We all know the codes, including that for an emergency, should we be compromised. Now, we should go. You must be in place by this evening, George. Stay safe, my friend. Continue to move daily to transmit, but you know that.'

Bernard rose, beckoning to the patron. 'Excellent mutton, patron, we will be here again, when we are next in Paris.' He paid for all three.

The patron took the money and gave half back. 'For when you come again.'

Bernard shook his head. 'Good food deserves good payment.' He left it, and more, on the table. The patron shrugged and pocketed it. George put on his beret.

Bernard picked up his pinched-out cigarette, stuffing it in an inside pocket. 'Filthy habit,' he muttered, drawing back Sarah's chair. 'Mama would be unamused, would she not, Cécile?'

George led the way onto the street. His bike was tucked down the side alley. Without a backward glance he pedalled away. Sarah could hardly bear to see him go. It could so easily be the last time, because he had outlived the period that a wireless operator was expected to survive.

Bernard walked with her. 'Meet me tomorrow; you know when and where?'

Sarah did. He strode right at the boulevard Haussmann, she to the left. On arrival at the hotel, she passed through the lobby and listened at her door for sounds of movement. There seemed to be none. She eased into the room. It was empty. She examined the hairs she had stuck to her suitcase. All was well. She slept until morning.

They took the train sitting separately, but in the same carriage. Bernard rose as the train slowed for a station and tucked his newspaper beneath his arm – her signal. Sarah followed. Some way from the station he eased into a barn, where two bicycles were propped against a rusted plough. On the back of each was a small crate in which a chicken scrabbled and clucked. Rope bound the top shut, and air penetrated between the slats.

Sarah sighed and pedalled after Bernard. Her revolver, tucked into the back of her waistband, felt cold, but she considered it necessary, here in the occupied zone.

They passed through two villages, jiggling over the cobbles. At the crossroads of one they were flagged down by a German patrol. They stopped, dug for their papers, resting the bicycles between their legs. While one of the Germans studied their ID cards, two others walked around them, stopping at the crates. They eyed the chickens through the slats. 'Why?' one asked.

'We take it for the farmer, to another farm.' Bernard shrugged.

'Why not two in the same box?'

Sarah said, tucking her ID card into her coat pocket, 'They peck one another, like quarrelling children.'

'This farm, you work there?'

Sarah said, as Bernard had briefed her, 'No. We have no work at the moment, so we do what we can. In return, we will be given eggs – six between us.' She gave him the name of the farm. If the soldiers checked, they'd be in trouble, but also long gone.

The patrol leader adjusted the rifle slung over his shoulder, as a priest left the church and headed through the village, perhaps for his lunch. Two women in headscarves left too, and a nun. The soldier gestured with his head. 'Don't eat all the eggs at once, or you will be constipated.'

The others laughed. Sarah smiled. Bastards, she thought. Bernard tipped his beret. They pedalled away, the chickens protesting at the bumpy ride. 'Shut up,' she growled. 'You could have been in a Nazi pot by tonight.'

Miraculously, the hens fell quiet. Bernard, riding alongside her now, laughed. 'You have the power of command. We're nearly there.'

She snatched a look behind. The village had disappeared, and so too the patrol. She and Bernard would find another way back. They pulled up 100 yards away, at a quite different farmhouse from the one she had mentioned to the patrol. They left the bicycles on the far side of the hedge, and the crates with the chickens too. It was their cover. Besides, the farmer wanted them back.

They flanked the farmhouse and came at it from the side, slipping around the house, listening. Bernard checked his watch. 'Dead on time.'

'Don't say "dead",' she snapped.

'I'll lead, and stop being prissy. It's only a word.'

He scouted ahead, and she watched as he slipped in through the huge doors of the barn. She would wait, because you never knew. There was no sound of shots, no shout. He would always shout, he had said, as indeed had she, because if they were captured, they were dead anyway.

He re-emerged and gave a nod. She skirted the farmyard and entered the barn. Bernard stood with a man whose tattered old trousers were tied with rope at the waist and with string at the knees, to stop rats climbing up. He was as old as his trousers, and as broad as he was long. Clearly 'tough' was his middle name. There was another, younger man standing in the shadows.

Sarah waited just inside the door. The old man looked at her. 'Ah, Cécile. I am François, and here is Hugo. He is eager to join us.' He called Hugo forward.

Bernard talked to him for a while, beckoning Sarah in. She and Francois sat on a pile of old logs, François fiddling with a piece of string.

She heard Hugo say, 'You can count on me. You need grounds for a parachute drop, you say? I know of one.' They shook hands and came over to Sarah and François.

They followed Hugo and François over a rise, south of the farmhouse, skirting the fields and woods until they reached level ground, about 300 yards in length, nicely shielded by trees from the road. Perfect and it matched anything she'd scouted out in the south. She and Bernard nodded to one another. As they walked back, Hugo and François conferred about possible hiding places for the supplies. Finally they agreed on an area only a few yards from the dropping zone: an unused potato-storage barrow.

Bernard asked if they knew men who could be trusted to help with the reception of supplies, and the securing of them at the barrow. Yes, it transpired, they did. Bernard made as if to leave, saying that a courier would come with details of the drop. Francois protested, 'No, no, my friends. Come, come.' Hugo left, but François led them into the farmhouse kitchen.

There they met Simone, Francois's wife. There were two grandchildren. Simone waved them to a chair. 'I have coffee – real coffee.'

Sarah closed her eyes and could almost smell it. 'Really?' she said.

'Sit, sit.'

She did, next to Bernard. He draped his arm over the back of her chair, touching her shoulder briefly. 'Half an hour,' he murmured. 'We need to be back by curfew.'

The beans were ground, the coffee made and drunk, and if she died that minute there would be no need of heaven, because that real coffee was food of the gods and she savoured every mouthful.

Beside her, Bernard did the same. He said, 'Even in England we do not have this.'

236

'Ah,' said Simone. 'But you've Winston Churchill, who has stood firm, he has not promised falsely; it will be hard, but we can win, we can take our country back.'

The children ran into the yard. 'How old?' asked Sarah.

'Six and eight.'

Sarah almost said that Lizzy was nine now. She put her cup down and asked instead, 'Where are their parents?'

'Their father is a prisoner in Germany, working somewhere – the bastards.'

François grumbled, 'The mother, pooh. She has another life, with a German. It is from there that we get the coffee.'

Immediately Bernard straightened, even more alert than usual. He checked his watch. 'We must go. We will tell you if we need you. Be safe, and thank you.' He shook hands, and Francois kissed Sarah on both cheeks, and Simone too.

Simone pressed some cheese into her hand. 'Go back safely to your home, one day.'

They rode back to the cycle drop and left the bicycles and the hens, before walking to the train. Sarah said, 'We can't use them; the children could say something to their mother.'

Bernard nodded. 'We try again tomorrow, or we move to Rouen. I will see George later, or at dawn. He will have moved, of course, and left notice of that at the message drop.'

They hurried to her hotel as darkness fell, using the back streets. Bernard stopped in the dark of the alley running along the side of the hotel. 'Come to the café and wear as many clothes as

237

possible; we might just leave here. Do not, I repeat do not, carry your weapon again for trips like these. If you are stopped, all the bluffing in the world will not help.'

'How did you know?'

'I know the shape of you, Cécile.'

The next morning Sarah moved to Rouen; Bernard did not. Why? The coded message at the drop had said, 'Change of plan.'

At Rouen, the Seine was its usual stolid self. Rouen's Gothic churches stood as though daring anyone to damage them, and its timbered houses probably looked as they did when Joan of Arc was tried for heresy. Sarah was focusing on this, because she hated being alone again. She felt the panic rising as she crossed the cobbled street. Everywhere there were German troops, and posters of wanted men and women pasted on the walls; some torn and weathered, others new. She saw one of George; it was new. Dear God, they must try and get him out of the country, but it wasn't a full moon, so no Lysander aircraft could be sent for him yet.

She went to the house designated in her in-structions, strolling past a machine-gun post at a corner. Her papers were checked, then again by a patrol. The second time she was searched. Thank God she carried no revolver this time, just her suitcase. This too was searched, but the false bottom was not discovered.

The door at the rear of the safe house was hanging half open. The windows were cracked and broken. It was unoccupied, cold. There was no furniture. Sarah slipped in. She felt cold, in spite of her layers of clothing. She carefully clicked open her case and removed the false bottom, withdrawing her revolver. Listening, she crept from room to room, ready to break a neck, kick legs from beneath any attacker or beat them with the gun. She didn't want to shoot, because it would alert passers-by more surely than hanging a sign out of the window.

She crept up the stairs, each creak seeming like an explosion. In the attic there was a note: 'Someone once lived here, but we don't know who any more.' She waited; 'once', 'who' and 'someone' meant that a contact would come. Shivering with cold, sitting on the floor in the attic and clasping her knees, she listened, and waited.

Through the broken skylight she heard the sound of Germans marching past, and one man shouted to another. There was the noise of passing lorries. Germany had been stalled at Stalingrad, and Montgomery had won at El Alamein, or so Bernard had told her. Maybe it was making the Germans nervous. Good, but it could impinge on the activities of the Resistance.

She waited, sitting on the floor of the deserted and empty house, but for whom?

At eleven at night, Sarah heard footsteps on the stairs. She eased herself upright and took up station behind the door, her hands ready, revolver in her waistband. Higher and higher the intruder was climbing. If it was the enemy, there would be more than one. She strained to pick out the sounds. The footsteps stopped, then started again. She listened until they reached the top of the stairs. She breathed through her mouth, put her weight on the balls of her feet. The floor of the landing creaked, and then again. He, or they were closer, so close. She waited poised behind the door.

Bernard whispered, 'I came by moonlight.'

She almost wept – Bernard, thank God. She whispered back, 'Indeed, and the wind is calm tonight.' She stepped out, and there he was. He reached for her, held her close and now, though there was no patrol, he kissed her, and it was such a long time since anyone had loved her that she kissed him back. They clung together, but then she pulled away. 'They have posters of George.'

He pulled her back, saying against her hair, 'I know, I was alerted. He is safe, for now. They will send a Lysander at the next full moon. If they can't land, then it will be next month.'

She didn't ask where, because there was no way he would tell her. Information wasn't exchanged. It was better that way. He held her close, whispering, 'We must stay here tonight. There are curtains at one of the windows downstairs; they'll keep us warm.' He left her, hurrying to the rooms below, and soon returned with the curtains. 'I don't like being up here, we're rats in a trap.'

He was arranging the curtains on the floor, and the dust from them caught in Sarah's throat. She said, 'We're not trapped. There's a way down from the window. We're better here than on the street. Just tell me: have we lost any more men?'

He shrugged. 'Come on, sleep. I'll stay on watch. Then I'll have some shut-eye, while you keep watch.'

They nestled beneath the curtains, shivering. She put her arms around him, and he around her, for warmth of course.

'Sleep,' he said. She did.

In the morning, stiff and aching, Sarah left her suitcase hidden in the eaves and wore two layers. She left her revolver. If she didn't return to the safe house, she would manage without it. They set out, heading for a shed where Bernard said they would find bicycles. They dodged patrols as they pedalled through and out of Rouen.

Yet again they headed for a contact; yet again it was a farmhouse; yet again they hunted out dropping zones. They met potential recruits, some to form a group that would carry out discreet sabotage, others who would stay passive until the allies invaded. At that point the groups would be awoken and their support action would begin. By the end of the week, Sarah and Bernard had the beginnings of a circuit, a group in the Bonsecours area. At the end of the next week, they had two. She and Bernard stayed in a safe house in a hamlet north of Bonsecours, one that no-one in either group knew.

On 21st November a courier left a message at the communications drop, a felled tree on the outskirts of a village. A coded message had arrived via the BBC: there was to be an agent and supply drop the next night. They'd need a reception committee at the 'zero dropping zone', as Bernard and Sarah had named it. Also a party to deliver the armaments and explosives to the hiding place within the woods that sheltered the 350-yard zone

241

from all eyes. Bernard went one way, Sarah another, informing their recruits of the time and place. They were to bring torches.

Soon they would be able to activate the plans to sabotage the ordnance factory to which a man known as 'Pierre' had access. Soon they would be in business, but no Germans must be killed. Absolutely no Germans, or they would have hostages on their conscience.

Any repatriation must wait for the following month, George would be told.

Chapter Sixteen

Kate stood at the attic window, the November day dawning. She wished she could see again the gypsies' summer wood-smoke spiralling above the trees. This time she would go with Andrei, just to live in a sort of peace. As she stood here, she could almost smell the smoke. She dug her fingernails into the ancient paint of the sill: hard, harder still, before holding her hands high, then letting them fall to her sides. There were indents where her nails had been.

So she did exist.

Pressing her nails into the paintwork of the windowsill was what she had done when she lived in London; it was what she had done when she returned here. She looked along the sill at all the indents. This was the evidence of her blood and flesh, but it didn't include a heart. She did not have one. She had thought for once that she had a friend, someone who knew about the world, heaven, hell; someone who was wise; someone who was scarred, as she was, and had known darkness, and who felt that to judge was wrong, whose role was to care, not to turn away.

Why had Tom's warmth turned cold? Why had he hurt Mrs B?

But this was what she was used to, this was where she belonged – in a place where nothing mattered or existed, not really. It was easier to bear living each day then.

Kate heard a distant knocking at the front door. Was it Sarah home unexpectedly? They'd had two vague letters. Well, they would be vague, and were probably written before she had left England. She checked her watch: eight o'clock in the morning. Well, not that early then, but if it was Sarah, she'd just come in. Standing here like a gormless log-jam wouldn't sort things. She threw on some clothes and climbed down the attic ladder, calling from the top of the stairs, 'Hang on, be there in a moment.'

She rushed into the bathroom. Lizzy came in, her hair tangled, her pyjamas rolled up at her ankles, bought by her mother with room for growth. 'Who is it, Aunt Lizzy?'

Kate said through the toothpaste, 'Not sure.' She was out of the bathroom in a moment, and tousled Lizzy's hair as she passed, 'The only way to find out is to go and see.'

She hurried down the stairs, calling, 'We're just coming.' She unlocked the front door and opened it a little bit. In London you never knew

243

who might be on the other side, but here? Well, it was wartime, and an escaped German prisoner-of-war had been reported last week. He'd been captured, but you never knew.

It was a ginger-haired army sergeant. He was pale, with dark circles under his eyes and a kitbag at his feet. He wore a sergeant's uniform; from some rifle regiment, by the look of it. He was twisting his cap between his hands. She didn't know him. He said, 'Mrs Baxter?' peering back at her through the crack.

'No, she's away. I'm the babysitter.'

Lizzy called, from behind, 'No, you're my aunt. Who is it?'

The man said, 'I'm a friend of Derek's.' His face said it all.

Lizzy was pulling at Kate. 'He knows Daddy. Let him in, come on – open the door.'

Kate was already opening it wide and gesturing the sergeant in. He entered the hall, the cold clinging to his uniform. It looked new, and it probably prickled. Kate thought of this, not of what news he bore, because she didn't want to be the one responsible for Lizzy when she heard. For how could she make Lizzy's pain better?

'You look as though you could do with a cup of hot tea. Put your kitbag down and come through to the kitchen, Sergeant...' Kate paused, as Lizzy jigged up and down beside her.

'Sergeant Jones. I'd have come sooner, but I've not long returned, you see. Was hidden for weeks – well, months – by some good Frenchies, then a bit of a trek over the Pyrenees into Spain, then interned, then escaped, and now here. I've been

244

in hospital; not well, you see. Not too sure in me 'ead what was what, who I was, that sort of thing.'

Kate gestured to the chair and set a cup before him, filling the kettle and heating it. She dished up two teaspoons of tea – fresh tea leaves only for this man, and for her, to help deal with whatever was to be said in the next few moments. She made Lizzy a cup of precious hot cocoa.

Lizzy sat opposite Sergeant Jones, staring from him to Kate, her lips set in a line, trying not to ask. She looked at her cocoa, then at Kate, then at Sergeant Jones and pushed her cup away. Kate picked it up and said gently, 'Drink this, please, Lizzy.'

Lizzy looked at Kate and clearly saw something in, her eyes, because she became very still and reached out her hand, but not for the cocoa. Kate gripped it, then released Lizzy's hand and gave this child her mug of cocoa. Lizzy held it between both hands and sipped it, while Sergeant Jones drank his tea with trembling hands. Kate made toast. The range was gurgling. She fed it with logs. She put the toast with a little butter on the table, and knives and plates. They all looked at them, and no-one moved.

Kate said, 'I think you have something to tell us, Sergeant Jones. We've had no news, you see.'

'There was no news because, once back in England, it took weeks in hospital for us to return to the land of the living.'

'Us?'

'Jonny and me – we made it back together, but not Derek. Sorry, missus, and little 'un; you will be getting it official like, but Derek, he died right at the start. His last thought was of you, Lizzy gal. You need to hold that tight to you, like you're 'olding that cocoa. He didn't suffer, it was just like going to sleep, and he said, 'Tell Lizzy and Sarah I love them.'

There was silence. Lizzy still held the mug to her mouth. Her tears were running through her cocoa-moustache. She licked them away. Kate took the cocoa from her. They held hands, then Kate reached out to put her arm around Lizzy's shoulder. Lizzy drew back. Kate nodded. The child needed her mother.

Sergeant Jones rose. He dug into his pocket and pulled out a pencil. It had been sharpened to half its length. There was a rubber on the top. 'He wanted you to have this back, Lizzy. You gave it to him, and 'e held it as he died. He carried it all through, you see.'

Lizzy just sat, unseeing. He placed it on the table, nodded at Kate. 'I'll see myself out.' She followed.

At the front door she handed him his kitbag and asked, 'So, he didn't suffer?'

He said, 'What else can you say? It gives some comfort. Thanks for the tea.'

She opened the door and he walked down the path. She called, 'Stay safe, and thank you. You are still a good friend to him.'

When she returned to the kitchen it was empty, and the cold was rushing in through the back door. The pencil was gone. She checked the waste bin and took it out, placing it on the table, and walked into the garden. Lizzy was urging the swing higher and higher, her face contorted. Kate watched for a while, until the child grew pale with cold, then she built up the range with logs, damping it down afterwards. She gathered their coats from the hall-stand and returned to the swing. She took up position behind Lizzy, slowing it. When it stopped, she handed the child her coat. 'Put it on. We're going to a place that might bring you some comfort. It's where I used to go when I felt alone, angry and lost.'

She had never been back, but today she must. She led her child through the back garden and then over fields where frost lingered, keeping to the hedge, as good walkers should. With her child, who sometimes looked like him; her child who was also so like her.

They reached the woods and she guided Lizzy under the beech trees, the dark-red leaves underfoot muffling their footsteps. They could see their own breath, and pigeons burst from the branches, startled at the intrusion. On and on they walked beneath the canopy in quietness, until finally, and for the first time in what seemed like centuries, Kate stood in the clearing. There was nothing to show that the encampment had existed, except the darker green of the grass where the fire had been. The fallen oak still lay on the far side, but now it showed signs of rot.

'Come with me.' She gripped Lizzy's hand and led her to the oak. They sat down together. 'It was a favourite place of mine. I came here when I was older than you, but still a child. It's where I found comfort.' Lizzy leaned against her, and now in this place, at her daughter's invitation, Kate held her close, and in her heart would never let her go.

They sat for all the hours that Lizzy needed.

It wasn't until two in the afternoon that they returned. Kate opened up the range vents, replenished the logs, ran a bath, a deep one – and damn the two-inch rule. She waited while the heat of the water brought feeling back into Lizzy's body, before rubbing her dry with a huge towel. She dressed her as though she were a baby, as she should have done, just once, before Sarah took her away. She brushed her hair, allowing herself to see the shape of Lizzy's head as it was when she was born.

She built up a fire in the sitting room and sat Lizzy there, with her colouring book. She made her vegetable soup, and they had it on trays in front of the fire. She brought in the cold toast from breakfast and they heated it on toasting forks. Kate cleared up the kitchen, then sat with Lizzy on the sofa. After a while Lizzy talked about how Derek had made her laugh so much.

'He'd chase me, Aunt Kate, and tickle me, but not too much or I felt sick. Mummy will be even sadder than me, because it was Daddy she loved most, and he loved her most. They both loved me, but not as much.'

She was colouring carefully, keeping within the lines. Kate said, 'I don't think that's quite true, you know, Lizzy. Your mum and dad would have moved heaven and earth for you, and you have such a place in their lives.'

Lizzy nodded. 'But they both went away in the end. Daddy had to, because he joined to become a soldier, but I don't think it was the same for

Mum. She wanted to. Lots of mums have stayed, after all.'

Kate knelt before Lizzy, putting her hands over the peacock she was colouring and making the child stop. 'In wartime, some people have special skills that the country needs. Sometimes they just have to go away, to keep their children safer than if they stayed at home. She is good with French, you know. I expect she is telling people what various signals mean, or something like that. Heavens, it doesn't matter where I am. Look, someone – anyone – can do my singing job in London, and my ARP patrol. So it's right that I have come here to look after you, and help with the school and the concert. People can sing anywhere, you know.'

'I thought she was driving a lorry or pushing a tea trolley?' Lizzy was leaning back on the sofa.

Kate sighed; she wasn't very good at lying. 'Oh, I expect she does some of that too, helping men like Sergeant Jones. Believe me, she will be home when she can.'

Lizzy sat up, her hand to her mouth. 'How will we tell her about Dad?'

'She left me instructions. Now, I'll go and see what she said, while you just have a little nap. I think it's best if you stay home, for this evening's rehearsal. Shall I stay here with you, or shall I ask Mrs Summers if she can come and look after you?'

Lizzy shook her head. 'You must go because you're wrong: not anyone can do your job, only you can. So, you see, you are the same as Mum. We all are, we're all helping, we're all important.' She lay down, almost asleep. Kate covered her

249

with a blanket, checked the fireguard, then hurried to the telephone box to contact Mrs Summers.

Later, while she waited for Mrs Summers to arrive, Kate found the envelope that Sarah had left for just such an eventuality:

Dear Kate

In the event that news is received about Derek, or even if Lizzy is unwell, or has an accident, please do not contact me unless there is something I need to do about it. I must concentrate. If, on the other hand, there is something I can do to help, please write to this address. I will be told.

Beneath her signature was an address in London.

Kate didn't write; what was the point? Because it was clear to her that Sarah was 'elsewhere', doing her bit, and it would be criminal to distract her. It could mean the difference between her life and death. Anyway, Derek was dead, so what could the poor girl do about that? The powers-that-be would probably filter the news through to London, and then it was up to Sarah's masters to make the decision.

By the time Kate arrived at the village hall, it had been set up for the final audition. Mrs B and her piano were to the left of the stage, and behind the panel Stella had sectioned off areas. In one area the costume team had congregated as usual around a large table, normally used by the chair-man of the WI; that was apt, because it was their members who comprised the costume team. Mrs

Woolton had a host of bits and bobs of fabric in her loft, it transpired, and had brought them to the afternoon WI meeting the week before and shown Kate, who was now a member.

In another section the stage manager, Bob Pritchard, the veteran of many an amateur dramatic performance, having cycled as usual from his farm near Stickhollow, was poring over designs with his team. In yet another, Fran Billings was gathering together the children chosen for the chorus.

Stella called, 'Sit down on the floor, children. Let Mrs Billings tell you what we have in mind for you this evening, and anyone who doesn't listen will not be in the show. Later Miss Watson will take you through the first of the tap-dancing rehearsals. Is that quite clear?'

'Yes, Miss Easton.'

Kate waved to Fran and winked. Fran grimaced in return, mouthing, 'You're late.'

Kate slipped across to her. 'We've just heard Derek's dead. I've left Lizzy with Mrs Summers. She's very tired and needs time to absorb it.'

Fran pressed her arm, but Stella was calling, 'We're behind, Kate. I hope you don't mind – we started without you.'

Two singers were coming onstage. It was Susie Fletcher, Adrian's wife, with the man himself. Kate hurried to the audition table. Tom sat next to Pauline, who had become a fixture on the auditioning team over the last few nights. Kate took the spare chair on the end, next to Stella.

'So sorry,' she muttered, leaning forward and addressing them all.

Pauline sniffed. 'I should think so. Everyone else makes it on time and, after all, you are the prime mover. I suppose it's different for you Londoners; the world is expected to wait on you.'

An evacuee mother, herding a child past the table towards Fran's group, spun round. 'I begs yer pardon? What's that supposed to mean?'

Tom put up his hand. 'Ladies, enough – let's get on. We have so much to do.'

Susie Fletcher handed her music to Mrs B, who had a quick look and called to the panel, '"Anything Goes".'

Stella made a note, then called, 'Excellent. Are you all right with that, Mrs B?'

'Indeed. I'll just have a quick run-through.'

Stella muttered to Kate, 'If Susie's already learned the words, then it shows she's keen. Let's see what she sounds like.'

Kate called to Susie, 'Just stay on the point, if you would please, Susie. We've marked the stage with tape.'

While Mrs B played quietly, Susie and Adrian settled into the centre of the stage, on the mark that Kate had created. It was a test to see if those auditioning were willing to take instructions.

Pauline spoke again. 'Where is Lizzy? We can't have one of the organiser's dependants letting us down.'

Stella put her hand on Kate's arm in warning, but too late. Kate was already leaning forward, the words tumbling from her mouth. 'She heard today that her father is dead. She is with Mrs Summers while I am here, and would rather be there. Is that reason enough, for the affianced of

252

the highly and indeed very Reverend Thomas Rees?'

Tom swung round to face her, and Kate just glared at him. He flushed, saying, 'I had no idea. I ought to go and see her.'

Kate turned back to the Fletchers. Mrs B was looking at her, shocked. She called, 'Oh, Kate. Oh, my dear.'

Kate smiled. 'Thank you, Mrs B, but the show must go on.' Her voice shook. She bit down on her lip.

Tom said again, 'I should go?'

Kate said, without looking up, 'That's entirely up to you, Vicar.' Her voice was as icy as his had recently become. 'Are you ready, Susie and Adrian?'

Stella took hold of Kate's hand and squeezed. While the Fletchers sang, the two women sat, hand-in-hand, immersed in their own thoughts, until the song and dance penetrated. They stared at the Fletchers, open-mouthed, as they now dived into a bit of a Charleston that they had clearly rehearsed. Mrs B rattled out the music, then seamlessly swung into 'Jealousy', to which the couple performed a tango. It wasn't perfect, but it could be.

Kate and Stella sat back; around them everyone had stopped what they were doing and had gathered behind the panel. So, this is what had brought these two together? Perhaps it would help them remain so.

When the couple finished, the room erupted in applause, led by Kate and Stella. Stella nudged Kate. 'Possible principals – what do you think?'

'I should say so. What about you, Tom?'

But his seat was empty, and only Pauline remained, reading a book, her lips formed into a firm pout.

Stella said, 'So that's two couples for a tango, if we can find someone to partner you. I've tried Tom again, because he's quite a dab hand. Pauline mentioned that his mother thought it an asset to a young man joining the army, even if it was as a padre.'

'Then Pauline can partner him.'

Stella whispered, 'Oh, please; she clumps about like an elephant, and I am having you in this, come hell or high water. We need you, my lovely. Your voice, your dancing, your presence, so you're not getting away with training everyone and then hiding out at the back.'

The Fletchers were still standing there, panting. Stella stood. 'The vicar had to drop in to see one of his parishioners, not to escape you two.' Those who were chatting behind them laughed. She continued, 'We love your act, and we have great plans. Rehearsals start in earnest next week; there will be three a week, if not more as time goes on, because time is short, and practice is all. We have to be ready for the twentieth of December. Can you manage that? We'll be having some rehearsals in the daytime too.'

The Fletchers smiled at one another. Now Kate saw Olive Fletcher off to the side, nodding gently, a determined look on her face. As Adrian and Susie left the stage, Kate wound her way through the gaggle to Olive's side. 'A talented couple.'

'Yes. They'd forgotten that part of their lives,

but this should kick-start it.'

'You're a clever woman, Olive Fletcher.'

'You're not so bad yourself, young Kate. Mind you, I always thought well of you, when there was all that nonsense being said. It's good to have you back, and Sarah's lucky to be able to share it with you. You're not doing a bad job with Mrs B, either. You need to do your tango, you know. I heard tell it's something special.'

Kate was about to turn away, but stopped. 'You did: who from?'

'Young Mr Moorhouse told us – you know, the one who holds our wills in his office in Yeovil. He saw you at the Blue Cockatoo. It made him go back the next night. He said he felt right proud to know you was a local girl. Right proud.'

Kate felt ridiculously pleased, but her back wouldn't withstand a tango now, not after all the washing, the turning of the mangle, the beating of the rugs. She was finding sleeping difficult, because the ache had become teeth-grindingly painful over the weeks. She just smiled. 'We don't need me, with your two.'

Mrs Fletcher patted her arm. 'Oh yes, we do, but there's time.'

Stella called, 'Earth to our singing-star producer. Get over here, please, Miss Katherine Watson.'

Mrs Fletcher laughed. 'You're wanted.'

Pauline's voice came over to her, loud and clear. 'Yes, her Burlesque Club must be missing her, when honestly...'

Stella's voice was even louder. 'Do shut up, Pauline; you're out of date, and no-one wants to

255

hear what you have to say until you say something helpful. Come on, Kate, we have the Bacon
twins playing the spoons. I think they could
actually be part of the band. What do you think,
Emily and Frances?'

The two twelve-year-olds were onstage and
replied, 'If we're good enough.'

'Then let's see.'

Stella pointed to Kate's chair. She sat, obedi-
ently, while the spoons prepared. After that it
would be time to take the little ones through the
rudiments of tap dance. It wasn't something that
exactly thrilled Kate, because she wasn't sure she
was much of a dance teacher.

The spoons began and were something the like
of which Kate had never seen or heard, but after
a whispered conversation, she and Stella suggested they should also be part of the band. The
twins were thrilled. Stella finished her notes,
while Kate changed into her tap shoes, then
herded the children onto the stage. She called
down to Mrs B, sharing her thoughts on the tap-
dancing chorus, which she wanted to perform
while the Fletchers led 'Anything Goes'.

Mrs B said, 'I think that would work very well.
But how are you going to even get them started,
let alone confident enough?'

Kate laughed, 'Look at them, they're clever –
aren't you, girls, and you two boys?'

The children grinned. One of the boys said,
'Not 'alf, Miss.'

Kate set them up in a line, mid-stage, then talked
them through the chorus requirements as she saw
them. 'Now, when we get to the bit where the

Puritans land on Plymouth Rock, you will all look up, shocked, with your hands to your mouths, and Mr and Mrs Fletcher will then move between you to take a place at the back and continue singing. Shall we try that?'

She sang, while Mrs B played until Kate held up her hand. Mrs B stopped and now Kate showed them how to toe-heel. 'You see, you toe-heel four times to the right, then four times to the left. Let's see you do it.'

Mrs B came in at the right time. Again, up went Kate's hand. Again the music stopped.

'Now, stand. So let's run through that again.' They did. She smiled, applauding them, but missing Lizzy and worrying about her. 'You see, it's not so hard, and let me tell you: we professionals rehearse just like this. Now shall I show you the other steps that I will be asking you to do?'

The children shot up their, hands. 'Yes, please, Miss.'

Kate asked Mrs B if she had the time, and the puff, to run through 'Anything Goes' from start to finish. Pauline was watching, almost with interest, so perhaps she tap-danced? If so, that might make her feel happier, which would help everyone.

Mrs B began and, as Kate danced, she explained to the children what it was that she was doing. 'Hand-to-mouth in shock, toe–heel, count out how many times?'

They counted aloud, 'Four to the right, four to the left. Stand. Move toes.'

'Now, make sure you stand casually, like this.' She put a hand on her waist and slouched. 'Now, step back to the right, tap, spring, tap. Stop, all change twice.'

She swung her arms; her head was up, looking ahead, to the far wall. The clock said eight thirty. She ignored the sharp and penetrating pain in her back, keeping her smile in place.

'Right, now follow me, shuffle, shuffle.' The people in the hall were looking as she tapped. She swung her arms. 'Pick up.' Tap-tap. Pain, pain. Her back should be healed, surely. She had always washed clothes for heaven's sake, but in the sink, and wrung them out, not heaved them on a mangle, lugging them out to the washing line, feeling the weight pull at her back, then stretching and bending to peg them on the line, with the pegs that Andrei's family and friends had made. 'Toe–heel, walking left, hear the tap. Mr and Mrs Fletcher will be singing, and so will you!' She heard the groan.

Stella laughed.

'Salute. Repeat that again.' She swung her arms. 'Now, star-jump.' She made herself do it and almost collapsed as the pain shot through her. It must just be a tightening of the scar. She kept upright, pushed her shoulders back. 'Salute. Shuffle, shuffle, twice.'

She nodded to Mrs B, who ended on a roll that would have done a jazz player proud. The children clapped, and in that moment Kate realised how much she missed performing, and how she had felt real, for a brief moment.

Chapter Seventeen

Tom dawdled through the village on his way to see little Lizzy. It was good to be free of those bloody women, even though he was cold, and there was so little moon that he had just walked into a cart heaped with aluminium pots, waiting to be taken to the collection point in the morning. He should have brought his torch.

He had prayed, but he hadn't been helped to forgive Kate, or ever trust her again. Should she be working with children? He tugged his scarf tighter, pulled his woollen hat down harder. Damn and blast the lot of them!

Why was Pauline still here anyway? She should have work to go to, but she said she had taken more leave. 'Compassionate?' he had queried when she arrived. 'I told you, I'm fine.'

'No, just leave.' Well, she had a lot of leave, that was all he could say; and he must do something about this engagement business, because he'd decided he'd had enough of the lot of them, and Pauline's nonsense was just making fools of them both.

He turned towards Melbury Cottage. There was a chink of light showing through the sitting-room window. Percy would be after them. He paused as he was about to step up onto the porch feeling furious again because he missed the knock that Kate used to give him. But now he made sure that

259

his blackout blinds were drawn properly.

He knocked. Mrs Summers opened the door. Tom stepped into the darkened hallway. 'I've come to see if I can help.'

Mrs Summers said, 'Yes, that's usually the role of men of God.' Her voice was neutral. Well, he had been difficult at the auditions, he knew that, and clearly, so did the rest of the village, but there was only so much a bloke could take, and who was this woman to criticise? 'Vicar?' Mrs Summers was closing the front door behind him.

He shook his head. 'So sorry,' he muttered. 'Just... Well, just...'

She led the way into the sitting room. Lizzy sat on the sofa, a colouring book on her knees, busy turning the dots on a clown's costume red.

Tom said, 'May I sit with you, Lizzy?'

She shrugged, not looking up. He sat. On the table there was the stub of a pencil. It had a rubber on one end, a sharp point on the other. He reached across. She shouted, 'Leave it – that was Dad's. His friend brought it back to me. His friend, do you hear?'

He let his hand drop onto his thigh. 'Your Aunt Kate told us the news. I came to say how sorry I am, and to see if there is anything you want?'

She continued to colour carefully, not going over the lines. The fire was crackling. He supposed they had been to the woods for logs. The woods...

He pushed past the image of Kate, and the lie. 'Anything?' he repeated.

Mrs Summers sat opposite. The wireless was chattering quietly on a shelf. She said, 'I'm waiting for *Germany Calling*. Lord Haw-Haw is good for a laugh. I imagine myself punching him on the mouth.'

Tom looked up, startled. He couldn't imagine Mrs Summers punching anyone.

She nodded. 'Oh yes, that would be my part of the war effort, Tom. Sometimes people need a good slap, you know.'

Lizzy lifted her head. 'Anything?' she asked him.

He forced a smile. Mrs Summers's words were resonating, but surely she didn't mean him? He turned to Lizzy. 'If I can.'

'Then stop being horrid to Kate, just because you're marrying that Pauline, who doesn't like any of us anyway. You used to be Kate's friend, just like Sergeant Jones was Daddy's friend.'

Mrs Summers said nothing, just looked from one to the other.

Lizzy went on, 'Aunt Kate'll be in the hall, working hard. She left her life to come here, and now you've made her miserable. I know you have, because she's quiet, like she was when she came. The second "Anything" I want is for you to go now.'

Mrs Summers moved to the sitting-room door. She held it open. Tom rose. There was really nothing else he could do, because they didn't know what he knew. He traipsed out into the hall. Mrs Summers moved ahead of him to the front door, opening it. She said nothing, just waited for him to leave. The moment he was clear of the porch, she shut it, quietly.

Well, that was him told; and he wished more

261

than anything that he'd never read the damned notebook, and that he was a better man of God. Damn it to hell, Mrs Summers was right. He was behaving badly, but he couldn't help it. He had been so disappointed in Kate, since he'd learned of her slandering Dr Bates. And then since they'd had that disagreement in rehearsals, the atmosphere hadn't thawed. It wasn't as though he hadn't prayed to God to help him separate the sin from the sinner, but nothing had happened.

He called into the vicarage on the way back and barged into the snug. It was cold, but he'd chuck the damned notebooks on the fire. It was time they were burned. He flashed on the light and rooted in the drawer. Two were there, but not the third. What on earth had he done with it? He checked the time. He ought to get back to the hall, but first those damned books must go. He carried them to the chair and lit the fire he made up himself in the morning, because Pauline and Mrs B knew better than to enter his lair.

He leaned on the mantelpiece, looking at the flames as they curled around the logs he had collected from the woods. He had never searched for the clearing where the encampment had been, and he never bloody would. He banged the mantelpiece, remembering Lizzy's words. Well, he too had thought he'd found a friend, someone who seemed to really understand him. So it wasn't one-sided, like the child thought.

He returned for the notebooks, but then saw the third. It was resting on the arm of the second chair. There were two bookmarks. He looked from the notebook to the drawer. He would never have left it out. He picked it up and read the pages where the first bookmark was lodged. He saw it was the part about Kate's lie.

He sat down, appalled. Pauline must have been in here and read these notebooks or, if not all, at least this one. How could she? He'd said no-one was to enter; it was his snug, his sanctuary. Yes, it must be her, Mrs B would not have so... The fire hurled out heat. He tore off his scarf and hat and shrugged out of his coat.

What would Pauline say to people – to Kate? He shivered. This was his parish, these were his people; and there were so many of Hastings's secrets that must now roost in that awful woman's head, for suddenly that's how he saw Pauline.

He flicked the notebook open again. What else had Pauline discovered, only to find a moment to blurt it out? He read as far as the second book-mark. There was little of interest beyond the affair that the previous postman had with a woman in another village, and both families had now moved. Fletcher was still abusing his wife, though Hastings had spoken to him. Tom read of births, including Sarah's arrival home with Lizzy, which Hastings felt was a satisfactory outcome. Hastings also applauded Reginald Watson's decision to give Kate some money for a head-start and encourage her to remain in London, never to return.

There were marriages and deaths, including that of Reginald Watson, who had a stroke. Tom had now reached the bookmarked page and threw both bookmarks onto the fire, but couldn't put the notebook down. He wanted an excuse not to return to the hall, or to Pauline, or Kate.

Three pages later he read Kate's name again. Hastings had written, 'Kate' – just the one name, on one line. Beneath it Tom read:

Today the Bishop telephoned me. He impressed upon me the confidentiality of what he was about to ask me, which was, 'Have there ever been complaints of a sexual nature against Dr Bates?' My heart didn't stop, though it should have done. Instead, it leapt almost into my throat. Apparently Dr Bates, now settled in his new 'parish', had visited a girl while her parents were out. He had, it was claimed, undone her clothes. He had said he would examine her. He had raped her.

She had told her parents. They had believed their daughter and asked the neighbours if they had seen the doctor's car. They had.

The Bishop explained that he was asking the question of all those parishes served by the good Dr Bates. So far, there were three more cases.

I will telephone immedia-

Nothing further was written. Tom checked the date that headed this entry. It was the day the Reverend Hastings was found dead of a heart attack. The following pages were blank.

Tom closed the notebook and laid it on his lap, the shame threatening to drown him. He was no better than all the others who had not accepted Kate's truth. He said aloud, 'And there is no health in us. But thou, O Lord, have mercy upon us, miserable offenders.' Never before had he said these lines with such feeling.

Tom walked to the village hall, his head pounding.

He entered into the light and the sound of happiness. There was Kate onstage, singing 'Anything Goes' as she tap-danced, but she was pale and was moving awkwardly. He saw her falter. He started forward, but she recovered. He watched for a moment but she seemed fine.

Mrs Woolton called out as he passed the sewing corner, 'We really do need another male tango-dancer, Vicar. I know you said no, unnecessarily firmly, but all hands to the pump, eh? We have Susie and Adrian Fletcher. They're just so good. There is whisper that you are a tango-dancer, and we so need a partner for our Kate.'

He watched the costume-makers as they cut material, with pins in their mouths. Two women were tacking sleeves to bodices. Finally he said, 'Mrs Woolton, I'm not nearly as good as Kate. I'm not to her standard at all, in anything.' He could hardly speak the words.

The parents of that other girl had immediately believed her. Kate's father had not believed her; the vicar had not, Sarah had not, but worst of them all, he had not. They had all accepted the appointments diary of a nursing home without question. Before coming out this evening, Tom had replaced the diary in the drawer, then telephoned the nursing home, which is why he was so late. He had begged them to check their diary, and indeed Dr Bates's appointment was written down for his usual time. Tom had implored them to check the sign-in book, if they had one for all those years ago. Thankfully they had. The woman on duty was bored, so she checked. Dr Bates had not signed in until an hour later than usual.

265

Tom had then telephoned the bishop's office, insisting on talking to the Bishop, though it was late. The bishop remembered the case clearly. It had been pursued, but without the need for involving the police, at the victims' request. 'Why?' Tom had asked, though he had guessed. The bishop replied, 'Because some had borne children, and how could these children be told they were the result of...?'

Apparently, the bishop explained, Dr Bates had 'retired' through illness. His wife knew nothing. A close eye had been kept on him and he had soon become disabled with a stroke, so everything had been satisfactorily concluded. 'For some,' Tom had said, thinking how fitting it was that both Bates and the verger had been dealt the same fate, a stroke; it was a very unchristian thing for him to feel.

The bishop had been sympathetic. 'I agree that "satisfactorily" is a misnomer. For those who are the victims, there is a legacy.'

Tom had replaced the receiver. Dear God, there was so much for him to learn. Part of it was to understand that God couldn't wave a magic wand; most of it was up to him, and whatever vestiges of humanity he possessed. Perhaps in time it would lead him to self-improvement.

He examined his feelings for the doctor yet again, here in the light and goodness of the hall, but his anger was mainly at himself.

Mrs Woolton was now looking at him strangely.

'I'm sorry, I was miles away,' Tom said.

'I said, I will make you a costume. Our Kate will get you up to scratch, you mark my words.'

266

'I don't doubt that.'

He moved on, towards the stage, but Pauline had risen and intercepted him. 'Where on earth have you been?'

'Looking for my notebooks. I found them, but so did you.'

'Indeed. We both know the truth now about that young lady, if one can use the term.' Pauline laughed. It was an unpleasant sound.

Tom said, drawing her towards the double doors of the hall, then out into the darkness of the lobby and finally outside, 'Truth?' He kept his voice calm, because who knew what made this woman as she was, and he must despise her actions, and not her.

'Yes, darling. I know you like your little snug, but I need to be part of everything in your life, as I'm to be your wife. It's appalling to read the truth of that little madam and her lies. No wonder you have changed your tune about her.'

'So, you didn't read to the end? If you had, you would have seen that you are wrong – we all are. She did tell the truth.'

Pauline laughed again. 'Nonsense. Her sort are no better than they ought to be. She asked for whatever happened to her in those woods, and now you say she told the truth. Exactly how do you know that?'

He sighed, because he was no better than this woman, not really. He said, 'Pauline, those books are private; they are not to be discussed.'

'Oh, darling, don't be such a softie. Use your common sense and take a look at her, showing off in there. I know you like to believe the best of

267

people, but honestly.'

Tom took off his coat. 'Put this round you. We are going to the vicarage to collect anything you have left there. We are then going to the pub, and you will leave tomorrow morning. This can't go on. You don't love me, and I don't love you, and if you ever so much as breathe a word about what is in those diaries, I will tell your employer that you have lied about needing compassionate leave. Please bear in mind that, in wartime, I expect there is some sort of penalty for not satisfactorily pursuing or performing war work.'

She pulled away from him, as he hustled her down the High Street. 'Have you gone mad?'

'I mean it, Pauline. I will phone whoever needs to know, if I don't get that solemn promise from you. And if I don't, I will also publish the truth about the diaries. You will be the only one to suffer.'

He waited in the kitchen while she collected her books, a pen and a scarf. 'If you have left anything, I will send it on.'

He marched her to the village hall and found her coat on the hook and her hat. He held her coat, and all Pauline could do was put it on. He wore his own, which smelled of her perfume, but he would air it tomorrow. He walked her to the pub.

'I will order a taxi for you. It will arrive at eight in the morning. I will not be there to see you off. Enjoy your life, Pauline. And I'm sorry I haven't spent more time with you and made you understand that we have no future together. You are a good woman, but the way you are behaving is sad beyond measure. Change, for your own sake, I beg you. Just as I must.'

She slapped him. It stung. 'You're hideous anyway, Tom Rees. And what makes you think that Kate will want you – because that's what all this is about, isn't it?'

He shook his head. 'It's to do with my failure as a man of God. I must do better. I must believe without proof, I must feel it in my heart.' He was aware that he was thumping his chest.

He turned on his heel and walked to the village hall. He hung up his coat, his scarf and hat and entered again into the light, making his way to the table at which Stella sat. She was making notes on one of her endless lists. The chorus was going through its moves, and they too had put on tap shoes, so there was a general clattering, but no uniformity, and no cohesion in their singing and swinging arms. He knew there would be. He nodded at Kate, who looked surprised. She checked behind her, then back at him. He mouthed, 'I'm sorry.'

She didn't understand, so he went to the edge of the stage and she bent down.

He said, 'I'm sorry to be so grouchy. It was unforgivable, but I needed to make some decisions. They are made.' He wanted to smooth her hair back. He held up his right hand. 'Friends again. A new beginning?'

Kate contemplated his hand, and for a terrible moment he thought she might not forgive him. He shouldn't have doubted her, and her integrity.

'I'm sorry,' he said again. 'Truly.'

She looked into his eyes for a long moment and

269

he held his breath as he waited. He'd beg, if he had to.

At last Kate took Tom's hand and shook it, nodded her appreciation of his apology, and then took her place back with the children. 'Just once more, then we must let you go home, children. And Mrs B too, who will immediately nip into the pub for a snifter.'

Mrs B called up, 'Really, Miss Watson, why would I stop at one, after a few hours here?'

The children and Kate looked at one another in surprise, then laughed.

Mrs B embarked on the introduction to 'Anything Goes', calling to Tom, 'And Pauline? Where's she disappeared to?'

He came and stood by her, turning the page for her. 'Home, Mrs B. It took me a while, but she's gone and is not returning.'

Mrs B sniffed. 'Ah, well, as long as you are happy with that.'

'Relieved, Mrs B.'

Happy? He looked around, feeling that he was on the way, now that he understood rather more about life, or God, or perhaps people. Or maybe all three.

Chapter Eighteen

On 24th November 1942 Sarah was given permission to proceed by the sentry, at a checkpoint on the outskirts of Rouen. All the while the hen clucked away in its crate. Perhaps the clucking would mean an egg one day. She lived in hope. She had said as much to Romain, whose hen it was, and he had shrugged, as a grizzled old Frenchman would. He kept them at the bottom of his rose garden. 'Manure for the roses and flesh for the pot, and eggs for omelettes,' he had said.

Romain was a Frenchman who was determined to risk his life to regain his country's democracy and sovereignty. One way was to leave the bike and crate for Sarah, in a different place every day; just in case. Everything was just in case, and if they forgot, it might be the last time they did.

She left behind the German corporal who had checked her documents and gestured her through. He called after her, 'Don't forget the curfew tonight, or the chicken might get shot and put in the pot. It might anyway.' His comrades laughed; Sarah laughed too, waving goodbye without turning. So often the same remarks, but as long as they didn't stop her, it was fine.

As she cycled away, she always felt vulnerable. She thrust the pedals round faster and faster, as though she could outrun a bullet. The thought made her laugh again. She did a lot of that at the moment, which was why Bernard said she was nearly due for leave. Her stint would be coming to an end in a month, which was when a Lysander would at last be arriving. She would be on it. But first there was the drop tomorrow, or perhaps the next night, whichever was clear of cloud and rain and allowed the full moon to beam down.

She cycled over cobbled road after cobbled road, passing tall French houses, each one seeming to prop the other up in long terraced rows. Soon these terraces thinned and she was in the countryside, heading for her Uncle Pierre's, or so she had told the corporal. She couldn't imagine what it would be like: going home, feeling safe, not sleeping with every sense tuned into the air temperature: is that a draught? Tuned into noise: is that a creak? Perhaps she'd even get rid of the cough she had acquired, and her chest would improve and stop wheezing.

It had all been worth it, because she and Bernard had gathered together four groups, and no-one appeared to have been lost to the Gestapo. But had they been turned? There was nothing to suggest it. She coughed, then smiled. Bernard should be returning from elsewhere today, having conducted a training session on explosives with one of the groups. Importantly, the new 'George' was still with them, moving from safe place to safe place every day. The old George had magically been transported south and over the Pyrenees, out of danger, as long as he managed to escape internment in Franco's Spain, which he was clever enough to do.

She stopped at a crossroads, holding onto her

bike as a German convoy tore along the top road. She tightened her tatty old headscarf and knotted it beneath her chin. She wound her woollen one round her neck again. German troops sat in the back of an uncovered truck, bringing up the rear of the convoy, scattering dirt and mud. One soldier waved. She lifted a hand in return. Her gloves had holes in the palms, her feet had chilblains, she had mouth ulcers, her hands shook.

The convoy passed. She crossed the main road on her way to give a third training session to Group 2. This time it was in sabotage. They should all be making their way to the woods that hid the landing ground from prying eyes. They would have created cover stories, and she had trained them to spot 'shadows' and to take a different route each time.

She cycled past the wood and then back. She waved as though towards someone and headed up a path. It couldn't possibly be called a track. She waved again. There was no-one, of course; she was acting. Kate would be surprised. Well, everyone in Little Worthy would be surprised to see the upright, morally certain daughter of the verger living a lie. She shook her head fiercely. Sarah was tired. She was Cécile: remember that.

She dismounted, once in the trees, and pushed her bike to the designated spot. There should be a lookout. Pierre stepped across her path. 'You were not followed,' he said. It wouldn't be his real name. He waved her through, his rifle on his shoulder, but she stopped to talk to him. He was young, vibrant and keen. He kept his eyes on the area through which she'd come, and which gave

273

him a view of the path and road. If a convoy came, stopped and the Germans swarmed towards them, he would let them know, pretty damned quickly.

'You are the first, except for Arnaud. He is guarding the north side. We have a good sweep, and all we see are gulls pecking the ploughed fields – though what fish will they find in the earth?' He shrugged.

'Ah, they have convinced themselves worms are a form of fish, I expect.' She rested the bike against her hip, coughing into her scarf.

'You have gulls in England?'

'We do, and they also follow the plough and look for... Well, what? Grain, worms? Derek loved to see them.' She stopped. God, she was tired, and she must not be. *Cécile* didn't have a Derek in her life, only Sarah did.

Pierre took her bike. 'Let me hold it for you. Is there an egg? Have you ever had such a thing as an egg as you travel?'

'Sadly, no.'

They stood back-to-back, watching, listening. She was early, as a precaution. She liked to see everyone who approached. Pierre pulled out a Gauloise, offering it.

Sarah shook her head and said, 'Better not. The scent of it carries on the wind.'

Pierre nodded and shoved the packet back into his pocket.

'But Gauloise? You're fortunate,' she said.

He shrugged; he was French, so it was what he did a lot. 'I have an uncle, he's... Well, he knows people.'

Did it matter that his uncle was in the black

market? Well, who wasn't? But she paused. She would mention it to Bernard. She smiled slightly. Would he kiss her cheek and say, 'I'll find out.'

The gulls were circling. Suddenly she wanted it to be next month, clambering into the Lysander and on her way home. But she wasn't the same person any more, so what would Lizzy think of her? She could kill a man, though she had not yet. She could train men to plant explosives, though they had not yet and wouldn't, until there was a reasonable target. They had thought they had found one, but the security had proved insurmountable.

So, would they notice on her return that she could lie and act, just like Kate, but couldn't sing? Derek could sing. He and Lizzy would sing together as they walked to school. She had stopped that, for it only led to mischief, it led to wildness; and besides, she couldn't join in, so she would have felt left out. What sort of and person was she, back then?

Pierre asked, 'Derek, your husband? You have left him behind?'

She shook her head. 'He's always with me, in many ways, and perhaps a prisoner-of-war too, here. I keep listening, but have learned nothing; perhaps one day...' She came back to herself. No, she must not talk about her life. Sarah saw movement, and nudged him. 'Three points east.'

A man was traipsing towards the copse, around the ploughed field. Pierre said, 'Raoul. And Florian two points east.'

'I'll go on. Send them through, Pierre, and thank you.'

275

Sarah made her way to a small clearing where Arnaud crouched, his rifle in his hand, two other men with him. She said, 'Stay on lookout, Arnaud.'

He looked up, tapping his watch. 'Renée is taking the watch at the moment. She clocks off in an hour.'

'Of course.' The guards rotated, and she needed to keep up, but Renée was as sharp as a knife, and no-one would get past her. For such a young woman, she was dependable and was admired by the whole group. Sarah's head ached with the cold. Raoul and Florian, the two newest members of the group, joined them, leaving Pierre on watch. They drew close together. She coughed into her scarf. 'Too many Gauloise,' Florian, a father of two, murmured.

'Too much cold,' she whispered back. They all nodded.

She explained that they would be talking about setting explosives. She insisted that only small quantities must be used, as they could be carried without discovery, or with a smaller chance anyway. As with everything I have said, you must avoid discovery, keep your intentions to yourself. Remember your pseudonym at all times. Do not involve anyone else,' she insisted. 'Not even your wife, or lover – or perhaps both.' It was a line Bernard always said broke the ice, and he was right.

The men laughed.

'The target must be specific, and the damage must be crippling. No point in risking your lives for something trivial. We need whatever the target is out of action for a long time, with the enemy

276

perhaps not even realising it is sabotage, which will minimise the taking of hostages.' She coughed again into her scarf.

'Why not let the RAF bomb it, if it comes to that? If we tell them the target?'

Sarah nodded. 'Good question, but we learned from the London Blitz, and the blitz of other cities, that much could be destroyed that way, but if nothing was critically damaged, teams could clear it up reasonably swiftly. If, however, there had been just one charge, tucked against one critical piece of machinery, all the clearing up in the world would not have got it working again for a long time.' She looked around. 'The task of the saboteur – you, and you, and you,' she pointed to them, 'is first to make sure that you will recognise the part of the machinery that is vital.'

She ticked off the points, stabbing her gloved finger into the bare palm of her hand.

'You need to infiltrate the factory, then smash that vital component – one that cannot be re-paired or replaced for months.' She stared at her exposed palm, then let her hands drop. 'So, what is required above all?'

The men looked at one another. One said, 'Intelligence.'

She said, 'Yes, so eyes and ears open, mouths shut. You will be told of specific targets, but you have a part to play there too. For instance, if you should receive information, use our communi-cation drops to let us know. You know where they are, and always use the codes. If you need help, use the drop and the codes. These will be changed for your own safety, regularly. Now.' She yanked at the grass in the clearing, and others helped, until there was just a small area of earth. Squatting, Sarah used a stick to trace a diagram. The men clustered around. 'One pound of high explosives will need to be applied, like so, to a critical part.' She rested, coughing again. She stopped. Was that a crack – a twig?

The men spun round, and revolvers emerged as if by magic. They melted into the trees, as did she. A deer bounded across the clearing. They waited, listened. Nothing, and no alarm raised from the lookouts. They re-emerged. Her heart was beating right up into her throat.

They clustered around the diagram again. She impressed on them the need to get it right the first time. 'Otherwise they will plug the loopholes in the perimeter which allowed you in.'

They talked amongst themselves, asking questions, some of which they answered.

Finally Sarah smiled. 'Full marks. If my hen has laid an egg, it is yours.'

They all laughed, but quietly, all of them alert, their senses heightened by the false alarm.

'So,' she said, 'if there is a boiler – say a steam locomotive – where do we place a *small* charge?'

'The boiler?'

'The wheel?'

She shook her head. 'No, all those can be repaired. Remember, we need to stop the transport of supplies, troops and heaven-knows-what, so a charge placed against the bare end of a steam cylinder, which is made of cast iron, will render it out of action for months. Cast iron shatters, and spare parts are rare, as cast iron does

278

not wear out.'

The men were nodding. They carried on for another hour, but then dispersed, heading back to their work and their homes whilst she cycled back to Rouen, reaching it long before curfew. She left her bicycle at the drop, checking for eggs: nothing. 'You wretched bird, but it's right that your master gets it.'

She walked, coughing, coughing, some 100 yards towards Romain's door, bending down when she reached it, shaking her shoe free of a non-existent pebble and moving a stone from the top step to the bottom. The chicken and bike would be picked up soon.

She continued, walking past tired, thin Frenchwomen, some clacking along in their wooden-soled shoes, and thick stockings, heavily darned, like hers. Others were in court shoes as worn and battered as her own, all with that look in their eyes. Were their sons, husbands, lovers still prisoners-of-war in Germany or had they been taken for labour? Were they collaborators; were they Resistance; were they just getting through as best they could?

Their coats were thin and wretched, their headscarves faded, their breath as misty in the cold. Many coughed, their shoulders rounded, though most straightened when they passed German patrols, looking ahead, not sparing these interlopers the time of day.

She passed the new safe house, walking on without a sideways glance. She rounded the corner, sneaking a look back. No-one was following, no-one was watching the house. She continued along the road and turned left, approaching the house from the rear. She stopped again at a gate, removed another invisible stone. Yes, the stick she had placed beneath the gate was still as it was. She entered, slipping along the side of the yard and into the house.

She waited under the stairs, listening. Nothing, just creaks. She slipped into the kitchen. There was a cellar trapdoor in the floor, covered by a rug. The house was no longer used, except by her, and by Bernard if he needed to move from his safe house. Just once, though, an escaping prisoner had been brought to her. She had mentioned Derek to him. He didn't know of him, but he was a pilot, so why would he? Where was her husband? It didn't seem to matter any more, but it should.

She sat at the kitchen table and put her head on her arms. She must not sleep, but she did.

Bernard woke her, stroking back her hair. He stood beside her. 'Don't get up.' He knelt, holding her against him. 'I can hear you breathing. Your chest is worse. It seemed quieter before we went our separate ways.'

'I'm fine.' Sarah coughed. He stood, lifted her up and carried her to the dining room, where she slept on a ragged mattress. He set her on it and let his canvas bag drop to the floor. 'I have food, and drink.' He joined her on the mattress, knees up, back against the wall. Both kept on their coats and shoes, and dragged over their legs an old coat they had found. Bernard shared bread, cheese, pâté and wine with her. 'I'm worried about you,' he murmured as he handed her the bottle. She drank from it, soothing her throat.

'Don't. This will pass. The men are ready for the drop tomorrow?'

He nodded, tearing the bread by the light of the full moon. He said, as he did so, 'It will be good weather next month, thank heavens. Or so my contact tells me, though how he knows...?'

She laughed, then coughed. 'A straight line to God perhaps?'

'Or a big mouth, and lots of hope. It's been approved that you return, just for a break.'

'And you?'

'Soon after you, perhaps,' he said. 'I have some things to sort out. Now sleep. We won't get any tomorrow night.'

She lay down beneath the coat.

Bernard said, 'Tonight, Cécile, I will stay. I'm worried about you,' he repeated. He lay close, for warmth; that was all. Just for warmth.

They stayed in bed throughout the morning of the next day, sleeping, waking, eating stale bread and drinking the remains of the wine, and water. Sarah ached. He said she was burning and put a cool wet cloth on her forehead. His handkerchief? He stroked her hair, kissed her forehead. She heard him say, 'I love you, my beloved, and you have been here too long.'

She thought: I love you too, but there is Derek. She had failed, because she hadn't found him, and even forgot him sometimes. She slept.

They left separately in the early afternoon, heading towards the dropping zone, reaching it as dusk fell, but before curfew. The men and Renée had already dug a pit for the parachutes, over to the right. Soon the group was gathered close. Bernard whispered, 'Watch me; when you see my torch, switch on yours. The moment the drop finishes, collect the containers, bury the parachutes.' The group already knew, because this was their second drop. They each waited in their places. Arnaud and Florian took the top and toe, and there was one person at each corner. She and Bernard took up position in the middle of the sides.

They lay on the frosty ground, listening, waiting, looking. The full moon beamed down. The moonlight was so bright it almost cast shadows. Sarah wrapped her scarf around her face, feeling too hot, then shivering with cold. The cycle ride had taken the last of her energy. Her head felt fit to burst. The men would take the supplies to the dump, then they'd melt back into their worlds. She would head for Rouen, whilst Bernard made for who-knew-where.

Sarah heard a faint rumble and raised her head, keeping as low to the ground as possible. There it was again, carried on the wind or whatever carried sound. It grew louder, but not yet, not yet. Then she saw Bernard's torchlight.

She sprang to her feet, hearing the sound of a Whitley, which was slightly different from a Lysander. How quickly she had come to recognise the different engines. Closer and closer, lower and lower. There it was, a dark looming shape approaching at 500 feet. Steadily it came, and then the parachutes were swinging down. She saw two parachutists and several containers. They all hit the ground, clunk-clunk-clunk.

The group rushed to them, detaching the parachutes and gathering them up as the Whitley flew off, dropping leaflets over Rouen, which was a cover that perhaps worked.

The group rushed the parachutes to the pit. They all took shovels and hurled in earth. Sarah's legs were trembling, her chest singing. Pierre was next to her. 'A train, you sound like a train.'

She laughed almost silently. 'Hush, and shovel.' He did.

Sarah saw Bernard shaking the hands of the agents, then hurrying them from the field. The stones in the earth clinked on the shovels. Bernard was now leaving the zone with the agents. She watched; he would leave her a message when he needed to. She coughed, and again. Arnaud took the shovel from her. 'Renée needs help. I'm quicker.'

He was. Sarah ran across the field to Renée, who was struggling to lift a container. She took the other end. It felt heavy enough for weapons. 'Renée, come on. Quick, quick.'

Together they hurried to the edge of the zone, into the woods, and then to the container dump, which was under a defunct charcoal kiln. Sarah had thought it would make a good container dump, the first time she had seen a kiln in the woods. It had been modified by them to reduce its weight and accommodate being moved, but even so, it took all their strength to shove the kiln off the dump. There were already containers in it, but room for more. They dragged the kiln back and then faded, each of them, into the woods, making their solitary way home, staying away from patrols or lying low until the morning and continuing after the curfew was lifted.

Sarah's plan was to do just that. It was too dangerous to try and cycle through Rouen at night. She propped her bike against the inside of the hedge, pulled her coat around her and waited in the piercing November cold until dawn. She sank her head onto her knees and waited another two hours. Then, at a time when people might be cycling to the town to find food, she dragged her bicycle back onto the road. There was ice at the bottom of the ditch, and frost in the furrows. She saw Arnaud and Renée in the distance on the other side, heading on foot up the hill. Why the hell hadn't they gone in the dark, for they only had a short distance to go?

She saw that Renée was helping Arnaud, who limped – even more reason to make headway in the dark. She would mention it when they next met. She cycled on with no energy to hurry, and had gone only a couple of hundred yards when a German armoured car approached, drawing closer and closer. She put her head down and ignored it, though she listened as it passed, relaxing as it continued. She always worried that the Whitley had been heard and the Germans were hunting possible dropped agents. The car continued along the road behind her, and she sweated, her back prickling. Were they suspicious? Had they seen Arnaud and Renée?

She heard the screech of brakes, just as another armoured car scorched out of a side road, blocking the way ahead. Soldiers spilled from it, straddling the road, rifles at the ready. Behind her she heard the armoured car reversing, revving forward, reversing again, revving towards her. She was trapped. She glanced up the hill and saw Renée and Arnaud throwing themselves to the ground. Had the Germans seen them yet? To her left was a gap in the hedge.

'Halt.' The call came from behind. Ahead, the soldiers raised their rifles. 'Halt.'

Any minute now someone would look up the hill. She flung herself from the bicycle and jumped the ditch, bursting through the hedge and groping under her coat, drawing the revolver she carried on drops, from the back of her waistband. She ran across the ploughed field, the soil dragging at her shoes, slowing her, making the terror boil within her, but she had done the arithmetic. She was only one person; Renée and Arnaud were two. The gulls lifted from the furrows.

Shots were fired behind her. She turned, aimed and fired wildly, at nothing, because the soldiers hadn't burst through the hedge yet, and she must create a diversion. She swept a look at the opposite hill. Arnaud and Renée were still lying low. She ran on, then turned. The Germans were forcing their way through the hedge now. Beyond, up the hill, Renée and Arnaud were crawling, heading for the top of the hill. They were almost there, almost, and still had not been seen. The soldiers were through into the field, aiming their rifles, firing but their shots were high. They'd want her alive. One had a machine gun; she heard its stutter as she turned and ran on. Bullets zipped past her. She fell, staggered to her knees, turned and fired again and again. Renée and Arnaud were disappearing over the ridge.

Sarah fired once more as the soldiers closed on her, but there was only a click. An order was shouted. There were no more shots, but the soldiers' rifles were held at the ready. An officer was in the lead. She staggered to her feet, threw the revolver to the side and readied herself, taking the knife from her pocket. One soldier was down just this side of the hedge; she could see the grey of his uniform, his helmet upturned beside him. How could that happen? She'd been careful. Oh God.

She readied herself. Step by step they were closing, their breath visible in the cold. They were big, their faces impassive, hate in their eyes. She shivered, her hands numb with fear. There was no escape. She wanted her mother. She wanted Bernard.

The officer smiled as he put one muddy boot in front of the other. He drew on his gloves. Why had he taken them off? The soldiers were closer now. She could see the mud on their boots. That wouldn't please them, for the sergeant would have them spitting and polishing. Above, the gulls called. Sarah looked up, wishing she had wings, wishing she was on a Lysander, heading home to Little Worthy. But she was Cécile Lamont, and her home was Limoges. Cécile Lamont, with 'miles to go before I sleep', as Robert Frost's last line said. Yes, it would seem like miles. She must hold out, but it would be better if they fired, right now.

The officer stood before her. 'Well, well. You will come with us.' The knife was in her hand. She brought it up, but he blocked her arm. She kicked his knee, brought up her other hand, caught him behind his ear. He went down. She held out the knife to the others, as the officer groaned at her feet. Kill me, she urged them, because I must not betray anyone, and I can't reach the pill we were given. It would be better – much better – if they fired, then she could sleep.

She heard breathing behind her, whirled too late, as an arm came round her neck and a hand grabbed her hair, pulling back her head. Her scarf was round her throat. The arm tightened. She choked, crumbling to her knees, the arm squeezing tighter and tighter. Her woollen scarf blew in her face. He pushed her head forward now. She looked into the officer's eyes as he struggled onto an elbow. 'Bastard,' she gasped.

He scrambled to his feet. 'Enough.'

The grip on her throat loosened, but the soldier kept hold of her hair. She felt sick, and her chest rattled.

The officer came close. 'So, we will find out who you are. We heard your Whitley. We will find out your plans, your groups. We will destroy you, but first you will want to die.'

'Bastard,' she repeated, but any courage she had was ebbing with her strength. She was dragged to the armoured car. Renée and Arnaud would be raising the alarm, even now. Supplies would be moved, the group would disperse, no-one would know where anyone else went, but a message would be left for Bernard. At least he would know; at least Lizzy and Kate would be told, eventually. She saw them for a moment and knew without a doubt that Kate would care for

287

Lizzy but would she tell...? She coughed, tried to catch her breath, but failed. Coughed and coughed again, struggling for breath.

She was dragged along, over the furrows. She couldn't fall because they held her arms so tightly. They shoved her through the hedge and pushed her down into the ditch. They laughed, looming over her as she lay helpless in the half-frozen sludge. She was hauled out, and into the car. The wind was blowing hard. She sat back. The gulls called above her. She watched them. They were free, as she never would be again.

As they drove along, with a revolver at her head, she wondered how the Germans had really known? Was it indeed the sound of the Whitley, or bad luck, or was there a traitor? If.so, who?

Sarah shook her head. That was not for her to decide, surrounded as she was by the enemy, on her way to a prison and interrogation. She must say nothing, for as long as she could. That's all she had to remember now. She was Cécile Lamont from Limoges, who had worked for a butcher in Poitiers. They would eventually break that cover, but they must not break her soul.

Chapter Nineteen

Kate looked at the bathroom tap. It had been dripping overnight and had formed an icicle. She called Lizzy to see. 'The hot tap works, so the pipes aren't frozen, thank heavens, but it will be best to use the kitchen sink to wash in. It's a shame that we can't sleep in the kitchen too – the air was so cold last night.'

'The sink is too small to sleep in, Auntie Kate.'

Ah, thought Kate. The first joke since Lizzy had heard the news about her father.

Lizzy reached out and broke off a piece of ice, watching it slowly melt on the palm of her hand. 'Perhaps it will snow at Christmas. It's only a few weeks, but it's cold for November, isn't it?'

'Yes, I suppose so, but it is December very soon, so perhaps that explains it. Come on, let's dress in layers, because it's no warmer at school. We can have omelette for breakfast.'

Lizzy headed for her bedroom while Kate hurried downstairs. She heard Lizzy call, 'I'd rather a boiled egg, please. But a soft one.'

'I'll do my best.' Kate smiled. It was the first time the child had bothered about food. Now, let's see if she actually eats it, she thought.

Lizzy did, as though she hadn't eaten for days, which she hadn't, not really, once the truth had sunk in.

Kate decided she'd nip out of school to reseat the tap after her reading session with the six-year-olds. She should have done it before, but what with finalising the choreography, and furious rehearsals every evening, for her at least as producer, the show date of 20th December seemed ridiculously close.

As she drank her tea she wondered where Sarah was, and if she was safe. She allowed herself to think about this every morning, but tried to keep it contained to this time, because the worry didn't

289

make anyone any safer. It didn't work, because her sleep was increasingly disrupted by thoughts of her sister being chased by the Germans. For some reason, she had come to feel that if the show was a success, and earned money for the war, it might pay for her sister's safety. But who was to be the arbitrator? Tom's God? It was at this point that she always gave up thinking and simply put one foot in front of the other.

Lizzy's plate was empty. 'Mr Manners will be enormously pleased with you, Lizzy Baxter,' Kate said, leaving the dishes in the bowl to soak. They could be dealt with after school.

'I wonder if there will be another letter from Mum?' Lizzy said, standing in front of the range, flapping her gloves to warm them up.

'Perhaps,' said Kate.

A telegram had arrived the day after Sergeant Jones's visit, informing Sarah and Lizzy of Derek's death, and Sarah's letter had not referred to the news in any way. Lizzy took Kate's reason at face value – the telegram hadn't yet caught up with her mum.

They dressed up in scarves, hats, gloves and two pairs of socks, because wellington boots were so cold. She wondered what Brucie would think of his glamour puss now, as she opened the front door. There on the doorstep were two eggs, left by some kind villager for Lizzy, to help her overcome her loss. It's what happened when someone was hurt, here in Little Worthy. There was never a note, never a need for thanks. Lizzy took them into the kitchen, and together they left the house.

They joined the Billings children at their gate

and waved to Fran, who had sailors' costumes to complete for the evening. The children slid on the frozen puddles, while Kate thought of Russia turning around the German invasion and Stalingrad holding firm. Good old mother winter freezing the invading troops where they bunkered down. What did it mean that the Germans were now occupying Vichy France? Was Sarah there? No more questions; it wouldn't help.

They joined others as they entered the school yard. The girls went through one door into the school, and the boys through another. The infants used the girls' entrance. All so orderly, and Stella's decree was that there was no need to queue in this weather. It was exactly the same pattern as the one she had grown up with. What would her father think about her teaching here?

She moved on from that thought.

Today Kate was teaching and reseating a tap; tomorrow she'd be washing clothes and mangling. At the thought she winced. She climbed the steps into the school, and one child rushed past her, knocking against her. She gasped at the pain in her back, doubling over, holding her breath. She reached for the door and clung to the handle for a moment. The pain eased a little, and she straightened and walked down the corridor. Stella was in the staff-room, wearing the look she always had when she'd received a letter from Bradley. They were few and far between, but somehow more precious because of it.

'Rehearsal at six, rather than six thirty – is this still all right with you, O tap dancer supreme?'

'Of course it is. You've cleared it with Mrs B?'

291

Kate hung up her coat, but then put it back on. 'It's so cold.'

'I know, it hurts my leg, I broke it three years ago, and the winter sets it off. Would you nip to the vicarage and remind her on your way home. I think it needs to be five thirty, after tonight.'

Kate sat down carefully. Of course, how silly not to realise it was the weather that was causing her back to play up too. How often on ARP duty had Frankie bemoaned his joints?

Stella handed Kate the register for Class A. 'Do you realise that our little War Bond fund-raiser has attracted people from as far as Yeovil?'

Kate levered herself to her feet. 'I thought I'd get the little ones to copy out the programme. With every seat sold, we need plenty more.'

That morning the children bent over their desks, tongues between their teeth, writing the programmes. It would take more than that, though, and she wondered if Tom could ask the congregation to put their pen-hands to the project.

At break time Kate hurried home, then used her tools to reseat the tap, replace the washer and put it together again. She stood back. Good, no drips. She called into the vicarage on her way back, drawing in a deep breath and thinking hard. How should she approach Tom? Yes, he was generally so much more himself, now that Pauline had gone, but she hadn't spoken to him on his own.

She knocked. Mrs B opened the door. 'Wipe your feet. He's in his snug, doing heaven-knows-what.'

'Snug?' Kate took her boots off, because her life

wouldn't be worth living if she left even a smudge of mud on the slate floor.

'The annexe, Kate. Keep up.'

Mrs B didn't smile, but she didn't frown, either. Kate smiled uncertainly and hurried to the snug. She knocked. Tom called, 'Who is it?'

'Kate.'

'Am I in trouble?' Ah, that's more like it, she thought.

'Not yet, but there are hours to go before dusk.'

'Enter.' He didn't sound annoyed.

She did, stepping down into the snug. He had the fire lit, and she warmed herself in front of it, not knowing quite how to start. Another deep breath. 'I need a favour.' He was at his desk, writing.

'Why am I not surprised? I've said I'll do the tango, but I can't sing.'

As he turned she said, 'I just need you to ask your congregation if, like all good men, women and children, they would be prepared to write out some programmes. We have such a large audience, we haven't nearly enough. I thought we could charge threepence per programme, which will boost our profits.'

He smiled, pointing past her to the fire. 'I thought I'd gone cold. You've blocked the heat.'

She said, 'I'll move when I have your agreement.'

'You have it – now move. You should be in school.'

She laughed, with relief more than anything, and headed for the steps, before adding, 'Just one more thing.'

Tom groaned.

'Mrs Woolton needs you to try on your tango outfit this evening.'

He sat looking at her. 'Not like the one poor Adrian has to wear?'

'The very same.'

'But, they've made his jacket so tight, and it's a bit shiny. So are the shoes. It's–'

'A tango costume, or would you prefer to wear the frock? I'm happy to change places.'

He grinned, gesturing her away. 'Go to work. I'll see you this evening.'

She shut the door behind her, then did something she had never dared to do before and knocked on the kitchen door. 'Yes,' Mrs B barked.

Kate said through the door, 'It's me. May I ask you something.'

'Open the door, I don't bite.' Kate pondered this, because Mrs B had always had a reputation for being on the verge of doing just that. Had she changed that much? She opened the door a little and looked round it. 'Will you be available at six this evening, and thereafter at five thirty? We have so much to do, and I know it's a nuisance, but we've brought it forward to an earlier time and...'

Mrs B held up her hand. 'Of course. I have blocked out my diary for just this eventuality. Timing gets tight as the date draws, near.'

'You sound as though you know all about it, which is more than I do.'

'I wasn't always a dried-out old prune. Once I sang and danced, but then the boys died of diphtheria, and John left. I forgot that I had once lived.'

Kate slid into the room. Should she hug this

woman for finally saying what everyone actually knew?

'I am fine, Kate. I am enjoying myself. It is most refreshing.' She paused. 'I liked your mother very much. I think you stopped living, in a way, when she died, and then your dog, and finally Melanie left. All gone.' She nodded.

Kate repeated, 'All gone.' She paused, and the words came in a rush. 'I felt I didn't quite exist, as though I was here, but not. And then it just got worse.' She stopped, saw the clock. 'I need to get back to school.'

She turned on her heel, and the pain caught her again. She reached for the door frame, and waited just for a second, then moved into the hall, breathing carefully. It would take a moment, but all would be well. It's what she told herself a lot of the time, these days.

Mrs B followed her. 'Kate, I don't think you look well, as though something is wrong.'

Kate pulled on her boots, opened the door and stepped onto the porch. She didn't turn, just waved. 'Oh, it's only the cold – it gets into my back.'

She reached the gate, opened it, moved onto the pavement, closed it and looked back. Mrs B stood there.

Kate said, 'The village needs you, Mrs B.'

Mrs B said, 'Thank you, Kate, and just look how we are beginning to need you. Everything will be all right.'

'The show?'

'Everything, Kate.'

As Kate walked back to the school, she knew it

never would be.

Tom Rees had listened to the conversation between Mrs B and Kate from the shadows of the doorway of the snug. He gently eased the door shut and slipped to his desk. He had burned all but the last notebook; this he had locked in the safe. Somehow, some day he would admit to Kate that he knew the truth of the rape, that he had Hastings's words written in black-and-white – well, navy-blue-and-white. He would ask her if she wished him to show the village, or at least her sister. He would ask Kate what she wished to do about Dr Bates: would she like to report him to the police or not? It was such a huge question, with children involved.

She had a right to that decision, though, after all that had happened to her.

He picked up his pen to begin a letter of condolence to Mr Smith the postie, whose son had been drowned on a merchant ship when his convoy had been attacked by U-boats. Later, he would visit them. He paused, staring at his calendar. Where the hell was Sarah Baxter? She was in the FANYs, but she hadn't been home for so long, not even when Derek was officially recognised as dead. She wrote, yes; or so Lizzy said.

Kate had merely shaken her head when he had asked at the rehearsal yesterday evening when Sarah would return to support Lizzy. 'She is doing important work. Had Derek been injured, she would have come.'

He had nodded and asked how she was doing. 'I'm all right, I'm always fine.'

296

But she wasn't; Mrs B was right: Kate looked ill and strained. Was it too much, with the show and Lizzy? Getting back to Sarah, hadn't the woman thought that if Derek died, her daughter might feel injured?

He threw down his pen. He'd go to see Mr and Mrs Smith; what good were scraps of paper when hearts were broken?

Kate left school at the end of the day, carrying about thirty handwritten programmes tied together with string. She walked behind Lizzy and the Billings children who talked among themselves, until they reached the letter box, when they clapped their hands together and did a star-jump. Then, as they walked on, they practised the shuffle, the toe-heel, toe-heel. She joined in, singing 'Anything Goes', swaying as she walked. Other children caught up and added their voices.

Mrs Woolton came to the door of her shop. 'You look like the Pied Piper, Katie Watson.'

Kate grinned and broke off from singing. 'Mum called me Katie.'

'She'd be well proud of you, my dear.'

Kate watched the children, saw where they were in the dance and picked up the song. Another three children ran to catch them up and joined in, the mothers laughing quietly behind. Kate let the children take over, and called over her shoulder to the women, 'Dress rehearsal tonight, plus endless other bits and pieces – even the tango. The vicar will be performing. I know you will have a note from Miss Easton, and there's another on the parish noticeboard, but it's six tonight, five thirty

297

from tomorrow, if you can bear it. Stage designers are working flat-out in the day.'

One of the women, Mrs Edgerson, raised her eyebrows. 'The vicar, you said – that'll be a sight for sore eyes.'

Mrs Williams's eldest daughter, Anthea, shrieked with laughter. 'Not that sort of performing, Mrs Edgerson.'

'That's a shame,' said someone else.

By now the children were humming, and the dancing had ended. Gradually they peeled off to their own homes, Kate calling after the mothers, 'Remember, six o'clock tonight; a lot to do. Bring your costumes. If you haven't yet got yours, don't worry; they will be there tonight.'

Fran's three ran into their garden.

'I'll pick you up at your gate at ten to six,' Kate reminded them.

Lizzy slipped her hand into Kate's. 'I like living with you, Aunt Kate. It's different – fun.' Her face was suddenly alight with energy again.

Kate squeezed her hand. 'I love it too, but it's fun because of the show. Your mum will be back one day, and clearly she is doing something of great importance, which is helping to keep us all safe, so we must be proud, and let her do it.'

They were at their own front door. Inside there were letters on the mat. She collected them up.

'Quick,' said Kate. 'Let's get the kettle on. You will have cocoa, and soup. I will have reused tea leaves, and soup. How about that?'

She added the letters to the programmes that she carried. Her back was aching even more, and no wonder: dancing with her arms full of paper, and a bag slung over her shoulder. She could hear her mother's voice: 'When will you learn to pace yourself, Katie darling.'

Once in the kitchen, warmed by the range, they sat at the table having their snack. As Kate drank the last of the tea she leafed through the letters, discarding the bills to be paid, with money that Sarah had left. She stared at Brucie's handwriting. Good heavens, she had almost forgotten London, and the Blue Cockatoo, and Bruce almighty Turnbull.

'Who's that from?' Lizzy was running her finger round the inside of her mug, then sucking it.

'It's rude to do that with your finger. Do you remember the Blue Cockatoo?'

'"Waste not want not," that's what Mrs Woolton says. And yes, I do. You were so good.'

Kate read the letter, then folded it and replaced it in the envelope. 'He's just writing to see how we are. And don't be cheeky. Mrs Woolton didn't mean that it was all right to forget your manners.'

'But, Aunt Kate, I want every last bit of the cocoa.'

Kate shook her head. '"I want" never gets, but I take your point. Just in wartime then, you may use your finger, but don't ask me how long that will be, because how long is a piece of string?' Lizzy grinned at her. Kate added, 'Hurry, though, because we need to be at the village hall in half an hour to help set it up. Poor Miss Easton and her helpers can't be expected to do everything.'

They collected their tap shoes and chorus costumes. Kate found her maroon tango dress and shoes. She took a selection of programmes and some paper, so that anyone with spare time could copy more. They hurried out into the dark, cold evening, and while Lizzy ran to wait at Fran's gate, Kate thought of Brucie's letter again. The GI's father would be over from New York and wanted to see her perform on 20th December, which was the date of the concert:

Get back here, babe, whatever you think of me. This is your chance, and there won't be another. Mr Oliver is the real deal, straight up, like his son said.

Fran herded her children out of the house and down the path.

Kate switched on her smile. 'Here you are too? You can carry some of the programmes, my girl.'

Fran groaned, and put them on top of the sailor costumes she carried. 'Just finished. Tell me again why on earth are we doing this?' she muttered.

Quite, Kate thought, because what is there for me, when the war is finished and Sarah is back? And why had she made a sort of bargain in her head with someone up there, that staying and making it a successful show would be a way of getting Sarah home safely? It was all too stupid, it was nonsense, but it had somehow taken root, so how could she break it?

They hurried on, through the cold to the village hall, where they found Tom chatting to Mrs Woolton, who was holding a black jacket against him. Fran whispered to Kate, 'All he needed to do was take his dog collar off. His work clothes would be fine.' They laughed together, but then Stella called, 'Come along, ladies. Much to do,

300

and Miss Watson, leader supreme: according to my programme, we have you onstage, leading the chorus, in twenty minutes, complete with costumes. Adrian and Susie are just changing into their sailor suits.'

Kate headed for the small committee room, designated as the girls' changing room. She hung up Lizzy's two costumes. One was a sailor suit and the other a girl's summer dress. She hung up her own dress, and the children gasped. 'You'll look like a princess,' Milly, one of Fran's children, said.

Fran nodded. 'I forget sometimes that you are a real singer. What must you think of us idiots?'

'I think you're the most amazing group of people I've ever worked with.'

Mrs Woolton came in, carrying another pot of kirby grips. '"Amazing" can mean many things, young Kate.' She set about some of the children, sorting out flyaway hair.

Kate was helping Lizzy to change into her sailor suit. 'Indeed, but this time I mean spectacular, talented...'

'Down, girl,' Stella admonished, standing in the doorway. 'Five minutes, gang.'

Kate pinned Lizzy's plaits to the top of her head, settled her round white hat on top and fixed it securely with grips, then joined Mrs Woolton in checking everyone else. Susie Fletcher was in a dress, and didn't tap, but wore low heels and just swayed about a bit, as she put it. Kate called, 'Susie, can you knock up Adrian from the other committee room. We're on, any minute now.'

She could hear the band warming up and

301

winced. They'd miss Mr Smith's saxophone. Susie disappeared, almost bouncing with confidence. Adrian should be wearing striped trousers, a jacket and a boater. Kate snatched a look around the room, as Mrs Woolton joined her, and Kate murmured, 'Is Adrian as he should be?'

'Oh, indeed, in more ways than one; sometimes death is of benefit, don't you think?' She swept out.

Kate lined the children up, waiting for Stella's gong, which she had taken to whacking with great gusto. Kate wondered if it was some sort of 'missing my Bradley' therapy. The music was playing, if you could call it that. Somehow the spoons and combs were out of sync, the recorders squeaky, though the drums were true, thanks to percussionist Ben Woodhouse, aged fourteen, of Star Cottage. Mrs B was banging out the tune on the piano, probably in an effort to drown the rest, but if she went on like that she'd break her fingers. Kate smiled at the children, and at Susie and Adrian.

'Whatever goes right, or wrong, smile and focus ahead.' She led them on, and they milled about as Susie and Adrian started to sing 'Anything Goes', then the children found their marks and formed two rows, chatting silently amongst one another, just as they should. At the crash of the cymbals they galvanised themselves. Kate forced herself to smile in spite of the pain in her back, and to relax, to start moving her feet, toe-heel, toe-heel. The children were with her. Here came the shuffle – it was immaculate. Everyone in the hall was watching, and the mums were in tears as their children outperformed Kate, who then melted into the wings, watching, hardly daring to breathe.

'Swing those arms,' she murmured. 'Now the star... That's it, you've nailed it, you've damned well got it.'

Tom's voice sounded just behind Kate as he came to stand close, his arm pressing against hers. 'Indeed they have. Will we? I haven't really practised – well, not with you; all you've done is stand in front and shout at me, and Adrian, when we get it wrong.'

She murmured, 'Feast your eyes. This is what makes it all worthwhile. Just look, all angels for a few moments.'

She longed to sit down to ease her back, but instead she must remain visible to her charges. Each day her back seemed to grow worse, but then each day the weather was colder. It couldn't be anything to do with her dancing, because her back was essential for the production, and for her future. She thought again of Brucie's letter; would she never really get another big chance? What's more, a job would take her across the Atlantic, so that when Sarah returned, she wouldn't have to experience exclusion again. But what about this show, these children and, damn it, perhaps even Sarah's safety? A brain was a funny thing. Why did it work in deals, and bargains, which were anyway just a trick of the imagination.

The children finished, counted to three and bowed. The hall erupted in cheers and applause. She gestured that they bow again and beckoned them off, leaving Susie and Adrian to take their bow. The children clattered past, looking to Kate

303

for her response. 'Bravo,' she said to each one. 'Bravo – so good, so wonderful.' Lizzy passed. Kate pulled her back and hugged her 'Wonderful, so good; your mother will be proud. Don't worry, I will write it all down and we can send the letter.'

Lizzy ran on, tapping her way along the corridor.

Kate turned to Tom, 'Now, our turn to get changed and–' She stopped. 'What's wrong? You look so sad.'

It was as though he woke from somewhere else, because he stared at her. 'You are a remarkable woman, a remarkable aunt.' He turned and walked into the hall.

She called after him. 'Quick change, young vicar. Flattery gets you absolutely nowhere.'

But it did; it helped. No-one had ever called her remarkable in quite that way.

She hurried to Mrs B and the band. 'Mrs B, shall we just manage "Jealousy" with you and the drums? Or, members of the band, would you like to give it a bash?'

The band did not want this, in any way, shape or form. 'We're just about perfect on "Anything Goes",' explained Arthur, the comb player, 'but need more practice for the others.'

Mrs B stared at him, her face impassive. Kate could see her thinking, Perfect? I beg your pardon? Once Mrs B would have said it, but not now; instead the housekeeper suggested that the band might like to go into the kitchen and have another run-through, starting with the one they felt most confident about and moving on through the others. They trooped off.

Mrs B whispered to Kate, 'It's chaos without Mr Smith and his saxophone, poor man. What on earth are we to do?'

Kate shook her head, leaning on the piano and trying to find a more comfortable position, arching her back, knowing immediately it was not a good idea.

Mrs B said, 'Kate, what is it?'

'Just a twinge, nothing to worry about. Now, about the band, we can't possibly get rid of even one of them; they have no idea how bad they are, and we can't upset them. They have improved, a bit.' The two women looked at one another, and neither needed to say that they couldn't have become any worse. Kate smiled; who would have thought Mrs B and she would ever reach a point where they could read one another's minds. 'We have three more weeks, almost, and I will just have to factor in some time for them. But I'm not a musician, that's the problem. However, don't worry, I'll sort something.'

Mrs B smiled. 'I know you will, and I'll think around the subject as well. Now, off you go and change, and I'll brush up on "Jealousy".'

Adrian and Susie were now onstage in their costumes and practising the tango promenade.

Kate walked carefully to the dressing room, which was, to her relief, empty. She slipped from her clothes and eased her back, before forcing herself upright. The door opened and Stella popped her head in and called, 'One minute, Kat–' She stopped. 'Oh, Kate, I didn't know.'

Kate had been about to step into her maroon dress, and continued to do so, saying just, 'I was an ARP warden, in the Blitz. Bombs were dropping, one whacked me, and a burning beam had the cheek to fall while I was in the way. There may have also been some shrapnel involved – a real wartime injury. It's fine, not a problem.'

Stella came and zipped her up. She said nothing, just turned Kate around and kissed her cheek. 'You are very fine, Kate Watson, very fine indeed.' Her lips were trembling.

'Don't cry,' Kate whispered. 'Please don't, because sometimes it hurts a bit, and that would just make it worse.'

Stella nodded, swallowing back her tears. 'Thirty seconds, madam.' She left.

Kate ran her hands down her dress, looking in the mirror. She was too pale, and her face was drawn in pain. She must smile. She did and found some lipstick in her handbag. She dug around and found powder. There, that was better.

She put on her high heels and walked out onto the stage, her back straight. Mrs B was warming up; Susie and Adrian were taking a long step, starting the promenade, hips to hips, she in her blue dress, he in his close-fitting jacket and trousers, his bow tie neatly tied. Tom was nowhere to be seen, but Kate could hear someone running up the steps on the far side of the stage. He arrived, his bow tie in his hand, looking frantic. He saw her and waved the bow tie, then stopped, his mouth open. 'Good heavens, you look wonderful, Kate.'

She walked towards him, laughing. 'Don't sound so surprised. Give me that, and let's sort you out.' While Tom stood before her, chin up, she tied the bow, finally pulling it straight. 'Very smart. Mrs Woolton's done a grand job with the suit.'

'It was Mr Woolton's, which she's taken in. She told me he died in it, after a good night out.'

'There's really nothing I can add to that,' Kate murmured, after the drum roll sounded loud and clear. 'Now, young man, let's see what you're made of.'

He took her in his arms.

She said, 'The tango is one of the most graceful dances known to man, so remember that it is deliberate and slow, majestic but passionate. Also remember that the stage is quite small, so we must accommodate the other couple. In other words, no barging, laddie.'

'Oh, bugger,' he groaned. 'You make it sound so difficult. I learned it before I joined the army, and just did it. I doubt I was graceful, majestic or passionate.'

'That's a penny for the swear box, naughty man of God.'

He realised what he'd said, but now Mrs B was into the introduction, with Ben, the young drummer, in accord. Kate glanced across at Susie, who winked, and at Adrian, who mouthed, 'We've been practising.'

They were all off and, to Kate's surprise, Tom's arms were strong and he led her in the closed promenade. She smiled, relaxing, at one with his body, because this was a dance she loved, a dance of love. He led her to the beat, gliding and striding, interweaving with Susie and Adrian, his head closer than it should be, his eyes on hers when they shouldn't be, and she should break away,

307

but couldn't, as he swept her into a fall-away whisk, but somehow he did it gently and the pain didn't overwhelm her. He guided her backwards, then into the break, and feet crossed into the turn, side-by-side, on and on, and then into the fall-away whisk again, but this time the pain sliced through her like a knife, so deep and hard that it took her breath, her strength.

She sagged, the darkness came and the agony endured. Tom pulled her to him, 'Kate, Kate...'

She heard a scream. Was it her? The music stopped.

Feet were pounding. He lowered her to the floor. 'Get an ambulance,' he yelled. Mrs B was by her side, patting her hand. 'Kate, dear. Kate, tell us where it hurts.'

Now Stella was here, holding her other hand. 'It must be her back. I've just seen it.'

Tom said, 'Lie still; whatever you do, don't move. If it's your back, don't move.'

Stella said, 'It's so badly burnt, and she said it hurt. I should have done something, but it's such a scar. I didn't realise it could hurt like this.' Then she was gone.

Kate heard them all, saw them all as though through a mist of agony. The hall was very quiet. Why? They needed to rehearse. She forced her eyes open. 'Get me off the stage, they need to use it – help me.'

It was Tom beside her, looking down at her, his face pale. 'Look at me, stay awake, Kate. Don't move,' he murmured.

She said, 'I must.'

He took her hand and held it to his mouth,

308

'You must not.' He kissed it. The vicar was kissing her hand, and now he was stroking her hair. Mrs B still held her other hand, shouting, 'Where is that damned doctor?'

Kate snatched her hand away and struggled to rise, but Tom held her shoulders. 'Keep still, there's something wrong.'

'No doctor,' she almost screamed.

Tom bent over Kate, holding her face firmly, saying quietly just to her, 'Listen to me, Katie Watson. I know the truth about Dr Bates. I know, do you understand? I read about it in a notebook the Reverend Hastings left for me. He discovered the truth, but died the same night. Dr Bates is a vile man, who raped you. No-one believed you, and I took my time to do so, but I finally got there. Can you hear me? It is written in black-and-white. Well, blue-and-white. Katie, listen to me, I believe you. You told the truth, you always do, but I was too stupid to realise.'

Her body was so hot, the pain so intense that it was drowning out his words, which came and went, but what she heard as she surfaced once more was, 'You must understand that I believe you. You told the truth, the Bishop knows, Reverend Hastings knew. Your father didn't, Sarah didn't, but Bates was clever. He created an alibi. He has done it to others. When you are better, you will decide what you want to do, but now you are going to hospital.'

Mrs B had reclaimed her hand, and gripped it. 'Oh Kate, I'm so sorry, just so sorry. I will go with you.'

Tom still held Kate's face and looked at her,

309

while his words were for Mrs B. 'I will go, Mrs B, and I will stay until they chase me away. Perhaps you will look after Lizzy. Please take her to the vicarage, so that I can telephone you there with any news. And this is between ourselves.'

'Indeed.'

There was a clattering of feet and Stella's voice calling. 'They're here. The ambulance is here. Everyone stand to one side, and soon we will continue.'

Kate smiled. 'The show must go on,' she murmured.

A stranger loomed over her. He had a stethoscope, like Dr Bates, but Tom said he believed her and would stay with her; had he said for ever? She hoped so. She gripped Mrs B's hand and held onto Tom's lapel with the other hand. She felt him loosening her fingers, one by one. She closed her eyes, then murmured, 'You see, I can't sleep in my bedroom because the ceiling is stained. It's what I watched while he was doing it.'

Then there was nothing, just darkness.

Mrs B and Tom walked on either side of the stretcher to the ambulance. It flashed no lights, of course. Tom climbed in, though the elderly doctor demurred. Tom looked at him. 'You'll have to throw me out. Don't be fooled by the bow tie and dancing shoes. I was at Dunkirk and can be as ugly as my face.'

The doctor nodded. 'Miss Easton gave me her background: a bomb blast, then a falling beam. Could be shrapnel that's moved, but I'd have expected the doctor at the hospital to sort that

310

out when it happened.'

Tom looked at him, his face deadpan, but his voice filled with fury. 'She was raped by her doctor when she was fifteen. She doesn't like you lot, so I expect she wouldn't stay. You'd better do a bloody good job, and I will be there to make sure you do.'

The doctor busied himself checking her pulse.

At the hospital a nursing sister asked if Tom was next of kin. 'I'm her spiritual advisor, the Reverend Tom Rees. I usually wear a dog collar, and this tango outfit belies a man of considerable strength and difficult disposition. Her present next of kin is at war, so I'm coming through with her. I promised, you see.' The sister – Sister Newsome, if her badge was correct – did see. It was in his face, and voice.

Tom watched in the emergency room as they turned Kate over, very carefully, and cut off her dress. He, like they, fell silent at the sight of her monstrous scarring. He now understood why she had touched his own scar and shown such humanity.

A young nurse muttered, 'Who will want this poor woman now?'

'I do, and always will,' Tom said.

She looked up at him, and his scar.

He said, 'We're still the people we once were, but wiser and kinder, perhaps, than you.'

Sister Newsome said in no uncertain terms, 'Out, until you can grow up, Nurse. Send in Staff Nurse Formby, if you will, who is far more suited to the task.' The nurse flounced out. Sister Newsome demanded, 'You too, Vicar.'

311

Tom went, saying, 'I am just outside, and listening.'

After half an hour the chair felt extraordinarily hard, and he heard Mrs B's voice in reception. 'I will not be told where to sit. I need to be with the vicar.' She swept into the corridor and sat with him, her handbag on her lap.

Tom said, 'I thought you were with Lizzy?'

'They are continuing the rehearsal – it's what Kate would want. I am to return with news, and not before. A note will be left, with information of who I am to telephone first. Lizzy will be taken to Mrs Billings's and will share the bedroom with Sandra, who is of a similar age, and they will support one another. I have brought us a sandwich each.'

She dug in her handbag for a package wrapped in greaseproof paper. It contained sandwiches filled with precious ham; was it from the vicarage ration, or from the back shelf at the butcher's? Who cared? Tom realised he was ravenous. Mrs B ate too.

The doctor popped his head round the door. 'We're off to theatre. She is stabilised and we'll have a ferret about, see what we can find.'

Mrs B stared at the closing door. 'Did my ears deceive me, or did he say ferret? Is this what the world is coming to?'

Tom patted her knee. She glared. He removed his hand swiftly. He said, 'He's a good doctor, I think. He allowed a harridan of a sister to sort out a young flibbertigibbet of a nurse. Now we wait.'

They did, for two hours; Mrs B sat upright the

312

whole time and only spoke once. 'I remember sitting somewhere like this when my little boys were brought in, so ill. I am not allowing anyone else I am fond of to die, Vicar, especially after her dreadful experience, so you'd better get some prayers said, d'you hear? Our Kate is due some fairness. I knew about her accusation, you see. I didn't believe her then, but clearly I was wrong. I think I had begun to realise that, because this young woman tells it like it is – or that is how a young American put it, in Taunton when I was there one day. It does us all good, you know, to hear Kate. It reminds me of her mother. So now get on and pray.'

Tom did, and he just hoped his God would listen.

At two in the morning Mrs B arrived at the vicarage by taxi. She let herself in. There was a note through the door from Mrs Woolton:

Phone me with your news, whatever time it is. I have set up the 'snow-line' we normally use for the WI to get the word round by telephone if we are snowed off. First stop this time will be Mrs Billings, so Lizzy knows the news, good or bad. She will then telephone the next on the list.

Mrs B immediately lifted the telephone.

'What number do you wish to call?' Sally at the telephone exchange asked, mid-yawn.

'Mrs Woolton, Sally. One-four-five, please.'

'And the news?'

'Shrapnel had moved and was fidgeting about

313

near Kate's spinal cord, or so the surgeon said. She is lucky. They have removed two pieces, stitched her up and tidied up some of her scarring.'

'I heard about that too. Poor wee thing.'

'Indeed. Poor wee thing.'

Mrs B held herself in check, and when Mrs Woolton answered on the first ring, she told her the news. Mrs Woolton said, 'Thanks be to God.'

Mrs B said, 'Don't forget a bloody good surgeon. Let the next in the snow-line know, if you would.' She slammed the receiver down. She seldom swore, but sometimes she needed to, because there was no rhyme or reason to life, she realised. Some lived, some died; it was how you went forward afterwards that mattered. Perhaps young Kate would find that she could begin to feel she actually existed, now that at least two people knew the truth. What's more, one of those was the young man who loved her, because Tom Rees most certainly did. Whether the boy knew it or not was another matter. Sometimes men were so slow.

As she removed her hat and gloves, she found, to her surprise, that she was crying. She moved through into the vicar's sitting room and sobbed for her children, and for the life she had subsequently lived, until Kate had reminded her that the children deserved more than grief as their epitaph. She slept in the chair that she had used to knit in of an evening, while the Reverend Hastings wrote his diary, neither of them requiring anything further of one another. It was one way to live, she supposed, but she was only fifty-seven and wanted more from now on.

Chapter Twenty

Sarah sat shivering on the stone floor, her chest wheezing and aching. She had been left for ... well, they had taken her watch, so she didn't know how long. Hours or days? Two guards had led her here, politely. The door had clanged shut behind her. There had been no food or water since then; no anything, in fact. She had peed in the corner. She heard comings and goings. She laid her head on her knees and dozed. She woke to someone tapping on a pipe. It was Morse code.

I am Paul, the taps spelled out. She didn't reply, for it could be a plant.

I am Cécile, Sarah said to herself, repeating her cover story, again and again. She dozed, then woke for a while, staring into the darkness, coughing, shivering, burning. She pretended she was still training and that she was safe.

Finally, boots clanged along the stone corridor. They passed. A cell door opened. Someone shouted, 'Get off me.' He was British. Was he Paul?

She called in French, 'Give them hell.'

He laughed, then grunted. There was the sound of more blows, of retching, then silence for a moment. After a beat or two of her heart, the boots clumped back along the passage, dragging someone between them.

She yelled, 'Someone cares, someone knows

315

you're here.' Her voice was cracked and hoarse, her throat dry and sore.

There was a thud against her door. 'Shut up,' in German. 'We'll be back for you, do not worry.'

She dug her fingers into her forehead. In French she said, 'I don't understand.' She did understand German, but every secret meant a vestige of power retained.

The darkness was a cloak. She dozed. The clumping of boots woke her. She stopped breathing, the wheezing ceased. Nearer, nearer. They passed. She drew in a deep breath and coughed. A door opened and then slammed shut. She waited. Nearer, nearer. They passed. She breathed again, coughing, again and again.

The taps came. 'I am still Paul.'

'Yes, you are,' she tapped.

She still didn't say who she was, because she trusted no-one. I will remember my training, she mouthed. Again she dozed, almost numb with cold, and parched, and now she saw shapes in the darkness.

Looming.

Moving.

She shrank into the corner. She tapped on the pipe. 'It is less than a month to Christmas, or it was when I was captured.'

'Thank you. Hard to know how long here, in the basement.'

'Yes.'

She didn't want to know how many days or weeks he had been here. There were no more taps.

She dozed, her head bursting, her chest rattling.

316

The shapes returned, coming closer, then receding. Closer, then receding. Were they real? But no, they were floating. She needed to drink. She tried not to pee, because she must retain liquid. She moved to the far corner. Peed. Returned, feeling her way around the damp, freezing walls. There was no sound for what seemed like hours. The boots came again, nearer, nearer. They stopped. Was it at her door?

There was a clanking. Dim light fell into the cell. She squinted, hiding her eyes with her hand. Then a shape loomed, a real shape. She laughed. It was a strange sound. Then a second shape. She said, in French, 'Good, you're real – just men.'

They said nothing. Simply walked her from the cell, almost like gentlemen. Almost, but their grip was savage. Sarah walked in bare feet. They had taken her shoes from her when she was processed. She was so cold that her feet were numb. They marched along the corridor, and their boots should be striking sparks on the stone, so violently did they slam them down. She could barely keep up.

They took the basement steps two at a time. She stubbed her toe, but her numb feet felt nothing. She was panting, her head was bursting, her chest rattling; she was coughing and she couldn't put her hand in front of her mouth. How rude, they'd catch her germs. Good. Very good. She coughed again.

Another guard stood at the top of the stairs and was doing what guards do: standing firm in front of a heavy metal door, his legs wide, his arms folded, his rifle slung over his shoulder.

'So this is the bitch who missed Gerhardt? Silly bugger tripped, so make sure you tell her or she'll think she's a good shot.'

Sarah didn't react. She was Cécile and knew no German, or English.

'Open the door, and shut your mouth,' one of her guardians grunted.

'Yes, Sergeant.' The guard stood to attention, drawing back the bolt on the door.

The sergeant said, 'Check cell four. He'll be dead by now. Cracked skull. He should have answered the questions with a civil tongue.'

Was this for her benefit? Again Sarah didn't react. She was marched along the corridor. She looked down. Her stubbed toe was smearing blood on the flagstones. Good, something for them to clean up. She still felt nothing. Her feet were white. Her mother would not put red and white flowers in the same vase. Blood and bandages. Death.

No. She was Cécile. Her mother lived in Limoges and would not, perhaps, have said that.

When the feeling returned to her feet, the pain would begin, but pain didn't kill.

Sarah walked as though she had a pile of books on her head, as their mother had said. That had got Kate laughing as they tried it, but Kate was always laughing, her blonde hair flicking, her eyes blue like their mother's, alive with such energy. Her father had come in and they'd stopped. Had they been frightened of him? Or was it just that it was a rule not to laugh, not to disturb, not to make waves? Had it, been her own rule with Lizzy? Was she her father in disguise? Was it

318

someone she really wanted to be? No, she was Cécile, from Limoges.

It grew lighter as they climbed yet more stairs, and this time the door was unguarded. 'Open it,' the sergeant instructed the private. She thought they were Wehrmacht, but wasn't sure because her brain wouldn't work; it was crackling with dehydration, not fear. Of course not fear.

The light was bright in this corridor, streaming in through large barred windows. They continued, clump-clump. Where were the sparks from their boots? Kate could have made a song of it. Go on, Katie Watson, make a song. Once upon a time Sarah had danced when Katie sang. When had it stopped? Ah, when her father didn't like it, but it hadn't stopped Katherine, Kate, Katie, lovely Katie. Yes, she used to call her that, but her father didn't like it, after her mother died.

Was it because her little sister was too like her mother? Did it remind him of her? Did he have to squash it out of lovely Katie, the part of her that was full of joy? Is that what she, Sarah, had done too? Is it what she was doing to her lovely daughter?

Her legs were tired now. Sarah just wanted to sag and let them carry her. Why not indeed? Why not? Because she was Cécile from Limoges and she didn't know Katie, or Kate, or Elizabeth or Lizzy. She pictured the map, the streets, the house where she had lived, the canary she had kept in a cage in the hamlet near Limoges. You had to put a cover over it, to stop it singing, and clean it out every few days. How many days? Three? She couldn't remember. And the butcher's in...

They stopped outside a door, a white door; no, a cream door. The sergeant knocked. 'Enter,' the man inside said in French.

They entered. An officer – was he Wehrmacht too perhaps? Were any of them? She couldn't think. He sat at a desk, his back to a barred window. The light shone in, too bright. Which way did the window face: south, north? She didn't know, so how could she work out the sun's position and therefore the time, if she was to escape? Was that snow on the roof opposite? He sat back, looking at her as she stood between the guards. Chin up, she told herself. Balance books. She smiled.

Surprised, he returned the smile and gestured to the chair on Sarah's side of the desk. 'Please, Mademoiselle.'

She sat, balancing the books on her head. Coffee steamed in a silver pot on a tray. There were two cups. If offered one, she would accept, though she should spit in it. She'd prefer water, as coffee was dehydrating, but she loved it, as long as it was real. She saw her reflection in the pot; it made her look like a gargoyle, but that was because it was a curved surface. She actually looked like a queen: upright, balanced. No books wobbled. She sat even straighter.

He looked at the tray. 'Would you care for a cup?'

She nodded. He waved his hand towards the coffee pot. 'Perhaps you would pour me one too.'

She reached out and poured. Her hand was shaking, but not through fear, just cold, that was all. She felt the guards move closer, and coughed. Were they about to knock it from her hand, scald

320

her? She didn't flinch, but passed a cup to the major, her shaking hand causing it to spill into the saucer. She placed it on the pristine blotting pad in front of him, then handed him a serviette that was folded on the tray. 'I'm sorry, I'm a little cold and therefore shivering. You might like to place your cup on the serviette to absorb the coffee, or it will drip on your uniform.' She sat back, the books still there. She stayed quite still.

He nodded, reaching for the serviette. His uniform sleeve rode up. She read the time: three o'clock, but which day?

She also took a serviette and placed it on her lap, lifted her own cup and drank. It was real coffee, and not too hot. It wouldn't burn, if knocked from her. She downed it almost in one and poured herself another. The major watched, smiling. 'Ah, we have a coffee lover. Yes, I hear that coffee is in short supply in England.'

Sarah shrugged. 'I do not know, I am Cécile Lamont, and have no idea why I am here.'

He took a cigarette from a silver box on his desk and lit it, smiling through the smoke. 'Oh, both you and I know why. You fired at one of my soldiers, and missed. You were not well trained.'

Ah, but Sarah was, and would remember every lesson.

He said, 'We need to chat until we reach the truth, Cécile Lamont, or, sadly, my men will have to take you across the road to our less respectful comrades.'

Sarah knew he meant the Gestapo. She shrugged again. 'Ah, the truth? You clearly do not recognise it when you hear it, Herr Major. I am Cécile

Lamont, from Limoges, and was frightened by your men, so I defended myself.'

'With a forbidden revolver.'

'Well, a girl out on her own is increasingly in peril, it seems.' Would she be here if she hadn't used her revolver? But if she hadn't caused a diversion, the other two might also have been caught. Do the arithmetic, that's what her father had always said.

He smiled again, sipping his coffee. He stared from one guard to the other, turned slightly to look out of the window. She checked his rotational silver calendar. It was 2nd December. He turned and slammed his cup down into the saucer, shattering both, then leaning across and striking the cup from Sarah's hand. She had been expecting it, and just stared at him as the cup, half full of coffee, hit the sergeant.

'Oh dear,' she said. 'That means another cleaning bill. Not the first, I suspect. I am Cécile Lamont, from Limoges.'

'Where in Limoges?'

Sarah told him, describing the hamlet, the shop next to their small house, and the canary, knowing it all existed and had been lived in by Cécile's family, now all dead, the house empty. 'I cleaned it out every three days. Was that right? What would you have done?'

The major nodded. The sergeant moved and dragged her head back by her hair. He spat in her face and released her.

Sarah used the serviette to wipe her face. 'Dear, dear,' she said. 'Perhaps you haven't a canary.'

There was another nod from the major. She

322

braced herself, but all that happened was that the guards gripped her beneath the armpits, lifted her to her feet and marched her from the room. There was blood on the floorboards from her toe. They marched her back to her cell and flung her in, but they had forgotten to take the serviette from her, so she sat on it. It gave a modest warmth, but it was a huge victory. This was only the first skirmish in the battle, though.

The next day they did not drink coffee. Later, she was dragged back to her cell, and Sarah reminded herself that pain could not kill her, as the throbbing of her ribs, and her jaw, and her head, where a clump of hair had been yanked out, threatened to make her groan aloud.

Sarah tapped, 'I am Cécile.' There was no answer, and loneliness almost drowned her.

Day followed day, and then she was dragged across the cobbled courtyard to the Gestapo, still without shoes. They interrogated her in a damp underground room, dimly lit. They showed her maps, wanted her to pinpoint where and who the members of the groups in her circuit were. 'Their container dumps, their dropping zones.'

'I am Cécile, from Limoges. I don't know what you mean.'

They shone the lamp into her eyes, like a spotlight. The tune 'Jealousy' began to play in her head and Kate danced, just for her. Sarah watched the fall and swing of her sister's beautiful blonde hair, her wonderful face, which shone with a sort of joy, but not as it had been when she was a child, not nearly, for it cloaked a sort of nothingness. She looked harder now. Yes, she could see that inside there was nothing. What did that mean?

On the fourth day the Gestapo had finished with her toes and started on her fingers. After an hour a guard held her hand, with its bleeding fingertips, out over the map. 'Show me, tell me.'

Sarah wouldn't. 'I am Cécile...'

His fist swung and 'Jealousy' played again: the saxophone, the bass, the piano, and Kate's voice, her dance, her partner. Was it Derek? No, of course not, he was missing; he was why she'd come, once upon a time, but... No, it was not Derek Baxter of Little Worthy; it was a young, young soldier. Sarah had watched him dance the tango with Kate in the Blue Cockatoo, harmonising the dance to the music. Did the young man still live? Please let him, so he could dance again.

On the fifth, sixth or was it the hundredth day, she wished her body was still numb because she was wrong: pain was more than just pain, it was something that coiled, smothered and must surely kill, and she could no longer lift her head and had long ago let the books drop. Again, she was dragged across the road after a night spent in the cell, feeling at one moment the cold of the floor, the burning heat of her body, the pain, and spinning with Kate in the spotlight while people threw white and red roses.

It was a different interrogator, a big man with stubble. He oozed even more hate than the others, and it burst from him, like a raging animal. 'You lie,' he roared.

'I am Cécile from Limoges.'

He slapped her with his great hairy hand. 'You

324

lie. You wouldn't know the truth if it stared at you.'

Suddenly Sarah was at Little Worthy. These hands and contorted face were her father's, and these words too. Kate's head had rocked back, as hers did. This man, this Gestapo slime, knew – just as all these men had – that she, Cécile Lamont, was lying. But now she saw Kate so clearly, and she wasn't lying. Kate didn't lie, ever. She never had. She had always braced her shoulders, held her head high and told the truth, just as her mother had always insisted.

'Oh, Kate,' Sarah whispered. 'Oh, my dearest lonely Katie, who missed our mother, what have we done to you?' For it was then, at that very moment, that her sister's nothingness had begun.

'What? What did you say?' The man behind came to her side. She didn't feel anything because she was not here; she was in Little Worthy, watching the hate and anger that had beaten against Kate. Through bruised, half-closed eyes Sarah looked up at the interrogator and round at the guards. Since she had been captured she had been amongst enemies, people who had no respect, people who thought the worst of her. Poor Kate had lived for years like this.

The man was busy, his great hands bunched, but she felt nothing, because she was thinking of Kate, who had re-entered a world that thought her wanton, where respect lay dormant and contempt reigned. Why? Because a child born of rape had need of her.

She gritted her teeth. 'Bastards,' she muttered. 'You all are utter slime. You are...' The map was held up. She shook her head.

Later, with a nod of the head, she was taken away. Was it over? Would she be killed? At least Derek might come home; at least Kate would look after Lizzy, teach her to dance, to sing, to laugh, to live. It was more than she had done, so determined was she to destroy the gypsy in the child, the wildness, lest Lizzy became as Kate had been.

She was flung in her cell. She lay there and, for some strange reason, she slept, and the pain flowed from her. It returned when the guards came for her yet again. She thought she couldn't bear it, but she must, for as long as she could. Bernard would suspect that she had been taken; he would know she wouldn't withstand too much, and would have enacted plans to disperse the group. But always it had been stressed that they must hold out for as long as possible.

She was taken to yet somewhere else, a light, warm office. A Gestapo officer in a grey-green uniform sat behind the desk. How strange. Previously they had been in civilian suits. He smiled; again, how strange.

'Ah,' he said 'I am Major Fischer, and for you, Cécile Lamont, we have welcome news about Derek.' Sarah stared. Derek?

'Ah, my dear Cécile, I will call you that, because you prefer it to your English name, but we have discovered that your Derek is in a Stalag. And I think, don't you, that it would be good to save your husband's life?'

Derek? Her mind played with his name, much as her tongue played with the cuts in her mouth and the broken tooth. Somehow one couldn't get

326

away from something in the mouth. Her toes, her fingers, everything else – well, somehow they weren't as bad. For some moments the major talked about Derek, how he was thin but well, how he sent his love.

'You could save him so much pain before his death. You could, in fact, save his life completely, and be with him. We would sort out accommodation until the war's end, after which Britain will be under German occupation. We would need something in return of course. You know what.'

She stared. Derek? She tried to see his face. He was thin? There were his brown eyes, his mouth. How did he look, now that he was thin? She couldn't think, couldn't remember; nothing would stand still, or stay in her head.

One of the guards gave her a glass of water. She held it with two hands and gulped it down, before it could be slapped from her. It wasn't. She replaced the glass on the desk. Her hands shook so much it tumbled over. Her raw nail-less fingers left blood trails on the desk.

She had come to save Derek. Now she could, and yes, she knew how. She would have to turn; glean information so that the Gestapo could haul in the whole circuit, and take over the transmitters to lodge misinformation, catching more agents as they arrived. But no, how could she? Yes ... no. Her mouth was dry, her chest hurt, everything hurt. She couldn't think.

He talked details. She tried to listen. She tried to think. She argued with herself. Derek? He was alive? It wasn't real. Nothing was real. She could hear her chest, feel the pain of her ribs, her cut lip, her black eye. Was her nose broken? Her ribs, her toes, her fingers... Her thoughts came and went. Derek? She couldn't see him. She saw Katie dancing, and heard 'Jealousy' playing. She saw Lizzy skipping with Derek. She smiled. Once she had lived in that world. Her lip bled. She licked it.

Derek? How could she let him die, when she had come to save him? But how could she kill Bernard? What about Pierre, Florian, Renée and all the others? They would be compromised, perhaps captured, certainly killed.

In her cell that night Sarah thought about so much. Bernard and Derek. Derek and Bernard. Pierre, Arnaud, Florian, Renée, all of them. She told the major the next morning that she had made no decision. He returned her to her cell, without further hurt, but as he left he said, 'Derek is not well. He has been hungry for so long. I advise you to save him quickly or it will be not at all, for he will not live.'

Sarah shook her head. 'How can I work with you? It is without honour.' The next morning she was taken to another room, with a comfortable chair, even a camp bed on which she lay. For the rest of the day they fed her plain food that her stomach would accept, and water, lots of it. They gave her medicine for her cough, and cup after cup of coffee. They explained their needs again, and talked of Derek's failing health. Her mind was too tired, it couldn't think; but overnight, back in her cell, it began to work.

The next day Sarah spoke to the guards. Her shoes were brought and placed inside the cell door. She forced the shoes on and walked unaided, the guards keeping pace, but not man-handling her. She crossed the courtyard and climbed the stairs, holding on to her thoughts this time.

The guards took her to the same office. The same Major Fischer was there. He poured coffee for her, and passed a plate heaped with biscuits.

Sarah drank her coffee and ate two biscuits while he watched and waited. At last she said, 'I need proof that my Derek – Derek Smith – really lives. If you give me that, then you will realise, because you have done it before, that I can't just walk out of here, for the others would suspect. I will need to escape, perhaps from a moving vehicle. Perhaps it could crash not too far from Rouen? So I can contact my group and resume my place, and find out about others. Family is all, I think you would agree.'

Major Fischer peaked his hands, nodding. 'Indeed, I would expect your conditions.'

Sarah was led away. She returned again the next morning. When she entered, the major gestured to the usual chair, reached into a drawer and with-drew a form. He passed it to her. She drew in a deep breath. The form gave a prisoner number and the name 'Derek Smith'. She nodded to her-self, her mind quite clear now. They did not have her Derek Baxter – her trick had worked. Items had been ticked on the form. Health: tick. Well-being: tick. Wife: tick. Capture: Tours. Crimes: none.

She folded it. 'I may keep this? It is all I have of him.'

The major hesitated. 'If you agree to work with

329

us, then it will not be all you have, for he will be returned to you in due course.'

She said, gripping the paper, 'I will work with you, if you bring him here now, and thereafter send me proof that he lives. Each day you must do that.'

He countered, 'You are in no position to bargain.' But she could tell from his eyes that it was what he expected. The tension built. He said, 'Deliver your first piece of information to the drop station, and then we will repay you with proof. Not before. He will be safe, but only until then.'

She nodded.

He went on, his eyes sharp, 'Had you been happy just to accept, I would have known that I could not trust you. You are to be our person on the inside. It will pain you, but it would be worse to be the cause of your husband's death. You have to learn to trust me, as our arrangement must be long-lasting. I repeat, trust me.'

Trust me, I'm a doctor, like Dr Bates, she almost said. She had thought about how all this could be done, sitting in the cell, her mind at long last crystal-clear, staring into the darkness. Lives were at stake, and she must get this right.

'I will,' she assured him. 'But I am not Mrs Smith, I am Cécile Lamont, and I repeat: we must create an escape for it to be realistic. If you follow me, be cautious, but there really is no need, because I can't be responsible for killing my husband. Who could?'

'So Madame Lamont, we must proceed without delay,' Major Fischer ordered. His eyes were without hate. Instead she could see satisfaction, and contempt.

Later that morning Sarah remained in her filthy clothes, but was given back her coat and woollen gloves. They drove hell-for-leather towards the outskirts of Rouen in a black saloon. Would Bernard attempt a rescue? After all, the traitor in the group could be telling him of her transfer, putting it down to 'intelligence'. But no, that same traitor would want the Germans' plan to work so would say nothing.

Ah yes, the traitor, for there must be one, or how else could they know about Derek? But the traitor didn't know her husband's surname. She closed her eyes briefly, relieved that she had not mentioned that detail to Pierre as they stood that day in the woods.

Pierre it was, and he must be stopped; Pierre, who must have alerted the Germans to the drop, after which she had been captured. Pierre, whose use to the Germans was limited because he did not know anything about the other circuits. She did, though, or could find out through Bernard. How clever it all was.

She braced herself as they approached the junction and the driver called, 'Prepare.' The expected truck came from a side road. Her driver stood on the brakes, skidded, careered into the corner of the house, spun round. The doors fell open and the guards half fell out, as though stunned. The officer in the passenger seat turned. 'Remember, your husband dies, the moment you fail to do as we tell you.'

Sarah clambered over the guards, as heads

peered from house windows. She ran like the wind, tearing back towards Rouen, taking the lesser roads, slipping into doorways, checking for shadows. There seemed to be none, but there probably were, because they knew they had not actually got Derek as a hostage. However, they thought she believed them, so they could be letting her run free. It didn't matter either way; she would be careful.

At last she reached the default drop box, the one she was to use if ever she was in trouble; the one no-one else knew about; the one she and Bernard had set up. She had written her note, in a code that Bernard had created for just this sort of emergency. Even if it killed her, she must protect the rest of the circuit by revealing the true situation to Bernard. She would hide in a place that only she knew; If she was being watched, it was what they would expect.

She received his reply the next day, at the second drop they had set up. She stole a bicycle and set off, cycling out of Rouen to meet Bernard and the remains of the group at the dropping zone. Her feet hurt, her bruises were still obvious, not to mention her swollen split lip. People looked at her strangely. She said to a fellow cyclist at a crossroads, 'I skidded on the ice and went over the handlebars.' He had shrugged, which was so normal that she smiled.

Snow lay on the verges and had drifted against the hedges, though it had largely thawed on the roads. She breathed in the cold, fresh air, loving it, unworried by the thought of shadows. The Boche must already know about this group from Pierre, so they wouldn't go to any great lengths to follow her, when they could pick them up at any time. No, it was the others in the circuit they needed. She thought about young, energetic Pierre. Had he done it for money? Was he a Nazi? Or was a relative a hostage? It didn't matter. He must be stopped.

She turned onto the track. Once at the copse, she left the bicycle propped up against a tree, just as Bernard had instructed. There was no guard. Perhaps further in? She hurried as much as she could towards the charcoal kiln. As she neared it, she heard a rustle to the left. She spun round. It was Pierre. He grinned, his blue eyes sparkling. 'Bernard has just told us you escaped – it is such good news that you are safe. Many of us have dispersed already. Bernard is to tell those who remain what to do next. First, we are to move the last of the containers. I am to remain on guard.'

She left him and made for the centre of the clearing. Bernard waited by the kiln. He took her hands gently, kissed her on both cheeks, then held her to him as though she was made of porcelain. He whispered, 'You are a clever girl. Yes, we had already moved most of the supplies. Arnaud and Renée will take you on from here, immediately. We have to wait for the next new moon, then you will fly out, as I always intended. I will see you tonight at the new safe house. Now go.'

'Pierre?'

'Leave him to me. The others have already disappeared, their task is over. We have the new George to fly out too. He's in hiding.'

'And the rest of the circuit?'

'It's safe, and I will be with you, for some of the time at least. Now go, and be careful. We didn't spot any shadows, but you never, know.' He had been talking for her ears only.

She left, slipping away with Arnaud and Renée, crawling along the soggy ditch leading to the stream, keeping below the bank, her knees cracking through the ice. At the bottom, they eased into the icy fast-flowing water. There had obviously been rainfall recently. How much one missed when kept in a windowless cell, she thought. They struggled against the flow, keeping below the bank for a half-mile or so, growing colder and colder. Sarah tried not to cough, and when she did, she held her gloved hand over her mouth. Her fingers had stopped throbbing because they were numb. It was a relief. A raptor circled above them. Would it give them away to any watchers? It disappeared.

Renée scrambled up the bank, keeping low. Sarah pressed herself against the bank, because a farmer was trundling a manure cart along a track beside the stream. She could hear the jangle of harness as the two horses thrust themselves forward.

Renée beckoned to the other two. Sarah shook her head. Arnaud whispered, 'The farmer is one of us.' This was what they had supposed about Pierre, she thought. The farmer eased down from the cart and called his dog, which had been loping alongside.

'Come,' Arnaud insisted. What alternative was there? She scrambled up as the farmer and dog wandered off.

'He will check bird traps,' Renée whispered.

Arnaud took the farmer's place on the cart. Renée hissed, 'Come, Cécile.'

Sarah followed as Renée eased up a corner of tarpaulin from the edge of the cart, holding it high enough for her to burrow beneath it. Renée followed. The weight of the manure bore down on the two women. Renée half laughed. 'It might dry us, and perhaps keep us warm.'

Sarah told herself she must not cough, or mind the pain as the weight pressed on her ribs and bruises. Arnaud called to the horses, and they lurched along over fields, heading into the unknown. He stopped at last and lifted the tarpaulin. They were in the yard of a farmer's supplier, on the edge of a small town. Renée covered Sarah's face with heavy make-up, obtained from who-knew-where.

Together they strolled to the station, arm-in-arm, in still-damp clothes and waited for a train to Le Mans. From there, Sarah would be taken on to a safe place, after which she knew she would not see anyone from the group again, except for Bernard. Pierre would be dead by now. Soon Sarah would be home. Please God.

Chapter Twenty-One

Tom cycled like a man possessed, immediately after Holy Communion, determined to reach the hospital and return in time for morning service. He took the steps into the foyer two at a time, then dashed up the stairs leading to the first floor on which Nightingale Ward was situated. He approached almost at a run, looking through the porthole windows of the double doors of the ward, meeting the face of Sister Newsome, who had been on duty on the night of the operation. She shook her head and pointed at her watch. 'Visiting is at two this afternoon.'

He stood his ground, panting, sweat beading his forehead, his scarf dragging on the floor. He snatched it off, bellowing through the glass, 'Please, Sister, I am Kate Watson's spiritual advisor, and it's Sunday after all, and she's had a second operation, and I need to see her.'

The sister sniffed, then barked, 'I believe you used the "spiritual advisor" bit on the night of the first operation, Vicar, when you made an infernal nuisance of yourself. You need to be more creative. Five minutes.'

She held the door open for him, and Tom felt he should tiptoe across the shiny and spotless floor, past women who slept, or read, or moaned quietly. Kate was on the right and had a sick-bowl at her side. She was pale. He sat with her, on the chair set up in front of the bedside cabinet. He had left flowers yesterday with the porter, and they were in a vase amongst many others ranged on the windowsill behind her. Most were chrysanthemums, their smell evocative of St Thomas's Church. Kate wouldn't like that. He took hold of her hand.

She opened her eyes, saw him and smiled. 'I feel very sick.'

'It's the ether, I expect. I felt the same when...'

He touched his face.

'You never did get the parrot.'

He grimaced. 'I've got you as my nemesis instead, to keep me on my toes.'

Moving her head slightly on the pristine and crisp pillows. 'I thought a nemesis pulled you down?'

'Then I'm wrong; you are my taskmaster, and a hard one at that, and you pull me up.'

Her blonde hair needed a wash, she had dark circles under her eyes and her brow was furrowed. But Tom still felt he had never seen anyone so beautiful. He lifted her hand to his lips. 'Dearest Kate,' he whispered against it. 'They had to go in again. They'd missed a bit. Just like you – you see, the shrapnel wouldn't be controlled.'

The sister's voice sounded from the end of the bed. 'Much as I suspected: "spiritual advisor", my Aunt Fanny. Now off you go, Vicar, time is up. Come later today, why don't you? We'll clean her up this time, poor wee thing, but she'll be much more comfortable with those nasty little bits of Hitler's nonsense quite gone.'

She was beckoning to him, and Tom didn't resist. He laid Kate's hand back on the counterpane. She was asleep again. He allowed himself to be marched out of the ward.

Sister Newsome waved him off at the double doors. 'She'll be up and about in no time, as good as new; or at least much better than she must have been feeling for months. She's bothering her head about a show or something, but I would guess she'll be treading the boards before you know where you are, and with her courage, nary a twinge will she feel. It was a close-run thing, though, young man. Someone needs to keep an eye on her. You can't leave everything to your boss. God, I mean, not her.' She nodded at Kate. He laughed.

The sister disappeared, the double doors swinging shut behind her. Well, Tom thought, as he started for home on his bicycle, no-one needed to worry any more, because he wouldn't be taking his eyes off Kate Watson from now until the sky fell down.

The wind was blasting through his jacket. Why the hell hadn't he worn a coat, for a scarf only went so far. He shut the front door behind him and Mrs B came out of the kitchen, with a steaming mug of tea. 'Here, drink this while you walk to the church. I have your vestments. How is she?'

She jammed on her hat and coat, as he sipped his tea. Together they half ran down the path to the side door of the church, into his St Thomas's snug, as he called the vestry. He handed Mrs B his empty mug; half the tea had splashed down his trousers, but at least it had been warm. 'You are a gem, Mrs B. Kate is feeling sick. Were those your chrysanthemums on the windowsill? She seems to have a lot.' He was shrugging into his vestments.

Mrs B tutted. 'Come here, you silly boy. Just look at your hair.' He bent his head, as she tugged it into some order. Then, extraordinarily, she kissed his cheek, the scarred one. 'You are a good boy.' She stalked away now, into the church, heading for the organ, because William Hall had decided his rheumatics had got the better of him.

Tom hurried to the church door and stood in the porch, welcoming in his flock. Each asked how Kate was. Each asked if she would be back for the concert, especially the children. He told them what Sister Newsome had said. Each grinned. 'I bet she's giving 'em hell,' Percy, the ARP warden, said.

Tom nodded. 'I dare say.'

He had chosen as the first hymn 'Love divine, all loves excelling'. His sermon was also about love. He stood quietly for a moment in the pulpit, wanting to tell his flock about the wrong done to Kate in the past, but that wasn't his truth to dispense. He read Matthew 22, verses 36-9, then leaned forward on the pulpit.

'We are fighting a war to defend our sovereignty, and our democracy. These two give us the power, and the right, to say and think what we wish, but remember the question asked in Matthew, chapter 22. "What is the greatest commandment in the Law?"

'You see, even though we have the freedom to speak and think, we need to consider our priorities. The first priority is that we should love our God with all our hearts and mind; but the second and, importantly, the one we should remember, is that we must love our neighbours as ourselves. Love is crucial, understanding too. Imagine our villages without it. There would be no gifts on doorsteps to show our love and compassion, no willingness to help, and understand. There would be no—'

Lizzy called from her pew, where she sat with Mrs Summers, 'There'd be no chrysanthemums in the hospital. Aunt Kate has lots, or that's what they said when Mrs B and I left some.'

He smiled down at her, as others laughed gently. He smiled at Kate's child, born of assault; but dearly loved by her biological mother, and her adoptive parents. How could the truth become known, without untold damage? But did that mean, that he should do nothing?

The congregation waited. He continued, 'So, sometimes gifts say without words what people mean, that the past – whatever it might be perceived as, or guessed at – is long gone. It is the present that remains and leads to the future.'

He looked across at the congregation. They were thinking, with furrowed brows. Mrs Summers smiled at him, nodding briefly. Did she know? Perhaps she had guessed? He turned to Mrs B, whose face was grave. She too nodded, her eyes fixed on his.

'Indeed,' she said. She knew, but of course would not speak of it.

'In the name of the Father... Now, hymn number three-seven-four: "Help us to help each other, Lord, each other's cross to bear".'

They all sang as though they would raise the roof. At the end of the service, before he sent them on their way, he spoke the Prayer of St Francis, and their voices were strong as they joined him: 'Make me a channel of your peace: where there is hatred, let me bring you love; where there is injury, your pardon, Lord, and where there is doubt...'

For the first time, as he gave the blessing, Tom

felt at one with his congregation, for they were good people. They did not shirk now from looking him full in the face; they quietly fought their own wars, not to mention the big, all-encompassing one that was raging, seemingly without end. But end it would, one way or another, and then they would continue to wake up each day and do their best.

He waited at the door, shaking hands, arranging to see them at rehearsals, and telling Percy he would take Kate's place on Tuesday nights, to do the rounds in her ARP helmet. He shook his head when Fran Billings asked if Kate had stopped being sick.

'So you've been?' he asked.

She shook her head. 'So many of us telephoned after the second operation that a harridan banned us again, and the snow-line to pass the news was reinstated.'

'Ah, that would be Sister Newsome. I think she breathes fire on a regular basis, but I'd want her looking after Kate in preference to anyone else. Her patients come first, and the rest of us can go about our business.'

Mrs Summers joined them. 'A good service, Tom, and a nice short sermon. Dear old Hastings did go on so, and then those temporary bods liked to give us a good verbal thrashing, so we couldn't even nod off. You're not moving on, I hope? The village wouldn't like that.'

Mrs Woolton, Mrs Martin and others clustered around like a gathering of sparrows. 'Surely you won't.'

'That won't do at all.'

341

Mrs Whitehead said, 'My husband and I will speak to the bishop.'

He held up his hands. 'What parish would have me, after I'm seen cavorting about doing a really, really bad tango? So I suspect I will be allowed to stay.'

Mrs Williams laughed. 'You've got a point there, Vicar. We need our Kate back, to teach you proper.'

The women went on their way and at last the church was empty. He snuffed the candles. The smell of melted wax was comforting and reminded him of Christmas when he was a small boy. He looked up at the stained-glass windows, with the thin, cold December sun casting coloured shadows. Turning, he took in the church. Mrs B was stacking the prayer and hymn books on the side table near the door. Doubting Thomas had been given St Thomas's parish, and now he realised he wasn't doubting any more. Little Worthy had worked its magic – a microcosm of life being lived in a time of despair, pain, hope and laughter.

He laughed at himself. Good grief, he sounded so theatrical he'd end up on the stage, at this rate. Mrs B switched off the lights. Tom looked up at the ceiling, which had been decorated just before he came. It reminded him of something important. He walked down the aisle towards the font. Mrs B waited. He said, 'I need paint, to cover the stain on Kate's ceiling, and I need it now. What can I do to get some?'

'Let's go and see if we have some at the vicarage, shall we?'

They rooted about in the sheds and the garage, which housed no car, and found a gallon tin of white emulsion. Mrs B discovered a screwdriver with which to prise off the lid. It was half full.

'Enough for the ceiling?' Tom asked her.

'How should I know, Vicar? I'm a housekeeper, not a decorator; but I know who is, or was, when he could still scamper up a ladder. Percy. But I have shepherd's pie in the oven and, though it's mainly parsnips, I'm not having such waste. So you'll cycle to him after lunch.'

He did, allowing Mrs B to visit Kate in his place. She then promptly arranged with Mrs Summers that they would both go with Mrs Martin in her car in an hour or so, taking Lizzy as well. He wondered just how much choice Mrs Martin had in the matter, but he was too busy thinking through his decorating to worry about it.

He lugged the emulsion to Percy's house, and the ARP warden reckoned that if they mixed the half tin with some of his paint, they could put a couple of coats on with no trouble at all.

'There's a stain on the ceiling, you see.'

Percy had a pencil behind his ear. It reminded Tom of the stub of a pencil that often had pride of place behind Lizzy's ear too.

'What sort of stain?'

'Water, I think.'

'Well, if you think emulsion is going to cover that, you have a lot to learn. Come along, I'll have to take over, I can see that.' He called to his wife. 'Ethel, just nipping out to put the vicar right on a few things.'

She replied from the kitchen, 'Lucky old vicar.

343

I'll be here by the fire. Give Kate my love, when you see her, and tell her I've almost finished the costume for the WI's song-and-dance routine. It's *de-lovely*, right enough.'

Tom laughed, but Percy was already out of the door, carrying his own tin of emulsion, bustling along East Street and turning right into the High Street. Tom picked up his tin and ran to catch up. At Melbury Cottage they nipped along to Fran. Lizzy was still there, and Tom explained why he needed to get into the house.

Lizzy said, 'The key is always under the pot that has geraniums in the summer. You know, Tom, the one by the fountain in the front garden – the one that doesn't work, the rusty one.'

Fran was laughing. 'Got that, have you, Tom?'

He saluted, and Percy followed him out. 'What does she use the pencil stuck behind her ear for?'

Tom smiled. 'It was her dad's.'

'Ah.' There was no need to say anything else.

Once in the house, they climbed the stairs. They found the bedroom with the stain. It smelled musty. Percy muttered, 'Ain't been slept in for many a long while.'

'She sleeps in the attic. She ... well, she keeps this room ready for a nanny, but there isn't one. Not sure there ever will be, at least not until the end of the war.' He stopped. Would Kate leave then? He couldn't bear the thought.

Percy was looking up at the ceiling. 'This needs papering, if it's to look all right, then painting.'

Tom looked at the walls with their old-fashioned wallpaper composed of a green background and large roses. 'But it will be so dark.'

'Not that, you daft lug; we'll use lining paper and paint it. That old stuff on the walls should be taken off, if you ask me.'

'I haven't papered before.'

'Look, Padre, you's good at spouting in a pulpit, but I dare say you're a load of old bollocks decorating. I'll paper the ceiling while you strip the walls, then at the end we'll emulsion the lot. Looks like a ruddy morgue in 'ere, and this old furniture doesn't help.'

Tom looked around, and at the bed. No, Kate wasn't sleeping there ever again. He and Percy arranged that the ceiling papering would begin tomorrow. Apparently Percy still had paste left from before the war. Tom set off on his bike, knocking on doors until he found all the replacement furniture he needed, but then he had to find someone who would like the old furniture and, what's more, take it away.

The publican rubbed his nose with his finger. 'Leave it with me, guv'nor.'

A van arrived on Monday morning and Tom helped a man he didn't know, but who heralded from Somerton, down the stairs with the mattress, the bed, the chest of drawers and the wardrobe. He then rolled up his sleeves and worked around Percy, soaking the wallpaper and scraping it off the walls. He had to stop at two, in order to rush to the school to teach Kate's class. He gave them more programmes to write, and when they groaned, he suggested that they coloured in the margins with whatever pictures they wanted. This they liked.

When school finished he had to cycle on his

rounds, before rehearsals at five thirty in the evening. He hadn't had a chance to visit Kate, but Mrs B reported that the sickness was passing and she was beginning to be a nuisance, so eager was she to be out.

'Not yet,' he warned. 'Her room isn't ready.'

'Don't you worry, Vicar. She's not ready either, the sister says, and even Kate can't best a woman like her.'

They laughed together and set out for rehearsals. Tom went in old clothes, and the others asked how he was getting on with the decorating. It was only after the rehearsal that he returned with Lizzy and Mrs Summers to Melbury Cottage. He rolled up his sleeves, clambered up the ladder and applied the first coat to the lined ceiling, but did nothing else because it would disturb Lizzy. He would check in the morning to see if Percy had been right and the stain was covered. If it wasn't, he would do whatever it took.

He was up early and changed into the same old clothes, but Mrs B caught him as he was leaving. 'Breakfast first, please. Lizzy won't be out from under your feet yet.'

He arrived at nine, when all were in school. Percy was there too and must have come straight off his ARP shift. Tom shook his head. 'Did you sleep at all?'

'Old 'uns don't need it like you young 'uns.'

They stood in the bedroom and examined the ceiling. 'Not a hint,' Tom crowed. 'You are a wise and exceptional man, Percy, and to heaven you will go.'

Percy rolled his pencil between his fingers,

much as if he was rolling a cigarette. 'Got a direct line to 'im, 'ave you?'

Tom muttered, 'How nice that would be. Bit of a smoker, are you, Percy?'

'*Was* I, you mean? Then came rationing, and the wife's tongue.' He picked out the sponge from the bucket of water. 'Hop up the ladder, and I'll clear the walls of the last bits. The plaster's good and won't need lining, so you can get painting.'

The two worked together all day, until both were finished. Percy's navy overalls were covered in a fine spray of white emulsion. 'There, that's your lot, lad. I'm off on my way to me bed now.' He shoved his hands in his pockets and left the room. From the landing he said, 'I always reckoned there was more to the poor girl's going, you know. I 'eard tell about something shocking in Great Sanders, some while after she left. About a young girl and that Dr Bates.'

Tom was silent for a moment, not knowing what to say.

Percy sighed and walked down the stairs. 'That's what the village reckon, now they've met Kate, now they remember, though it's taken time. But they won't say nothing. There's Lizzy after all, ain't there?'

'What do you know?' Tom asked.

'I reckon the women have come to know it all. Them weren't born under a gooseberry bush, they have eyes to see, and ears to 'ear. If they know, then so does the rest of 'em.'

The front door slammed.

Tom worked hard, painting the woodwork. He would leave the windows open, put another coat on the walls tomorrow and move in the new furniture. Then Kate could come home, if she was allowed, and have a proper bedroom. Mrs B would be round before then to help him move Kate's clothes, which he'd heaped into boxes.

As he washed the brushes in the bathroom he heard a knocking at the door. 'Damn.' He shut off the tap and hurried down the stairs. Had the furniture come early? But no, a villager would have shouted. He opened the door. A large man stood there in a homburg hat and an expensive grey wool coat, with an astrakhan collar.

'Yes, can I help?' Tom asked.

The man stuck out his hand. 'Bruce Turnbull at your service, sunshine.'

Tom checked his hands. 'Sorry, they're wet. I've been freshening up the bedroom.'

'Oh well, when you've finished, tell your boss I've come to fetch her. I sent a letter about an agent coming across from America to gather up singers for his Broadway shows. I ain't heard from her. She's my main girl, Kate Watson is. This is her big chance. Tell her to give me a tinkle at the pub, Squire. I'll be there to take her back, so we have time to get the act right.'

He dug in his pocket and drew out half a crown. 'There you are, lad. For your trouble.'

He spun on his heel and sauntered down the path. Tom watched him go, the man's words resonating through him: Kate had received a letter; her big chance. Had she read it? Perhaps. But what if she hadn't? He should let her know, but then she might leave.

Bruce Turnbull was shutting the gate. He tipped

348

his hat at Tom, who couldn't bear the thought of Kate going, so why say anything? Even as he thought that, he called out, 'She's in hospital. She had an operation on her back. They say she'll be better before too long.'

As Bruce turned, Tom told him how to get to the hospital and the name of the ward, then shut the door. He would put the half crown in the collection on Sunday.

Chapter Twenty-Two

Tom received the furniture the next day. After school Lizzy helped him place it in the room.

'No, not so far over, Vicar. This way a bit.'

He pushed. There was the sound of screeching. He stopped. He had scratched the floorboards.

Lizzy put her hand to her mouth. 'Put it back and hide the scratch, but lift it, Vicar. Lift – don't be so weedy.'

Mrs B poked her head round the door. 'Trouble?'

He shook his head, but Lizzy pointed. 'Just look, Mrs B, he shoved it.'

'I'm not a circus strongman,' Tom grumbled.

Mrs B nodded, 'Well, that's abundantly clear.'

Mrs Summers entered with a vase of chrysanthemums. 'Now, now, Mrs B. He can't help not having biceps.' Tom watched Mrs Summers put the vase on the windowsill. The rain was pouring down, and the smell of gloss paint was slowly dissipating. He hurried across and opened the windows wider. 'Don't do that,' shrieked Mrs Summers. 'The rain might damage the paint.'

Lord, save me from this regiment of women, Tom thought, as he closed it to, within an inch. 'Will that do?'

'Perfect,' Mrs Summers said, standing back and admiring her flowers, while she fluffed her hair. She had always reminded Tom of something, and now he knew what: a fluffy chicken that busied itself around the chicken coop. He decided that as he was becoming vaguely wise in the ways of women, he would not share that with her.

Mrs B had taken all the drawers out of the new white-painted chest and had laid them on the bed. She now lifted the carcass, with Lizzy at the other end. 'That's how you do it, Vicar, for another time.'

She replaced the drawers. There was new bedding, found in various bottom drawers and donated at the rehearsals over the last two nights, because no-one had spare ration coupons. Mrs Summers smoothed the patchwork quilt. 'I sewed this last year. It kept me calm when the war news seemed so hopeless. It's bright and cheerful, Vicar. And you and Percy have done a magnificent job. Our Kate will be so pleased.'

Why did no-one ask why Sarah hadn't visited Kate, or even come home on leave? Did they know she was up to something? He didn't doubt it for a moment, knowing this village, and at last he was catching up with them, and knew that Sarah had lived and worked in France for a couple of years before she was married.

He checked his watch. He was supposed to visit Kate this evening, but he couldn't bear to. What if she told him she was leaving? What if she wouldn't be here to dance, gently, with him, to grow to like him? What professional performer wouldn't at least go for the audition? But if she did, would the village see it as betrayal? What example was it to the children who shone, just for her? What about Lizzy?

Mrs B came to stand next to him, with Lizzy on the other side, while Mrs Summers plumped up the cushions on the small armchair at Kate's bedside. The blackout blind had been replaced, the curtains were new, and the small flowers on the white background contributed to the cheerfulness of the room. Even the lampshade had been changed for an almost-new cream one.

'I think it's ready now,' said Lizzy. 'The only trouble is: Kate likes to stand at the attic window and remember how she climbed out and ran to the woods, feeling free.'

Mrs Summers eased her shoulders. 'Well, perhaps she will feel she won't need to any more. We can but hope. Now come on, Vicar, you did say you'd visit. I think Kate's been expecting you.'

They shooed him down the stairs. He changed into his better trousers in the kitchen, plus a sweater, put on his coat, wound his scarf round his neck, pulled down his woollen hat and checked that the slit paper was in place over his bicycle lamp. He set off, using the back road. He should be at the hospital within the hour. The bitter wind was behind him, so he felt as though he flew, but that could be because he wanted to

351

be there, with Kate, while there was still time.

He toiled up the hill, 'A Foggy Day in London Town' playing through his mind. It was a song that all the cast would sing as their finale, though it had nothing to do with *Anything Goes*. At the moment the run-throughs were messy, but that was because Kate wasn't there to herd them into shape. As he pedalled over a bridge he smiled, picturing her conducting with every fibre of her being.

He reached the hospital, chained his bike to a lamp post and entered the blacked-out door, telling the night porter where he was going. 'That's all right, sonny. Been in action, have you?'

For days at a time now, Tom forgot about his face. 'Yes, it keeps me out of the firing line, but then we do have a lot of women in the village who make a good imitation of the enemy. Or at least aren't a million miles from the sergeant-majors I worked with.' The porter's laugh followed him up the stairs.

In the ward there was a buzz of chatter. Sister Newsome sat at her table, writing. He skirted her post, but she had eyes like a hawk.

'Ah, you are here to deliver some more spiritual guidance this evening, are you, Vicar? You've been a bit remiss, haven't you? On the other hand, Kate's survived with just we nurses ministering to her and absolutely no heavenly choir in the background.'

He stopped and laughed. 'I'm quite sure, Sister Newsome, that nothing would dare to go wrong in this ward whilst you ministering angels are on duty.' Her loud, long laugh was a surprise.

'Get on with you. Men of the cloth shouldn't

sweet-talk, should they? But I have to say, she's got her voice back. She's been practising for her big night, or so she tells us. The trouble is, it doesn't stay a solo for long, but ends up as an ensemble with quite a number of the other patients joining in – I've even been known to harmonise with her myself. A sing-song does everyone a power of good.'

He almost turned and left, because he couldn't bear to hear what he suspected the big night was. Instead he approached Kate's bed. She was reading music, but looked up and grinned at him. 'Ah, I thought I'd scared you off, what with the dirty hair, and Lord knows what else. Thank you for all you did for me. You kept me immobile, I hear, but if you hadn't, what on earth would have happened?'

'Perhaps we wouldn't have been able to dance the tango, even be it most carefully, at the show.' He waited.

Kate said, 'Ah, the rehearsals, how are they going? I should be up and at it, very soon. I walked about the hospital today, you know, Tom. Up and down the stairs too and there was no pain, just the stitches pulling. It's as though I've been given a new life. Can you believe what that is like?' She looked closely at him, and gripped his hand. 'Of course you can, because look at you. A new eye, and there's a spring in your step. You look different, sort of alive. That's how I feel too, as though the world has opened up for me. Now, tell me about Lizzy? She was in yesterday and seemed to be brimming with news she absolutely refused to tell me.'

'Ah, that's because the tap dance is looking so good.'

They talked of this and that, until time was called. Kate still held his hand, but Tom didn't know what it meant, and she said nothing at all about things he wanted to understand. Nor did he ask; he didn't dare. They just sat quietly as the sound of the bell faded.

After the other visitors had left, Sister Newsome stood at the bottom of the bed, tapping the watch-brooch pinned to her chest.

Tom asked, 'When will she be coming home, Sister?'

'You can pick her up on Sunday, but of course you will be busy doing what you do, so perhaps someone else can.'

He stood. 'In the morning?'

Kate released his hand.

He stooped and kissed her forehead and smoothed back her hair, for what could be the last and only time. 'See you on your return. I'll come round.'

'Pastoral visit, eh?' She looked at him and waited.

He didn't know what to say or do. He nodded. 'Yes, of course.'

He left, wanting to run back to Kate and carry her away with him, but what would he do then? Put her on his crossbar? A girl like that deserved so much more than a parish, the duties of a vicar's wife and very little pay. He'd been mad to think for a moment that he had anything to offer her, with the bright lights within reach.

On Sunday 13th December Tom finished morning service, all the time wondering if Mrs Martin and Lizzy had brought Kate home. Mrs B had left a neck-of-lamb casserole in the oven at Melbury Cottage first thing that morning, so all the bases had been covered. He stood in the church porch, shaking hands. Most parishioners wondered if Kate would be up to directing the rehearsal. 'We must wait and see,' he said.

He walked along the path with Mrs B, who patted him on the back. 'She will come and see you, don't you worry. Or you could go to her: faint heart never won fair lady.'

'You're a witch – you have second sight.'

'No need for that; first sight is quite sufficient to see how you feel.'

They entered the vicarage by the back door, wiped their feet and Tom sat at the kitchen table, wanting to put his head in his hands like some lovelorn prince. Instead he shook out his napkin. 'I have nothing to offer a potential star of the stage.'

'I know it's been worrying you, ever since you told me of the agent arriving, but you don't know she'll go. Kate hasn't said anything to intimate that she is not attending rehearsals or the show.'

'But she hasn't said she is.'

Mrs B placed the casserole on the table. It was also neck of lamb, because she had brewed up two in her 'cauldron', as Tom had said at the time. She had not been amused, so he didn't repeat it. 'Why would she? If she's turned down that ghastly man, then nothing has changed.'

She dished up the casserole and although there

355

wasn't a lot of lamb, the parsnips were, yet again, plentiful. In the vegetable dish there were sprouts and cabbage, with a few carrots, plus a baked potato. Tom wasn't hungry, but he wasn't about to tell Mrs B that, or he'd be wearing the casserole dish. Steam was rising from it, and the smell began to tempt him.

He downed the lot, eating the last sprout as the doorbell rang. Mrs B rose. Tom waved her down, but before he could get up and go to the front door, Kate called from the hall, 'I let myself in, but I bet you're eating. So sorry, but may I use your telephone? It's rather urgent, and there's a queue outside the phone box.'

He sat quite still. Mrs B cocked her head at him. He said, 'Would you do the honours, Mrs B?'

'Lizzy is quite right to call you weedy,' Mrs B whispered.

'Kate hasn't said anything about the room,' he whispered in reply.

Mrs B was by the door and whispered back, 'Give the girl a chance. It's a miracle she's made it here.' She returned in a moment. 'She's on the telephone, to the Blue Cockatoo. Get out there at once and listen.' It was still a whisper.

He shook his head. 'She'd see me.'

'Then come here.'

Mrs B opened the kitchen door just a fraction. Unable to help himself, Tom joined her. He heard Kate's lovely voice. 'Yes, Frankie, it's me. I'm so much better, my wonderful friend. I feel a new person, full of beans. Please, Frankie, do me a huge favour. I need Stan to come to the village on the night of the twentieth – before, if possible.

356

Our band is, I fear, rather depleted because our saxophonist postman is grieving and hasn't the puff. The village needs help.'

Mrs B poked him with her elbow. 'I think she's staying.'

He whispered back, 'She hasn't said that, only that the band needs someone.' He didn't dare hope, and how could Kate put her dreams to one side? Perhaps she and Brucie had discussed another date?

'Yes, Roberto and Elliot too would be a miracle, but I know it's a big ask. Hello, hello. Oh, Brucie, you shouldn't snatch the receiver off people, it's rude. I know, I meant to write, but I've only just made a decision. Look, I can't come to any audition. We have our own musical. No, no, stop shouting for heaven's sake, it will get you nowhere. No, really, our concert is just as important. A great many people have put in a lot of work and, what's more, they're worthy, but I doubt you understand what that means?'

Tom murmured to Mrs B, 'I can't bear it for her – it's not fair.'

Mrs B pulled at his sleeve. 'Trust her. I reckon she's going to send him on his way.'

There was a long silence, then, 'Goodbye, Brucie. Yes, by all means let Cheryl have her chance, why not? It will put an ocean between her and me.'

Mrs B nudged Tom again, so hard it hurt, but he didn't care because none of this was right for Kate, though he longed for it to be so. He wrenched open the door. 'Don't hang up, Kate. You must take this chance. It might not come

357

again, and you deserve it. We'll be all right.'

But it was too late. Kate had replaced the receiver. She stood still for a moment, then turned towards him. She spoke quite calmly, as he stood in the doorway, with Mrs B right behind him. 'If you think that an audition is of any importance, when a dear, kind man tells me to lie still and stops me from being paralysed, then tells me of Hastings's diary, you have another think coming.' She moved a step closer. 'What's more, this wonderful friend protected me at the hospital, along with the equally wonderful Mrs B, standing up to the formidable Sister Newsome, which is above and beyond the duty of any man. Sister Newsome told me this man insisted on staying until my operation was over. So, if you think I would choose not to dance the tango, enormously carefully, with him, you are sadly mistaken.'

She walked across the hall, her coat hanging open, her hair awry from the wind, her cheeks flushed, and she had never looked more beautiful to Tom. Mrs B shoved him, and he was striding towards her. Kate stopped a pace from him.

'This wonderful man has wiped the past from my room. In more ways than I can possibly imagine, he has brought me peace, and you will have to prise me from him, from this day forward, and nothing will change my mind.'

Her words melted his heart, and he longed to tell her he loved her, and would until the day he died. He reached forward and she took his hands in hers, pulling him towards her. He stood against her, kissed her, and now his arms were around her, holding Kate so closely and carefully that he felt they could become one; and it was all that he had thought it would be. Her arms were round his neck, and then Tom was holding her face between his hands.

'I love you,' he said.

'I love you too,' she replied. Her lips were soft against his as she spoke. They clung together, kissed again, and then she kissed his scarred face, her touch tender and loving. He traced his finger from her hair to her eyes, to her mouth.

'I'm so happy,' he murmured.

'As am I, far more than you.' She was leaning back against his arm.

He responded, 'No, I am happier.'

They were both laughing. Behind him, Tom heard Mrs B say, 'Oh, for goodness' sake.' The kitchen door slammed. They laughed harder still.

Then he said, 'Truly, darling Katie, I love you up to the sky and back down again, and that's an end to it.'

'But there is something we have to do,' she said, all laughter gone.

He nodded. He knew what that would be. 'Today?'

'Of course.'

'I will order a taxi.'

He heard the kitchen door open and Mrs B called, 'I don't know what you're talking about, but Mrs Martin will lend you her car. Just pay for the petrol. It's funny-coloured stuff; I think it should only be used by farmers, but they like her.'

Dear heavens, Tom thought, does everyone know everything about everything. It wasn't a question.

Kate had discovered Dr Bates's address and gave Tom directions as he drove, her hand tucked under his arm. They talked a little, and let the silences fall as they willed. Eventually they drew up outside Dr and Mrs Bates's house. Tom let Kate lead the way up the path. The doctor's brass plate was dull, old and pitted with green. Kate knocked.

After a while Mrs Bates opened the door. She was a woman in about her mid-fifties, wearing an apron. She wiped her hands down her front. 'Yes, can I help you?'

Kate said, 'We were passing, Mrs Bates. It's Kate Watson, I'm home for a while. I thought I would just drop in quickly to see Dr Bates.'

'Oh, my dear, how very kind of you, but I'm afraid dearest Joseph died two months ago now. He had a stroke some years ago, of course, so it wasn't altogether a surprise. Come in, don't stand there letting in the cold.'

She shut the door behind them and led the way into the sitting room, where a fire burned in the grate. There were some early Christmas cards on the mantelpiece.

'I thought you had left to go to London, Kate. I know that Joseph valued his friendship with your family, and of course with your father. They built up that golf club together, but then somehow they drifted apart. I was surprised when dear Joseph retired early, but he said he was suffering from nervous exhaustion. Who did you say your friend is, dear?' Mrs Bates gestured to the sofa. They both shook their heads.

Kate said, 'We can't stop, Mrs Bates. This is

360

Tom Rees, the vicar of Little Worthy. We are to be married.'

Tom smiled. Oh, he did hope so, but was this all part of the patter?

He moved to the fire, where photographs stood on the mantelpiece, half hidden by the Christmas cards. There was one of Mrs Bates and the doctor, on their wedding day. He saw Lizzy in the doctor's smile, but the rest of the face was emotionless, superior, without life. He wanted Kate away from here, but only she could decide when it was time. He hoped, though, that she wouldn't tell all to Mrs Bates. The woman presumably knew nothing, so why destroy her life?

Kate was shaking Mrs Bates's hand. 'We must get on our way, I'm so sorry to disturb you.'

'I like being disturbed, I see so few people now. Somehow our friends have disappeared. Perhaps it's something to do with Joseph being a doctor and knowing their problems.'

'Probably,' Kate said.

Mrs Bates saw them to the door. They walked back to the car. Tom started the engine. 'Well?' he asked.

'It's over.'

'Lizzy?'

'She can't ever know. If she asks, then the father is my friend, Andrei, the gypsy. I think she'd like that idea. But that's up to Sarah, if – no, when – she returns.'

Tom drove off. 'You'll marry me then?'

'I rather think I pushed you into that. So wait until you're sure.'

He could have banged the steering wheel in

361

frustration. Did she or did she not want to marry him? She really was the most infuriating woman, but he loved her more than he had ever thought it possible to love anyone.

She leaned against him. 'I'm happy, which I never thought would be possible.'

Well, what could be better than that, for now? As they drove along, Kate knew that even if she had been able to leave Tom, and the children, and all the villagers, she would still have forfeited her audition because she feared that Sarah would not survive, if the show collapsed. It was her own bargain, with whoever it was up there in the ether. She laughed at herself. How absurd even to think that a bargain that she herself had devised would make a difference, but she couldn't take the chance.

Chapter Twenty-Three

Sarah sat wedged upright by Renée as the train left the station and trundled towards Le Mans. Both women rested books on the wicker baskets Renée had bought at the station. Both of them wore gloves, and thank goodness, because Sarah's fingers would give the game away. Especially as she had new forged papers in the name of one Adèle Carron, so she had to be very careful not to stand out.

The train chugged through countryside Sarah vaguely recognised. But only vaguely, because it was as though there was a mist she couldn't

362

brush to one side. Every time this mist fell, Sarah raised her hand to brush it away, and Renée grasped it, drawing Sarah's attention back to a page in her book, before replacing her hand in her lap. Why? She hadn't the strength to ask.

As a fellow passenger left the train at her station, her basket reeking of leeks, Renee whispered, 'Don't touch your face; your make-up will transfer to your gloves and reveal your bruises. Neither must you remove your gloves, or people will see your fingernails. Well, where they once were.'

Sarah sat, letting the book rest on her basket, her hands too painful to hold it; everything too painful. She could hear her chest rattling, and her breath wheezed in and out. She was as hot as a furnace, which made her lucky, as there was no heating in the carriage. She half laughed. More snow had fallen early or even overnight, and it hadn't thawed.

At Le Mans they left the train, muddling in with many others as German soldiers guarded the ticket office, checking tickets and IDs. Sarah smiled as she handed hers over. Her hat was set at a jaunty angle, as was Renée's, and Renée launched into a flirtation with the men. The French citizens glowered at her and shoved the two women. The soldiers checked their papers, waving them through. The younger of the two smiled. The elder did not.

They hurried out of the station. It was swarming with troops and police, all alert, all scanning the crowds. For her? Sarah kept her mind on being Adèle Carron from Paris, who had just been to see her mother. How did Bernard get the papers? How had he arranged for her to be here?

They strolled along the narrow cobbled streets, in shadow from the typically tall town houses. The cathedral loomed, and the River Sarthe fed the damp and cold wind battering their coats and trying to snatch their hats. Another German patrol yelled, 'Halt.' They did. Renée's flirting knew no bounds, and Sarah tutted her disapproval, snatching her away.

'Excellent,' murmured Renée as they clattered along on their wooden soles. 'You feel better now, Adèle?'

'Of course,' Sarah lied. She didn't, and wondered how much longer she could walk as though untroubled. Renée walked on, and somehow Sarah kept pace until they stopped at one of the tall, thin houses. Renée knocked twice, then once, then once again. They waited as Renée counted under her breath. She knocked twice more. The door swung open.

Renée spun on her heel and walked away. A woman reached out and took Sarah's wrist. So, whoever it was must know about her hands. She was drawn into the darkness and the smell of lavender and polish. The wide oak floorboards shone in the slits of light shining through the shutters.

'Come,' said the elderly woman, still holding her wrist. She pointed up a wide staircase. Sarah couldn't manage another step, but somehow she did, agonisingly slowly, not caring any more what lay at the top. Did another traitor lie in wait? Or was this an angel at her side, careless of her own safety? She coughed, clung to the banister, and now a strong arm was around her, half carrying her upstairs. She saw in the dim light that the elderly woman was in front. How strange. How very strange. Did angels exist?

They moved along a landing until they reached a wall, decorated by a running alabaster frieze of roses. The woman pressed a rose. Part of the wall swung open, like a door. They entered a bedroom. Sarah was led to the bed. The woman said, 'You must lie down. I will care for you until you go home. You are safe – as much as anyone is.' The woman took Sarah's weight now and eased her to the bed. The scent of lavender was all around. She heard the floorboards creak. She turned, and all she saw was a man disappearing onto the landing. The door closed.

'Thank you,' she croaked.

'Shhh,' the woman soothed, stroking her hair, like Bernard. Like Derek used to. Derek Smith, Derek Baxter – Derek, whom she now felt was dead. Somehow, after all this time, Sarah felt that was the case. It meant nothing, because the darkness was growing, though there was daylight streaming into the room from the window. There were shutters, but they were open. She saw roofs and sky, and birds flying free, but then the darkness took her over.

Sarah slept, sweated, burned up and coughed. A doctor came, just as Dr Bates had come to Kate but this one was kind, and proper. Dr Bates had not been, though no-one had believed her poor little sister. Sarah believed her now. Or was she Cécile, or Adèle? One of them, or all of them, knew the difference between a lie and the truth.

They could see it in the eyes, but it had taken too long to reach this point. She had failed her younger sister at the time and done little better ever since, because she simply hadn't thought about it: She should have known during her training, when lying became an art. Derek *Smith* – so said that fool of a major who wasn't a man, but a devil. Did he think she couldn't read him? She should have read Kate like that.

She stopped. It was all so long ago – a lifetime – but if she survived, she would make it up to Kate. If.

Later, how much later Sarah did not know, but the sun still shone and deep snow gleamed on the roofs, she heard a soft French voice. 'Be calm, we have the doctor here again, to help. This is your third day here, and you are not quite well, but you know that.'

Sarah breathed in the scent of lavender, and coughed; her chest rattled, her head was bursting, her body hurt, her feet and hands throbbed, her eyes were dry, her belly ached. Was that a new pain? She felt an arm beneath her, and her crisp white pillows were changed. She was lowered gently.

The doctor examined her, his stethoscope cold on her chest. He pressed here, there. He looked closely at her fingers, and laid her hands gently on the bed. 'Bastard,' he hissed. He moved from her sight, pressing her hips, her legs, lifting the sheet, which was all she could bear on her toes and feet. 'Bastards,' he hissed again.

She said, 'I am alive. I am lucky, I am grateful.'

366

Her voice was a croak, a husk of herself.

The woman stroked her hair, like Bernard, and like Derek.

The doctor came to her. He was old, his eyes deep-set, his hands trembled.

She said, 'You are brave. I thank you, but you must not come again. They could...' She coughed until she could barely breathe.

The doctor was saying to the elderly woman, 'My love, we can do little, but it will be easier for her if she stays raised, for the coughing at least. Pneumonia, infected fingers and toes, cracked ribs, perhaps a damaged spleen. We can't risk hospital. Soon she will leave. We will, between us, keep her alive till then.'

'Of course.'

The doctor touched Sarah's arm. 'You will soon be home, Adèle.'

She wouldn't believe that. She could be betrayed again, and these two with her. She wanted to be in a barn somewhere, alone, like an animal creeping away to live or die. She had lasted almost three months, the life-expectancy of an agent. She repeated, 'I'm lucky.'

She slept and woke when darkness had fallen. The shutters were closed, and a blanket had been draped over them, like a blackout. Ah, a black-out. Was she home? No, she was here, being hidden, but what if...? She slept again, then woke to increased pain. How could it be worse, when she thought she had reached the heights?

The woman, whose name she did not know, but whom in her mind she called Madame Lavender, whispered, 'Be still, my child, let me care for you.'

She bathed Sarah's hands by the glow of an oil lamp, before soaking her fingertips in warm water. They stung. Sarah flinched.

Madame Lavender murmured, 'It will help; sometimes it hurts to make things better.' It was what her mother had said. Madame Lavender gently patted her fingers dry before laying them down on some gauze. She moved to her feet, sponged them, then laid a soaking flannel over them. It stung. The woman said, 'Salt water. It is all we have. It is good, it will help.'

'Thank you, but I must go elsewhere and hide. We are trained to do so. This isn't fair on you.'

The woman put her finger to her lips. 'Shhh, you must allow me to help. It is my wish.'

Sarah slept.

The light was streaming through the windows. Another day, but her chest was worse. She tossed and turned, dozed, and woke to see the door was ajar. Should it be? She heard voices, a laugh. Pierre? She sat upright and groaned with pain, retched. 'Pierre?' He should be dead. He had betrayed her. 'Pierre.' It was a scream. 'Pierre.' Another scream. She slept and saw his face, his eyes so blue, peering down, his hands busy on her sheet, a cool flannel on her forehead. She struggled to sit, but he held her down. No, no. She felt his breath on her face, but he said nothing, just smiled, then whispered, 'Don't be afraid.' No, no, she tried to say, but no sound came.

She slept, and woke to a sunny day. It was so often a sunny day, or was it just that she saw so much of the sky? Madame Lavender helped her from her bed, as she did three times a day, and to the bathroom off her bedroom, then left, saying, 'Call me if you need help.'

There were some things she must do alone, Sarah had said. She finished, stood at the sink and stared in the mirror, as she did every morning. Who was this woman with a black-and-blue face? What would her mother think?

She would fold Sarah in her arms, as Derek would have done, and Bernard. What would her father have done? Told her it was her fault? She should not have misbehaved? 'But I haven't, Daddy. It is Kate who did that.'

But Kate hadn't. No, she hadn't. Lizzy was Dr Bates's child, and he should burn in hell for hurting little Katie, but what could they do? For Lizzy must never know.

She returned to the bedroom, exhausted, her chest rattling. She crawled into bed and slept. When she awoke it was dusk, though the shutters were not closed. The moon was no longer a slice. Soon it would be full and she could go home, but it was too hard to hope. She turned from the window, and a man sat in Madame Lavender's chair, deep in the shadows. She shrank from him. Pierre? No, he was dead. Bernard had killed him. Pierre was a traitor. But she had seen him, here. No, don't be silly; it was in her head, as the shapes in the basement cell had been.

'Sleeping Beauty wakes.' It was Bernard. He leaned forward. 'Soon the Lysander will come.'

'Am I safe?'

He shrugged. 'As are any of us.'

She hated herself for having asked. Was she a

coward, a fool?

He said, 'No, of course not. You are ill, and hurt.' So she had spoken aloud. He leaned nearer, and laid his hand on her arm. 'I have news I should tell you. Before the new "George" signed off, he was told that Derek is confirmed dead. So he is safe, after all. In a sense.'

She slept and Derek was with her, in the garden at Melbury Cottage. He was swinging Lizzy. Poor Lizzy, who would look after her? 'Well,' Derek said, 'you, of course.'

Of course, she was going home, and how could she have left Lizzy at all? How could she? Had she done any good here – had she kept her country, and therefore Lizzy, safer?

She felt Bernard's hand on her arm. 'Yes, without a doubt. Never doubt that you have played your part, Adèle.'

She slept, and wept, and slept again, but she couldn't really see Derek; she hadn't been able to for months. He didn't come in her dreams again. Lizzy did, and Kate, her hair shining and blonde as she sang. She heard her sister's laughter as she played with Lizzy. How, though, because she hadn't really seen them together? Because she just knew that although her sister had been despised and cast out, she was like their mother and would love a helpless child.

She woke to Madame Lavender standing by her. 'Ah,' Madame Lavender said, 'chicken broth, you smelled it, I think.' There it was, on the side table, steaming in the cold room; Sarah moved her arms, which did not ache so much. Her chest was quieter. Perhaps she was even hungry. Now she felt that she might live, if she was allowed to.

'Madame Lavender spoon-fed her, after tying a large napkin around her neck.

'How can I thank you?' Sarah asked, when the soup was finished.

'You have, by finishing your soup. It is the first thing you have eaten in days. Soon, my dear, you will be safe.'

'But you will remain, Madame Lavender?' She looked at the elderly woman, who had piercing blue eyes and a smile like...? Who? She couldn't remember. She had fulsome white hair, coiled in a French pleat.

Madame Lavender shrugged, but what French person didn't? 'I will remain. There is more work to do, but you have completed yours, and paid a price. It is time you go home to ... someone?' There was a question in her eyes, which disappeared immediately.

Sarah just smiled, because this woman should know nothing about her. It was safer for everyone.

Now it was night and she lay watching the ever more spherical moon. Soon, if God and the Germans allowed, she would be home.

The next day Bernard came again, with the doctor, who brushed aside Sarah's protestations about his safety and examined her. Bernard stood by the window, looking at the roofs and saying, 'When I was at school, our art teacher would tell us to look at the roofs, study the angles against the sky. He had been in the trenches, and had frequently viewed the world from slits in the ground.'

The doctor finished, tucked the sheet and eider-down up around Sarah's shoulders. He joined Bernard at the window. They talked quietly to-gether. The doctor came to her, lifted her hand gently and kissed it. 'Goodbye, Madame, we will not meet again, but a doctor must see you on your return. You will require an operation, but I believe you will return to full health, in body at least. Your mind, my dear, might take longer. You must be patient with yourself.'

He left. Bernard came across and sank into the wicker chair. She watched as he leaned back, closing his eyes. He was drawn, tired, but then he sat straighter and looked at her, his usual smile in his eyes as he said, 'Our good doctor should be air-lifted out with us, as he is a Jew, but he re-fuses. He is sure that he can remain in hiding and work for the good of people like you, until the allies prevail.'

The goodness of people stimulated too much emotion; it made Sarah want to moan with grief, and worry for their safety. Instead she said, 'Air-lifted out with *us*?'

'Yes, us. I am coming home, for a while at least. Though it is winter, it can be hot out there.' He nodded at the window, and shook his hand as though it burned.

'When?' she asked.

'You can tell that yourself. Just look at the moon.' He rose, but at the door he turned round. 'Your work is done, Sarah. You are compromised, contaminated – whatever you like to call it – as are the group, but you know that. The circuit remains, though.'

She picked at the sheet with her bound fingers. 'Pierre? Did you kill him?'

'Don't worry about Pierre.'

'I dreamed I saw him. I screamed. He pinned me down with the sheets.'

Bernard didn't look surprised. 'You must have been delirious. Fever does that to you.'

He left and she stared at the door. Was she safe? Why wasn't Bernard surprised? It was Pierre who was the traitor, wasn't it? Or were there two of them?

She slept, but fitfully.

The next day she made herself stumble around the room even though it brought on coughing fits. But she must become fit, just in case. She peered from the window. It was at the rear of the building. The roof sloped, but another roof cut across at an angle. She could make it, just, if she built up her strength. It would require a drop to the ground. The Germans would be back and front, but at least she'd die fighting, not caught like a rat in a trap.

She checked the wardrobe. Her shoes were there, cleaned, and her clothes, laundered. The door began to open and she stumbled to the bed, coughing. Madame Lavender entered. 'Bravo, you take exercise. It helps to keep the blood flowing.'

Sarah lay back on the pillows. Her ribs and belly hurt. She was sick over the sheets.

Madame Lavender came. 'No more walking. Hush, hush, I will change the sheets. Here, if you can, sit in the chair.'

She could. Madame stripped the bed and

bundled the sheets out of the door. Sarah heard the key turn in the lock. Oh God, they were locking her in. Within five minutes Madame Lavender had returned, and Sarah was halfway to the door, through which she intended to escape.

Madame Lavender changed the sheets. 'Now, you must come to bed, please, my dear. Take your medicine – it helps you sleep. You look agitated.'

Sarah sat on the bed, looking at the medicine. She had taken some every day. Was this why she slept? She nodded. 'Yes, I will, but please do not let me hold you up, and I'm so sorry for giving you extra work.'

She poured the sleeping draught into the sink when Madame Lavender left the room, turning the key in the lock, as she must always have done. Were they all traitors: Pierre, Madame Lavender and Bernard; perhaps even the doctor? Why else would they lock the door? Were they getting her better so that the Gestapo could start once more? Would she ever see Lizzy again? Was Derek really dead, or was Bernard lying?

Sarah wept, frightened. She was alone, so alone, and she wanted Kate, because she never lied.

Chapter Twenty-Four

It was 17th December, just three days before the concert, when Kate received Stan's letter:

Hey you

We'll be down for the concert, just let us know the songs. By 'we', I mean Roberto and Elliot and me. Do not, and I repeat not, thank Brucie, because he is kicking up like a pimp who's lost his tarts. We intend to be there at midday. I gather it will be a cast of 5,000, so presumably you and your vicar will produce five loaves and two fishes. I prefer alcohol, but you know that.

Your pal
Stan

PS Tell your vicar we expect a free pass through the Pearly Gates.

It was the school holidays, so Kate waved the letter at Lizzy, who was practising her tap shuffle on the kitchen floor, which would never be the same again.

'We have three more coming down from the Blue Cockatoo, Lizzy.'

Lizzy looked up, frowning with concentration. 'Three what?' she panted.

Kate laughed. 'Musicians: Stan on saxophone,

375

Roberto on piano and Elliot on bass.'

Lizzy stopped, but her frown remained. 'But what about Mrs B? She is our piano player.'

Kate was aghast. 'Of course. Oh, heavens, what on earth can we do?' She stuffed the letter into her pocket. 'I'll have to stop them.'

Lizzy stood with her hands on her hips. 'Oh, Aunt Kate, stop fussing. We just need to think – or that's what you always say.'

The pair of them stood looking at one another, then Lizzy shook her head. 'You're right, but we do need to fuss, and two heads aren't enough, so we must go and talk to the vicar, but we mustn't let Mrs B hear.'

They put their coats on. One of the paper-chains had come unstuck from the picture rail and dangled on the floor. Kate stopped to hook it up, but Lizzy shouted, 'Not now, Aunt Kate; we haven't a moment to lose, and you mustn't bend and stretch.' She had already opened the front door.

Kate followed, holding this amazing child's hand as they hurried along the road.

'I'm nine now, Aunt Kate. I don't need my hand held.'

'Ah, but I need to hold it, because I could slip, and so could you, and we both need our feet in prime condition. I'm not letting go, you little wretch.' They were both laughing as they waved to Mrs Williams, who was hurrying to Percy with a pot of paint. Was it the red he needed for one of the flats? The backcloth, an ocean-going liner, was complete, but it had to be, for there were only three days to go.

They spun into the vicarage and round to the back door. Kate knocked briskly and, as always, waited to be invited in. One only went so far with Mrs B.

'Remember, say nothing.'

The door opened. Lizzy pushed forward. 'Hello, Mrs B. We need to talk to the vicar, about something secret.'

Kate sighed as Mrs B raised her eyebrows. 'Well, I suggest you go through to the snug. He's trying to catch up on his correspondence. He's been dancing that wretched tango for what seems hours, on the hall floor. At least he's not doing a tap dance, or I dread to think what state the floorboards would be in. It's all your fault, Miss Kate Watson.' She led them, smiling, to the snug door. 'But I have to say, he's a smarty-pants at it now.'

Lizzy put her hand to her mouth. 'Oh, you said "pants".'

'Well, so I did.' She left them.

Lizzy grimaced at Kate. 'I think this concert is making people very naughty.'

'Yes, and I think I'm looking at the naughtiest. Who said we mustn't let Mrs B know what the matter was, and there you are – saying we must talk to Mr Rees about a secret.'

Lizzy put her hand to her mouth. 'Oh, I did, didn't I?' They knocked. Lizzy said, 'We'll get her flowers, and that can be the secret.'

'Flowers in December?'

Tom called, 'Come in, if that's my favourite woman; otherwise, please go away.'

Lizzy looked up at Kate. 'I think love makes people soppy.' She raised her voice. 'It's the favourite woman's niece, so do I have to go away?'

Kate pulled one of her plaits. 'That's enough.'

'Then my two favourite women may enter.' Lizzy grinned and opened the door, skipping down the steps.

Tom came to meet them, ruffling Lizzy's hair, then picked up each plait. 'Perhaps I should tie these together and hang you from a peg.'

'Then I couldn't be in the chorus.'

He laughed. 'Kate, what are we to do with this monster?' He gestured to one of the chairs. 'Sit, Lizzy, there's a book you might like. *Peter Pan*. Have a scan.'

'We have a problem: a *secret* problem,' Lizzy said. 'We thought three heads, not just two, would be better.'

Tom raised his eyebrows at Kate. 'Oh, so no *Peter Pan*, but you have something pressing that your local vicar may help with?'

Kate explained. He raised his eyebrows again. This time he gestured Kate to a chair too. She sat, while Tom took his place at the writing desk. Kate leaned forward, her elbows on her knees. 'I can't hurt Mrs B. I'd rather cancel the boys.'

Tom turned his pen over and over, deep in thought. 'So,' he said, 'what have we in the band?' He ticked off the instruments. 'Comb, two spoons, several recorders, saxophone, bass, drums and piano, but no violin?'

Violin? Kate shook her head. Why would they have a violin? Tom cocked his head at her. 'You won't know, I suppose, though perhaps little Miss Know-it-all sitting opposite me, aged nine,

378

might. What other instrument does Mrs B play, which is, actually, her forte?'

Lizzy leapt to her feet. 'I knew you would have an answer. I expect it's because you are close to God, and He whispers in your ear. Come on, Aunt Kate, we can tell Mrs B, because she plays the violin.'

Kate was laughing quietly as Tom looked heavenwards, presumably for help. 'Out of the mouths of babes and sucklings,' she said, to the man she loved.

'Indeed, now out: the pair of you. I have work to do, if I'm to make the rehearsal tonight. What on earth are we going to do when this all-consuming shenanigans is over?'

Lizzy was standing on the top step, tapping her foot impatiently. Kate went to Tom and kissed his mouth, saying against it, 'I love you, Mr Rees.'

He kissed her back. 'Go, before we shock Miss Elizabeth Baxter. And I love you too.'

Lizzy sighed. 'Oh, come on, we haven't got time.'

Kate hurried, her back remarkably free of pain. Her stitches pulled, just a bit, but otherwise: virtually nothing.

The day of 20th December dawned crisp and clear. Kate hadn't slept very well, and neither had Lizzy, who had slipped into her bed in the early hours, murmuring, 'I will have bags under my eyes and look a fright.'

Kate had laughed herself to sleep. Clearly Mrs Fellows had been chatting to the girls as she did their make-up for the run-through.

At lunchtime, Stan, Roberto and Elliot arrived by bus from Yeovil. Elliot was outraged that he had had to pay for a seat for his bass, even though it stood up all the way. They ended up at the pub, ordering whatever was on offer – for medicinal purposes only, they insisted. Kate stayed with them for half an hour, paying for their sandwiches and a watery pint each, and putting bus money in Elliot's pocket, as though he was a little boy. Meanwhile Stan dug out a bottle of Scotch from his pocket. 'Courtesy of Brucie, not that he knows it.'

Roberto saw the alarm on Kate's face. 'Don't worry, we know we have to perform, but the party might run on afterwards, back here at the pub. We're bunking up, you know, just in case we get plastered.'

Cynthia, the barmaid, winked at Kate. 'There's no "just in case" about it, I tell you now. Go on, I'll send 'em along in an hour, almost stone-cold sober and in time for their run-through.'

The trio arrived promptly at two. Kate introduced Mrs B, who shook hands firmly. 'I hope you're not drunk. I won't play with people who let me down.'

Kate shut her eyes, but Stan roared with laughter. 'It's like meeting my mum. You play the fiddle, I hear.'

'Young man, I play the violin.'

Roberto was warming up the piano, and the spoons and comb were rehearsing quietly in the corner. The recorders were squeaking. Stan and Elliot looked at one another. Mrs B said, 'We four just need to play up, that's all.'

Stan saluted. 'Yes, sir.'

They took up their positions in the roped-off orchestra pit on the left of the stage. They started with 'Anything Goes', but then Stan waved them to a stop. 'Sing it for us, lovely girl.' He beckoned Kate over.

She said, 'Susie will be singing it.'

Elliot said, 'Maybe, but we need a reward for leaving our pints on the bar.'

She stood, her arm on the piano, and sang along. It felt good to be with the boys again and she relaxed into the song, drifting carefully across the floor and back, letting the words flow, coming alive. But that was wrong, because these days she had never felt more alive in her life. Mrs B's violin was jaunty, the recorder players squeaked just a little, and the comb and spoons fitted in remarkably well.

Tom watched with Lizzy, who leaned against him. Lizzy looked up and said, 'She looks really happy, doesn't she, Reverend Rees?'

'She does.' He felt nervousness sweep over him. He loved this woman with all his heart, far too much to keep her in the straitjacket of a vicar's world if she'd really rather be elsewhere.

At three thirty, Kate clapped her hands and chased the cast home, and the boys back to the pub, with dire warnings to keep sober, while Fran took Lizzy to her house for a quick tea. Kate had to help Percy and Mr Pritchard, the stage designer from Stickhollow, to adjust the flats, which had been a problem during the run-through. Tom stayed too, and the three men manoeuvred the flats into place, securing them with screws to the stage floor, and by rope to the overhead pipes.

She and Tom walked back through the village. Kate was so nervous that she could hardly speak, and her stomach was churning. Would people really come? Would the chorus remember to smile, and keep in time? Would Susie hold the notes? Most of all, would everyone have fun? Tom held her hand and when they reached the gate into the vicarage she turned to him. 'Thank you,' Kate said. 'For loving and saving me.'

He kissed her as though it was for the last time. 'You will be wonderful, and we will dance that tango as though we were born to do so, but still carefully, my post-op girl. Thank you for coming into my life, for making me whole again.'

She kissed his cheek, his mouth. 'Break a leg,' she whispered.

Within an hour they were back at the village hall, changing in the dressing rooms. Kate busied herself hurrying from pillar to post. Her task was to direct things, not perform, except for fronting the tap routine for 'I Get a Kick Out of You', as chosen by Stella and approved by the children. The WI had hastily produced a sailor suit. Then Kate would dance what she feared would be a tentative tango, before she sang the finale songs, 'A Foggy Day in London Town' and 'Begin the Beguine', at which point the audience was to be encouraged to join in and leave the hall on a high note.

At the hall, the doors opened at six thirty. There were buckets in the kitchen, which would be placed at the exit afterwards, for donations towards the War Bonds. The villagers had donated a teaspoon of tea from each family, so that tea could be served in the interval. All this Kate ticked off on her list. She did her rounds of the changing rooms, calling outside the doors, 'Everything all right?'

Everything was.

At seven prompt they began, with the chorus taking its place behind the closed curtain, while Susie and Adrian stood at the front, waiting for curtain up. The band began, with Roberto, Stan and Elliot in their dinner jackets, bless their hearts, and Mrs B in an evening gown; the others in their best bib and tucker too. Kate could have hugged them all, but instead she marked time in the wings, mouthing, 'Smile.'

The curtain rose. Susie started to sing. Anything Goes', with the two lines of the chorus moving toe–heel, toe–heel as Kate directed from the wings, until the couple moved to the back and then the children were joined by Kate herself. The children swept into their routine, tapping it out, swinging their arms and smiling as though their lives depended on it, while Kate's performance was more circumspect. She had no intention of undoing the good the operation had done. Their turn ended and the audience stood, the parents in tears.

The ballet turn followed, which Kate had handed gratefully to Mrs Major's daughter, the local dance teacher. On and on it went, as the scenes changed, the gangster became a minister, and then back again, and the American accents tended to fade in and out of Somerset and the

East End.

The curtains closed for the interval. Kate was exhausted, but so far nothing had gone wrong. She and Stella helped the children to change again, while Susie slipped into her tango dress, before creeping round to the men's room, to help Tom and Adrian with their bow ties.

The curtain rose on Kate, still in a sailor's suit and tap shoes, and behind her the children in two rows again, on their marks for another tap routine, for 'I Get a Kick Out of You'. She looked at the band. Roberto grinned. The music began, she started to sing while the chorus behind launched into the dance with gusto, swinging their arms and singing along with her.

She laughed at the end of the song as the children took their bow, clapping them along with the audience, looking from one row to the other, until she reached the back. And there was Brucie, standing with another two men, one of them in GI uniform. It was Tim, the son of Mr Oliver, so the other must be Mr Oliver himself. The GI waved and whistled. Stunned, Kate bowed her head to them especially.

The chorus tapped off the stage and she followed to change into her dress. The band played the introduction to 'Jealousy' and the audience settled as she and Susie entered the stage from the right, whilst the men sauntered on from the left. Susie and she sang 'Jealousy' as the men, slick in their dinner suits, circled, talked, circled again, then reached for their women who were beckoning to them, centre stage. The men clasped them as the lights faded a notch or two, and all stood motionless, elegant but passionate until, in response to the music, both couples turned into the promenade. Tom's face was suddenly too serious for the requirements of the dance.

She said, 'I love you' as he swung her into a gentle fall-away whisk rather than snapping her into such a move, as Adrian did for Susie.

He whispered, 'I phoned Brucie. He hired a car to bring the Olivers down in time for this. I can't ask you to stay here and be a vicar's wife, when the world could be at your feet.'

They pivoted a quarter left, then swung right in a pivot arc. Kate squeezed his hand tightly and looked at him, heedless of the required head stance. 'Sorry, Vicar, but you're stuck with me. If you don't marry me, then you will condemn me to fallen-woman status, because I'm moving in.'

He eased her into a fall-away whisk again, looking into her face, long and hard, which was also a non-tango stance.

'For the rest of my life,' she finished.

They performed the chassé, interweaving with Susie and Adrian, and now Tom and Kate's passion was overflowing as they swept from step to step as though in some other universe until the music sliced to a stop, and they stood body to body, heaving breath to heaving breath. At last, as though awakening, he slipped his arm around her and held her close as they all bowed to riotous applause. The men and Susie left the stage, and now it was Kate's turn to end the evening.

Bob, who was in charge of the lighting, lowered the stage lights further and caught her – like a moth, as Brucie used to say – in the spotlight.

She sang 'A Foggy Day in London Town', beckoning to the audience to join in, although no-one did. Lizzy called from the wings, 'We want to listen to you, Aunt Kate.' The audience laughed, so Kate sang and slipped into 'Begin the Beguine', which was supposed to be the last song; instead, the band played 'April in Paris'. She sang it for Sarah. They played 'Love for Sale', followed by 'All the Things You Are'. This was for Tom, and she held out her hand to him, as he stood in the wings, his face a picture of love and pride.

Stan looked at her now, and nodded. She beckoned all the cast onto the stage, not knowing what song was about to be played. It was 'We'll Meet Again', and this time the audience joined in, and by the second verse sadness and longing had gripped them all, but somehow they kept singing.

As the last notes died, there was a moment's quiet. The cast bowed and still there was silence, and then the audience were on their feet, cheering and applauding. Again she heard the GI's whistle. What a shame to have made a wasted journey. As she bowed again, she felt a little hand in hers. It was Lizzy, who said, 'Do you think we'll ever meet Mummy again?'

Kate lied deeply, deliberately and believably. 'Of course.'

Chapter Twenty-Five

Sarah eased into her clothes after a lunch of bread and chicken soup taken, as always, in her room, although now she was strong enough to sit at a small table. She was tired, though, because she did not sleep for more than a few hours at night without the medication that might merely be used to drug her. When she did sleep a little, the shadows loomed, moving, hiding. The pain racked her, but she trusted no-one. It was what they had been taught, and why would she begin to trust now, held a prisoner, as she was, inside this room?

It had been a full moon last night, and there would be another tonight. Would Bernard come today to take her to the dropping zone or would he take her back to the monsters? She continued to be compliant, to smile at Madame Lavender, longing to rest her head on her shoulder and accept her kindness as genuine. But how could she? She had walked around the room over the last few days, enflaming her toes, but perhaps she was a little stronger. Her toes were infected again. Madame Lavender had tutted this morning, 'Soon you will be home. I do not wish to risk danger to our doctor again, so we will continue with salt and water. But why are they infected?'

Sarah had lied, as she did so easily. 'I don't know.'

She pushed the table to one side, moved to the door and listened. No voices, no clump-clump, spark-spark. The darkness of the cell seemed to close around her. She walked back to the bed, unscrewed the bed knob and kept it with her, in case they came. Madame Lavender entered. Sarah held the bed knob behind her. The elderly woman smiled. Again there was a memory, a resemblance... Then it was gone. 'Thank you, Madame.'

An hour passed, and then another. She heard a voice – male. She stood, and in her hand was on the bed knob, ready. It might help her protect herself, because her hands were not strong enough on their own now. The key turned in the lock, the door opened. It was Bernard, wonderful Bernard. Or was he? She trembled. The knob dropped to the rug and rolled across the boards. Bernard looked from it to her. 'It's only me. You are safe, remember.'

She nodded. 'Old habits die hard. Sometimes...'

She rubbed her forehead. Her chest still rattled, though not as much; and her thoughts were still jumbled, perhaps even more than they had been. He held up a coat, old but wool. 'Slip into this. We have transport most of the way. The Lysander will be at the zone, or so we hear. If it cannot be there, we will be back at the zone tomorrow.'

She slipped first one arm into a sleeve and then the other, feeling captured as Bernard did up the buttons, because her fingers were too sore and swollen. Her thoughts were slipping again. She started to laugh. Well, if they thought she was well enough for more torture, they were wrong.

Just one more day would kill her, because she could face no more. Trust no-one, she had been told. No-one.

Bernard held her arm.

Sarah said, 'I won't run away, I can't.'

He kissed her cheek. 'You won't need to. I am with you, and will be for as long as you need me.'

He urged her forward, pulling the door open. There was no lock visible, and no key. She stared and touched the door. He said, 'The lock is hidden, beneath that moulding.' He pointed to the rose frieze. She thought she remembered it. He shut the door behind him while she watched. He took the key from a hidden hole in the skirting board, locked it and replaced the key. The rose swung back into place, hiding the keyhole.

As he straightened he said, 'This safe room was created in the First World War for escapees. It is being fully used in this one.'

He held her arm and led her to the staircase. No-one else appeared. The hallway seemed too far away, but somehow she reached the bottom of the stairs. Bernard led her towards the back, through the kitchen and out. She braced herself for soldiers with guns. There were none, just a bitter wind and snow lying on the cobbles. Sarah felt sick and ill. A horse and cart drew into the yard. It held logs, a few of which the carter began to unload and stack in the log shed. They waited in the shadows until one side of the cart was clear.

Bernard helped her up, into the space. 'Lie down,' he instructed. She obeyed, because she must do as she was told, until she could escape. Stay alert, the trainers had said.

He covered her with what looked like a coffin, but lighter, because he lifted it himself. Then she heard the sound of logs hitting the coffin. The air-holes were clear. Then it was as though the world lurched, but it was the cart; and Bernard's voice came, sounding rough, strange and old. 'Come on, old mare.'

She heard Madame Lavender call, 'Thank you for the logs, Henri. Good luck with your other drops. May your day go well.'

Sarah was knocked and bumped as the cart lurched over cobbles. Truth or lies? Genuine or not? She would know only when a Lysander came, or did not.

The cart stopped after some hours – and yes, it was hours, because her watch told the truth, and perhaps it was the only thing that did. She could hear Bernard talking to another man. There were other voices in the background, all low, some no more than a murmur, but they were French, she realised. French, not German. How clever, or was it the truth?

The cart creaked as someone jumped down. Bernard? Then there was the sound of scratching, as logs were removed, and finally the coffin was lifted. She stared up into a bright moonlit night, with barely a cloud in the sky. An owl hooted. Bernard stood over her, smiling, his finger to his lips. He helped her to sit up. She was sick over the side.

'Something hurts,' she breathed. 'I'm sorry.'

He jumped down and held up his arms. She couldn't jump, but sat on the tailboard and let him lower her to the ground. Behind him, in the moonlight, men were talking, heads close, while one gestured to the four points of the landing strip. Some of the men melted away. She listened. It seemed to be a proper drop. She brushed bark and woodchips from her coat, shivering, as Bernard saluted someone who came out of the dark.

'Good evening, Adèle.' She recognised the voice before she recognised the man, and she wrenched free from Bernard, who clapped a hand over her mouth. 'Shh,' he breathed in her ear. It was Pierre standing before her. Pierre, who was dead, but whom she had heard and seen, and who had held her down on the bed at Madame Lavender's. He smiled, and now she realised it was the same smile as Madame Lavender's.

She couldn't struggle. They'd have to kill her, because she was too ill, and too tired. And what was the point of living when you could barely trust anyone ever again. 'Lizzy,' she said against Bernard's hand, which tasted of wood.

Bernard spoke against her ear. 'Pierre risked his life to put into play our plan. He played the traitor, but could only give the Gestapo Derek's first name. We hoped that when the bastards only talked of Derek, you would understand and test them with a false surname. So we waited. I am going to take my hand away. Be quiet, because I can hear the plane.'

He removed his hand. Pierre supported her on one side, Bernard on the other and they started to walk. She couldn't think. 'But I was locked in.'

Pierre whispered, 'If the Gestapo had come, they wouldn't know the door was there, but it's only totally secure when locked.'

'Who else is to leave?' she whispered.

'George, who is blown and already at the zone; another incoming operator will be on the Lysander. Pierre is to leave with us too. The bastards think he is dead: charred remains and his hat were found at the copse. You don't need to know whose body, but the man was already dead from an earlier fracas. Your "Madame Lavender" remains in place, but they do not know about her, yet.'

'She should leave.'

Pierre shrugged. 'My grandmother is her own person. I hope perhaps another time.'

'And Derek?'

'An agent was dropped elsewhere. He relayed the news that Derek has been officially notified as dead. I'm so sorry, my dear.'

She waited with these men, whose story sounded right, but ... but... Words were easy, her thoughts were muddled, and until she was in the air she would not believe a word of it.

Inside the fuselage of the Lysander the smell was that of the Whitley, oily and tinny. The moonlight was shut out, and the aircraft began to move. Bernard sat with his arm around Sarah, holding her as it accelerated along the bumpy landing strip. There was still time for them to be stopped, still time to be shot out of the sky, but somehow, it didn't matter, because she had been wrong; she could indeed afford to trust, but that certainty came and went, and there were shapes that loomed, moved and then danced away.

She gradually became used to the darkness and exchanged salutes with the blown wireless operator, who was real, and lucky to have survived, just as she was. Next to him Pierre grinned that grin of his, but looked thin, strained and years older than a few months warranted. They all did, but that was the way of it, and they still had to reach England. As they gained height she wished those who had been brought in the Lysander to replace them all the luck in the world. Dear God, they would need it.

They flew on, and drank the water the despatchers brought them. She poured some of the water over her fingertips and eased off her wool gloves, which had stuck to the raw, throbbing, nailless digits. And she slept in Bernard's arms.

The ack-ack woke her as they left France's shores and headed across the Channel. The despatchers moved about, and one brought Sarah coffee in a tin cup. It was real coffee. She took it from him, and in the dim light the RAF despatcher saw her fingers. His face set, but he said nothing. But a moment later he returned with a biscuit. He said, 'My mother bakes them and sends them to me. It is her whole sugar ration. She would be pleased if you accepted it.' Sarah shook her head, but the man murmured, 'Take it. It is all I can do for you.'

She took it. 'Please thank your mother, but you know, young man, you are taking me home, so you are doing a great deal for me.' He was probably her age, but she felt very old.

He nodded and returned to his post. She ate the biscuit, still feeling sick, but so grateful that she could have wept at his kindness, for what could she do for them, these brave young pilots and despatchers who died too often, and too young, transporting people like her?

She was barely aware that they had landed, because she couldn't wake up properly. She found the strength, however, to say that Lizzy must not see her until she looked better. 'But tell them both that I am safe and will be home soon. But wait. Wait.' She looked around for the despatcher. 'Thank you, I will never forget any of you. And thank the pilots. I owe you all my life.'

The despatcher nodded. 'I will. Don't you worry about a thing now.'

She was handed down from the plane into Bernard's arms. He carried her to the ambulance. The moment they reached the hospital, the darkness that had been growing cocooned her in silence, and then there was nothing.

She woke into the brightness of a quiet room. A nurse in a grey dress, white apron, white cuffs and white muslin veil said, 'It's Christmas Day – you are safe, you are almost home.'

'They must not see me until I am better.'

'I know, we have been told; and your dependants have received notification. You are in a military hospital, and we are like soldiers and are likely to shout, extremely loudly, if you misbehave.' The QA's voice was stern, but she smiled.

An elderly doctor came, his white coat gleaming, his stethoscope round his neck. Sarah turned from him and looked out at the grey sky – so much grey. She tried not to cough.

He said, 'A Merry Christmas to you.'

'Don't be bloody ridiculous,' she snapped.

The nurse laughed and, after a moment, so too did the doctor.

Bernard said, from the corner, 'This young woman never used to swear. How things change.'

She peered towards the voice. 'You're here.'

The doctor said, 'He's a bloody fixture, if I may join you in your adjectival adventure.'

The nurse agreed, 'We disinfect him, as well as the floor. One day he will leave.'

Bernard sat up. His coat was over his knees. 'Out into good old England I will now go. Grey, as per usual, damp and bloody cold.'

'Oh my,' the doctor said, listening to Sarah's chest. 'Yet more adjectives pertaining to the Anglo-Saxon, if my ears deceive me not. So out you go, young man, just for a moment. I need to listen to the orchestra that is playing into my stethoscope.'

Bernard came to Sarah, who was propped up on pillows. 'I will be back. I will always be back.'

She snatched at his hand, then let go; her fingers hurt too much. 'Don't go, not yet.'

'I must. I have to see someone, but I will be back before I go anywhere, *if* I go anywhere.' He bent, kissed her lips. Into her hair he said, 'I love you more than life itself, so, I repeat, I will be back.'

Derek had said he would be back too.

She watched as Bernard left. He'd be off to be debriefed, and then what? Surely he was finished in France. Please, please, he must be. She sighed. Soon someone would come to debrief her too.

The doctor took her pulse. 'We had to open you up to have a bit of a butcher's inside. There were a few concerns about your spleen. Some little toerag

395

had whacked you pretty hard. It's swollen, but not irreparably damaged. Rest, rest and more rest. Your chest is already showing signs of improvement, but that will also need rest.' He pointed at her fingers. 'The nails will grow back, and so too those on your toes. Let's say that in anything from six months to a year you will be tickety-boo. But for now...' He raised his hand as though he was conducting.

She said, like a good girl, 'Rest.'

'Indeed.'

Kate had received the letter on Christmas Eve and put it beneath the tree, for Lizzy in the morning. There were a few other presents, including chocolates from Mr Oliver, who had offered her a contract at any time of her choosing. He said he would have taken the whole cast and caboodle, if he could, for nothing had quite touched his heart-strings as that evening had.

Tim Oliver, the GI, had grinned as Kate touched his father for a donation to the War Bond fund before they went on their way. He had given her twenty pounds, but she kept out her hand.

'More?' Mr Oliver drawled.

She nodded. 'The church clock is stuck, not at ten to three – and neither is there honey still for tea – but it has been broken for too long.'

The Americans had looked blank, but not Mrs B, who recited the last verse of Rupert Brooke's poem, 'The Old Vicarage, Grantchester', ending:

...is there Beauty yet to find?
And Certainty? and Quiet kind?

Deep meadows yet, for to forget
The lies, and truths, and pain? ... oh! yet
Stands the Church clock at ten to three?
And is there honey still for tea?

The two Americans, and even Brucie, had listened to Mrs B's quiet voice. Mr Oliver swallowed and handed over another twenty pounds. Brucie drove them to Exeter, where Mr Oliver knew someone who would fly them back to London. His final words were, 'Any time you want to tread the boards again, on a bigger stage, call me, Kate Watson.'

On Christmas Day morning, the sitting-room door stayed shut until Lizzy had eaten a soft-boiled egg and toast, unburnt, which Kate said was Lizzy's main Christmas present from her.

Lizzy laughed, but then saw Kate was serious, and slumped back in her chair, her arms crossed.

Kate couldn't keep up the pretence. 'However, Father Christmas will have brought just a few things.' Lizzy pushed back her chair. Kate stopped her. 'No, not so fast. Dishes first.' They washed and dried them in the quickest time possible.

Once in the sitting room, Kate gestured to the Christmas tree hung with decorations, some of which Kate had made with her mother and Sarah. 'There's a little pile there. Why not start with the letter?'

Lizzy flung herself onto her knees and fingered the envelope. 'It's open.'

'That's because it's addressed to me, but it contains something that very much concerns

397

you: read it and see.'

Kate sat cross-legged on the floor, watching as Lizzy pulled out the typed letter. Her lips moved as she read it, and then she started at the beginning again. 'We *will* meet again, Aunt Kate. You told the truth.' She threw herself at Kate. 'She's coming home, Mummy is coming home.'

Kate rocked her backwards and forwards, cradling her. 'Yes, your mum is coming home, when she's better – and not before. But we know she's safe, and that's all that's important.' Yes, that *was* all that was important, because Sarah was Lizzy's mother, though Kate wished with all her heart that it was not so, and that she could tell her child who her mother really was. But that would never happen.

They stayed quiet for a while, but then the wrapped presents called out to Lizzy. She was allowed two chocolates before morning service, but then they had to run to the church or be late. Kate handed out hymn and prayer books, as a vicar's fiancée should. What was so surprising was that she enjoyed the fun and the gravity of her role, the sense of being important to the village, of responding to the villagers' needs and being part of a team.

She grinned across the church to Mrs B, and to Lizzy in the choir stalls. Together with Tom and Stella, they had dressed the tree that stood in the corner of the church. And soon Sarah would return, and resume her role of mother. It was enough that Kate would then be secure in her position of aunt.

Tom came from the vestry and announced,

'Merry Christmas to one and all, and we start with hymn number fifty-nine: "O come all ye faithful, joyful and triumphant".'

Kate sang to Lizzy, to Mrs B, to Sarah and to Tom. Perhaps it would be to God one day. He was definitely a bit closer than he had been for a long time.

At the end of February 1943, when the cold was deep and bitter, and the British had begun to push back the Japanese in Burma, the Germans had surrendered at Stalingrad and the allies had taken Tripoli from the Axis, Sarah returned to the village in her FANY uniform. She was brought by open army jeep, which was freezing, but that didn't matter because she had been cold before, though now she wasn't lonely, hurt or frightened. Now she was coming home, with Bernard.

They drew up to Melbury Cottage, but before she was able to clamber from the jeep, Sarah saw Lizzy running down the path, then jumping up and down, as Sarah eased herself to the ground, opening her arms. Lizzy threw herself into them. 'You're back. You must have served millions of cups of tea, and driven thousands of lorries.'

Sarah hugged her child, so tightly that Lizzy wriggled.

'I can't breathe, but you're back, and that's all that matters.' She slid from Sarah's arms and looked behind her at Bernard. 'Oh, dear me, I think you two are going to be soppy, like Aunt Kate and Tom.' She reached out a hand.

Bernard shook it. 'Good morning. I'm going to marry your mother, if you will both have me.'

Lizzy shrugged. 'Well, there's room, I suppose. Do you dance?'

Bernard looked taken aback. 'Well, not really.'

Lizzy beckoned them towards the house. 'Don't worry, Aunt Kate will teach you, and you too, Mum.'

She slipped her hand into Sarah's. 'I expect Daddy is looking down and is glad we will have a man about the house. That's what he liked to call himself, isn't it?'

Kate watched from the doorstep, holding the door open. Her sister looked strained and exhausted, but there was a light in her eyes that Kate hadn't noticed, ever.

Sarah smiled at her, reached out a gloved hand and touched Kate's cheek as she entered the hall. 'Dearest Katie.'

Kate took Sarah's coat from her and hung it on the hook.

Bernard shook his head when she reached for his. 'I can't stop – places to be, people to see.' His mac was open, and he wore a uniform of what looked like a Guards regiment. 'I just wanted to see Sarah safely home.'

Lizzy was dragging Sarah into the sitting room. 'Come on, Mum. Aunt Kate lit the fire and she has the kettle on, and Mrs B got some of the ladies to donate sugar, so there are two small cakes, but only two. One for you, and one for me, if Bernard really isn't staying.'

Bernard laughed and began to head for the sitting room too, but Kate barred his way. 'So?'

He dug his hands into his pockets. 'I can't tell you much, but she's home for good.'

'No more gallivanting then, to pastures further away than a canteen on a railway station, or the cab of a lorry?' Bernard said nothing, but she liked his steady stare, one that she felt invited the real question: 'Is she in one piece, mentally and physically?'

There was a world of love in his smile. 'She will be, but she still has dreams, and a touch of paranoia; but that goes with the territory and is hard to leave behind. Who is the enemy, who isn't? It should improve. I can say no more.'

Lizzy slammed the sitting-room door shut. Kate said, 'When you say dreams, you mean night-mares.'

It wasn't a question.

'Nightmares,' he confirmed. 'Perhaps you could stress that she is now safe, that whatever happened will eventually be in the past, but I'm not sure if you can understand what I mean.'

Kate stood firmly in front of him. 'I understand very well, and I'm telling you now that Sarah will not enter your world again or, if so, it will be over my dead body. There is a child to consider, and she has done her bit. Do you understand, Bernard – or whoever you really are.'

'Sarah wouldn't be allowed. And yes, I under-stand.'

He walked from her to the door of the sitting room and knocked. Kate was hot on his heels as he entered. He stood in front of Sarah and said gently, 'I have to go.'

Sarah nodded, standing in front of the fire. Bernard held her. She laid her head on his shoulder as he kissed her hair. He turned and as he left

401

the room he called to Lizzy, 'I will be back; remind your mother of that.'

Lizzy said, 'My daddy said that.'

Kate followed him into the hall. The jeep hooted, but she dragged at his sleeve. 'You'd better come back.'

'I fully intend to, but look after her for me. You've done a splendid job with Lizzy.'

Kate smiled at him. 'Flattery is always nice,' she said. 'However, it's easy to do a splendid job with Lizzy. I, however, have a bark and a bite, where the family is concerned, so just you remember, when you come back again.'

The front door closed behind him. Kate made tea, and carried in the tray. The cakes were on a plate. She set the tray down on the small table next to Sarah's chair. 'It's so good to have you home, Sarah.'

Sarah was comfortable in the easy chair – her chair – to the left of the fireplace. She smiled at Kate. 'Thank you,' she said. 'Thank you for everything, especially when I didn't believe you, but I have learned the difference now.'

'Difference?' Lizzy asked, while Kate poured. She had saved her ration of tea leaves over the last month or two, determined that her sister should have as many decent cups of tea as she needed.

Sarah still wore her gloves, and hesitated to take the cup and saucer that her sister offered, so instead Kate placed the cup on the table.

Lizzy repeated, 'What difference?'

Sarah said, 'Between what one thinks and what really happens, Lizzy.' She looked hard at Kate. 'I'm sorry, Katie.'

'It's over; the past is dead, just as it will be for you too, Sarah.' The two sisters sat quietly for a moment, just looking at one another.

Lizzy said, 'You can take your gloves off, Mum. It's warm in here.'

Sarah flushed. 'Well, you see, I stubbed all my fingers on a door – how silly was that – and, hey presto, off came my nails.'

'We don't mind that, do we, Aunt Kate? I can tell my friends at school. Billy's dad came home from the army with only one leg. The stump is horrid.'

'Oh, well, this is nothing then.'

'You're home, so take them off. You need to be comfortable.'

Sarah shook her head as her daughter pulled the fingers of her gloves, one by one, then yanked both gloves off at once.

'Ugh,' Lizzy said. 'That's revolting. Wait until I tell Billy.'

Kate stared at fingers that had been nowhere near a door. What could she say to her sister, who was not allowed to discuss her past? So she merely said, 'Try the cakes. I forgot the napkins. Just a moment.'

She left the room and rooted about in the cutlery drawer, where she knew there were none, but the clatter hid any noise she might make as she cried. War was such a ghastly bloody business, but damn it, sometimes it had to be fought.

And this is what Sarah said to her as well, when Kate responded to her cries in the night.

'I regret none of it. Not my feet, my hands, any of it. It has to be fought, you see, Kate: to keep

403

our children safe from these people. You have no idea what they are doing, how they are behaving, the races they are targeting. Billy's dad, Derek, you, Tom have all given so much. And no, I don't regret it.'

Kate held her until she slept.

Chapter Twenty-Six

Churchill broadcast to the nation at three in the afternoon on 8th May 1945, declaring that the war in Europe was at an end. It seemed such a small speech for an end to such a terrible time, one that had witnessed sustained courage, endurance and suffering beyond belief. Tom said this was why the bells should ring out in Little Worthy. The bell-ringers were a little rusty, after such a long lay-off, and the cacophony woke Kate's daughter, Amelia Lavender, named after someone Sarah had known rather well in the war, and Pierre's grandmother – or so Sarah had referred to her.

Kate pushed Lizzy's old pram backwards and forwards as she and her husband, the Reverend Tom Rees, stood with the congregation who had collected on the green to listen to the broadcast. Bernard had arrived, battered and bruised in late 1943, with an escape story he would never be able to tell. Tom had married Sarah and Andrew – which, it transpired, was Bernard's real name – in early 1944. Lizzy was the bridesmaid, wearing a dress produced by Mrs Woolton. It looked suspiciously like Cinderella's ballgown, made from parachute silk for the 1943 village pantomime, directed by Kate.

Pierre – or Claude, his real name – had been Andrew's best man. Shortly afterwards, word came through that Madame Lavender had been betrayed and shot, along with her lover, the doctor.

In the spring of 1947, which ended one of the coldest winters in living memory, Kate and Sarah walked together towards the woods. They talked of the severe rationing that was designed to get the country back on its feet, and of the formation of the welfare state, but fell silent as they walked further into the woods, beneath the budding beech trees.

The buds were bursting, the sky was blue above the branches and the birds were singing as they reached the clearing. They laid flowers where the gypsy camp fire had been, in memory of Andrei and his friends who had not returned and had perhaps died at the hands of the Nazis, as so many gypsies had. For a long moment they stared at the circle of rich green grass, which seemed to be a legacy of the wood ash.

'It must never happen again,' Sarah said, as Andrew, Lizzy, Tom, Amelia Lavender and Mrs B, with her paramour, Frankie from the Blue Cockatoo, stood with them.

Kate remembered Andrei's mother patting her breast and saying, 'Feel it – feel the music, my little bird. Dance with your heart and you will be brave and free.' She remembered the dancing

405

and singing, the life and energy.

Tom put his arm around her. 'Their spirit remains.' She nodded. It certainly remained here, in this clearing, for her; and always would.

She looked at Sarah. 'Come along, everyone, we have Colonel Bill Secker and his wife coming to the vicarage for lunch. Do you remember, I danced the tango with him at the Blue Cockatoo when you came to summon me home, Sarah?'

'I do.' Sarah remembered the young, young soldier, remembered how he'd appeared to her in her darkest times. She was so glad to hear he'd survived. Then suddenly, snapped from her reminiscing, she realised what Kate had said. 'You said "home". Is it?'

Kate laughed softly. 'Can you doubt it, when I'm surrounded by my family and friends, including those who come down regularly from the Blue Cockatoo.'

The two women walked on together, as Tom strolled with Andrew.

Kate said, 'Roberto and the gang will be down in the summer.' She added in a whisper, looking behind her, 'I wonder if Frankie and Mrs B have danced the tango?'

The two of them were still laughing as they re-entered the village.

Tom caught up and put his arm around Kate, who repeated her question. He laughed. 'Which one is going to be brave enough to ask?'

No-one volunteered.

The publishers hope that this book has given you enjoyable reading. Large Print Books are especially designed to be as easy to see and hold as possible. If you wish a complete list of our books please ask at your local library or write directly to:

Magna Large Print Books
Magna House, Long Preston,
Skipton, North Yorkshire.
BD23 4ND

This Large Print Book for the partially sighted, who cannot read normal print, is published under the auspices of

THE ULVERSCROFT FOUNDATION

THE ULVERSCROFT FOUNDATION

... we hope that you have enjoyed this Large Print Book. Please think for a moment about those people who have worse eyesight problems than you ... and are unable to even read or enjoy Large Print, without great difficulty.

You can help them by sending a donation, large or small to:

**The Ulverscroft Foundation,
1, The Green, Bradgate Road,
Anstey, Leicestershire, LE7 7FU,
England.**
or request a copy of our brochure for more details.

The Foundation will use all your help to assist those people who are handicapped by various sight problems and need special attention.

Thank you very much for your help.